Anessia's Quest

Written by
Karen Arnpriester

Reviews

Get your box of tissues ready, sit in your favorite chair, swing, etc. and begin a journey that will stay with you long after you've finished the book. Karen Arnpriester has definitely been blessed with the gift of writing. ... The characters could be anyone around you whether you know them or not. They are well defined. You get to know them and their hearts. Your heart breaks for them and rejoices with them. The situations are so realistic. They are situations you see or hear about each day. Some of them may beexperiences you have dealt with yourself. For this reason the book stays with you. You will always see yourself in this book in some way. I look forward to reading more from this author. Her book most definitely blessed my heart and spirit.
Sandra Stiles - 5 Stars www.goodreads.com

This story is one of joy and sadness, triumph and tragedy, love and forgiveness. I laughed, I cried, I found myself wanting the story to continue at its end… to know what lies beyond for Pagne as she continues turning pages in God's unending story. Truly inspiring, Pagne's journey is an amazing reminder that we each have a destiny and role to play in God's eternal plan. Needless to say… I'm a fan! Looking forward to the movie!!!
Pam Rich

This story grabbed me from the start. The characters were well developed and so incredibly real. You really get drawn into their lives. The storyline was creative, captivating and unpredictable, especially the ending! The book was an emotional rollercoaster and touched my heart in so many ways. I highly recommend it to everyone, regardless of your faith.
Barbara Strand – Amazon 5 Stars

This book was surprisingly refreshing for me, since my favorite type of reading is learning manuals or true stories. I read a lot but took time out to read Anessia's Quest. It came with me on a vacation and I just could not stop reading it. I felt emotionally attached to the characters and was feeling their joys and their pains. I even thought about them later wondering how they were doing. The author has a real knack for keeping your attention. I hope there is more to come from this author, she is on to a great start! Two thumbs up!!!
Ava Peterson – Amazon 5 Stars

I Loved this book! I did not want to put the book down. The author did a great job at catching my attention. I definitely laughed out loud with some of the funny moments in this book. Most of the characters in this book really touched my heart. To sum it all up it is a great heart warming, funny, and inspirational book. I hope to see more of Karen's books in the future.
Crystal Quiro – Amazon 5 Stars

It is a very powerful book that points out God is in our lives. It is a book of redemption. I could not put it down!!!
Trisha Timosh – Amazon 5 Stars

I read this book in two sittings. Up to eighty pages the first time, then took an entiremorning to finish the rest. And I did need tissue. The story is an emotional ride, the characters are real to you – you care or you hate them or you have hope for them. The author is a natural story-teller.
Jennifer Locke – Amazon 5 Stars

A novel of real-life trials and triumphs, "Anessia's Quest" is an inspirational, well-written, magical story of God's love. Spanning over an entire lifetime, we get to know these characters so deeply. We share their pain, joy, excitement, and shame… but their faith shines above it all. Karen Arnpriester expresses the power of healing as each endures to be the person they want to be, rather than the person they think they are. I am captivated by Anessia's strength and compassion. Truly a book I didn't want to put down…. And when I finally did, I found myself wanting more from this author.
Jana Adams – Amazon 5 Stars

See more reviews and book trailer at anessiasquest.com

Introduction

This is my first attempt at writing, and I can't tell you why this story, or why now. I only know that I had an idea for a beginning, and an end. The characters took me on a sweet and emotional journey. I believe this book is part of my quest, one of my ripples in this realm we call life. I pray that it touches your spirit and gives you pause to consider God's destiny for your life. Are you brave enough to trust and allow God to fulfill His plans in your life or does the ripple stop with you?

I hope that you enjoy reading this book as much as I enjoyed writing it.

karnpriester@gmail.com
www.facebook.com/karen.slimickarnpriester
twitter.com/KarenArnpriester
amazon.com/author/karenarnpriester
Blog: http://karenskoncepts.com/mythoughts

anessiasquest.com

In the Heavens

Psalms 91:11

"For he will command his angels concerning you to guard you in all your ways;"

Draken walked swiftly through the marble passageway, lit only by a warm, golden glow whose source was unknown. The excitement was building as he weaved his way through the network of stone halls, intricate stained glass panels, and vines with incredible cobalt and purple blossoms. Each flower's center had a spray of tendrils that shimmered and flickered with light. They pushed their way in through small openings and cracks, covering the ancient stone walls with their winding tendrils. He had the ability to think himself to her instantly, but instead he savored the journey through the tabernacle. As Draken entered the great hall, he sent groups of colorful butterflies scattering. Some of the butterflies were tiny and flashed bright yellow and orange light, while others were massive and moved almost as in slow motion. Their deep-purple and metallic gold wings didn't shine brightly like the others, but had a velvety luster that picked up the room's light with each flutter. The spaces in between were filled with every size and color of these delicate creatures. This room never failed to take Draken's breath away. There were exquisitely detailed sculptures, cast or carved from every precious metal and stone, encrusted with jewels and pearls. Above him were strings of glowing orbs that didn't appear to be connected in any way, glistening shades of pink, lavender, blue, and green. Beautiful birds of every description dove and soared in the upper dome. Draken would spend hours in this room, simply appreciating its beauty.

As he came upon an area of comfortable chairs, he saw Anessia sitting on the hard floor in her usual position, both legs folded under her with feet twisted out to the sides. She would sit this way for hours.

"When will you ever discover the comfort of these lush chairs?" he teased her.

She just grinned and said, "Probably never." Draken shook his head. She liked the coolness of the stone floor on her skin.

Draken sat down in his favorite chair, an opulent purple satin with three times the stuffing most chairs would contain. He waited for her to speak, but there was only silence. After a few anxious minutes, he could wait no longer.

"Well, Anessia. You summoned me here. You said you were ready."

She hesitated and seemed unsure for a moment, then handed him the delicate gold scroll. Draken, a regal man with long white hair and a full beard, took the scroll and fingered it gently, knowing the importance of its content. He took a deep breath and looked into Anessia's eyes. He loved her eyes, so large, so engulfing.

"I am ready," is all she said. Draken felt the contradiction of relief and dread. This would be a difficult quest, filled with many hardships and pain.

"You will have a lot of sadness to deal with, but you were selected with the knowledge that you are capable. You have a strong sense of justice and love."

"Oh, Draken, I want to make a difference, to be part of these miracles!"

"Once you leave, you realize you will not be able to change your mind. The quest will not be recalled," he reminded her.

"I totally understand. I know that I can do this. I know I can make you and our Father proud. I believe I am the one to help fulfill the destiny described in the scroll."

Draken truly adored Anessia and her tender heart, but she was fierce, one of the most committed wards he had responsibility for. He also knew that the quest was a journey filled with love, joy, and an incredible outcome.

"I will make the arrangements. Prepare yourself; your time here is short." They both came to a stand and, with a hug and a kiss on her head, Draken disappeared to carry out the necessary details.

~

Anessia stood alone and waited until she was sure Draken had left the chamber. She could contain herself no longer. She spun around, her hair flowing and gleaming in the light that was radiating down from above. It was wonderful to have a destiny. She giggled and hugged herself. Anessia mentally willed her beautiful wings to engage and she flew out of the windows near the top of the upper dome.

She didn't have to fly very far. There, by the glimmering pools, was Ennett. She slowly dropped down behind him, so quietly that he didn't know she was there. Anessia crept up behind him and jumped back as Ennett whirled around, but not quick enough. His folded wings smacked her in the face. "Oh Ennett, I thought I got you this time," she said, as she rubbed her cheek.

"Do you forget that I can read your thoughts? You need to work on shutting down that brain of yours when you plan to attack," he pouted at her, while touching her tender cheek. They both laughed and sat down on the cool grass next to the pools of crystal-clear water. They slipped their feet in and giggled loudly as the fish nibbled their toes. Anessia loved the landscape outside the main tabernacle. It had sumptuous gardens, streams, and trees that bore delicious fruits. Flowers of every size, color, and scent. Some were deep shades that were fuzzy and glimmered, while others were tucked under the shade of the trees with transparent petals that glowed with pulsing light. The aromas were so delicious.

She couldn't count the different species of animals that roamed through the gardens. Every visit was a new discovery. These unique and exotic creatures would wander the gardens and come when beckoned, allowing her to pet and love on them.

"Well, I assume it is time?"

"Yes, it is," she acknowledged.

"Anessia, it is a different realm there," he warned. "There is darkness, despair, and pain."

"I know. I can do this. Draken and our Father do not send me to fail."

"I have faith in you but, please be careful!"

They both sat quietly for a short time. "I need to go prepare," whispered Anessia.

"I love you Anessia, I will be here for you always." They held each other for what felt like an eternity but it was only moments in another time.

Chapter 1

Leah thought she could bear it no longer. Why didn't this baby come out? She had been pushing and writhing for hours, hurting so bad that she wanted to die. Finally, the nurse came in and said she was ready to have the baby. Leah knew that she would have feelings for this kid eventually but, right now, she almost hated it. They wheeled her into delivery and after thirty more minutes, the miracle of birth happened. A little, white-skinned, red-haired girl with blue eyes. She looked at her and felt numb. She may have connected better if the baby had looked like her. If she had gotten her golden skin, dark, curly hair and chestnut brown eyes. This baby looked like a stray, not her kid.

Leah had endured a difficult life and tried to bury it with alcohol, drugs, and sex. During her drunken months of pregnancy, she thought it would be funny to name her baby girl Champagne, after her favorite beverage. Champagne Marie Crenshaw. Champagne would carry her mother's last name since Leah didn't know which John was the proud papa. Leah had considered having another abortion, but this time was different. This baby would change her life. She just knew it. Leah wanted to be loved and wanted someone to love. She'd convinced herself she could be a mom. When Leah was in her seventh month, she had stopped hooking and left Los Angeles. She moved north for a fresh start. Champagne would find out quickly that her mom failed miserably at being a mother. She would also find out there was someone watching over her, protecting her.

When the hospital determined that Leah was ready for release, she was indignant and annoyed. Three days was not nearly long enough if you asked her. She figured she deserved and could use at least another week of leisure and strong pain meds while the nurses cared for Champagne. Upon leaving the hospital, Leah brought the baby back to the disgusting motel room that she had rented with her assistance checks. She figured they would do okay, since the amount written on those checks would increase with the birth of Champagne. She might have been able to afford a nicer place, but the majority of her money went for her alcohol and drugs. *How was she going to take care of a baby all by herself?* Looking around the room, Leah realized that she should have prepared a little more for the baby. She pulled out a drawer, dumped it, and laid Champagne in it. The strong pain meds were wearing off and they had only prescribed glorified aspirin as far as Leah was concerned. Luckily, she had stopped on the way home to pick up a big bottle of cheap wine.

"Well brat, I guess the closest I'll come to champagne for awhile is changing your crappy diapers." She laughed to herself, *"That was a good one Leah. You haven't lost your dazzling wit yet."*

~

Several years crawled by and, somehow, Champagne survived her mother's indifference. On one summer evening, Leah finally could not take it any longer. The pounding on the door was killing her head. What a hangover she had. When she jerked the door open, she looked into the chest of a police officer. Behind him stood her neighbor, *Miss Nose Up My Butt*. She could tell it wasn't good by the smirk on Miss Butt's face.

"We got a call that you have a toddler playing unattended on the landing," said the officer.

"Well, I don't see no kid out here, do you?" shot back Leah.

"Not at the moment, but your neighbor called quite concerned. She said that it is not unusual to see your front door wide open and your small daughter playing out here by the stairs. Do you understand how dangerous that is?"

"Well yes, Officer, I do. I'm not an idiot. I am always just inside the door, watching her every move. The kid has gotta have some fresh air and sunshine right?"

"Ma'am, unless you use better judgment and find a safer place for your daughter to play, we will be back out with Child Services," threatened the Officer.

"Okay. I will figure out something."

The officer filled out his paperwork and handed Leah her copy. "This call will be documented." He held the paper for a delayed moment, making eye contact with Leah.

"Thank you, Officer," Leah said sarcastically as she snatched it from his hand.

As the officer moved down the stairs, Leah looked over at Miss Butt as she was turning to head back to her door. Leah smiled a big smile at her, flipped her off with both hands, and then slammed the door as loudly as possible.

"Thanks, Pagne, just what I needed." She glared at her sweet face and grumbled, "Worthless brat." Leah had decided when Champagne was a year old that she did not deserve the name Champagne. She hadn't improved Leah's life, but complicated it. Leah called her Pagne, pronounced as "Pain." The fact that Pagne was showing signs of freckles to go with the red hair from her nameless father didn't help either. Leah hated freckles with a passion. She plopped down on the ratty couch that folded out to their bed and turned on the TV, filling a tumbler with wine.

~

Leah's lust for drinking didn't allow her to survive on the meager assistance she received, so she'd begun hooking again shortly after Pagne was born. Pagne's childhood was a whirlwind of her mother's customers, late nights, and the consequences of being the child of an alcoholic. One thing was consistent, an anchor that Pagne could rely on, her mother's total disregard for her. As time passed, Pagne had no choice but to be self-sufficient. She kept herself clean, got herself ready for school, and made sure the trash in the room didn't pile up too high.

When Pagne was eight years old, Adam Williams was her mother's new flavor of the month ... good looking, funny and he actually had a job, a nice change for Leah. Adam always brought a bottle of quality champagne for her and Jack Daniels for him. A few drinks, some laughs and then "Good lovin'," as her mother would say. Leah considered him a boyfriend, so she didn't charge him for her company. Pagne learned to keep out of the way when Adam or other men were there. The close quarters of the motel room made it difficult, but Pagne would lock the bathroom door and climb into the tub, pretending she was in a boat heading to a strange new land.

She would also read with a passion. She loved stories about fairies, faraway places, or brave characters who saved the day. She read whatever she could bring home from school. Her mom certainly wouldn't bother to take her to the library or buy a book. When the tub was too disgusting to get into, Pagne would pile up dirty laundry on the floor and make a nest. The width of the floor space fit her and her nest perfectly. She wished the walls were more sound proof though. The loud laughing and sexual noises from the other room made it hard for her to read, pretend, or sleep. Pagne wasn't sure what they were doing, but she felt uncomfortable hearing them. Sometimes, the men Leah brought home would hit her. Pagne knew to stay very quiet. She didn't want them to know she was there. Some mornings, Leah's face would be swollen and bruised. When Pagne would look at her with concern, Leah would shrug and say, "Comes with the territory."

Adam never hit her mom. He would always bring Pagne a toy or candy when he came over. He was nice enough, but something made her uneasy about him. He didn't do anything bad, but he always wanted Pagne to sit on his lap.

She didn't like it and she wasn't sure why. Even her mom didn't like it. Leah would jerk Pagne off of his lap and plop herself down there instead, giving Pagne the evil eye. Leah didn't realize how grateful Pagne was for removing her from the awkward situation.

Even at the age of eight, Pagne was independent. She could get her own breakfast and lunch, toaster pastries or cold cereal. It wasn't so bad when the milk hadn't soured, but usually she ate the cereal dry. She got free hot lunches at school when she started first grade. Leah wasn't hungry until late evening, since she drank her meals during the day. She would throw something together for dinner, but in her drunken stupor, usually burned it. Pagne didn't eat much. She didn't talk much either and doctors thought it was because of Leah's frequent drinking during her pregnancy. But, according to Pagne, she just didn't have anything much to say.

One hot summer evening, Leah drank herself into another stupor and passed out on the bathroom floor, leaving Pagne alone with Adam. He grinned at her and turned on some cartoons. Their TV only had three channels. Luckily, one was cartoons... most of the time. Pagne loved cartoons. She could watch them all day and pretend she lived in the TV where she could fly like a super hero. Adam sat down in the old recliner and motioned for Pagne to come over to him. When she came close, he reached out and grabbed her by the waist, pulling her onto his lap.

"Your mommy is outta service, so maybe Adam and Pagne can have some fun? You wanna play with me, sweetheart?" Her instincts told her it wasn't good. Adam's breath stunk from the liquor. She felt his arms tighten around her. Pagne began to whimper and tried to pull away. Adam was whispering and sputtering spit into her ear.

"Be quiet. I'm not going to hurt you. Trust me, you'll like it ... well, I will." She felt one hand slipping between her thighs and the other sliding up her belly, lifting up her t-shirt. Pagne brought her leg up and slammed down hard, kicking him in the shin with her heel. He grabbed her even tighter, squeezing her painfully. She kicked his shin again and this time he let go. As he grabbed at his leg, Pagne was able to slip off his lap and head to the front door. Adam jumped out of the chair and lunged at her, screaming with anger and pain. He was behind her and grabbed her arms. It hurt terribly and she began kicking and screaming. Her screams woke Leah who came stumbling into the room, yelling for Adam to shut the brat up. She was confused when she saw Adam and Pagne struggling by the door.

"What the hell is going on?" She bellowed.

Adam released Pagne and spun around to Leah. "Nuthin', kid just went nuts on me, she tried to run away." It took a few minutes for Leah's drunken brain to absorb the situation.

"So, my little Pagne didn't wanna play with you huh?" Leah showed no reaction as she tried to remain standing. She managed to focus on Pagne's face and gave her the most hateful glare Pagne had ever seen. Pagne pulled open the front door and ran out, tears filling her eyes and clouding her vision. Through her tears, Pagne thought she saw white wings fluttering around her. Then blackness.

When Pagne woke up, she hurt all over. Every part of her was bruised and sore. Her head was pounding with pain. She could hear voices, but she didn't want to open her eyes. She could hear a sweet lady's voice speaking to her at times. She was curious about the woman, but decided it was better to pretend that she was somewhere else. Sleep, she just wanted to sleep. It didn't hurt so bad when she slept. In her dreams, she could fly with wonderful white wings as others flew around her, laughing, dipping, and gliding.

Pagne woke up to her mother's voice, speaking close to her ear. "You gotta wake up. What am I going to do with a brain-dead kid? I can't deal with this Pagne. Wake up now!" Pagne opened her eyes and looked at her mother. Her face was not haggard and worn from worry, but the familiar face of someone hung over. Leah's breath reeked of wine. "Well it's about time. What took you so long... sweetheart?" Sweetheart was thrown in for the benefit of the nurse who had just walked in. "Me and Adam have been worried sick. You scared your mama something awful." As the nurse finished her duties and left the room, Leah moved in closer, so only Pagne could hear. "Pagne, they think Adam hurt you. We both know that's a big fat lie, right? The police are going to talk to you. Mommy can't lose Adam, baby. You gotta fix this."

Later that day, several officers and a very nervous, skinny woman named Miss Lament, came into Pagne's room. The officers tried to be friendly and brought a teddy bear with them. It was very cute and Pagne found it oddly comforting to hug. Miss Lament, who didn't smile and had very tiny, beady eyes, was trying to ask Pagne what had happened with Adam. Pagne decided she didn't have anything to say. She knew that Adam was a bad man but, even at her tender age, Pagne intuitively understood that it was her mother's truth. Leah needed him.

The officers and Miss Lament left very frustrated. Her mother had been waiting in the hall and slipped in. "Good girl. Now we just have to convince the judge. We're going to move in with Adam once this whole mess is cleared up. He's going to take care of both of us. Won't that be nice? We'll be a family real soon!" Pagne didn't respond. "We hit the jackpot, baby," cooed Leah.

That evening, the sweet-talking nurse was on duty. She took Pagne's temperature and adjusted her tubing. While she worked, she talked softly to Pagne, assuring her that she would be fine. As she turned to leave, Pagne grabbed her hand, squeezing it tight. The nurse, who's nametag said "Mrs. Greenly," looked into Pagne's eyes. She saw fear and worry in them. She asked, "What's wrong, hon? You in pain?" Pagne took a deep breath and spoke in a whisper for the first time since waking up.

"What happened?" she asked.

"Oh honey, no one has told you what's going on? Well, I'm not sure why, but you ran out your front door and then you fell down three flights of cement stairs. You broke your leg and your arm, cracked your head, and have lots of bumps and bruises. You are very lucky that you didn't hurt yourself even worse. I believe you have a guardian angel, dear. Yep, an angel that cushioned your fall. We all have an angel, you know. Talk to mine sometimes, when I'm sad or scared. You should thank your angel for protecting you. They have a thankless job!"

Pagne asked when she would be going home. "You should be able to go home in a few days," the nurse answered. Pagne began to weep softly. "Oh sweetheart, that's not that far away." The nurse looked into Pagne's face and realized this was something different. "Don't you want to go home?" Pagne just closed her eyes and let go of the sweet nurses hand.

After she left, Pagne whispered quietly, "Thank you." She did see wings, she was sure of it.

~

Pagne lay in her bed, a cast on her right arm, a cast on her left leg, bandages here and there, and a dull headache as Leah filled out all the paperwork for her release. Leah looked at the prescriptions for Pagne and was grumbling that nothing was strong enough to do her much good. "The least they could do is give us Valium." Several nurses entered the room and helped Pagne into a wheelchair. Pagne's doctor and a police officer walked into the room. "Now, Miss Crenshaw, there are some requirements you must meet to have your daughter home with you," said the officer. "This Adam Williams is not to be within 300 yards of your daughter or your residence."

"But he didn't do anything," Leah insisted.

"That might be, but until the judge makes his determination, the restraining order is in effect," the officer responded.

"Yes, of course," Leah snapped.

Pagne's doctor stepped toward Leah and began speaking. "Here is the treatment plan for Champagne's after care. Her therapy is crucial if she is to have a full recovery. I also want to stress that she will need a balanced, healthy diet and a safe, clean environment. Obviously, the stairs will present a safety issue. Have you made arrangements for assistance?"

"Yes, I have taken care of everything," She lied.

"Mrs. Crenshaw, a child services worker will be checking in," reminded the officer.

"Yes, I know, another person up my butt. Can we leave now?"

"Yes, you may. But remember, your court appearance is at three o'clock today. We will remove Champagne from your care if you fail to appear."

"Yes, I know, I know," replied Leah, disrespecting the officer.

The nurses put Pagne into the cab for the ride home while Leah had a cigarette. Once her nicotine fix was satisfied, she climbed into the cab next to Pagne. She shot the nurses a hard glare when their faces revealed their disapproval of her indifference. Pagne sat quietly while Leah went on and on about their new life with Adam. Leah talked about how Adam really cared about them, how happy they would all be together, and how Adam would bring money into the house. Leah finally shut up and drifted into her fantasy of a wonderful future with Adam.

Pagne considered telling her mother what Adam had done, but she was a smart girl. She knew there was no point. Her mother already knew. When they got to the hotel, Leah struggled to get Pagne upstairs, cursing with each step. Once inside the room, Pagne looked around and wasn't surprised to see that nothing the doctor had listed was done. Pagne hopped over to the couch and sat in silence.

"Wanna toaster pastry, doll? Know how much you love them." Pagne shook her head and turned on the TV.

A few minutes later, there was a tap on the door. Leah opened it and Adam's head popped in.

"Hey, my two favorite girls. Just wanted to stop by and bring Pagne a get well gift." It was a tin of mints from the liquor store down the street and a car air freshener in the shape of a rose.

"What did you bring mama?" asked Leah with a little girl voice and a giggle. Adam slipped a big bottle of champagne around the door.

"Can I come in for awhile?" he asked.

"No baby, not till the court says it's okay. My neighbor next door has big ears and eyes. This should all be resolved this afternoon. You gotta be patient." Leah laughed as Adam tried to grope her through the opening. "We'll all be together soon," assured Leah. Adam looked over at Pagne and winked with a disgusting lick of his lips.

"Okay, but I miss you guys. Good to have you back with us, Pagne." Pagne turned the TV volume up and turned away to look at the screen.

"She'll warm up to ya, baby, just give her some time. I'll call when I get out of court." Leah closed the door, giggling. She looked over at Pagne. Pagne could feel Leah's eyes on her, but she refused to respond.

~

Pagne was very nervous sitting in the courtroom, waiting to find out what they expected of her. Everyone was so serious, except her mother. She whispered insulting comments about everyone. Sticks up their "you know what's" and other such childish remarks. When it was their turn to appear before the judge, Leah bounced up, flicking her hair. Once she was at the front, she suddenly seemed to realize that Pagne was still struggling to get out of her seat. She smiled and loudly proclaimed, "It's okay baby, Mommy is here." She went back and, very graciously, helped Pagne into the aisle. Her performance impressed Pagne. Once she made it to the front, Pagne sat at the table facing the judge.

Leah began by explaining that the whole thing had been a misunderstanding. She explained that Pagne had been throwing a temper-tantrum and Adam had been trying to keep her from running out of the room. When the judge asked if she was in the room at the time, she admitted that she had not been because she was suffering from one of her migraines and was laying on the bathroom floor for relief. "The cool tile is soothing," she explained.

They called forward Pagne's doctor and he described the extensive bruising on Pagne's thighs, chest, and arms. In the photos they showed, a large man's handprints were clearly visible. Leah did not have any explanation for the bruises. The judge looked at Pagne and asked if she had anything she wanted to say. Pagne just looked out the windows at the beautiful blue sky, wishing she could fly away.

The lawyer representing Pagne's interests made a good case that the events before her fall were clearly assault and possibly molestation. The judge agreed and ordered the restraining order to stand pending further investigation. Adam had been picked up and interviewed after Pagne was admitted to the hospital. He wasn't arrested, but he did have a court date.

Leah went into a rage. "This is ridiculous. You are punishing a good man, my man, for something that was very innocent. This isn't fair," she yelled.

"Well, Miss Crenshaw, if you want to have your daughter in your home, you must honor the restraining order. If you disregard the order, Champagne will be placed in the care of the state until this case is resolved," responded the judge with obvious distain.

"Well, I don't think me and Adam should suffer because of this brat. We have a life to start. You guys can deal with her," Leah said as she looked at Pagne in disgust. Leah then turned and walked out of the courtroom.

Everyone stood there in shock. No one knew what to say or do. Pagne hobbled over to the window and allowed one tear to roll down her face, just one. Then she looked to the skies and flew far away.

Chapter 2

The noise at Langston Hall was incredible, all the screaming, laughing, and yelling. But, even harder to bear was the crying at night. Pagne had a room with just three other girls. Since she was still recovering from her injuries, she didn't have to stay in one of the dorms. Her mother had been gracious enough to hand the social worker a box of her belongings before slamming the motel door. She had her few items of clothing, some personal papers and drawings, some costume jewelry she had collected here and there, the bear from the police officer, and Adam's gifts: the candy tin and the stinky rose. These last two items she quickly tossed in the trash. The staff said she could go through the donated items to find more clothes and shoes, but she was comfortable with what she had. Pagne settled in to begin a new chapter of life.

This storage facility for broken hearts and dreams was clean, but stark, no softness or textures. Washable surfaces of mustard gold and brown. A local art class had come in and attempted to brighten the main playroom. They'd painted a large, underwater mural on the longest wall. It was a good attempt, but inconsistent styles and levels of ability made it look second best, much like the lives of the children living there. The food was good, better than Pagne was used to having, but institutional and a bit bland. The staff was helpful, but Pagne could feel the wall of detachment they erected to protect their hearts.

Her healing progressed slowly and she eventually had the casts removed. Her arm and leg were thin and weak. The facility got her therapy started and she was thankful that they had not left it up to Leah. The county decided that Pagne would receive better care at Langston Hall during her recuperation. There were no attempts to place her in foster-care.

They asked her several times if she wanted her social worker to try to set up visitation with her mother, but Pagne declined. The facility ended up being her home for nineteen months. Pagne looked at her healed limbs. Her leg looked almost identical to the other except for the scars where they had run a metal rod through her shin for traction. Her arm, however, was a different story. There was scarring and she had difficulty bending it. Most of the time, it hung straight at her side. The doctors had to operate to remove bone fragments and repair some of the tendons. The therapist was pleased with the progress Pagne was making, excited actually, and this made Pagne realize just how serious her injuries had been.

Pagne enjoyed her time at Langston Hall. She became friends with several of the kids and started to trust them. Her best friend was Bree, who was wild and crazy compared to Pagne. Bree had long, blonde hair and pale blue eyes. Pagne somewhat envied her straight hair and flawless skin and no freckles. Bree laughed and giggled at everything, especially if someone farted or burped. Pagne didn't see the humor in these rude body functions, but would laugh with Bree because her giggles were infectious. Bree would sneak into Pagne's room late in the evening and they'd sit in the dark whispering and sharing their stories. Bree was one year older than Pagne. She also had a lot more to talk about than Pagne. Bree's family had died in a car crash several months ago and she didn't have any other family to take care of her. Her years with her family sounded magical to Pagne. Bree had her own room, a little brother to play with, good food, but best of all was her stories about her mom and dad. They were huggers and cuddlers. Bree talked about the stories her mom would read to her. Bree and her mom would snuggle in Bree's bed and use a flashlight to read in the dark. Her dad would take her fishing and hiking. After Bree would sneak back to her dorm, Pagne would lie in bed and pretend she was in her own room with her parents just outside, discussing family plans. She would drift off to sleep.... until Leah would show up at her beautiful house, banging on the door, demanding to get her kid back.

~

Bree ran into Pagne's room early one morning, very serious. This was unusual for Bree.

"I'm leaving today. They found a foster-home for me," she explained.

"You don't look very happy, I thought that is what you wanted."

"I do, but some of the kids have told me how bad their foster-homes were. What if I get a bad one, Pagne? What if they don't feed me, or hit me, or worse?" Pagne wasn't sure what to say.

"The social worker said we just have to tell them if something is wrong or call 911," reminded Pagne. "Besides, a nurse explained to me that we each have a guardian angel. So, you have one, too. You'll think I'm crazy, but my angel wrapped me in her wings when I fell and kept me from hurting my brain or my insides."

"Seriously?" asked Bree. Pagne nodded dramatically. "I hope you're right, I would love to have a guardian angel. I guess I'm just nervous. Kinda weird having a whole new family."

"I'm going to miss you, Bree," Pagne said, sadly. This was her first experience with truly losing someone that was important to her. She did not miss her mom. Bree left with the social worker later that morning. She was laughing and hugging everyone as she made her way to the large, front entrance. Bree looked over and saw Pagne, tears rolling down her cheeks. Bree blew her a kiss and was gone.

Miss Renee, the only adult Pagne trusted at Langston Hall, slipped next to Pagne and put her arm around her shoulder. She didn't say a word, and just stood next to her. Pagne appreciated the gesture and leaned into her. Miss Renee was young and had just started working at Langston Hall. She hadn't built a wall around her heart yet. Pagne thought she was beautiful. Miss Renee was tall, her dark blonde hair cut in a short bob, and she had green eyes that sparkled when she smiled.

Bree's absence left Pagne with only one other close friend, Itchy. Itchy wasn't his real name, but he was always scratching. He said it had started when he had lice so bad that his skin was raw. They had shaved his head and made him take baths in foul smelling medication. When Pagne asked him if he still itched, he said only once in awhile, but it was so bad, he would stop in his tracks and just start scratching everywhere. The bugs were gone, so Pagne figured it was just the memory of the bugs that haunted him. Afterward, he would go on as if nothing happened. Most of the kids teased him terribly and acted as if he had bugs that would jump on them. His real name was Arthur, but everyone called him Itchy. He kinda liked it. He had always dreaded hearing his name when he was at home. He usually got screamed at or hit. Arthur had been saved from an extremely abusive dad. His mom abandoned him when he was very small and he had lived with his dad for seven years and suffered terribly. Itchy wouldn't talk about his dad or his life at all. If anyone tried to talk to him, he turned bright red, clinched his hands, and locked his jaw. Pagne saw the pain and horror in his eyes.

They had better things to discuss than the past. They didn't get to see each other a lot. Boys and girls were in separate sections of the facility. When there was shared time and space, they were stuck like glue. When they did talk, it was about their dreams and their plans.

Itchy wanted to be a policeman, a fireman, and a rock-star. Pagne had decided this particular week that she wanted to be a circus performer, the flying trapeze. She figured this was the closest she could get to flying without wings.

It was Pagne's tenth birthday and, after lunch, the staff brought in a glowing cake with ten candles and "Happy 10th Birthday Pagne" written in bright pink on chocolate frosting. Everyone sang the birthday song and Pagne actually felt special in those few moments. As soon as they finished the song, the kids began screaming "Cake! Cake!" The cake was wonderful, so chocolaty. Pagne loved chocolate. This was only her second birthday cake and both were here at Langston Hall.

As the kids moved out to the playground, Miss Renee walked over to Pagne. "Happy birthday, sweetheart," she said, as she kneeled down. "Ummm, this is kind of unusual, we weren't expecting her, but your mother is here. She wants to see you. You can say no, but you should know that she is working with the court to get visitation and parental rights reinstated. It might be a good idea to talk to her. I can stay in the room with you if you'd prefer." Pagne's face fell. Her mother? How can that be? She gave her to the state. So many questions raced through Pagne's mind. Could they really give her back to her mother? What about Adam? Pagne dreaded the thought of being in the same room with Leah, but she needed some answers.

"I'll see her, Miss Renee," Pagne responded. "Would you please stay in the room with us, at least at first?"

"Of course, Pagne." They walked the long hallway, holding hands.

When Pagne and Miss Renee stepped into the waiting room, Miss Renee released Pagne's hand and moved to the chair in the corner. Pagne stood there face to face with her seated mother, the woman who gave birth to her, who was supposed to protect her and love her. Pagne felt nothing but disappointment and building anger. Just then, she felt a light brush against her cheek. She looked and saw nothing, just smelled a lovely scent that quickly melted away.

Leah rose from her chair and squealed loudly! "Oh, my baby! I've missed you so much!" She moved closer to Pagne and squeezed her in a crushing hug. Pagne pulled away, pretending her arm was still tender. Leah stared into her eyes and grinned. "You've gotten taller, Sweetie. You're such a big girl. Did you miss your mommy? I sure missed you," Leah lied, as she plopped back down in her chair.

Pagne moved over to a chair on the opposite side of the table and sat down, not speaking or looking at her mother. Leah shot Miss Renee a nasty look. "Whats with the guard honey? You in trouble in here?" asked Leah. Pagne realized that she would have to speak to her mother.

Quietly she confessed, "I asked her to be with me." Leah looked shocked.

"You afraid of me baby? You know I wouldn't hurt you," said Leah, glancing over her shoulder at Miss Renee. "I'm hurt that you don't trust your own mama." Leah had a ridiculous pout on her face.

"What do you want?" asked Pagne, coldly.

"Well, you didn't think I'd miss your birthday did you? I brought you a present. Sorry it looks so messy. The old bat outside had to search it before I could give it to you. Just like a prison in here, huh Pagne? Bet you can't wait to escape!" Pagne looked at the gift bag her mother was holding, obviously a recycled bag. Pagne didn't think a bag with storks and rattles printed on it was standard for a tenth birthday. The tissue paper was bunched up and Pagne could see bright orange knit pushed down in the bottom of the bag. Leah pulled out a sweater, size eight. *How appropriate, Mom,* Pagne thought, *much too small, middle of the summer, and stained.* Her mother had probably found it at the local thrift store or in the lost and found at the motel office. To make matters worse, Pagne hated orange. Her mother looked pleased with herself and held the sweater up to Pagne. "Looks a little small, sweetie, but sweaters stretch! It's the thought that counts right?" cooed Leah. *This is so ridiculous. There was no thought to it,* Pagne told herself sarcastically.

Leah leaned in close, speaking in a quiet voice, thinking Miss Renee could not hear. "I want to bring you home, baby. It's just not the same without you."

"What about Adam? I thought you two were starting a new life," asked Pagne.

"Oh Adam. Well, that ended months ago. Caught him cheating on me with a fourteen-year-old tramp. Not gonna let some slime dog sneak around on me."

Pagne was so angry. *He can fondle and attack your daughter and you keep him, but he cheats on you and you dump him. Guess it's not cheating if it's your kid,* thought Pagne. "Sorry," is all the response Pagne could muster.

"Well, I've met several generous men, but no one I can count on. Figured you and me can take care of each other and be two single gals. It'll be fun Pagne. You'll see."

Pagne looked at her mother in disbelief. "I don't want to come home with you!" Pagne said. Leah jumped up and stepped back.

"I can't believe you... you ungrateful brat. How dare you. I am your mother!" exclaimed Leah. "How do you expect me to live, I need the money your sorry butt brings in from the county. I have rights. You are my kid. No one is going to keep you from me." Leah grabbed the sweater and stormed to the door. "Get used to it, Pagne, you're mine and there's nothing you can do to change that. So quit pretending you get a different life. This is what fate dealt you. You're mine and we're stuck with each other!" Leah quickly stomped out of the room. Miss Renee had moved in closer when Leah jumped up and after Leah left the room, she reached out for Pagne and tried to comfort her.

Things were normal for the next few weeks, then Miss Renee came into Pagne's dorm early one morning. After recovery and therapy, they had moved Pagne into one of the eight-bed dorm rooms. "Good morning Pagne. We need to go see Mr. Phillips in the administration office. We need to discuss your case." Pagne felt a lump in her throat. The other kids had warned her that when you went to see Mr. Phillips, big changes were going to happen. The courts had decided either you were going home or you had been placed in foster-care. Pagne was praying that it was the latter. She didn't know what she would do if she had to go home. She noticed a sweet scent again, the same wonderful aroma that she had smelled when she saw her mom. It calmed her, gave her a sense of peace.

"Okay, Miss Renee. Let me put on my shoes." Once she was ready, they headed over to see Mr. Phillips.

When Pagne and Miss Renee got close to the office, Pagne stopped and looked up at Miss Renee. "Will my mother be there?" she asked cautiously. Miss Renee looked at her sweet, freckled face and assured her that she would not. Pagne was relieved and moved toward the office. She had seen Mr. Phillips before but had not talked to him. He looked like a kind man. "Well, hello there, Miss Champagne. Please have a seat. That is an unusual name … Champagne."

"Everyone calls me Pagne, sir."

"Okay then, Pagne. Do you know why we are here today?"

"I think so, sir. You're gonna tell me where I am going."

"Yes, dear. We have discussed your case with the judge, your attorney, your mother, your social worker, and Miss Renee. How would you feel about going home?"

"I thought my mom had to do a lot of stuff before I could go there. The other kids said the parents have to take classes and get tests, lots of stuff. I don't think my mom did any of that."

"Well, your case is a little different. The state did not remove you from your mother. Your mother felt she was unable to provide a good home for you at the time, but now she believes she is able to be a responsible parent. Apparently, the person in question, this Mr. Williams, is no longer involved with your mother. The case against him was dismissed due to lack of evidence." Mr. Phillips paused, "It is the goal of this office to reunite parents and children whenever possible."

Pagne felt her heart clench. "Sir, do I get a vote?"

"Well, Pagne, we certainly want to hear what you have to say, but this is a decision for adults." Pagne wondered if telling Mr. Phillips about the men coming in all night, the beatings her mother endured, and the drinking, would make a difference, then decided it wouldn't. Her mother was a good liar. *Who would believe her? She was just a kid.* Pagne leaned back in her chair. She didn't have anything more to say.

Pagne went into a deep, dark place. She spent a long time staring out the windows wishing she could fly away into the clouds. She started to wonder why she was even here. What was the point of her life? Was she just to be a yo-yo for her mother to play with? She wanted to know what was going to happen next, but dreaded knowing at the same time. Miss Renee tried to comfort Pagne the best she could, tried to get her to talk, but Pagne had shut down. One afternoon, Pagne approached Miss Renee. She had to try to reach out to someone before it was too late. "Miss Renee, you heard her. She doesn't love me. She just wants the money she gets for me," Pagne reminded her.

"Oh Pagne, I am sure she loves you. We all say things we don't mean when we are angry or hurt."

"Miss Renee, you don't know my mom." Pagne walked away, defeated.

She moved out to the playground and went to her favorite spot. There was a tree there with huge branches that sheltered her from the sun. One branch curved low and was easy to climb onto. From that branch, she could climb way into the bowels of the tree. She felt safe there. She laid back on one of the large branches, staring up into the streams of light that filtered through the leaves. She watched as butterflies lazily glided through the glittering light. She thought she could smell the flowering vines growing up the trellis close by, but the scent wasn't right. No, it wasn't the vines. She knew this scent, the same scent she had smelled twice before. The scent of her guardian angel? "Are you here?" Pagne asked. "Is that you?" The scent grew stronger as it swirled around her, filling her nostrils with glorious delight. "It is you. I knew you were real!" She felt soft feathers brushing against her cheek and arm. Pagne closed her eyes tight and pretended she could see her angel. Then she heard a whisper, "I am here." Pagne almost fell out of the tree. She was so surprised to hear a voice. But, did she hear it? It didn't seem to come through her ears. It felt like a thought, a thought that wasn't hers, a breath that fluttered through her brain. She quickly looked around, thinking one of the kids might be messing with her, but no one was there. It was her and her angel. Pagne smiled and knew everything would be okay.

Several days later, Pagne went to Mr. Phillips' office again. Miss Renee was already there when she came in. They invited Pagne to sit, which she did slowly. "Am I going home now?" asked Pagne. Mr. Phillips looked at her quite seriously for a few minutes and then glanced at Miss Renee.

"Not today, Pagne. We revisited your case and have some concerns about your mother's ability to provide you with a safe place to live."

Pagne was not aware of it, but Miss Renee had done some investigating after their last talk and found out that Leah was arrested three times for public intoxication. She also had pending charges for prostitution. They attributed the county's oversight to a mix-up in social security numbers on Leah's police files.

"We have decided to give your mother more time to resolve her issues. Rather than have you stay here during this time, we have released you for foster-care placement. Miss Renee will explain the process and your rights after our meeting here. Do you have any questions you would like to ask me?"

"No, sir, but thank you, sir."

Mr. Phillips dismissed Pagne and Miss Renee. Pagne felt a huge dread lift, but a new anxiety quickly replaced it. What was coming next?

Chapter 3

Miss Renee explained all the rules and safety precautions to Pagne. She would be leaving today. "Pagne, you will love Mrs. Buttonhook. She is an older lady who has been a foster-parent for many years. She is a lovely person, and she absolutely adores her kids. She has three foster-children living with her now. I know she will provide you with a wonderful home." Pagne went back to the dorm to pack up her few belongings. She hugged the girls and asked for permission to see Itchy before she left. Itchy came into the rec room and saw the look in Pagne's eyes. "You're leaving me?" he asked.

"Yep, they found a nice home for me... at least for awhile. I didn't want to leave without telling you goodbye."

"Sure glad you did." Itchy got very quiet and looked down. "I'm really going to miss you, Pagne. Not going to be the same around here without you."

"I'll see if they will let me visit."

"Yeah, that would be cool. Good luck, Pagne. Hope they don't figure out what a brat you really are!" He smiled at her with a crooked grin.

"You are so mean." she laughed, as she slapped his arm. Pagne watched as he headed back to the boy's area. She thought she saw him wipe his eyes with his T-shirt.

The social worker delivering Pagne to her new home had a name, but Pagne was too distracted to remember. The lady was really chatty and just talked and talked. Pagne let her ramble, too nervous to have a conversation anyway. They pulled up in front of a cute three-story house. It was painted bright yellow... banana yellow. Pagne noticed the purple door and shutters. The yard was full of brightly colored flowers. It even had a white picket fence with an arbor to walk under. Pagne smiled and thought, *this is just too cute!* As they walked up the sidewalk to the front door, Pagne smelled freshly cut grass, flowers, and chocolate chip cookies baking.

When they stepped onto the porch, the social worker rang the bell and Pagne felt her whole body stiffen. She felt a flush in her cheeks. A young girl, maybe a year older than Pagne, with white powder on her face and t-shirt opened the door.

"She's here!" she yelled as she ran back into the other room. Pagne got a strong whiff of her angel, which was quickly overtaken by the smell of baking cookies.

As soon as they stepped into the living room, Pagne liked what she saw. It was bright and cheerful. Mrs. Buttonhook came in from the kitchen. She was older than Pagne expected. She was also very short and very wide. Her gray hair was styled in very tight curls.

"Well, hello there, my lovely. You are just adorable. I love freckles! My name is Ophelia Buttonhook, but all my kids call me Grandma." Pagne realized that she had never thought about grandmas or grandpas. She didn't even know if she had any. "You can take your time and figure out what feels good to you. I answer to just about anything." Grandma, which was the name Pagne would chose to use, suddenly swept Pagne up in her arms and gave her a big hug. Between the fleshy arms and her full bosom, Pagne thought she might suffocate. "Forgive me, sweetie, I just gotta hug," Grandma giggled. "God built it into my DNA! Nothing I can do about it."

God? Who or what was God? He built her? This was a very odd woman indeed, but Pagne felt an instant connection with this crazy lady. She felt herself grinning, without knowing why.

After the social worker talked Grandma's ear off for an hour, she finally left. Grandma then focused on Pagne and smiled as she said, "Boy that woman can gab. I didn't think anyone could out talk me. Let me show you around, sweetheart." She took Pagne upstairs to the third floor, to an attic room with steep angles on the walls. The stairs came up into the middle of the room. On each end was a window with a twin bed underneath it. There was a small dresser at each end and a large cabinet in the middle. The walls were painted a soft blue with white trim and there were large bulletin boards on each end of the room. One was empty but the other was filled with wonderful items that all meshed together.

"Well, sweetie, this bed is yours," she said as she pointed to the twin bed underneath the window that faced onto the back yard. "You can put your clothes in this dresser, and you have more room in the cabinet there. Macey will be sharing this room with you. You met her at the door earlier. Let me show you around the rest of the house, and then you'll have time to put away your things while I fix dinner."

They moved to the second floor. There was a large bathroom with a shower and tub.

"We all have to share this one bath I'm afraid. We came up with a schedule that works out fine. In here is the boy's room. They're at softball practice right now. You will meet them at dinner. Tad and Chad are twelve and they're twins. My room is right here. If you ever need anything, don't be afraid to knock on the door. Be sure to knock nice and loud. I take my hearing aid out at night. If I don't, I end up laying on that side and my ear aches for hours when I get up. Lord knows you'd think I'd roll over." She chuckled to herself as she moved back to the stairs. "Now, downstairs is the living room and kitchen. You've seen the living room, so let's go check on how the cookies are coming." Pagne loved the sound of Grandma's voice, so kind, joyful, and full of energy.

"Macey, this is Pagne. Pagne, this is Macey."

"Pagne, unusual name. Is that short for something?" asked Macey.

"Well, yeah. My mom named me Champagne after her favorite booze," replied Pagne.

"Well, I like Pagne better. I consider myself a pain, too!" Macey gave Pagne a big, warm smile. Pagne knew she would like Macey right away.

"Ohhhh my goodness, Macey, let's get this last batch of cookies out of the oven before they burn. You girls can only have one now because we'll be eating dinner soon. Pagne I hope you're not picky. We eat very simply here."

"I'm not picky at all," Pagne answered, as she helped Macey take the cookies off the sheet to cool. "These cookies smell so good! Sure we can just have one?" Pagne asked, as she stuffed one in her mouth.

Grandma chuckled. "You're gonna fit right in here, Pagne."

Tad and Chad exploded into the house just as they started to put dinner on the table. "You boys go get washed up quick," yelled Grandma. "Dinner is ready!" Tad ran straight to the stairs, and Chad froze, looking at Pagne.

"Who's this?" he asked.

"This is Pagne. You can dazzle her at dinner. Get up there and wash those hands and face. You're all dirty and sweaty." Pagne felt her cheeks warm as she sat at the table.

It seemed like only a few seconds had passed before Pagne could hear the boys pushing and stomping down the stairs. Tad made it through the door first and sat down with the rest of them. Chad was right behind him. He slipped on a sly grin and stood at the table with arms crossed over his chest.

"Why is she in my chair?" he asked. He tried to look injured and sad.

"Oh Chad, leave her alone. You know you always sit here next to me," Grandma said, waving him toward her. Chad looked at Pagne and grinned his biggest grin. Once he was seated, Grandma asked them all to hold hands and bow their heads. Macey leaned over and whispered in Pagne's ear, "Sometimes this can take a long time." Grandma started her prayer, thanking her God for the food, for the weather, for her health, for all of them, and for all the beauty in the world. After about five minutes, she apologized to God for being so short-winded and promised to make up for it during her evening prayers. Macey breathed a sigh of relief.

The dinner was delicious. Roasted chicken with baby potatoes, fresh green beans, and a wonderful fruit salad.

"Grandma, this is so good," said Tad through a mouth full of potatoes.

"Just eat and you can talk later. We got cookies for dessert. Macey made them this afternoon," Grandma announced. Tad and Chad started groaning and grabbing their guts as if they were in horrible pain. "Now you boys quit teasing her. She is a fine cook."

Pagne felt comfortable joining in. "I had one earlier and they are good, so if you don't want yours, I'll take them." She smiled at Macey.

"Noooo, we want them!" both boys exclaimed.

With an evil grin, Chad asked "Are you?"

"Are I what?" Pagne asked back.

"You know, a pain?" he asked with a snicker. This started a wave of laughter from Tad and Chad.

Pagne wished she had a dollar for every time she was asked that question. She decided Chad deserved a sarcastic answer. "No, but I can bring it!"

"Ewww, I'm scared," Chad responded with mock shaking.

"Now, now, boys, that's enough. Pagne is a fine name. You leave her alone!"

The boys stopped their teasing, but broke out in giggles every time they looked at each other. After dinner was done, each of them rinsed their plates and set them in the dishwasher.

"Will you kids finish up the kitchen please, me and Pagne need to have a conversation."

"Sure Grandma," they all chimed in.

Grandma fixed two big glasses of lemonade and a plate of cookies. She handed Pagne one of the glasses and moved out the back door into the yard. Pagne had never lived anywhere but in the motel and Langston Hall, so a yard was a new experience for her. She looked around at all the flowers, vines, bushes, and trees. There was an apple tree and a pear tree and, over in one corner, was a vegetable garden.

"We grew those beans you had tonight. We get a lot of our vegetables out of that garden. If you like gardening, I'll let you help tend it." Pagne had no clue if she liked gardening, but she liked the idea of making something grow, especially if you could eat it.

"I'd like to learn, Grandma." Grandma made her way to a little patio of large flat stones. Pretty moss grew in-between the stones with tiny purple flowers. There was a small table and chairs where they could sit. They were made of scrolled metal and the paint was chipped and faded. Grandma had placed brightly colored cushions in the chairs.

"Have a seat, hon. I'd like to discuss the house rules." Pagne listened attentively while Grandma explained the bathroom schedule, the chore rotation, laundry, and all the daily functions of a family. "I don't have a lot of rules about behavior but the ones I do have are important. Number one is to be respectful of our family. No name-calling, hitting, or insults. There is enough of that outside our house, we don't bring it in here. Second, we respect each others' personal possessions. Do not borrow or use anything without getting permission. If you need something, let me know, and I'll do my best to get it for you. The last is no lying. We can't deal with the issues of life if we're all lying up in this house. We are a family and we gotta have the facts if we're going to take care of each other." Pagne agreed to the rules and was happy to be part of this family.

As if they had radar, or they just knew Grandma's body language, the kids headed out the back door as Grandma was finishing. "Can we show her the tree-house now, Grandma?"

"Of course, children. Come in when it starts to get dark. You've got school tomorrow." Grandma took the glasses and headed into the house.

"Come on, Pagne, you're gonna love this!" Macey grabbed her hand and pulled her toward the backside of the yard. As they came around the wall behind the garden, there was an open field. A short distance away was a huge oak tree, gnarled and reaching to the sky. The boys were quite a ways ahead and got to the tree first. They scampered up the rope ladder like two squirrels. Macey and Pagne got there as the boys disappeared into a huge wooden shack sitting in the tree. Macey showed Pagne how to climb the rope ladder so that it didn't swing too much. When they got into the tree house, Pagne was amazed. There were chairs, a table, shelves with books and rocks, dead bugs, and all sorts of treasures. On the floor were huge pillows that now held the twins. "Beat ya again," they taunted.

"So what," Macey threw back. "You had a head start."

"Yeah right," Tad threw in response.

"Stop it you guys. Remember Grandma's rules!" Chad said sarcastically.

"What, you guys don't like the rules?" asked Pagne.

"Nah, they're fine. Grandma is really good to us, and we are all crazy about her, but she didn't tell you the most important rule," explained Macey.

"What's that?" Pagne asked.

They looked at each other and then turned to Pagne.

"Can we trust you to keep a secret?" Macey asked in a whisper. Pagne nodded her head emphatically.

"Gotta promise," Chad said.

"I swear," said Pagne.

"Grandma is bonkers!" Tad exclaimed.

"Tad, that isn't funny. She has some issues and we help to look out for her," explained Chad.

"What kind of issues?" asked Pagne.

"She forgets a lot and we just help her."

"Well, forgetting isn't that big a deal, right?" Pagne suggested.

The three of them looked at each other and Chad nodded, giving the group permission to reveal the severity of the problem. Macey proceeded to explain. "Well, she forgets what day it is so, we have to be sure to get to school during the week. She forgets to buy food sometimes. She loses everything: keys, her shoes, everything. We try to put things she needs out where she can find them. But, the worst thing is, she will forget the stove is on or food is cooking. She can forget and leave water running in the tub. We make sure her baths are scheduled when we are home, that way we can check the water so the house doesn't flood. We offer to help cook and clean the kitchen so we can be sure everything is turned off. We worry about her during the day, but we can't miss school."

"Why don't you guys tell the social worker?" asked Pagne.

"What! Are you crazy? This is the best place I've ever lived. She is good to us. We just have to look after her the way she looks after us," replied Tad with such passion. "So Pagne, you can't tell. They will move us out of here so fast your head will spin off."

"I won't. I already like it here and I don't want to go back to Langston Hall." The group of survivors pinky swore and Pagne officially became a member of the alliance.

~

Her first Saturday there, the kids were hanging out in the backyard where they were supposed to be weeding the garden, but they had gotten distracted with horseplay and teasing. The twins didn't fight or argue much, but they loved to wrestle. Pagne and Macey were cheering them on and would clap when one pinned the other. Pagne wasn't sure how it happened, but she got dared to square off with Chad. Tad and Macey were laughing hysterically as the two of them stomped around in a circle like sumo wrestlers. It was fun and Pagne got into her character. She grunted and growled as she stomped and flexed her thin arms. Chad made a quick lunge for Pagne and missed as she jumped and turned to one side. He was up on her again and grabbed her arms from the back. The harder she struggled, the tighter he held. Pagne's emotions shot back to the day in the motel room, to Adam's brutal grip on her frail arms. She remembered his reeking breath next to her face. She began kicking and screaming and she lashed out at Chad with everything she had. Grandma ran out back, yelling for Chad to let go of her. He was afraid to because he was not sure what she would do when he did. He finally released her, jumped back, and tucked himself into a roll. Pagne fell to the ground, sobbing. Grandma shooed the other three into the house. Chad whispered "I'm so sorry, Pagne" when he passed her. Grandma pulled Pagne up and just held her. "You're okay, sweetie.

I know Chad wasn't trying to hurt you."

"I know, Grandma, I just panicked when he grabbed my arms."

"It's okay, baby" soothed Grandma. She held Pagne and let her crying slow down, her breathing come back to normal.

They moved to the table and Grandma asked, "Would you like to talk about what is so upsetting?"

"I don't know. I'm afraid to say it out loud. I can pretend none of it is real if I don't talk about it."

"I know it feels like that, sweetie, but you know it's lurking in your memories and your heart. You know if you don't want to talk to me about it, God will listen."

"You keep talking about this God. I have never heard about him before. Why would I want to talk to him?"

Grandma took a deep sigh. "Well, this is gonna take some time, why don't you go get us a piece of that rocky road cake we made and a big glass of milk. Let the kids know you're feeling better. They're worried."

"Okay, Grandma, I'll be right back." After reassuring the others she was okay, especially Chad, she prepared a tray with two big slices of cake and some cold milk. Pagne made her way carefully back to where Grandma waited for her.

As they ate cake, Grandma chatted about insignificant things, encouraging Pagne to join her in conversation. It didn't take long for Pagne to become comfortable and to trust Grandma. She realized that she ached to talk about the years with her mother, the men that frequented their house, and how unloved she felt. She told Grandma all about Adam and his attack, her injuries, and about how her mother had picked Adam over her. Pagne revealed how afraid she was that the courts would send her back to her mother. She shed many tears and reduced the tissues in Grandma's apron to pulp. Grandma sat quietly and listened, frequently squeezing her hand until she was able to get it all out. Once Pagne was calm and had said everything she felt in her hurting heart, Grandma took a deep breath and looked up, as if to summon help from the Heavens.

"Pagne, I don't know your mama, but she sounds like a broken spirit to me. Most of the time, when people are hardened and selfish, it has come from needing to survive. You say you have never met your mama's family? Maybe she suffered great harm in her life and now she is doing the best she can. I am not saying that it is acceptable or fair but, when someone is broken, they do unspeakable things. That is why God is so important. He can mend broken spirits and he can change who we are and how we live."

"But Grandma, who is God?"

"That's a big question, hon, and I'll do my best. God is a living power that rules, and He created Earth, our universe, and all the universes. He created man to be his companion. He is love and compassion and he hates sin, because sin destroys his creations. He will remove all sin someday."

Grandma took a moment and continued. "Once our lives are done here, we will dwell in Heaven for eternity with him and all the angels. We only have to believe and accept his son, Jesus, as our Savior", explained Grandma. Pagne's face lit up in recognition.

"I have heard about baby Jesus before. His birthday is Christmas, right?"

"Yes child, that's right. God is his father, and He also wants to have a relationship with you. To help you get through life and the troubles we all will have to endure. God loves you, Pagne, you are his daughter."

"I guess I don't understand why God gave me to my mom. She doesn't love me. Why didn't he give me to someone wonderful, like you?"

"I don't know all the answers, sweetheart, but I do know that he has wonderful plans for you and me, for everyone who will follow Jesus. I know he helped bring us together and that he wanted us to know and love each other."

"Grandma, you mentioned angels. Do you really believe in angels?" asked Pagne.

"I sure do. I believe everyone has a guardian angel that helps them through life."

"So do I. Grandma, would you think I was crazy if I told you I can smell mine and, sometimes, I can see her wings or feel them brush against me." Pagne wasn't sure how much to share but felt safe with Grandma. "What if I told you she talked to me?"

"Why, child, I don't think you're crazy. I just think you are a special young lady that has an open mind and heart and this allows you to see beyond other folks. You are blessed. "

"Grandma, is it okay if I talk to my angel?"

"I think your angel would like that very much. Must get boring hanging around all the time when no one talks to you," Grandma said. They talked awhile longer and saw that the sun was setting. "Next time, Pagne, I'll share my life with you. It's longer than your story and a little sad in parts, but it is my story and I wouldn't change it for anything."

"Okay, Grandma."

They walked into the house holding hands and feeling like this moment in time changed them forever. Pagne stopped Grandma just inside the door with a question. "How would God fix my mother?"

"Well, he knows what is in her heart and what she has endured. He also wants her healthy and in a loving relationship with you. I would say praying for her is the best way to start." Pagne gave Grandma a squeeze and ran off to find the others.

~

The next three years were wonderful. Pagne came to love this crazy family of hers. She believed that eight eyes could certainly look out for one old lady. She also liked her school and her teacher. Her family went to church on Sundays and they all shared the work, laughed together, and grew closer and closer. Macey told her that she was going to be a dancer when she grew up. The girls would crank up the music in their attic and dance for hours. Grandma would take out her hearing aid, the boys just had to suffer. Sometimes, Tad and Chad would come up to laugh at them and would end up joining them.

Tad wanted to be a baseball player. He hoped he could go pro when he was old enough. Chad played because Tad wanted to. He enjoyed it, but it wasn't his passion. He was a science geek. Chad would talk for hours about microscopes, chemistry, and bugs. He loved bugs. He would tell them about every bug in the yard, what they ate, how they multiplied. He would drive them crazy until they ran away screaming… no more… stop! Chad would eventually give in and they would play endlessly.

The tree house was their sanctuary. They spent hours up there playing games, teasing, laughing, and debating. It was their place to be in control and set the rules.

Pagne loved that she could put her past behind her. It was all about now. No one talked about why they were there. They just were and they were happy.

Each of the kids would make sure Grandma had lunch for the day before they left for school, so she wouldn't cook while they were away. The kids always made sure one of them came right home if the others had after-school activities. Several times, they found the stove on or the freezer door left open, but it wasn't anything they couldn't handle. It was a good life, loving and caring for each other.

~

While sleeping, Pagne was having the most beautiful dream. She was in a lush garden filled with flowers, butterflies, and birds. The birds were singing beautiful songs and one flew up and sat on her shoulder. There were also angels flying and fluttering about. Pagne realized her angel was near. She could smell her. The scent was so amazing and it got stronger and stronger. Pagne kept turning and twisting, looking around for her angel. "I know you're here. I can smell you" she yelled in her dream. Then she heard her angel's voice.

"Pagne, wake up, now!"

Pagne sat up and realized the lovely angel smell had turned into stinking, choking smoke. Now that she was awake, she heard the smoke detectors wailing. How did they all sleep through them? She jumped up and woke Macey.

"Get downstairs now. Wake Grandma. We have to get out of the house." Pagne saw the little white Bible from Grandma on her nightstand and stuck it in the waist of her pajama bottoms. They both ran to the second floor. Macey threw open Grandma's door and woke her by jumping on the bed. Pagne ran into the boys' room and jerked them from their deep sleep, screaming their names. Grandma and Macey were first into the stairwell, heading to the first floor. Pagne was close behind with the boys following her.

As Macey and Grandma reached the bottom step, Grandma lost her balance and fell hard. She screamed in pain, then whimpered "My hip is broken, my hip." Tad pushed ahead of Pagne to help Macey pull Grandma out the front door. Pagne looked back to tell Chad to hurry but he wasn't behind her.

"Where's Chad?" she screamed.

Tad looked up, confused, "I don't know. He was right behind me."

Pagne ran back up the stairs, screaming for Chad. The flames had now made their way inside the walls and were breaking through into the hall. Chad was in his doorway with his microscope and an armload of papers. "What are you doing, you idiot?" screamed Pagne.

"I can't leave it behind," he screamed back. As Chad moved toward Pagne, a portion of the ceiling fell, pinning Chad to the floor. Pagne moved in and began pulling the debris off of him. Feeling the heat and finding it harder and harder to breathe, she was struggling not to panic. She finally got him free, but he didn't appear to be breathing. Pagne had no clue how to do CPR and there was no time. The heat was becoming unbearable. She dragged Chad to the top of the staircase and pushed. He rolled down and landed at the bottom of the staircase with a loud thud. Just as Pagne headed down the stairs, the flames broke through the wall, and engulfed her. She had no idea what to do, so she ran down the stairs not realizing that she was feeding the fire that consumed her clothing and skin.

Pagne was in such a panic that she tripped over Chad on the floor and rolled across the room. As she tried to sit up, she saw several firemen enter the living room. "Chad! Get Chad! He's right there." One of the fireman lifed Chad and disappeared out the door. The second fireman quickly reached Pagne and wrapped his jacket around her to smother the remaining flames. He then lifted her up and carried her out of the house. Soon, she was lying on the neighbor's front lawn. Pagne looked over and saw their lovely home crumbling in the flames. She knew that she was burned and wondered why it didn't hurt more than it did. She closed her eyes and smelled the lovely scent of her angel, then she heard someone screaming, "She's in shock!" as she went back to her lovely dream. She would not understand the importance of her selflessness that night for sixty-seven more years.

Pagne woke up disoriented in a strange, brightly lit room. As her eyes and brain focused, she realized it was a hospital room. She could hear the equipment beeping and quiet voices in the hall. Her chest hurt and it was very difficult to breathe without making the pain worse. She found the buzzer on her bed and summoned the nurse. As the nurse entered, Pagne tried to sit up, but found it very painful. She hoarsely whispered, "Where is my family? Are they okay?" She saw movement in the corner of her eye. Leah leaned in next to her head from the chair by her bed. "Why, I'm right here honey. All the family you need." Pagne wanted to scream in despair, but she didn't make a sound.

Over the next few days, she found out that everyone survived the fire. Grandma had in fact broken her hip and was placed in a nursing home. It would take several months for her hip to heal, but her foster-care days were over. She had gotten up in the middle of the night to make a cup of tea and left the burner on. Unfortunately, a dishtowel was close enough to the stove to ignite and start the fire in the kitchen. The firefighters said that Chad had barely survived. Rolling him down the stairs had saved his life as it had gotten him below the worst of the smoke. He was bruised and had some smoke inhalation issues, but would be fine in a few weeks. Pagne, however, was not so lucky. She had suffered third degree burns on her neck, chest, arm, and shoulder. They would heal with painful treatment, but the scarring would be extensive. She thought about her rotten luck; *of course, it was her perfectly fine arm that was burned.* Pagne would fluctuate between self-pity and anger. Sometimes, she could smell her angel, but ignored her or told her to go away. "Where were you? Why didn't you protect us? Why didn't you protect me?" Then she would cry softly.

Pagne was so sad that her time with Grandma and the kids was over. She had never felt so loved and connected in her life. She tried not to blame God, to wonder why he let her be so happy just to take it away, but there was no one else for Pagne to blame.

To make matters worse, Leah was an every day annoyance while Pagne was in the hospital. She was rude and demanding of the nurses, ordering extra food and drinks for herself while she sat in Pagne's room, going on and on about how she was going to sue the county. What were they thinking? Letting an old, deranged woman care for her precious baby. This should be worth quite a bundle. All the pain and suffering she had endured, all the days in discomfort she had spent sitting by her child's bed, the embarrassment she would endure when everyone stared at her disfigured child. It was just unbearable, the burden she must now carry. The local news and paper were willing to give Leah a very public soapbox to vent her rage and suffering.

Pagne almost looked forward to the painful water treatments for her burns because her mother wasn't allowed in the treatment room. The nurses were kind and Pagne could see they truly felt her pain - physical and mental.

One afternoon, while still in the hospital, Pagne heard some familiar voices in the distance. She looked up and saw Chad and Tad standing in the doorway. She squealed in delight to see them looking so healthy and here to see her.

"How did you get here?" she asked. They moved close to her bed.

"Our new foster-parents brought us. After all, you saved Chad's butt. You look good Pagne, for almost being a crispy-critter," Tad said with relief. Chad stayed very quiet and just kept looking at her arm. Tad talked excitedly about their new home and filled Pagne in on all the details. Pagne was happy for them, but her regret and the pain from her own circumstances showed on her face and in her smile. There was that awkward silence, the one you could cut if you had a knife. Pagne didn't have any good news to share and she felt Chad's discomfort. Chad cleared his throat and asked Tad to give him a few minutes alone with Pagne. Tad headed out of the room, making kissing sounds, as he went looking for a vending machine.

Pagne knew Chad needed to unload his feelings and she patiently waited for him to speak. After a long, painful delay, he finally spoke. "Pagne, I am so sorry. We could have all gotten out of the house in time if I didn't go back for my stupid stuff." The tears began to roll down his cheeks. "I should have been the one burnt, not you." Pagne looked into his sad face and felt her own eyes tearing up.

"Chad, I am just glad that we are all okay." He reached over and gently touched her bandaged arm.

"Does it hurt much?"

"Some," she lied. It hurt a lot.

Chad stood there in painful silence. They were both relieved to hear Tad coming back. "Get the mushy stuff over with?" he asked with a mouth full of chocolate candy. Chad turned and jabbed Tad with his elbow.

"Shut up, Tad."

"Pagne, it was good seeing you alive but we gotta go." Tad leaned in, gave Pagne a soft hug, and moved to the door. Chad was trying to hold back more tears.

"I'll try to come again," he whispered, but this would be the last time they would see each other. Chad reached for Pagne's copper curls and gently twirled them in his fingers. He mouthed, "I am so sorry, please forgive me." The pain in his eyes mirrored the pain she was enduring. Pagne took his hand with her good hand and squeezed. She smiled and nodded at him, knowing that if she spoke, it would release fountains of tears. The boys left as quickly as they had come. Pagne laid back and shut her eyes, trying to close out all the pain. Then she heard the unmistakable screech of her mother's voice coming down the hall. *"God, if you are there, please take me now,"* Pagne prayed to herself.

Eventually, they released Pagne from the hospital into her mother's care. She guessed that her mother's threat of a lawsuit was being taken seriously and the county didn't want to aggravate the situation further. Leah had played the outraged and concerned mother very well on the five o'clock news and had acquired a high profile lawyer.

Pagne was surprised to learn that her mother had gotten a job as a retail clerk nine months earlier. Leah's drinking and lifestyle had taken its toll on her looks and she found it difficult to find men willing to pay her what she thought she was worth. Leah pretended that she'd left the business while she was still on top, on her terms. This new job gave Pagne some precious time without her mother around. With the small income her mother was making and the assistance she received for Pagne, they were able to move into a small, one-bedroom apartment. Pagne slept on the couch. It was some time before she could return to school. The pain medications she needed kept her groggy and unable to focus.

She was a local celebrity for a short while because of her heroism. The city and the local fire departments established a college fund for Pagne. Luckily, they made sure no one had access to it unless it was used by Pagne for college tuition. Her popularity was short-lived when a local politician was caught buying drugs from an undercover cop. Pagne was no longer the main attraction for the local news or the newspapers and the media had tired of Leah's ranting. Her battle would now be fought in the courts.

Pagne's mother still drank, but it seemed to have slowed down a lot. Life was much calmer with Leah. She was home alone most evenings and Pagne actually preferred that. As she was laying in the dark, she thought she smelled her angel but, no, she had sent her away. Surely, she had insulted the angel and the angel would have moved on. But, the scent came again, this time stronger. "Are you still there?" Pagne asked quietly. The smell swirled around her. It was as if it was dancing. Pagne felt an emotional pull on her heart. "Oh angel, I am so sorry I was mad at you. The fire wasn't your fault. You tried to save all of us." Pagne smelled her angel's scent surrounding her, saturating her t-shirt and her pillow. "I'm so glad you didn't leave me."

Pagne began to pray again for her mom, Grandma, and the kids. She also prayed for Itchy and Bree. She wondered where they all were. She hadn't thought to get a phone number for the twins when they visited. She asked about Itchy and her social worker said that he had gone to live on the east coast with an aunt. Bree had just disappeared. Grandma suffered several strokes while in the nursing home and didn't know who anyone was. She wasn't able to track down Macey either. Everyone had been taken from her, but she couldn't lose Leah if she tried.

School was her sanctuary. Pagne was now thirteen and in the eighth grade. She was making friends, but she was cautious. She'd lost everyone that ever mattered and she didn't think she could survive if it happened again. One boy intrigued her though. His name was Lenny. He was cute, funny, and so smart. Pagne would catch herself daydreaming about him in class. She found his dark hair, olive skin, and deep brown eyes mysterious. Lenny had a broad, white smile and he was charming; he reminded her of Aladdin in the animated movie.

They had several classes together. She felt a dark side to Lenny though. He didn't talk about his family and never seemed to be looking forward to anything. Maybe that's why Pagne was so drawn to him.

They became best friends over the next few months. They would hang out after school every day, sitting under the trees talking about their plans. Lenny wanted to be a writer and he would let Pagne read some of his short stories. They were wonderful, but none of the characters seemed truly happy. Some kind of barrier always kept their joy away.

Monday, after school, Pagne asked Lenny to meet her at their place. She really needed to talk. He showed up with several candy bars from the school's vending machines. "Thanks, Lenny. Can I save it for later?" she said softly. Pagne was visibly upset and Lenny moved in closer to her.

Pagne looked deep into Lenny's eyes, looking for trust. "I need to talk, but this might change things for us," she whispered. Lenny took her hand with a reassuring squeeze. "Pagne, you're my best friend. Nothing you say will change that." They both sat down in the cool grass in the shade of a large tree.

Pagne began sharing her story with Lenny. She explained that her mother had been a prostitute, how they'd lived, and about Adam and the fall. Her tears would come and go. When she talked about the fire, the painful treatments, and the permanent scarring, she fell into quiet sobs. Lenny wrapped her in his arms and held her while she cried. "Pagne, I know the scarring is a crappy thing, but you have to know that you are beautiful," Lenny said lovingly. "I love your eyes," he whispered as he gazed into them. "You are beautiful inside and out." Pagne relaxed and just lay against Lenny's chest, feeling her heartbeat line up with his. It soothed her and their deep connection became even stronger. Pagne was young, but she knew she loved Lenny. She needed to love him. Someone.

"What's going on Pagne? Why tell me this now?" Pagne looked at Lenny and then dropped her head.

"My mother is seeing Adam again. I saw him drop her off last night and, the way they were talking, it sounded like they have been seeing each other for awhile. She doesn't know that I know." Pagne felt a sense of hopelessness fall over her again. She was just beginning to feel normal. School was fun and challenging and she had friends. She had Lenny. Pagne knew that she was old enough now to fight Adam if she had to, but she could envision the nightmare that her home life would be.

"I don't know what will happen, Lenny. I can't live around both of them, but I don't have anywhere else to go except for Langston Hall or maybe foster-care. I have no idea where they will put me. I could lose everyone again." She moved as tight as she could into Lenny's arms and whispered. "Lenny, I can't bear to lose you. They could send me anywhere and I might never see you again. Except for my angel, I will be all alone again."

~

Lenny held her, totally confused. How he could proceed with his plan? He had thought that when he left school today, that he would never see Pagne again.

Lenny knew every bit of Pagne's pain. He had just found out that his father, Leonard, was coming back home. His dad said he was clean for good this time, no more meth, but Lenny didn't believe him. He had seen the cycle too many times. It would be good at first; the honeymoon Lenny called it. But, it would change quickly and dramatically. His father's favorite hobby was beating and humiliating his wife. When his dad thought she'd had enough, because he certainly didn't want to kill his meal ticket, he would focus on Lenny. First it started with taunting, jabbing, and slapping. When Lenny wouldn't man up and hit him back, his dad would get rougher, calling Lenny insulting names. These sessions would always end up with punches and humiliation. It didn't matter if Lenny defended himself or not, his father would work up in a rage and become vicious. The beatings became more brutal as Lenny got older.

When Lenny was small, he thought his life was normal, that all daddies were big, mean, and violent. When he got old enough to realize his father was an animal, Lenny tolerated it because he felt the need to protect his mom. After seeing her allow this man back into their home and back into her bed time and time again, Lenny figured she liked it and deserved it. She never pressed charges and she never stepped in to shield Lenny. He eventually decided she was on her own because she didn't protect him.

His dad would tire of them eventually and would disappear for months at a time, flopping wherever he could and bingeing on whatever drugs he could find, but meth was his drug of choice.

Lenny had found out that morning that his dad would be home when he got back from school. He had decided that tonight would be the night of resolution. His dad would be settled in by the time he got home. He would be sitting on the couch watching his wrestling. Mom would be so happy that her man was back. She would be convinced that this time would be different, wonderful, normal. She would be cooking his favorite dinner: steak and baked potatoes. They lived on macaroni and cheese or hotdogs when he was gone, but Mom made sure Dad ate the best.

Lenny struggled with the decision, himself or the animal who was his father. If just himself, his pain and anger would be done, but the animal would still be free to roam. If he only killed his father, Lenny would have justice and revenge, but he would be locked up the for the rest of his life, knowing he could never be with Pagne. A heavy price to pay. Lenny had stolen an old gun from his friend Rob's house. He could picture it in his mind. His mother would dutifully set up a TV tray and bring Lenny Senior his dinner and beers while his father screamed at the wrestlers on TV. Lenny would calmly walk in, aim, and then pull the trigger. He would be at close range, sure to kill. He wanted to see the shock on his father's face. Lenny decided he would then take his own life, finally peace, he hoped. His mother would get to live with the guilt and heartache of their deaths. All would be fair in the world. He was ready. He had a plan.

But, then Pagne had needed to see him and he would get to smell her and touch her one last time, dream about what could have been. Then goodbye. It would be the last goodbye. Once she revealed why she was upset, he realized she needed him. He had to protect Pagne. She said that she couldn't bear to lose him. This changed everything for Lenny. All of his plans vanished. He broke and let all the rage and hurt and pain gush out. Pagne was alarmed and thought she should get someone to help, but Lenny grabbed her hand. "Please don't leave, just stay with me." Pagne sat quietly while Lenny cried softly at times and punched the ground.

They ended up lying on their backs side by side, looking up at the late afternoon clouds that drifted by. Pagne encouraged him to open up to her, but he wasn't ready. He couldn't even find the words to describe all the emotions and feelings he had. He did know that he felt drained and oddly relaxed. "Guess I just needed to unload," is all he would say. "You said something weird earlier, Pagne. Do you really have an angel?"

"Oh yes," Pagne confessed, as she turned and propped up on her good elbow, well the better one anyway. Her face lit up with a glow. "You'll think I'm crazy, but I can smell her. Sometimes I see the edges of her wings. They have brushed my cheek and she's even talked to me a couple of times." He looked at her with a big grin on his face.

"Are you serious? Pagne I knew you were a little ditzy but I never thought you were crazy."

"You can laugh, but it's real. You have one, too. You're just too stubborn to smell him."

"Why a him? Why would I want to smell a guy? What if I want a girl angel?" he asked with a wink.

"They are with you all the time. Do you want a girl angel in the bathroom or shower with you? That would be creepy!" Pagne said. Lenny began to laugh quietly as that mental picture developed. Pagne looked at him with irritation and Lenny finally burst out laughing. Pagne joined in and allowed the stress to be relieved with their shared peals of laughter. They both were amazed that they could laugh. The laughter became giggles and then quiet again.

"Nice thought, having someone watching your back. Mine is fired, he hasn't helped me any."

"I don't know how it works exactly. I know that they don't keep you from everything bad, but if you try to listen, they will warn you," Pagne explained. "My angel woke me up the night of the fire. We all would have died if I hadn't smelled her and heard her."

Lenny took Pagne's hand in his and gently felt the softness of her skin. "Pagne, I don't know if I believe you, but it sounds good enough to pretend that I do."

What Pagne didn't realize was that her needing Lenny gave him a glimmer of hope, a reason to endure. He would not be taking anyone's life to end his pain today.

"Kinda strange really. When I lived with Grandma, she talked a lot about God. How he gave us these angels to guard us. I don't know everything about Him, but I believe that there is something after this life, something incredible because, so far, this living thing sucks!"

"Amen to that," said Lenny with conviction.

~

It was so difficult to leave. They found sanctuary in each other. They agreed that Pagne would not do anything hasty. She would make sure that Adam really was dating her mom. Lenny said he would never leave her and he would follow her wherever she ended up. Pagne thought this was a romantic, ridiculous pledge, but it filled her with joy. She had no clue how serious Lenny was.

Pagne ran up to the apartment, filled with excitement and disbelief over what she and Lenny had shared that afternoon. She truly felt happy. What a wonderful feeling that was! As she reached for the door to unlock it, the door swung open. She was suddenly overcome with the smell of her angel. It was overwhelming and made her dizzy. She grabbed the doorjamb to steady herself. There stood her mother with a ludicrous grin on her face. "Oh baby, you're finally home. We've been waiting to share the good news." Her mother whipped her hand up in front of Pagne's face, displaying a pathetic ring. Pagne was speechless. "Isn't it beautiful? Adam proposed to me just this afternoon." She reached for Pagne and pulled her into the room. Leah leaned in to whisper in Pagne's ear, "It's a real diamond, baby." Adam sat on the couch with a huge smile on his face.

Pagne, still recovering from shock, looked from one face to the other. "Mom, what are you talking about? How did this happen?"

"Well, baby, I didn't want to upset you. You and Adam got such a rocky start." Leah paused to get her breath. Pagne could see that she was excited. "You can call it kismet or fate, but a couple of weeks ago, Adam came into the minimart where I work, to pick up some beer, and we were shocked to be looking at each other over the counter. He stopped drinking the hard stuff, hon. We got to talking and we decided to go get a beer after work. Well, all that chemistry was still a churnin' and we've been dating ever since. I wasn't sure how to tell you and I wanted to see if it was going to last before I said anything." With that, Leah floated across the room and plopped down next to Adam. His hand immediately settled on her upper thigh and squeezed. Pagne felt her face flush hot and surely red. They looked like a couple of hyenas grinning at each other. "Aren't you going to congratulate us, dear?" her mother asked.

This was insane. They both acted as if nothing had happened. That they would even think she would be happy for them was bizarre. Pagne ran from the apartment and didn't stop until she reached the schoolyard trees. As she ran out the door, her mother's words swam in her head. "Don't worry, darling, she'll adjust. After all, it's about my happiness right now."

Pagne fell to the ground. She didn't cry because there were no tears left. She just felt numb. It was interesting. She barely smelled her angel, almost as if the angel was testing to see if she was welcome. "Hello, Angel. I really do need to give you a proper name if we're going to keep this up. How about Angelica? Nah, that's too corny. You're a tough angel right? Cause I certainly needed a tough one. How about Chantal. That's pretty and strong. Okay, Chantal, you have my permission to enter my space." The smell flooded in. Pagne arched her back, breathing Chantal's glorious aroma deep into her lungs. Pagne felt calm and so full of love. How did a creature she couldn't see face to face fill her with such love? Now Pagne had a plan. She had choices!

"God, I don't know if these are the right words, but I can't do this alone. My angel helps me, I know, but I need everyone I can get to make it through this life. I need you, God. I accept your son, Jesus, into my heart. Oh yeah, I think I'm supposed to ask you to forgive all my sins. Okay, hope that does it. Not sure what I do next, but maybe the angel can give me a clue." she whispered. Pagne didn't realize how powerful her words were, from her mouth to God's ear. She was not alone, nor had she ever been alone.

Pagne waited until dark to return home. Not really home, she reminded herself, but a dwelling. Yes, that suited it much better. Pagne quietly went in, hoping to be unnoticed. Her mother, sitting on Adam's lap, turned a drunken glare at her. "Go ahead and sleep in my room tonight," she said. "Adam and I will be up late celebrating our engagement and we don't need you around spoiling the mood." Pagne was relieved and slipped past them to the only bedroom. She couldn't help but notice the half-empty bottles of champagne and Jack Daniels sitting on the coffee table. *Guess he broke down for this one night of celebration,* she thought sarcastically.

Pagne was in a deep sleep, dreaming of her and Lenny flying through the clouds. She sniffed all the angels that whipped past them, trying to find her angel. "That's her," Pagne shouted. The closer they got to the angel, the stronger the scent was. Suddenly, it became overpowering, and nauseating. Pagne's eyes flew open. There in the doorway stood the silhouette of Adam. She couldn't see his face, but she could hear him licking his lips. "You awake Pagne?" She said nothing. "Ahhh Pagne, I see your eyes are open." The light from the kitchen was shining in her face. "That's okay, baby, just heading out, but I wanted to tell you how happy I'm gonna be when I'm your daddy. You're developing quite nicely. You have a very cute little figure. I can get past those scars, especially in the dark. I'm looking forward to finishing what we started!" With that, Adam turned around and staggered out of the apartment. Pagne ran to the front door to lock it behind him and saw her mother, almost naked, sprawled on the living room floor, her mouth wide open, drooling as she snored loudly. Pagne looked down at Leah, felt utter disgust for her mother, and then spat on her. She went back to the room and braced a chair under the knob since there was no lock.

Pagne left early the next morning, before her mother was even awake. She ran all the way to school and waited for Lenny to get there. He finally showed up early, too. His face was red and puffy on one side. Pagne looked at him and touched his cheek. "What happened?" she asked with concern.

"Oh, just tripped in my room, landed on my face. I know, a real klutz." Pagne almost challenged this lame excuse, but knew Lenny was not ready to talk.

"Oh Lenny, it's happening. They're getting married." Pagne repeated all the gory details starting from the blast of smell at the door, the ring in her face, the flying dream, and Adam in her doorway. She didn't tell him about spitting on her mom. Pagne didn't want him to see that side of her.

"I'm so sorry! What are you going to do?"

"I know a lady I trust at Langston Hall, Miss Renee. I'm going to cut afternoon classes and take the bus across town and see if I can talk to her."

"Want me to go with?" he asked. After his emotional displayyesterday and the bruised face this morning, Pagne thought it would be a good idea. In fact, she had hoped he would offer to come. She played helpless and said, "If you'd come, I would be so grateful. I've never taken the crosstown bus alone before." She said and batted her eyes.

"You're a goof, Pagne. You don't have to play me to get me to go." They agreed to meet at lunch break and slip off the school grounds. Pagne had gone through her mom's purse before she left and had found enough to pay for both of their fares. She was prepared in case Lenny would go with her.

It was a stealth operation. They met at the designated time and place and nonchalantly walked to the trees that lined the edge of the schoolyard. Lenny had enough change on him to buy two bags of chips for their lunches. They were starving since both had left home without eating breakfast. They watched the kids run and play, then slowly head back to the school entrance. Lenny and Pagne didn't speak the whole time, almost as if they thought they would be invisible if they didn't make any noise. When the final school bell rang, they casually strolled off the grounds. Once they were out of view, they ran to the closest bus stop and jumped on the bus, panting and feeling very adventurous.

"That was easier than I thought!" Lenny proclaimed.

"Yeah, we're regular super-spies, we are." They both laughed.

"How are we going to explain not being in class this afternoon?" Lenny asked.

"Don't know yet. I'll have to think about that on the way home."

~

When they reached Langston Hall, Pagne was feeling a little nervous. She wasn't sure what she would say or what Miss Renee could really do for her. Pagne went up to the main entrance and stepped into the lobby. Lenny was a few steps behind her. The secretary slid the glass window open and spoke, "Good Afternoon dear. How can I help you?" Pagne didn't recognize her.

"I would like to speak with Miss Renee, please. Can you tell her that Pagne is here?"

"Well, I would, but Miss Renee no longer works here." She started to slide the glass window closed. Pagne put her hand in before it shut. "Please," she said, "Can you tell me how to find her? It is very important."

"Of course, dear. I should have one of her cards." Pagne heard the sound of shuffling papers. "Here it is," the receptionist said and handed Pagne the card.

"Thank you, very much," Pagne said before they stepped outside. Pagne looked at the card, and read Miss Renee Landor, Court Appointed Special Advocate for Children. She was familiar with the address on the card. "Her office is close to the courthouse," Pagne explained to Lenny.

"How far is the courthouse from here? Can we walk?"

"Oh sure, it's only about five blocks." They headed in the direction of the courthouse.

When they found the building, Lenny explained that Suite 300 on the address meant she was on the third floor. They took the elevator and came out on the landing, just in front of Miss Renee's office. Her name was on a metal plate on the door. Pagne tried the door, but it was locked. She felt a dive in her stomach. "Oh no, she's not here," whispered Pagne.

"Well, let's try knocking," Lenny suggested. They both tapped on the door and waited, but they heard no one inside. "Let's wait for a while. Maybe she'll be back." They both sat quietly with their backs to the wall. Pagne felt her hope slipping. This was a bad idea. *They would both be in trouble for cutting school. Her mom would just yell, but Lenny might get it much worse.* They waited for an hour.

"Lenny, we'd better head back. We're going to be in a lot of trouble as it is and the ride home will get us back even later." As they got up to leave, the elevator bell rang and the doors opened. There was Miss Renee, searching her bag for her keys. "How could I forget those papers? I am such an idiot," she muttered to herself. She almost ran into Pagne and Lenny. "Oh my goodness, I'm sorry..." she paused before recognition came. "Pagne? Pagne is that really you?"

"Yes, Miss Renee and I need your help." Miss Renee motioned for them to follow her while she found her keys and unlocked the door.

"Please, come in." She flipped on the light and moved around to her chair behind the desk. This had to be the smallest office Pagne had ever seen. There was room for a small desk, a small bookcase, and two small chairs in front of the desk. The room had no windows. "Welcome to my closet," she said as she twirled around with her arms out, like someone displaying a grand room. "How long has it been Pagne? I almost didn't recognize you. You've grown up so much." Miss Renee settled in to her chair and motioned for them to sit down. "Who is your friend?" she asked.

"Oh, I'm so sorry, this is my best friend, Lenny." Lenny reached out to shake her hand with flushed cheeks.

"So nice to meet you, Lenny." Miss Renee then focused on Pagne, "How have you been, dear? I heard that you were hurt in a fire and that you've been living with your mom."

"Yeah, I messed up my good arm and shoulder but we all got out alive."

"I'm so sorry, Pagne. I know burns can be very difficult to treat." Miss Renee could not help but cringe when she saw the scarring on Pagne's exposed lower arm.

"I wanted to find you to see if you could tell me what my rights are. The lady at Langston Hall said you weren't there any more and gave me your card. Back with my mom has been okay but I just found out that she is going to marry Adam." Pagne went into the details and her fears. After Pagne finished, she felt as if some of the burden had been lifted from her.

"Well, Pagne, this is quite odd that you would come looking for me now. After knowing you and seeing the struggles you and other children were having, I wanted to be able to do more for kids like you. I left Langston Hall and started training to become a children's advocate. I just recently opened this office. I would love to help you. Let me contact your social worker and get your current details. This will take me a little while, but they will not notify your mother of my investigation until we have a plan worked out. Okay? Can you hang in there for a little while longer?"

"Yes, I suppose."

"I also need Adam's full name. I want to run a criminal check to see if he has any prior charges that we can use in our arguments. Please fill this out so I have all your current information." Miss Renee set a piece of paper in front of Pagne.

After Pagne finished the form, she and Lenny stood up to leave. Miss Renee walked them out of her miniature office. While waiting for the elevator, Miss Renee hugged Pagne and whispered in her ear, assuring her everything would be fine. She shook Lenny's hand and told him how nice he was to help Pagne and that she was a very special young lady. Lenny agreed. She gave Lenny one of her cards and told him that if she could ever be of help, he should not hesitate to call her. She then lightly touched his swollen cheek.

Pagne and Lenny made a mad dash for the bus stop. It was almost four thirty and Pagne didn't know if her mom would blow up or not even notice she was late. She could tell Lenny was very nervous but he pretended he was fine. Lenny's stop was first. He held Pagne's hand for several seconds, just gazing into her eyes, and then he bolted out the door. When Pagne reached her stop, she began a frantic prayer as she got off the bus and walked the three blocks to her apartment. When she got home, no one was there. *Ahhh, such a relief,* she thought, but there was a note on the refrigerator:

OUT WITH ADAM, WILL BE LATE
SCHOOL CALLED
YOU GOT SOME EXPLAINING TO DO
MOM

Crap, thought Pagne. She thought she would have until tomorrow before she had to explain cutting school.

Pagne wasn't sure where she should sleep that night. She didn't want to make her mom even more upset by being in the bedroom, but she didn't want to be asleep in the open living room when they came back either. She would feel vulnerable if Adam came in with her mom. Pagne decided to pull the couch away from the wall and make room to curl up behind it where she wouldn't be seen. Pagne wrapped the blanket around herself and squeezed into her cave. She quickly slipped into deep, fitful sleep.

The next morning, she woke up to snoring, loud snoring. She slipped out from behind the couch and the room was clear. She tiptoed to the bedroom door and heard two distinct snore patterns. Pagne guessed that Adam and her mother had come in so drunk, they had passed out with no regard for where Pagne was. She quietly cleaned up and dressed for school. She grabbed a toaster pastry and thought she was going to make a clean getaway but, when she turned around to leave, there stood her mom. She looked terrible, eye makeup smeared, bed hair to the worst degree, and huge bags under her eyes. Pagne had to think quickly.

"Hey mom, you need a Bloody Mary?" This was her mom's self-treatment for a bad hangover. "I can make you one," Pagne offered.

"I do need one but don't think you can butter me up. The school left a message and I wanna know why you cut school yesterday? You off lying with the boys? We don't have any room for another bastard kid here," Leah said in disgust. Pagne wanted to scream at her and remind her that she was not like her mother, but she held her tongue.

"I wasn't doing anything wrong. I got some really bad cramps and I knew the nurse couldn't give me anything. I came home and took some medicine at lunch. I laid down with the heating pad and fell asleep."

"Sounds like crap to me, Pagne. You weren't here when I got home from work. Adam wanted to take us both out for Chinese," Leah challenged. Pagne got the sense that her mother thought missing Chinese with her and Adam was supposed to disappoint her.

"I woke up about four o'clock and was feeling better so I went to the library to work on my history report." Pagne was hoping Leah would want that Bloody Mary more than explanations. The lies were getting thick and she was afraid she'd slip up. Leah never bothered with Pagne's homework so she had no clue what Pagne was supposed to be doing. Her mom looked at her for a few seconds.

"I think you're lying to me, Pagne, but I guess I don't have to worry about no boy knocking you up with all the scars you got. Make me a drink and then get to school. I'm not writing you a note for this. It's your problem." Pagne made the Bloody Mary and headed for the door. She escaped, feeling exhilarated because she'd managed to slip through the minefield without blowing up. She hoped that Lenny fared as well.

Pagne decided that her story would work for the school, too. They warned her and threatened detention if it happened again, but they cut her some slack because she was a good student and was always in class. Pagne watched for Lenny all morning, but he wasn't in their science class. She didn't know exactly where he lived or his phone number. She was worried sick but couldn't check on him. She ate lunch alone, picking at the free food. By the time PE started and there was still no Lenny, Pagne was frantic. The gym teacher kept yelling at her to get her head in the game, but Pagne just couldn't focus on softball.

After school, Pagne ran to their spot, the cluster of trees. She saw someone sitting on the ground with his head on his knees. It was Lenny. Pagne ran to him. "Lenny, where were you today? I imaged all kinds of terrible things." As she was standing in front of him, Lenny slowly looked up. His face was terribly beaten up. He had a swollen eye, gashed and clotted with blood, a busted lip, and several chunks of hair missing. "Oh, Lenny." Pagne dropped to her knees and sobbed uncontrollably.

"I'm okay," he said without any conviction. "I didn't know the school would call my mom so quick. Dad was waiting for me. He had a lot of time to get worked up." Pagne moved to his side and tried to hold him but he grimaced. "Careful, Pagne. I think I might have some broken ribs."

"When did this happen?"

"Last night. I got out of the house and hid behind some dumpsters. Guess I finally fell asleep. I came here when I woke up."

"Lenny, we gotta call Miss Renee. Your dad can't do this and get away with it."

"No," Lenny said. "They will take me away and then I won't be here for you."

Pagne got very brave in those next few moments. "Lenny, if you're dead or in the hospital, you won't be here for me anyway. I need you alive and safe. I'll be fine, but we have to get you some help. Please let me call her." Lenny was lost in those pleading eyes of hers and he knew how close he'd come to dying this time. If the neighbors hadn't banged on the door until his mom opened it, he wouldn't have been able to get away.

"Okay," he agreed.

Lenny was too embarrassed to walk into the school office, so Pagne helped him to the nearest public phone. When they reached Miss Renee, she insisted they call 911 immediately and she would meet them at the hospital. When the police arrived, they asked a few questions and rushed them to the local county hospital. Miss Renee was already there. The nurses took Lenny into an exam room and Pagne waited outside with Miss Renee. They examined Lenny, took x-rays, and got him started on pain medications. By the time Pagne was able to see him, he was already getting his color back and looking like himself, except for the swollen half of his face. She moved one of the chairs up by his head and held his hand. Lenny assured her he was going to live and was feeling better.

Miss Renee came in with the doctor and he listed Lenny's injuries. Along with the stitches for his eye and face, Lenny had three broken ribs, a cracked jaw, several fractures in his hand from hitting has father, a damaged spleen that would require surgery, and multiple deep tissue bruises. Pagne thought Lenny's father was truly a monster to beat his son so viciously. Lenny would have to stay in the hospital for five to seven days.

The police picked up Lenny's dad and the neighbors agreed to come forward as witnesses. His father still had Lenny's blood on his knuckles and clothing. He was screwed. Lenny had given him a black eye and knocked out his two front teeth. Leonard tested positive for meth and the police found meth amphetamines in the apartment. He was looking at serious charges and Pagne hoped they would let him rot in jail.

Pagne stayed by Lenny's side every day after school until almost dark. Leah didn't argue because she and Adam were focused on themselves. On the second day of his hospital stay, Lenny's mom walked into his room and froze. Seeing the damage to Lenny in the bright lights must have shocked her. Pagne could see the tears welling up in her eyes. "Oh Lenny, my baby, I'm so sorry your father hurt you." She moved to the side of Lenny's bed and reached for his hand. He pulled it away and turned his face toward Pagne.

"Want me to leave?" Pagne asked.

"No, please stay," he said with a tone she had not heard before.

"Lenny, I know you're mad, honey. I should have protected you. I didn't know he would hurt you so bad." The tears started to roll down her checks.

"Mom, where were you yesterday? Why weren't you here?"
She didn't say anything for a few minutes.

"Well, you know he is my husband." She paused for a few moments, "I was trying to find a lawyer for him and to see if we could make bail. They said he has to stay in jail until his court date."

Lenny closed his eyes, and took a deep breath. When he opened them, he looked up at the ceiling. He spoke coldly, rage just under the surface. "Mom, thank you for giving birth to me, but you've never been a mother. I want you to get out. I don't ever want to see you again."

"No, Lenny. Please. I love you," she wailed. "You can't leave me all alone!" Several nurses came in and escorted his mother out, explaining that the stress was harmful for Lenny. Things would be sorted out, but not today, not in his room. They could hear his mothers sobs fade as she was taken away.

Lenny squeezed Pagne's hand. "Thank you for staying. I needed your strength and both of our angels," he said. "Think I could have a little time alone?"

Pagne leaned over, hesitated a moment, then lightly kissed him on the forehead. "I'll be back tomorrow morning. It's Saturday." Lenny nodded as his eyes filled with tears. As Pagne walked out of his room, she began to pray that his heart would be able to bear the pain. She caught a faint whiff of her angel. "Please stay with him right now," she asked. "He needs you more than I do." Pagne left the hospital to face her own nightmares.

When Pagne returned to the hospital Saturday morning, Miss Renee was in Lenny's room. He seemed to be dealing okay with his mom and everything that would take place when he was ready to leave the hospital. His first stop would be Langston Hall. They were considering foster-care or possibly a group-home. After Lenny had all of his questions answered, Pagne and Miss Renee went down to the cafeteria to discuss her case. Lenny told Pagne not to be gone too long. He missed her and the good cartoons were coming on. Pagne just rolled her eyes.

Miss Renee ordered coffee and some orange juice for Pagne. They sat down and Miss Renee pulled out Pagne's file. "Well," Miss Renee started, "I'm surprised. No criminal charges have come up on Adam. He's had a few tickets, several divorces, but nothing we can use. Your mother did fulfill all the court's requirements and isn't in violation. At this time, I'm not sure that we have any legal grounds to remove you."

"Can't I just say that I don't want to be there?"

"They will certainly listen, but..."

"I know. It is a decision made by adults."

"I'm sorry, Pagne. You know that if Adam or your mother are abusive, we will move on it quickly."

"Why did I get her as a mother? What did I do so wrong?"

"Nothing, sweetheart. It's not you. Your mother is broken."

"Yeah, but does that give her the right to break me?"

"I wish I had an answer that made sense, Pagne," Renee said sadly.

Pagne went up to Lenny's room. He was watching silly cartoons and smiling. It was the first time Pagne had seen him smile since the beating. He asked her how things were going with Miss Renee. "Fine, will take some time, but fine." She didn't want to pile any more on him right now. He had more than enough to deal with already. Pagne took comfort in her circumstance; she could be there for Lenny while he recovered in the hospital. He had become her first priority.

Pagne knew that only God could help her and she prayed at every opportunity. She so wanted to smell her angel. Where was she?

Pagne left Lenny's room Sunday evening to head home. She was later than usual. When Pagne opened the front door, the apartment was dark and she thought no one was home. She walked in and switched on a light. She saw her mother sitting at the table. Her mother whispered, "Turn it off." Pagne turned off the light and shut the door. It made her nervous. Her mother never sat in the dark. She was afraid of the dark.

"What's going on Mom?" she asked.

"Well, where do I start? Oh yeah, got a letter today. The lawyer says we don't have a strong case for your burns. He said that you kids contributed to the accident by not reporting Mrs. Buttonhook. He's not taking the case and advised me to let it drop. So nothing, zip. Luckily, the county covered the medical bills." Pagne just sat quietly, not knowing what to say, waiting to see if her mother was going to explode. Maybe she would end up in the hospital next to Lenny. She knew her mother had big plans for the money and thought everything would be wonderful when the county paid up. "So, I'm real angry and I called Adam to vent, thinking he'll step up and say that we don't need it. He makes enough to take care of us." The calmness in her mother's voice confused Pagne. It was haunting, as if she was telling a story about someone else. Leah was also sober, which confused Pagne even more.

"Adam then tells me that he doesn't have a job. He lost it months ago. He's been living on his credit cards. He saw us in the paper when you got burned. He read that I was suing the county, found out where I worked, and just happened to come in. Chance meeting and all that crap. He was counting on our settlement to get him square again. He was only marrying me to get his share. He told me that I'm a dried-up, old woman and he has to be drunk just to look at me or touch me." Then the calm broke. Leah began crying so profoundly that Pagne's eyes began to tear up as well.

"Oh, Mom. I'm so sorry." She really was. Her mother's pain was so intense that it engulfed the room.

"Well, he's worthless and we're better off!" Leah hissed, but Pagne could tell these were just words. "Go to bed now. It will be better in the morning," Leah assured her. Pagne moved toward the bedroom doorway. "Oh yeah,"

Leah continued, "I told him I wouldn't give him back the ring and he laughed. He said it was the cheapest thing he could find at the pawnshop, eighteen ninety-nine. Ain't that a hoot? He says I should keep it as a reminder of how much he valued me. I might head out for a while but I'll be back before morning. Go ahead and sleep in the bed. I changed the sheets. Didn't want any of that man's stink left."

Pagne didn't know whether to comfort her mom or just go to bed. They had never been affectionate so she decided to go to bed and slept fitfully. She tossed back and forth with her dreams, nightmares really. Lenny's dad showing up in Lenny's room, blood flowing, diamond rings shattering when hurled on the floor, and tears in the dark. When Pagne woke up, the sky was cloudy and it looked like it was going to rain. She lay in bed, trying to remember what day it was. She dozed off and when she woke again, the rain had started. She could hear the drops hitting her window. Then, there it was, the scent of her angel, mixed with the smell of the rain. "Hello" Pagne cooed with a silly smile on her face.

Then she heard her whisper, "You shall endure." Pagne jumped up, knowing that something was terribly wrong.

Her mother was not in the apartment. There were no notes or messages on the phone. Pagne didn't know where her mom had gone. She was probably passed out somewhere and sleeping it off. Pagne realized that it was Monday, so she got ready for school and left. Why did the angel tell her she would endure? It haunted her all day. Pagne went by the hospital after school but only stayed a few hours because she was oddly worried about her mom. When she got home, the apartment was exactly as she had left it. There was no sign that her mother had been home. She called Leah's job to see if she was at work. The owner answered and was very agitated that Leah had not come in and hadn't called.

Pagne knew that her mom could party for days without checking on her, but she hadn't missed work since she got the job. It was the only thing that made her feel good about herself. Pagne knew if she called Miss Renee or the police, they would remove her from her apartment and take her to Langston Hall. Pagne wouldn't be able to spend the afternoons with Lenny and that just wasn't an option for her, he needed her. That was evident by how he held her hand and wouldn't let go, and became sullen when they were told visiting hours were over. She was all he had and he was all she cared about. Pagne locked herself in the apartment and decided to wait it out.

Several more days came and went and Pagne went to school as usual. It was Friday and during third period, she was called to the principal's office. When she stepped in, she saw two police officers. "Hello Pagne," one officer said. "We need to know when you last saw your mother?" Pagne debated about lying but realized in her gut that something was wrong or they wouldn't be here.

"Five days ago," she admitted.

The principal looked very upset. "Have you been alone all that time?" he asked.

"Yes sir, except when I was in school or visiting my friend in the hospital. Have you found my mother?"

The second officer led Pagne to a chair, "Please sit down," he said. Pagne knew that in movies, when someone had died, they told you to sit down.

"Is she dead?" Pagne blurted. Tears welled up in her blue eyes, making them bluer than normal. Pagne was surprised at her reaction to the possibility that her mother was dead.

"No, honey. She's alive. Someone found her in an alley and the police brought her to the hospital. Does your mom drink a lot?" Pagne nodded her head. "Well, she got very sick from all the alcohol in her body. The doctors are taking care of her and she will get better. She isn't making a lot of sense right now and we don't think you should see her yet. We are going to take you by your apartment and let you get some things. You've stayed at Langston Hall before, right?"

"Yes, a few years ago."

"So nothing scary, just a safe place to stay for a little while until we can figure things out," the officer said gently.

Pagne packed up her few belongings and the officers took her to the hall. Miss Renee was waiting for her. Pagne was so relieved to see a face that she trusted. "Hello Pagne, I'm quite upset that you didn't call me when your mother took off."

"I couldn't leave Lenny alone, Miss Renee. I didn't mean to do anything wrong, I thought my mom would come back."

"I know, but you being alone in the apartment all that time was not safe."

"I'm sorry," said Pagne quietly, even though she was not.

"Let's get you settled in. I don't know much about what happened with your mom except that she is very sick, but she is doing much better. She is sleeping a lot and doesn't want any visitors. Can you tell me what happened?" Pagne shared the events with Miss Renee.

"Lenny doesn't know I'm here. If I don't show up after school, he will be really worried."

"I'll call him and let him know where you are. You okay here?" asked Miss Renee.

"Yes, I'll be fine."

"I have to leave, but I'll keep in touch and let you know when I have news about your mom."

"Thank you, Miss Renee," Pagne paused, "I love you."

"I love you too, Pagne."

Pagne was taken to her dorm room so she could settle in before dinner. She waited for an update on her mother before she went to bed. Miss Renee called and explained that Leah was doing well and they thought she would be released by Tuesday of next week. The doctors were testing her for liver damage and other complications common with excessive drinking and alcohol poisoning. Leah still insisted on no visitors and Pagne was hurt, but relieved at the same time. She found it difficult to sleep. She would see Lenny tomorrow and that was great, but added to her insomnia.

Pagne woke up early and took extra time to fix her hair and select her outfit. She wanted to look her best when she saw Lenny. The morning dragged. She had breakfast and met with her social worker to discuss her situation. Just as she guessed, the court would determine her fate once her mother was stable and could appear before the judge. The limbo would normally drive her mad, but waiting for Lenny overrode anything else in her head. Why wasn't he here yet? She prayed that there were no problems leaving the hospital and that he was fine or that he wasn't going to another facility and that his mother hadn't figured out a way to take him home with her. All these concerns melted away when she saw him coming into the cafeteria at lunch. Pagne couldn't contain her squeal of delight. He was beautiful, still swollen and purple in spots, but beautiful. His head had been shaved very close. When Lenny heard Pagne, he looked embarrassed and thrilled at the same time. They ran to each other and held one another. After a few minutes, they realized that everyone was staring at them and giggling. They broke away quickly and said hello in unnatural voices.

Pagne led Lenny over to her table. "How are you feeling? Get your room assignment yet? Are you hungry? What do you think of the place?" So many questions bubbled up. Lenny was grinning at her.

"Slow down, Pagne," he said. "To answer your questions, I feel like crap, yes, no, and if you're here and my family isn't, it's great." Pagne started to laugh, but the seriousness of his last answer brought her back to why he was here. She kissed her fingertip and touched it to his lips. He closed his eyes until she pulled her finger away.

"One last question… why did you shave your head? I love your hair."

"Well, I don't think having chunks of scalp showing is the latest rage, although I'm cute enough, it might have caught on." Pagne rolled her eyes at him. "Figured I'd let it all grow in together. It should grow quick, ya think?" Pagne ran her hand over his short stubbles,

"I don't know, Lenny, it's kinda growing on me." Pagne felt embarrassed by the physical contact and pulled her hand away. "If you're not going to eat, come with me." She jumped up and led him out of the cafeteria to her favorite tree in the yard area. "This is the tree I told you about." She climbed up onto the sweeping branch and motioned for Lenny to follow her, but she didn't move any higher. Pagne didn't know how sore he still was. Lenny pulled himself up without too much pain, but they stayed on the bottom branch. Lenny looked up into the heart of the tree.

"Pagne, this is incredible. I can see why you would love this tree. Maybe in a few days, I can climb higher."

"No rush," Pagne soothed. "This tree has been here a long time and it isn't going anywhere. Each limb can be a step up every day."

Lenny grinned at her. "I like the sound of that."

The next few days were wonderful. She couldn't see Lenny as much as she wanted, but they cherished the time they had. Each day, Lenny would go up another branch in their tree sitting. They would lie along the thick, woody arms and daydream about life and their futures. Pagne was comforted knowing she was always a part of Lenny's plans and he was part of hers. While in the tree, Pagne heard someone call her name. It sounded like Miss Renee.

Pagne yelled down, "Yes?"

"There you are. This is such a great tree," Miss Renee said, as she stood under them, looking into the canopy of branches and leaves. "I wish I had my jeans on. I'd join you up there." She paused a long time before speaking again. "Pagne, I have some news. Mr. Phillips is waiting for us in his office." Pagne slowly climbed down while looking at Lenny's scared face. "She won't be long Lenny. You okay up there by yourself?"

"Sure, Miss Renee. I'm feeling pretty much back to normal."

"Wonderful, Lenny. I'll send her right back."

"Okay" he whispered.

Pagne was silent as they walked to the front office. Miss Renee seemed to want to be quiet too, so they continued without a word.

"Hello again, Pagne," Mr. Phillips said, as he motioned for her to sit. Miss Renee pulled up a second chair next to hers. They both faced Mr. Phillips as he sat behind his desk. "Pagne, we brought you in here today to discuss your case and what we think is the best plan. Miss Renee will give you the update on your mother and the court's position."

Miss Renee turned toward Pagne and laid her hand on Pagne's knee. "Things are a little complicated Pagne. Your mother was feeling much better and left the hospital last night without letting anyone know. They found her bed empty on the early morning check and notified the police. The police went by your apartment and all of her things are gone. We have no idea where she is and she withdrew what little she had in the bank early this morning. They found this note on the kitchen table."

CHAMPAGNE
I HOPE YOU CAN FORGIVE ME.
MOM

Pagne didn't know what to say. *Why would she call her by her full name? Why didn't she say more? Why couldn't she say Love, Mom?* Pagne brought the note to her nose, thinking the note would smell like her mother. Instead, she could smell a faint scent of her angel. She cried as Miss Renee held her and assured her she would get through this. Mr. Phillips left the room to give them some privacy. Through her sobs, she asked Miss Renee what this would mean for her. Where would she go? Miss Renee told her that she would stay here until the courts could confirm and declare abandonment. Once the legal issues were resolved, they would place her a foster-home. Miss Renee assured her that she had a wonderful home in mind for her and that she would be safe. It was here in town and she could stay at her school. Pagne dreaded to ask, but she had to know. "Will Lenny stay close by if he goes into a foster-home?" Miss Renee looked into those hurting eyes and put a hand on each cheek. "I will do everything possible to keep him close Pagne. I know how much you both need each other." Pagne hugged her and asked if she could go back to the tree, back to Lenny.

"Sure, hon, we'll talk soon."

Pagne ran to the tree, praying that Lenny hadn't left and he hadn't. He saw her face and knew that she would share when she could. For now, they just laid in the branches, watching the light flitter through the leaves. Lenny reached over and intertwined his fingers in hers. "Always, Pagne. Always," he uttered, almost soundlessly. She closed her eyes and thanked God for Lenny.

It had been two weeks since Pagne's mother left the hospital and there had been no word from her. They did a search to see if any family could be located, but there was no one. The judge finally declared abandonment as cause to give the county guardianship over Pagne. Miss Renee came into Pagne's room early one morning. "There is an opening at the foster-home I told you about. I'd like to move you in there tomorrow. This is a special family, Pagne. I believe you could be there a long time."

"You're sure I can stay at my school?"

"Yes, same class, same teachers. We worked it out with your principal. They are excited to have you back." Pagne missed her friends and teachers.

"Have any decisions been made for Lenny?"

"Not yet. We're waiting for a local family to have an opening. Lenny can stay here till we can work something out."

Pagne met up with Lenny and headed out to the tree. "I saw Miss Renee earlier. Did she come to see you?" asked Lenny.

"Yes, the home she's been waiting for has an open bed. I'll be leaving tomorrow at noon."

"You're sure you can come visit?" he asked quietly.

"Yes, Miss Renee promised. I will come as much as I can. We can talk on the phone, too," Pagne added with encouragement.

"That will be great." Lenny responded with very little enthusiasm. "My mom keeps requesting visitation," Lenny said suddenly.

"Think you might agree to see her?" Pagne gently asked.

"Nah, too much has happened. She made her choice and it wasn't me."

They heard the call for dinner and scrambled out of the tree. Tonight was pizza night and they didn't want to be last in line.

Pagne had mixed emotions, both excitement and trepidation. She didn't want to leave Lenny, but she knew he could leave Langston Hall at any time. If she stayed, she could be without Lenny and miss out on this home. She trusted Miss Renee when she said it was the perfect place for her, so she packed up all her belongings. Lenny had given her one of his t-shirts so she could smell him while they were apart. He also gave her a notebook full of his poems and stories. He had written many just for her. She treasured this book more than anything she owned. Miss Renee was ready to leave, so they traveled the twenty miles to Pagne's new home. Miss Renee filled Pagne in on the dynamics of the house. The family consisted of a father who was a defense lawyer and a stay-at-home mother, a nine-year-old son, and another teen girl that had just turned fourteen, a year older than Pagne. They also had twin babies that were going through heroin withdrawal. The twins' mother was currently in a rehabilitation program and, since she was doing so well, the twins would return to her in a few months. Pagne had never been around babies before and thought it would be fun.

When they pulled up to the house, Pagne was surprised to see that it was a newer home and in a nice neighborhood. They walked up to the porch and rang the bell. A woman in her mid-thirties, not beautiful, but very striking, opened the door. Her name was Pam Masters and she had bright amber eyes and deep raven black hair. "Hello Pagne. That is what you like to be called right?"

"Yes, Ma'am. Pagne will be just fine."

"Well, Pagne, please come in. I'm really happy to meet you."

Pagne and Miss Renee stepped inside. The living room was simply decorated, but it was warm and inviting. There wasn't a lot of clutter or knick knacks like at Grandma's house. They took a seat on the couch. Pagne knew the drill. Miss Renee and Mrs. Masters would review Pagne's case file, discuss any health or education issues, and then Pagne would be left in the unknown environment that she was supposed to call home. Strangers for parents. Self-pity began to slip in. She was a discarded charity case.

Chantal, her angel, startled her by nudging her, and then spoke to her in a whisper, "You are loved!" Pagne felt the bitterness melting away as she remembered Lenny, Miss Renee, and everyone at Grandma's. Pagne smiled to herself and thanked Chantal, knowing that the love of God and her angel was powerful and consistent.

When the adults were through talking, Miss Renee stood to leave and, as she hugged Pagne, she felt some tension in her body. "Don't worry, Pagne. You will love it here," she whispered in her ear.

"Thanks, you'll call if there is any news on my mom?" Pagne asked.

"Yes, dear. Just as soon as I hear anything."

Miss Renee left and Pagne was now alone with Mrs. Masters. "Let me show you the rest of the house before the twins wake up." Mrs. Masters started to pick up Pagne's bag, but Pagne insisted on carrying it herself. Pagne followed her up a wide, carpeted staircase to a balcony of sorts. The landing split off in two hallways, one to the right and one to the left. There was a set of double doors in the center of the landing. "This is our room," she explained. "This room is by invitation only. We decided that when we became parents, we needed one space that was private for me and my husband."

"No problem," Pagne said.

Mrs. Masters turned down the hall to the left, pointing to the first door, "Here is the bathroom you girls will share. There is plenty of room for your things." Pagne peeked in and saw a huge jacuzzi tub. She was anxious to try it out. "Here we are," Mrs. Masters announced with some pride as she opened the door at the end of the hall into a large, lovely, sun-filled room. There was a twin bed on each side of a huge window with a pillow-filled window seat. Pagne could see herself curled up, watching the skies and the clouds. The primary colors in the room were black, gray, and lime-green on the left and bright electric blue on the right. The window seat had a mixture of black, gray, blue, and green pillows. The walls were black at the bottom and faded up to a light gray at the top. There were wonderful, framed drawings hung on the left side of the room. Pagne noticed that the right wall displayed empty frames. Mrs. Masters motioned for Pagne to put her bag on the blue bed. "This will be your bed, sweetheart. Half of the closet is for you." Pagne noticed a long, gray desk with a computer. The room was incredible.

Suddenly, they heard a loud squall. "Oh my, that's it for the tour, I'm afraid. Bree will be home soon. She can show you the rest of the house. You can get settled in or come with me to meet the twins."

"I'll come with you," Pagne answered. She was excited to see the babies. *Bree, Hmmm,* she thought. *Could it be?* She hadn't noticed any pictures while in the room. The screaming got louder as they reached the twins' room. Pagne's heart melted when she saw the tear streaked faces of Matt and Mattie standing in their cribs. "They are adorable," she cooed. Matt and Mattie were cookie cutters of each other except Mattie had a girlie look that Matt didn't have. They both had golden brown eyes and black hair that fell in glorious curls. They were healthy and chubby, but not fat. "How old are they?" Pagne asked.

"Well, they were ten months last week." Mrs. Masters answered. Pagne looked around the room. There were bold crayon colors everywhere. One wall had a hand-painted mural of an adorable bear standing on a tree stump, holding onto another bear that was drifting up with a balloon tied to his tail. Clouds on a blue sky filled the rest of the wall. "We got them when they were a month old. They were hospitalized for their first month due to the drugs in their systems. I'm trained to work with babies born with drug complications. It's a difficult first year for them. They go through withdrawals and have other issues we try to work through," Mrs. Masters continued.

"How long do you keep them?"

"That depends. If the mom can get herself clean and functioning, the court tries to reunite them. If the mother does not complete everything required by the courts in a set timeframe, the babies are available for adoption. They don't want these little guys caught up in the system for very long. They need extra love and attention."

"Isn't it hard to give them back," Pagne asked.

"Yes, very, but what we do is really important. It isn't about us. It's about helping these babies have a safe, loving environment that will give them a great chance at life. It's wonderful when you see a baby reunited with a mother who has worked hard to get her life back on track. Our son, Richie, he's nine, wasn't so lucky. His mother wasn't able to stop drinking and died from alcohol poisoning when he was just over a year. He knows we aren't his biological parents, but he knows we couldn't love him any more even if we were. The alcohol his mother used while she was pregnant has permanently affected him and we knew it would be difficult to find an adoptive family for him. We adored him so much and decided to adopt him ourselves. He has been such a blessing. I hope you'll be patient with him. He has issues with remembering so we have to remind him of important things. Richie also has difficulties with controlling his impulses and judgment. It can be hard at times, but we have to remember that Richie doesn't make mistakes on purpose."

"I understand," assured Pagne. "My mom drank when she was pregnant with me. They think that's why school has always been a challenge for me."

"Oh, hon, I'm so sorry you have that burden. I think you might be very good for Richie. He is very bright but, he gets so frustrated. He knows that he isn't like the rest of the kids his age. Here at home, we use the K.I.S.S. approach with Richie. Keep It Simple Sweetie. Richie responds much better if we use few words and only one instruction at a time. We may have to remind him several times. We can ask him to go pick up his room and he will make it to his room then forget why he went in. We'll find him rearranging his socks."

Some things were beginning to make sense to Pagne. She had always needed to make notes and use a checklist when she had lots of things to do, especially in school.

"Richie is getting a lot of help at his school. They have some special classes for kids that struggle like Richie."

Pagne was looking forward to meeting Richie. And Bree. She wanted to ask about Bree. "Mrs. Masters?" Pagne said, not sure what she should call her. "I knew a girl at the children's home a few years ago named Bree. I'm wondering if she could be your Bree?"

"What was her last name? Bree is a very popular name."

"We were pretty little. I don't think I ever knew. Her family died in a crash."

"Could be. Why don't you ask her yourself? She just came in the front door. Bree!" Mrs. Masters yelled. "We're in the twin's room." Mrs. Masters lifted Mattie out of the crib. "Gotta change these wet diapers." Pagne heard someone running up the stairs and as Pagne stepped into the hall, she saw her Bree. They both squealed and grabbed each other laughing.

Chapter 6

"It is you!" Pagne said breathlessly.

"Oh my gosh, Pagne, I knew a new girl was coming but, I never imagined it was you."

"This is wonderful," Mrs. Masters yelled out. "You girls can catch up in a minute… Matt is trying to climb out of the crib and I'm up to my elbows in baby poop." Everyone started laughing and Bree ran in the room to grab Matt. As Pagne came back into the room, she saw a loving family. Bree was throwing Matt into the air while he giggled and grabbed her long blonde hair. Mrs. Masters was patiently redressing a wiggling Mattie. Pagne wanted to be part of this family so badly, but she was scared to assume they would feel the same. After all, they already had each other. What if they only had an empty bed to fill, but the space in their hearts was all used up?

Bree whirled around and saw Pagne standing there with a look of longing on her face, a look Bree knew all too well. "Hey Pagne, wanna hold him?"

"Let me give her Mattie, so I can change Matt. I'm sure he is soaking wet," said Mrs. Masters.

"Yeah," said Bree as she sniffed Matt's behind, "and he stinks, too! Ewwww Matt," teased Bree, "you sure can dump a stinky load." As Mrs. Masters handed Mattie to Pagne, she groaned. "Bree, you lucked out this time. Give Pagne the rest of the tour, but you get poopie duty next time."

"Okay, Mom," Bree cooed. She shook her head at Pagne and twisted her face into a grimace.

Bree, Pagne, and Mattie moved into the hall and began the tour. "Have you seen our room yet?" asked Bree.

"Oh yes, it is awesome! I love everything about it. I haven't put anything away yet."

"Did you see the closet?" Pagne shook her head no. "Oh my gosh. It's a whole other room. It's incredible." Pagne laughed knowing she wouldn't need more than two drawers. They moved from one lovely room to another. Richie's room contained books, videos, and trains. Trains were on the sheets and his walls and an actual train set was set up on a narrow ledge close to the ceiling and encircled the whole room. Pagne guessed Richie was a train fanatic.

One wall was painted like a blackboard and covered with drawings. Some were obviously Richie's, but some were beautiful, detailed sketches. Pagne asked, "Who drew these?"

"Me," beamed Bree. "I had to stop though. Richie won't erase them and I didn't want to fill up his wall. They did the wall for Richie, to encourage his coordination and his ability to express his feelings. If it was up to him, he'd have me cover the whole wall."

"Bree, these are really good! Those were your drawings on the bedroom wall?"

"Yes, Mom decided I needed a gallery and got all those frames for me to fill. I didn't want to use up the frames on the new girl's side of the room, in case she had her own drawings or pictures. The last girl, Nancy, couldn't care less, so I used all the frames."

"I don't have anything to hang either so feel free to put them back up."

"Maybe I'll do some new ones that you can keep. Then you'll have something of your own to hang." Pagne told her she would like that, a lot.

Mattie was starting to get heavy and tired of being held, so they did a quick peek of the Masters room. It was breathtaking, decorated in purples, royal blues, greens, and gold. It looked like a room out of an interior design book. "Mom and Dad have asked us to give them this space so, we don't enter without knocking."

They moved downstairs. Mrs. Masters and Matt were already in the family room, a room clearly designed for family living. The door was gated to keep the babies from wandering the house or crawling up the stairs. They had toys and things to climb on in one corner of the huge room. It was a virtual playground. Matt was already crawling into the mini playhouse. Mattie squirmed and fussed and Pagne gratefully set her on the floor. She was surprised how heavy a baby could get. The rest of the room was designed for fun. There was a large, flat screen TV mounted on the wall, comfy couches, huge pillows on the floor, and shelves full of every game available, with a table close by to play them on. Wii and PlayStation were set up on another large TV. Anything breakable was high enough that the twins couldn't reach, which created a wonderful room that allowed everyone to relax without having to watch the little ones every second. Their home was warm and comfortable but visually delicious.

The kitchen was also huge, the pantry filled with everything you could ever want or need. Bree whispered that, while both of her parents were incredible cooks, Pagne should be prepared for some odd foods. They loved to experiment with foods from other countries. "For the really strange meals, they only ask that we taste it and then we are free to heat up a pizza. Dad encourages us to cook, too. It's a lot of fun. Mom stays out of the kitchen and lets us go crazy. We mostly make desserts. Dad has a real sweet tooth!" Pagne looked forward to these evenings of group cooking.

"Bree, why don't you show Pagne the back yard, then I'll need some help with dinner and the twins."

They headed out the patio door and walked into a beautiful, but functional, oasis. There were flowers and trees everywhere with several fountains that emptied into rock beds. There was a large main deck and several smaller decks that were scattered through the yard, one with lounge chairs and another with a small table and darling chairs. This deck was in the center of a lovely shade garden. A huge mulberry tree created a canopy over the deck and garden. Outdoor furniture, a large table, and a built in BBQ grill that had a sink, fridge and stove partially covered the main deck. "Dad loves to BBQ," Bree commented.

Over in one corner was a fort and jungle gym setup. It was one of the nice ones made from wood, with a canvas roof on the fort. "You can find Richie up there when he's not playing his games," Bree shared. "You'll love Richie. Did Mom explain about his issues?"

"Yes, some," Pagne answered.

"He can get worked up and sometimes he lashes out. It's not often, but you can tell before it happens. He'll start to tense up and turn red in the face and he won't talk to you. When this happens, we stop whatever we're doing or saying and give him a minute to calm down. If that doesn't work and he comes at you, we just hold him very firmly and talk softly to him. He rarely has these outbursts any more. When I first came here, it was really hard to deal with." Pagne's apprehension showed on her face. Bree saw her concern and assured her that it had been a long time since his last outburst.

"How long have you been here?" Pagne asked.

"Well, a total of two years, but they adopted me eighteen months ago."

"I just figured you had been here since you left the Hall."

"On no," laughed Bree. "This is my fourth foster-home placement. Tonight, we'll catch up. Let's go help, Mom." Bree turned to go back into the house and Pagne followed. They found Mrs. Masters in the kitchen, trying to prepare dinner with Matt on one hip and Mattie hanging on one leg,complaining loudly.

"Help!" she yelled, laughing, out as she saw the girls.

"Wanna cook or herd?" Bree asked.

"I'll herd," volunteered Pagne. These little ones intrigued her. Mrs. Masters handed Matt to Pagne. Bree scooped up Mattie and took her over the play area. Pagne followed her. The twins were adorable. The more comfortable they got with Pagne, the more they climbed on her. Pagne lay on her back and sat them both on her stomach. While holding her knees to support them, she would buck and wiggle, which made them both giggle loudly. Pagne loved to hear them giggle.

Much too quickly, playtime was over and it was time to feed them. Each one had their own highchair. Mrs. Masters liked to feed the twins first so she could actually eat dinner with the rest of the family. Bree and Pagne each fed one of the twins. Bree was quick with the twist of her wrist to catch the food that Mattie spat back out, but Pagne got more food on Matt's face than in his mouth. Matt had food in his fingers and in his hair. It was a mess. "I'm sorry. I'm so bad at this," Pagne admitted.

"That's okay, hon. It does get easier. They are very quick and love to wear their food." By the time the meal was done, Matt had managed to get food from his ears to his toes. "We need to take him outside and hose him down," Mrs. Masters teased, smiling at the squirming ball of flesh covered in sweet potatoes and turkey. She came over with a warm, wet cloth and had him sparkling clean in a matter of minutes. "There, that's better. You did great for your first time. The first time Bree tried, she ended up with food in her own hair, on the floor, and Mattie was still starving."

"Did not," laughed Bree.

"Well almost. It was a sight!"

Pagne liked this woman, her kind face and her ability to tease without humiliating. She hoped she would be here for a while.

"When will Mr. Masters and Richie be home?" asked Pagne. She was anxious to meet them.

"Very soon," answered Mrs. Masters. "Richie has tutoring two days a week after school. Mr. Masters, Brent, picks him up on his way home from work. Let's get the table set. They should be pulling up about now."

No sooner were the words out of her mouth, the door flew open and Richie yelled "Mommm! I got a B!" Richie flew into the kitchen and grabbed his mom around her waist. "I got a B, Mom. I didn't think I could even get a C and I got a B!"

"That is wonderful, Richie! I am so proud of you." She leaned down and hugged him with a grunt.

Richie quickly ran to Bree and they did a loud high-five. Richie was big for his age, with brown hair and honey colored eyes. He was adorable, a few freckles sprinkled over his nose. You would have taken him for ten or eleven, but the pitch of his voice and his behavior were clearly that of a younger boy.

"Good job Richie. I knew you could do it!"

Richie then saw Pagne. He looked at her oddly and grinned. "You're the new kid they said was coming," he said with no shame.

"Well, yes, I am. My name is Pagne."

"That's a silly name. That's not a girl name."

"Well, it's a nickname."

Richie looked at her, squinting and tilting his head to one side, then he slid into a chair at the table. "What's for dinner mom?" His interest in Pagne abruptly ended.

"One of your favorites," she said. "Liver and onions." Pagne quickly got a sick feeling in her stomach. She could never swallow liver.

"You're teasing, Mom. You hate liver."

Mrs. Masters laughed. "That's right, I forgot." Pagne was so relieved as baked pasta, fresh green salad, and French rolls were placed on the table.

"Where's your dad?" asked Mrs. Masters.

"The car was sounding funny so, he's yelling at it."

"Oh nooo!" Mrs. Masters exclaimed. "Guess the mechanic didn't fix the problem." She looked at Pagne and explained that the car had been in the shop last week. Mrs. Masters and Bree removed the trays from the highchairs and pulled the twins up to the table. *How sweet,* Pagne thought, *they included them even though they had already been fed.*

A few minutes later, Mr. Masters came in, wiping his hands with a rag. "You'd think for the amount of money they charge, you could count on them to fix the car," he muttered.

"Dear, I'd like you to meet Pagne. Pagne this is my husband, Mr. Masters. I mean Brent." She seemed a little flustered.

"Hello, Pagne. Unusual name."

"Yes, Sir. I get that a lot."

"I'm sure you do. Nothing wrong with being unusual. I like it." He grinned at her.

"Wash up, hon. Dinner is already on the table," encouraged Mrs. Masters. Mr. Masters quickly washed his hands in the kitchen sink and joined the rest of the family at the table. He was an average-looking man. Six foot, sandy blonde hair, and not fat, but a few extra pounds. His eyes were striking, bright green with splashes of gold. He had a broad smile with perfect, white teeth. Pagne could see the joy in his heart through his eyes and his smile. He grabbed Mrs. Masters's hand and leaned in to kiss it.

"Smells wonderful, doll. I'm starving." Mrs. Masters glowed. Pagne saw the connection between Mr. and Mrs. Masters immediately.

"Well, hello all. How was your day?" Mr. Masters said to everyone else. "Mine sucked and I'll bore you with every detail when you're all done describing yours!" Everyone but Pagne groaned.

"Not again, Dad. We don't want to know," teased Bree.

"You guys are killing me. The only good thing about a bad day is getting to complain later to all the people who love you!" He chuckled.

They ate dinner with light conversation, laughing, and teasing and had seconds on all the wonderful food. The twins were given pieces of bread, some pasta, and anything they could have without choking. They were so cute, with food all over their faces and fingers. Pagne was relieved that she wasn't getting the third-degree right away. She knew they would have questions and house rules to discuss. She didn't mind that, but she enjoyed being included and not treated as the new kid.

Mrs. Masters suddenly remembered, "Want to hear something very cool?" she asked Mr. Masters.

"Sure, hon, what?"

"Pagne and Bree already know each other. They were at the Langston facility at the same time."

"Wow, that's great. Small world!

"Yeah," Bree added. "We even liked each other."

"Good," said Mr. Masters, "then no arguing over the bathroom."

"Well, don't count on that, Dad. After all, we're teenagers now!" Bree responded with conviction.

After dinner, everyone but the twins got up, rinsed their dishes, and put them in the dishwasher. In about ten minutes, the kitchen was clean and the twins were wiped down and playing. *How nice to have everyone helping. It made it so much quicker, thought Pagne.*

Mr. Masters was looking through some paperwork on the desk, "Hon, know where the mechanics number is? I'm going to have to see when I can bring the car back in. He better not try charging me more to re-fix his mistake."

"His card is on the fridge, Babe." Pagne loved the pet names they had for each other.

"After you call, why don't you join Pagne and me in the living room. I think she might have some questions for us."

"Sure, I won't be but a few minutes."

Mrs. Masters spoke to Bree. "Will you bathe the twins for me so I have some time with Pagne?"

"Sure, Mom. I'll yell if I need help."

"Thanks, hon. Richie, I need you to take care of two things for me."

"Okay," Richie agreed.

"Put away your school bag and jacket and empty the kitchen trash. Then you can have free play time."

"Got it, school stuff and trash." Richie jumped up to grab his things.

"Pagne, want to get something to drink before we sit down?" asked Mrs. Masters.

"No thanks. I'm fine."

Mrs. Masters fixed herself a glass of iced tea. "Let's go in here where it's a little quieter." Pagne followed Mrs. Masters into the living room. Normally, she would have been nervous but, instead, she felt very peaceful. She sat in one of the comfy chairs that faced the couch. "Well, Pagne, you've seen a typical day around here. Do you think you could be comfortable living here?"

"Oh yes," Pagne said. "I have never been around babies and they are so much fun. I think Richie and I have a lot in common and we can learn from each other. Bree was such a good friend and it feels like a miracle to be back with her! I haven't been in a real family before." Pagne felt awkward. "You know, a mom and a dad with kids?" Pagne said, which made Mrs. Masters smile.

Mr. Masters came into the room, shaking his head. "The mechanic is trying to tell me it must be a new problem. I told him, that's odd when it acts the same way. Sheshhhhhhh. I'm taking it back in on Friday. Can you follow me over and drop me off at work? If he can finish Friday, I'll have Mike from the office run me over to pick it up."

"I hate to load the babies up only to turn around and come right back. Can we go over early and drop of the car and the keys? That way I can get back before the girls leave for school, and they can be here with the babies."

"Sure, hon. That'll work out fine."

"Well," Mr. Masters said to Pagne as he sat next to Mrs. Masters. "What do you think of our little tribe here?"

"I think it is wonderful," Pagne let slip. She tensed as she scolded herself. *Pagne, this is not your family, not your life. You are just a visitor!*

"I'm glad. I get good vibes from you, Pagne. I think you will fit right in but, we have something very serious to resolve first."

Pagne was a little concerned, "Yes?"

"What would you like to call us? I know it's awkward to know what to call someone when you hardly know them."

"I'm not sure," Pagne admitted.

"Well, we are too young and too cool to be Mr. and Mrs. Masters. Those were my parents."

Mrs. Masters smiled and lightly smacked his thigh. "We would prefer Pam and Brent for now. Okay with you?"

"Yes, I'd like that."

"If and when you feel comfortable enough, you can call us mom and dad if you'd like, but no pressure. Only if you decide to, okay?" said Pam. Pagne nodded her head as she thought of how she would love to think of these people as her mom and dad, but that would open her up to so much disappointment if they didn't want to keep her. She couldn't get attached. Using Pam and Brent would suit her just fine.

"Has Pam gone over the house rules?"

"No, we just started talking," Pagne answered.

"Okay, good. We are a family here and we want everyone safe and happy.

No matter what is going on out there in the world, we want to share joy and love in our home. The rules are simple: be kind, help out, take responsibility for what you do or don't do, and laugh… you gotta laugh!" Pagne liked these rules. "As things come up, we will discuss and resolve them as a family. Sound like a way you can function?"

"Oh yes, definitely yes." *Again, too much enthusiasm,* thought Pagne.

"Good. I'll let you and Pam finish up with the details. I'm gonna go help Bree get the babies ready for bed. Gotta get my twin time in." Brent kissed Pam on the head and patted Pagne's shoulder on his way out of the room. He stopped, turned around, and looked straight into Pagne's eyes. "We are so glad that you're here, Pagne. We look forward to getting to know you," he said sincerely. With that, he ran up the stairs, yelling, "Where's my babies?" Pagne heard Matt and Mattie squealing with excitement.

Pam watched him adoringly as he went up the stairs. "He is such a good man, Pagne, I am so lucky."

"I think you both are very lucky." Pagne's heart was softening, even as she fought to stay indifferent.

Pam looked at her with surprise and then reached over and squeezed her hand. "Yes, we are, aren't we? I wanted to talk to you about how we deal with chores, schedules, laundry, school, and other boring stuff. I won't keep you long; I know you and Bree have a lot of catching up to do." Once Pagne had a good understanding of the workings of the house, she felt comfortable enough to ask a few questions.

"You and Mr. Masters… I mean Brent, seem to love kids so much. Why don't you have any of your own?" Pam's eyes suddenly teared up. Pagne felt so bad. She realized she had touched on a very tender place in Pam's heart.

"We both wanted kids but, I found out when I was very young that I would never be able to have children."

Pagne thought about how sad Pam must have felt when she found out she couldn't have a baby. She cautiously pressed, "Is it too personal to ask why you couldn't have kids?"

Pam looked down at her hands. "No, but it's hard to go into all the details. Let's just say I was hurt many times as a young girl and it left me unable to have children. I don't know if Bree told you, but I was in the foster-care system all my life. Now my family is something I never take for granted." Pagne was shocked. Pam was so lovely, smart, giving, and happy. Pagne never would have guessed that she had been an abused kid in the foster system. It gave Pagne hope that she, too, could be a survivor, like Pam.

"Well, enough seriousness for tonight. I see Bree hovering at the top of the stairs. Get up there before she pops!" Pagne rose from her chair, turned to leave the room, and then turned back toward Pam. She was still sitting there staring at her hands in her lap. Pagne came up to her and lightly touched Pam's hand with her fingertips.

"I am sorry if I upset you," Pagne quietly whispered.

Pam looked up at her with a deep sadness in her eyes. "It's okay, Pagne. I don't think about the past very often anymore but, it's good to remember. It reminds me that what Brent and I are doing is very important." She patted Pagne's hand gently. "Better get going... I swear to you, she could pop!" Pagne grinned at that and watched as a tender smile appeared on Pam's face.

Pagne realized she had forgotten to ask about Lenny and church but decided this wasn't the right time. Pagne left the room, ran up the stairs, and was suddenly face to face with Bree. She had her hands on her hips and exclaimed "Finally!" The girls ran to their room, giggling with delight that they had found each other.

Once they got into their room, they both fell down on their beds. "This seems like a miracle, Bree. You don't know how many times I wanted to find you. I asked a few of the staff but, no one could tell me anything or wouldn't."

"Well, I believe in miracles," said Bree "and this is proof." Bree put her finger to her lips and said "shhhhh." The girls tiptoed to the door and listened. Suddenly, Bree swung the door open and there stood Richie with a glass in his hand. He had it pressed up to the door until Bree pulled it open. "Richie!" Bree yelled. "You know that is not cool!"

"I just wanted to know what you were talking about. You coming down to play Kingdom of Hearts with me?"

"Not tonight, Richie. This is my friend and we haven't seen each other for a long time. We want to talk about girl stuff like boys and clothes."

"Boring," Richie said.

"Tell you what. Give us tonight to talk and tomorrow you will have two sisters to play with. How does that sound?"

Richie looked at Bree and then at Pagne. "You promise?"

"Cross my heart!"

"Okay, guess I can play alone." Richie looked forlorn and then his face brightened. "Maybe Dad will play."

"I think he will. Go ask. You gonna let us talk tonight without hanging outside my door?"

"Yes," Richie agreed as he ran down the hall yelling. "Dad!"

"The girls kick you out, buddy?" Brent asked as he stepped out of his bedroom.

"Yep, they wanna talk about girl stuff."

"Ewwww," Brent said. "Let's me and you go have some man-fun!"

"Yeah," said Richie, "man-fun!" He turned around at the top of the stairs and stuck his tongue out at Bree. She laughed and closed the door.

Once she was sure they were gone, she motioned for Pagne to come by the closet. "You gotta see this!" Pagne went over to the closet and Bree opened it with a "Tada!" Pagne had never seen a closet so big. It would make a perfect room for Pagne and everything she owned. One side of the closet was full of clothes, shoes, jackets, hats, and anything else a girl could want.

"That's all yours?"

"Sure is. You're close to my size. You can borrow whatever you want."

"I'd be afraid I'd mess it up. I can't replace it you know."

"I'm not worried," assured Bree. "While Dad was putting the twins to bed, I snuck some stuff up here for us to snack on." Pagne saw cookies, chips, sodas, and fruit.

"Wow, Bree, how long you think we'll be in here?"

"Well, I didn't know what you liked, so I got a little of everything I could find. I figure it's going to be a long night and, as long as they don't hear us moving around, we can stay up for hours."

They decided to get their pillows and blankets and make nests in the closet. It was very private and cozy.

They did rock, paper, scissors to see who would start. Bree won. Pagne's first question was "Why four foster-homes?" Once settled in with their snacks of choice, Bree began her tale. "You remember when I left that day? The day you cried your eyes out," teased Bree.

"I didn't cry over you… I had something in my eye, I mean eyes."

"Yeah, right. That meant a lot, Pagne. That was the first time I felt loved since my family died. Anyways, I went to a family… I'll call them 'The Deranged!' It was crazy, no order and no schedules. There were four other foster kids and no one seemed to care what any of us did. Cold cereal, macaroni and cheese, and peanut butter sandwiches pretty much summed up most of our meals. 'The Deranged' really played it up when the social worker was coming. They acted like we were one big, happy family. I didn't know what foster-homes were supposed to be like so, I didn't know to complain when the social worker would ask me how things were going. They had us do lots of chores, which wasn't so bad. At least it was something to do. I was only there four months because the social worker suspected what was going on and made a surprise visit. Neither of 'The Deranged' parents were home and we were there alone for the weekend. That is not cool with the workers! Well, they pulled all of us out that day and they lost their license. I didn't really get to know the other kids that well. They were older and didn't really seem to want to get to know me. That was good in a way, I guess, I didn't miss anyone when I left. They took me straight to another foster-home instead of back to Langston Hall."

"The second family was much better, Mike and Susan Baker. They had a teenage daughter, Lisa, that still lived at home. She was really nice. I was the only foster kid for a while, until they took in Megan. We became really good friends. The Bakers were sweet, and I had a good life there. Just when I thought it might be permanent, their son, Ben, got real sick. He got cancer, which shocked everyone because he was so young, only twenty-three. He couldn't work anymore. The Baker's didn't want to stop doing foster-care, but Ben, his wife Anne, and their two little kids had to move back in with them. There just wasn't room in the house for all of us. Mrs. Baker cried for days before we left; it broke her heart. I went back to the Hall for a week, I think. Somebody told me that you were back with your mom and I hoped it was better for you this time. While I was there, Itchy went to live with an aunt back east. Boston, I think."

"The third family, the Sneckinbackers, were a nightmare. Howie and Estelle fought all the time! Howie's son, Paul, lived with them. Estelle couldn't stand Paul, and didn't want him there. Then Howie would get mad at the way she treated him. Me and another boy, Stevie, were strictly income and slave labor for Estelle. Howie, at least, would be nice sometimes. They fed us okay, but nothing extra. Howie was gone most of the time and Estelle lived on the computer."

"Well, one night, Estelle found out that Howie had posted dating ads on four different websites or, at least, those are the ones she found. Oh man, did she explode. When he came home that night, they started yelling, throwing things, and then Estelle jumped on Howie's back and was just beating the crap out of him. We were all watching from upstairs. Paul called 911 and the police arrested Estelle. Howie was all bloody. He had scratches all over his face and she even bit his ears. He was a mess." Bree started to chuckle. "The funny part was Howie was very muscular but only about five feet tall. Estelle was almost ten inches taller and weighed at least three hundred pounds. I don't know why Howie didn't collapse when she jumped on him, but he just kept running around screaming and swatting at her head. She looked like a giant cowboy riding a bucking, Shetland pony."

Pagne looked at Bree and they both started howling with laughter. They laughed and laughed until they heard a knock on the bedroom door. "Girls, time to get some sleep," suggested Pam.

"Okay, Mom," yelled Bree.

"Goodnight," Pam called through the door.

"Goodnight" they both yelled back. Bree put her finger to her lips and went into the bedroom. She shut off the lights, laid on her bed, flopped around so the bed would creak, and then slowly rolled off. Pagne was covering her mouth so Pam wouldn't hear her giggles. Bree crawled over to the closet and shut the door slowly from inside. "Okay, now we gotta whisper. No laughing!"

"The police stayed at the house until our social workers could come pick us up. So, that was home three. My social worker was upset that I was getting moved around to all these different homes, so she made some calls and told me that we were coming here. She knew Pam and Brent and she convinced them to take me in that night. It was three o'clock in the morning by the time we got here, but Pam was so kind to me. I lived here for six months and I felt like this was my family. They were so loving. They sat me down one evening after Richie was in bed and said they had a proposal for me. They had fallen in love with me and wanted to know if I would let them adopt me. Pagne, I was so excited that I screamed and then cried like a baby. It was disgusting! They started crying and then Richie ran down and started crying because he thought something bad had happened. When he found out I was going to be his sister, he started screaming, too. It was an emotional blood bath!" Pagne hugged Bree and told her how happy she was for her, yet she felt a twist of jealousy. How she wished she could have a family like Bree's.

"Okay, so that brings you up to speed on the major stuff. It would take days to tell you all my stories like school, friends, and Jimmy!"

"Jimmy? What's up with this Jimmy?" asked Pagne.

"Oh, nothing. He's just the most gorgeous boy you'd ever want to meet. I think he likes me... I hope he likes me."

"Tell me more," begged Pagne.

"Not tonight. We'll have lots of time to talk about my Jimmy!"

"Yours huh," teased Pagne.

"Okay, enough stalling. Inquiring minds want to know," prompted Bree.

Pagne took a deep breath and then said, "I really have to pee."

Bree slapped her playfully and said "Okay, but be quiet and quick!"

Pagne slipped out of the closet and tripped over her unpacked bag, almost falling over in the dark. "Shhh" she heard from the closet and then giggling. Pagne made it to the bathroom and debated whether to flush and wash her hands. It would make noise and they would know that she was up. However, she decided that if Pam came in before she woke up in the morning and found pee and tissue in the toilet, she might wonder if Pagne should stay, so she flushed and washed her hands quickly. She slipped back into the closet and saw Bree stuffing her face with chips and dill pickles.

"Yuck," groaned Pagne.

"You'll love it," insisted Bree. Bree handed Pagne a chip with a pickle sitting in the center of it. Bree's "I dare you look" convinced Pagne to tough it up and try it. She closed her eyes and shoved it in her mouth. After a few chews, she realized it was actually pretty good, so they made quite a few potato chip and pickle sandwiches that night.

"Okay, okay… spill it girl!" Bree whispered impatiently. Pagne began her story, slowly and quietly. Her voice was almost soundless, but Bree was very close and could hear every word. She told her about her time at the Hall after Bree had left. She tried to explain her broken heart when her mother left her in the courtroom, her home with Grandma, Tad, Chad, and Macey. She then told her about the fire, the burns, the treatments, and the pain. She rolled up her long sleeve and showed Bree the scars. She pulled down the collar of her shirt so

Bree could see how far they came up her body. Pagne shared the wedding plans and the pity she felt for her mother that night in the dark. She then went on to the story about Lenny and the beating, which led to the arrest of his father. Pagne was surprised that even though Bree quietly cried on and off, she herself could tell the story without tears. She wondered if she had cried every tear she was given in a lifetime and would only have the suffocating ache in her heart to confirm the pain she endured. Pagne had saved the story of her angel for last. Bree looked at her in shock and amazement as she described her encounters and her relationship with this winged creature. When Pagne had finished, she realized Bree had not asked her one question, but had just sat there focused on Pagne's every word. Bree held her hand through the toughest parts, shoved a pillow in her face while she laughed at the funny parts, and provided an endless supply of tears. Bree leaned over and put her arms around Pagne and Pagne could feel her warmth, her love, and her strength. It felt so good!

After about ten minutes, Bree whispered, "Now I gotta pee." Both girls felt a giggle building. "Oh no," they both whispered and then shoved their faces into their pillows as an explosion of laughter cut loose. Not that it was hysterical that Bree had to pee. It was more about releasing the tension and laughing to prove that they both had survived their lives.

Bree came back to the closet and Pagne looked at her with mock disgust, "You didn't flush or wash your hands!" Pagne accused!

"I didn't want to wake them up. It's two o'clock in the morning! I just hope I don't stick my fingers in my mouth while I'm sleeping!" Both girls could not contain their laughter. They were unaware that Pam was laying in bed, smiling at the joyful noise coming from the closet.

~

The next morning, Pam let the girls sleep until ten o'clock and then knocked on their door. "Okay, girls, time to get up." No response. She opened the door and peeked in to find they weren't in their beds. She heard deep breathing from the closet and, when she opened the closet door, she had to chuckle. Both girls were curled up together in a pillow and blanket nest surrounded by junk food. "Okay, girls, party is over. Time to get up." Both girls stretched like sun-soaked cats and opened one eye at a time, blinking at the intrusive daylight that was flooding into the closet. "Now, don't go back to sleep. We have things to do today." Pam left the room, shaking her head with a big grin. She knew she'd be back in their room at least one more time before they got up. She decided to give them thirty more minutes.

~

After the girls cleaned up the closet mess, Bree got into the shower first. Pagne decided to unpack. She put her few items in the closet's wire drawers and had about five tops to hang. She placed her two pair of shoes on the closet shoe rack, which looked sad compared to Bree's twenty or so pairs. Pagne put

Lenny's book under her mattress, so she could pull it out at night to read, and she put his shirt under her pillow. While Bree was finishing up in the bathroom, Pam knocked on the door and stepped into the room. "I heard you guys laughing last night," she said with a grin. "You and Bree get caught up?"

"Pretty much, I guess. She says she has lots more stories."

"I'll bet she does. Did you get unpacked?" Pam looked around for Pagne's belongings in the room, then glanced in the closet and saw Pagne's meager wardrobe. "Is this everything, hon?"

"Yes," Pagne answered.

"Well, dear, when Bree gets out of the bathroom, get cleaned up and we'll discuss the plans for today. You and Bree want breakfast?" She knew the answer before she asked.

"No thanks, Mrs. Masters, I mean Pam. We're feeling very yucky after all the junk last night."

"You think?" commented Pam with a tone of sweet sarcasm. "See you both downstairs as soon as possible. We got a big day ahead of us."

As Pam reached the family room, Brent was playing video games with Richie while keeping one eye on the twins. "Hon, think you can cover the kids if me and the girls take off for a few hours?" asked Pam as she struggled not to cry. Brent looked at her and squeezed her hand.

"Sure. What's going on?"

She swallowed hard. "Pagne has nothing, just a few hand-me-downs."

"Take all the time you need, hon. We'll be fine here. Might look like a tornado landed when you get back, but all the kids will be alive." She smiled at her sweet Brent and knew he wasn't kidding about the tornado.

When Bree and Pagne made it downstairs, Pam looked at them sternly. "Much too much laughing last night. You stayed up way past a decent hour. I'm going to have to punish both of you with some hardcore... shopping!"

Chapter 7

Both girls squealed and hugged Pam until she almost passed out. "Come on, so many stores, so little time!" All three of them ran to the car. Brent grinned as he watched them, laughing as they piled in the car.

Pagne had never been on a shopping spree before. Pam and Bree tried on enough items that Pagne didn't realize it was about her. She couldn't remember when she had owned a new outfit. Her mother only took her shopping at second-hand stores. Of course, Leah wouldn't be caught dead wearing anything from a second-hand store herself. Pagne felt a slight tug when thinking about her mom.

They went into a boutique that catered to teen girls. Bree insisted she had a cute figure and kept showing her darling tank tops and short little t-shirts, but Pagne kept finding excuses why they wouldn't fit. Pam had been warned about Pagne's scars and she realized that Pagne was embarrassed. She reminded Bree that she needed new bras and panties and sent her over to find her sizes. While Bree was occupied, Pam took Pagne aside and let her know that she understood how she felt about her arm showing in the warmer weather clothing. "Pagne, it is important that you understand that your arm is a badge of honor. You saved a young man's life. Probably everyone in that house." Pagne didn't know that Pam knew about the fire. "You are a beautiful, brave young lady. Please don't ever limit yourself out of shame." Pagne looked into Pam's face and believed her.

"Okay, Pam, bring them on. I love purple, blue, and teal."

Pam smiled, "You got it. I'll keep them coming."

Pagne found lots of clothes that were fun and suited her taste. She would step out in each outfit and wait for their reaction. The first time Pagne stepped out, revealing her burnt arm, she saw Pam struggling to hold back her tears. Pagne wasn't sure how many items she could get. Pam had her start three piles: "I love," "I like," and "No Way." After Pagne had tried on nearly everything in the store, she had three piles with tops, dresses, pants, and shorts. Pam picked up the "I love" pile and gave it to the sales girl. "Okay, now we vote on the 'I Like' pile." As Pagne held up each item, the three of them voted yes or no. If an item got two or more yes votes, then it was purchased. Several more items were handed to the sales girl. The unwanted items were returned to the lady at the dressing room counter. "Sorry," Pam said as she laid down the big pile.

On their way out of the mall, some wonderful scents caught their attention. They entered the bath and beauty store. Each of them found a set of bath products that suited their personalities. Pam got White Linen, Bree got Citrus, and Pagne got Lavender. They took turns sniffing each other as they made their way to the car with arms full of bags.

When they got home, the girls carried their bags up to their room. Bree announced that a fashion show would start in exactly ten minutes. Brent, Richie, and the disinterested twins sat facing the family room entrance. Pam grabbed a chair at the kitchen table. Bree came in, announcing the first group would be "casual wear." Pagne timidly entered the room and froze. She had on deep-purple cotton shorts and a lavender, lace patterned tank top. Brent's smile flickered when he saw Payne's scars. Richie blurted out, "Hey, what's wrong with Pagne's ..." but Brent quickly said "Shush. You're interrupting the show."

"But, her arm, it's all messed up," continued Richie.

Brent and Pam shot a quick look at Pagne to see her reaction. Pagne looked down for a moment, brought her hand up to her arm, rubbed it lightly, and looked right at Richie.

"Well, Richie, this is a badge of honor. I got this saving my friend's life and it shows the world that I am brave."

"Cool," said Richie. "Tell me what happened?"

"After the show, okay? I have a lot more clothes to model."

"Okay, but right after!"

"Sure," she smiled.

Pagne modeled every outfit. She started to relax and posed, curtseyed, and flexed like a body-builder to Richie's delight. Everyone was laughing and clapping. Even the twins were clapping along each time Pagne donned a new outfit. Bree glowed as she watched Pagne get sillier, each of her poses more dramatic than the last.

After the show, Pagne asked Richie to help her put her new things away while she told him about the fire. Richie raced her up the stairs. Bree followed them to hear the fire story again.

~

Brent leaned down to teasingly kiss Pam's ear, then whispered, "Do I want to ask how much?" Pam smiled to herself, "No. No, you don't, but I will say this... well worth it!"

"I'll trust you on that," he said, as he placed a long, hot kiss on her neck. They shared a moment of "Them," the chemistry they still shared, but then the twins decided they had been ignored long enough and insisted some attention.

"A good day," Pam said as she picked up Matt. "A good day!" After a big bear hug, Pam handed Matt to Brent and moved to the fridge to prepare dinner while he bounced Matt on his right knee and Mattie on his left.

After the clothes were all put away and every one of Richie's questions, the kids headed down to help with dinner and the twins. When they made it to the top of the stairs, Richie reached for Pagne's hand.

Once downstairs, Bree picked up Mattie and Brent set Matt on the floor so that Richie could lead him to the toy area. Pagne assumed she was helping Pam with dinner. "Great show Pagne," said Brent. "You guys got it covered in here? I'm going to take a few minutes and clean out my car if you guys can survive without me!"

"Sure, Dad," Bree answered.

Pagne moved into the kitchen and shyly asked Pam what she'd like her to do. She didn't know how to act around someone who'd just given her a lifetime of Christmas and birthday gifts in one afternoon.

"Can you help me cut the vegetables for the salad?" Pam asked as she handed Pagne a knife. They stood next to each other, not saying anything, listening to the rhythm as they chopped.

Pagne finally said, "Thank you so much!" Pam just bumped her with her hip and smiled. Pagne felt herself longing to lean into Pam, and to touch her, but her years of physical isolation prevented her.

When dinner was ready, homemade pizza, salad, and a shimmering gelatin dessert firming in the fridge, they all came to the table. Everyone was starving and they crammed the food in their mouths. There wasn't a lot of conversation during dinner. Pagne liked the quiet at times because she could focus on the taste and texture of her food.

As the meal was wrapping up, Pagne brought up Lenny. "Pam, do you think I can earn some money to take the bus to Langston Hall? I have a very good friend that I would like to visit."

Bree grinned with a devilish gleam in her eyes. "Yeah," she teased, "Lennny." Pagne kicked her under the table. "Ouch," Bree yelped.

"It would mean a lot," pleaded Pagne.

Pam glanced at Brent. "The Hall is very far from here, Pagne. I don't know if it would be safe for you to ride the bus alone all that distance." Pagne tried not to smile. She had traveled the network of buses alone since she was seven. Leah never had an issue and welcomed the fact that Pagne didn't bother her when she needed to get around. Pagne liked that Pam worried about her, because it let her know that Pam cared about her. "I think I might have a better idea," Pam said thoughtfully. "The twins will be starting extended visits with their mom each week. Her facility is over that way, just a few blocks north. You could ride over with us, visit this young man Lenny while the twins are with their mom, and have a ride home. The babies have only had one-hour visits, but starting Friday, they will increase to four. Would that work for you? I can pick you up after school." Pagne confirmed that Pam's plan was perfect.

"Oh, yeah," Pagne said, "I was also wondering what time we will leave tomorrow." Everyone looked confused.

"Leave? What's tomorrow?" asked Brent.

"Church" Pagne explained.

Pam's face went flat and she spoke with a brooding tone. "We don't attend church Pagne,"

"You don't? But, you are all so loving and kind, I just assumed you attended church. Most nice people I know do"

"Not everyone has to have God telling them to be good," said Pam, almost irritated. Pagne knew that she had stumbled into another touchy subject.

"Okay, I just really enjoyed it when I lived with Grandma. We all went to church and then came home to a big lunch. A picnic in the back yard when the weather was nice." Pagne looked down at her hands and decided to drop the subject. Pam looked at Brent and cleared her throat.

"Just because we don't go, Pagne, doesn't mean you can't. There is a lovely church just down the street. The music is wonderful. We can hear it out back sometimes. I believe the service starts at ten o'clock and is over at twelve o'clock."

Bree cautiously suggested "I could go with her, Mom, so she knows someone. I miss going to church. My family went all the time when we were together." Pam didn't respond. Brent stepped in and told Bree that would be very kind of her to keep Pagne company.

Richie burst out, "I want to go, too!"

Pam's face tightened. "Not this time, Richie," she said, somewhat angrily.

Pam excused herself and went to sit outside. Everyone could see that she was working through some feelings and Brent said that she needed her space. Bree brought out the dessert and served the others. It was delicious; marshmallows, nuts, pineapple, cherries, peaches, and bananas surrounded by shimmering green slime. So cool and sweet. Pagne asked Brent if she could take a bowl out to Pam.

"I think she might enjoy that." He answered. Pagne scooped a healthy portion into a bowl and headed outside to the sitting area under the big tree.

Pam looked up when Pagne approached. "Would you like some dessert, Pam?"

"Sure, hon. Thank you for bringing it out. Knowing those guys, there wouldn't be any left by the time I came back in." Pagne stood awkwardly for a moment as Pam looked at her. "Would you like to sit with me?" she finally asked.

"Yes, please." Pagne sat in the other chair as Pam slipped a spoonful of the transparent treat between her lips. It was hard to be grumpy with sweet slime swishing around in your mouth. Pagne started slowly, "I'm sorry if I upset you again. I seem to keep doing that." Pagne was concerned that if she kept upsetting Pam, she might want her to leave the house.

"Oh, Pagne, it's not you, hon. I just have a lot of skeletons in my closet, and they like to pop out at times." Pagne wasn't sure if she was treading on thin ice but decided to ask.

"Do you believe in God and are mad at him or do you think God is pretend?"

"That's a very heavy question Pagne. I used to believe in God, I would talk to him often. But, when I really needed him, He didn't help me so, I'm not sure if He just doesn't care about me or if He isn't real. If he's real, then I guess I am mad at him." This made sense to Pagne.

"I wonder where he is sometimes too, but I guess my angel keeps me from being mad at him. After all, he did send her to protect me." Pam looked at her, intrigued.

"You have an angel?"

"Yes, I named her Chantal. Figured she might like a name instead of being called hey you, angel. Kinda like being called kid all the time." Pam couldn't help but smile.

"Have you seen this angel and why did you name her Chantal?"

"I haven't actually seen her. I see the edges of her wings sometimes and she has talked to me a couple of times. Mostly I smell her."

"Smell her, hmmm that's different."

"I know. I haven't found anyone yet that can smell their angel. Guess I'm special that way."

"Their angel? You think others have angels too?"

"Oh yes. Everyone gets an angel. It's easier to know they are there if you believe. If you don't, they are still there but they are invisible. They still look out for you, but it's a lot harder job for them." Pam loved the picture of angels floating all around, but it was a child's fantasy. "My angel has a beautiful smell. I can't even tell you what it smells like. Nothing else here on earth smells like her. She protected me when I had a really bad fall and she woke me up when Grandma's house caught on fire. She shows up when I'm really happy and when things are sad or dangerous. I know she is with me all the time, but I don't always smell her. She's here right now." Pam found herself looking around, hoping to see a shimmer in the evening light.

"I'm very glad you have your angel, Pagne. That must give you a lot of joy."

"She does," Pagne said and then was quiet.

"You didn't explain why the name Chantal," reminded Pam.

"The name Chantal sounds strong and beautiful. Someone with this name would be brave and fierce. I need a powerful angel, not a sweet, frail one," explained Pagne.

Pam saw the desire for protection in Pagne, so very similar to her own longing for all those painful years. "Pagne, I have a question for you. You have had many hard things to deal with in your short life. I realize you believe God has given you an angel but, why aren't you mad at God about the fact that you need an angel? Don't you wish He would take away all the bad things?"

"I suppose so. I think this life is important, but it's like the cartoon before a movie. It's a little part. If the cartoon isn't that great, it's okay because your best friend told you how good the movie is. So you just watch it, laugh when you can, and look forward to the movie." Pam was impressed how well Pagne could express herself.

"The movie is Heaven?" asked Pam. Pagne nodded her head. "And how do you know this movie is good enough to sit through the lousy cartoon?"

"Because my best friend, Jesus, told me and I trust him."

"So, you're not mad at God about the fall or the burns?"

"No, He didn't do it to me. He tried to warn me so I would be safe. We are going to get hurt and bad people will sometimes find us. God isn't happy when it happens, but He stays with us so we have his strength to get through. He gave us our angel, too." They both sat quiet for several minutes.

"Well, I would love to talk more about this later, but it's getting chilly. Why don't we go join the rest of the family?"

"Okay, so you've had enough space?"

Pam smiled, "Yes, Pagne, I just want to share space with you guys now."

With that, they both walked into the house, taking turns bumping into each other, each trying to throw the other off balance. Pam slipped her arm around Pagne's shoulders and Pagne leaned into the curve of her side.

That evening, Bree and Pagne selected their outfits for the next morning. Pagne was looking forward to visiting God in his house. She loved the music. The words the preacher said were kinda hard to follow sometimes but, Pagne liked it when they told the Bible stories about Noah, Moses, Jesus, and Abraham. There was also a lady named Esther that was very brave and Pagne wanted to be like her.

The girls decided to try to match the best they could. Bree and Pagne both picked out denim skirts and pink tops. Bree's had little flowers with short puffy sleeves, while Pagne's had elbow-length sleeves and a striped pattern in shades of pink. Pagne was feeling better about her arm but, she didn't want to shock everyone by showing most of the scars her first time there. The girls were exhausted from their late night the night before and passed out by nine o'clock.

~

Pam came in the room when she realized how quiet they were. She moved through the space and collected their cups to take down to the kitchen. As she reached to turn off the light, Pam saw where the girls had laid out their outfits for the next morning and smiled at their effort to match. She then saw Pagne's little white Bible next to her clothes. Pam picked it up and opened the front cover. In a lovely cursive handwriting she read:

My dearest Pagne ~
May Jesus always be your best friend, a friend who waits to show you His Heaven. What a joyous day that will be.
Your Grandma for Eternity.

This was followed with xoxoxoxo. Pam felt a tear forming because she wanted to have this hope. *But, no, it's a lie.* She wouldn't be deceived again. She set the Bible down and left the girl's room.

~

The next morning, the girls were up early, fluttering around with hair and last minute wardrobe changes. They had found the service times online. Nine o'clock for Sunday School and ten o'clock for church service. Richie was quite put out that he wasn't going. "Let us check it out, Richie, and maybe next Sunday Mom will let you go too," Bree said.

"Okay," he said, reluctantly. "You promise?"

"Well, Mom has to say it's okay, but if she says yes, then you can come with us." The girls grabbed some toast and juice and rushed off to brush their teeth and apply clear lip gloss. They looked at each other critically and agreed they were the "Divine Duo." Bree's long, blonde hair was pulled to the sides with tiny braids that met in the back with a bright pink scrunchie. Pagne had let her hair dry naturally and the copper, shoulder length hair fell in beautiful ringlets. Pagne actually loved her hair. She caught her reflection in the mirror and saw her face, sprinkled with golden freckles. She liked her face, but the arm, it leaped out at her and mocked her. She called on Jesus to give her strength to accept the scars. She left the house with Bree to walk the few blocks to a new adventure.

Chapter 8

The church was small. As they came up to the front doors, a sweet elderly man welcomed them. "You two are new here, aren't you?" he asked.

"Yes, we are," declared Bree. "Our first time."

"Well, Sunday school is about to start. What grade you girls in?"

"I'm in 7th," said Pagne, "and she's in 8th."

"Well, you both are in the Jr. High and High school class. Go down the first hall on your right and it's all the way to the end. Can't miss 'em."

"Thanks," the girls said in unison.

They moved through the church taking in the people, the structure, and the sounds. They entered the large room at the end of the hall. It was the coolest room they had ever seen. There was a huge tag wall where some of the kids were adding their input, an area with couches and large beanbags on the floor, and another section with long tables with chairs all around. There was a counter at the end of the room with donuts, fruit, and juices. A tall, thin young man made his way over, extending his hand. "Hello there. I am the Youth Pastor, Eddie Johnson. You can call me Eddie." They both shook his hand and introduced themselves. He seemed genuinely glad they had come. If he noticed Pagne's arm, he didn't act like it. "What brought you guys here today?"

Bree piped in first, "Well, Pagne just moved in and she likes to go to church. She was coming and I didn't want her to come by herself so, I said I'd come too. I used to go to church when I lived with my real family but that was a long time ago. My new family doesn't go to church." How did she say all that without even breathing, Pagne thought.

"Well, Pagne, I am so glad you thought of our church and that you came with her, Bree. Do you both know Jesus?" *What an odd question,* thought Pagne.

"Well, I did the prayer," Pagne admitted. "Don't know if I did it right and I can't say I know Jesus." Eddie grinned but quickly caught it so he wouldn't insult her. Bree jumped right in.

"I know some Bible stories, but I don't remember much else. I'm sure I didn't do a prayer or anything."

"We love to tell young folks about Jesus and his love. I think if you give us a chance, we can make some things clear for you about who Jesus is and what he wants from you. Let me introduce you to some of our kids. We'll be starting class soon."

With that, Eddie led them around the room introducing the girls to some of the kids. Everyone was nice but, when one girl made a disgusted face while looking at Pagne's arm, Eddie poked her in the side. She suddenly looked up, embarrassed, and then planted on a fake smile. Pagne was sure they thought she didn't notice, but overall, everyone was kind and seemed to take the scars as any other feature on a kid. She knew they all wanted to know. Maybe, someday, she'd share, but not now. She didn't even know yet if she would be back.

Eddie had everyone sit on the couches and pillows. Pagne and Bree both liked the casual atmosphere. It was so much better than rows of hard, metal chairs. Eddie began by welcoming the new kids. Everyone said hi and then Eddie opened with prayer. He thanked God for such a beautiful day and every blessing he could think of. He asked Jesus to meet them there and bless the lesson. One of the boys played his guitar and the group sang worship songs. Actually, the other kids sang and Pagne and Bree just listened because they didn't know the words. Eddie said this was the time to worship God and that God liked it a lot and he would hang around even longer, or something like that. After the songs, they had announcements about things that would be happening. School would be out for the summer in just two weeks so, they were planning lots of fun stuff. Pagne and Bree also found out that the kids met on Wednesday evenings for youth. They were interested but didn't know what Pam's reaction would be. After the announcements, Eddie began teaching from the Bible. They were studying the book of John. It was all about the birth of Jesus and how he died on the cross. Today's lesson was the part where Jesus could've jumped off the cross if He wanted to but He didn't because He loved them too much. Pagne noticed that Bree was listening very closely and hung on every word.

When Sunday School was over, everyone headed to the main sanctuary where the service started right away. The choir sang really well and the musicians were awesome. Pagne felt herself almost floating and she could smell her angel, very faintly, but she was there. Pagne closed her eyes and let herself feel the presence of God in his house. It was a pressure of joy that overcame her.

They took the offering and shared family related announcements. Bree looked at Pagne and whispered, "too bad our family won't be there." Then Pastor Tim began to speak. He was young and funny and he didn't have any shoes on. Pastor Tim talked about how God wanted them to take care of each other. They were his hands, his arms, his wallet, his eyes, and his mouth.

After church, the girls said goodbye to Eddie. He asked them if they would like to come Wednesday night. It was open-mic night. They could sing, dance, share a poem, anything they would like to do. There would be pizza and ice cream, too. Youth started at six-thirty and ended at nine o'clock. "We will have to ask our parents," they said. "We would like to come."

"Think we'll see you next week?" asked Eddie.

"Absolutely," they said in unison.

"Do you girls have a Bible? It helps in the classes if you have one to follow along in." Pagne said that she did, but forgot it this morning. Bree admitted that she didn't. "Wait right here," Eddie said. He came back with a teen Bible and handed it to Bree. "You can have this. Try to bring it every week. It's also a good idea to read a little each day, maybe when you pray." Bree looked at him oddly.

"I thought you prayed when you needed something," Bree shared.

"That's what a lot of people think," he said. "But if you had a friend that only called you when she had a problem, would that be a good, loving relationship?"

"No," Bree admitted.

"God wants us to treat him like a friend we love, someone we share our good and bad with, our dreams and our secrets. You do that by talking to him every day." Bree was starting to get it. They said bye again and headed back home. On their way, they decided they would read together each night and pray. The closet would be their place.

When they got home, they ran into the kitchen where Pam was pulling a raspberry basted ham out of the oven. "Hope you girls are hungry."

"We're starving. Can we eat upstairs?" Bree asked.

"Okay, but bring your dishes down." They each filled their plates and headed up to their room. They sprawled over their beds and shared thoughts about their morning at church. They agreed that they both wanted to go back. They tried to figure out the best way to approach Pam about Wednesday nights and about letting Richie go.

"I think we shouldn't make a big deal out of it, kinda like we almost forgot about it. If we make it sound too important, it might worry her." Bree said. "I think it may take some time before she lets Richie go."

"I think you're right," agreed Pagne.

Monday morning, the girls grabbed a quick breakfast. Pagne walked the first block with Bree until she reached her bus stop. Bree would walk the remaining three blocks to her school alone. Pagne saw a bird struggling on the ground because it couldn't fly. It didn't appear to be hurt but was very weak and limp. "Don't touch it," warned Bree. "Birds can have a disease that you can get. It kills the bird. I don't know if it can kill people but it makes them really sick." Bree continued on her way to school. Pagne couldn't stand to watch this bird flopping and suffering on the ground. She pulled some binder paper out of her backpack and picked the bird up with it. She talked to it and held it until it died. Pagne was so sad. She thought about putting it back on the ground but that seemed mean. She saw a trash barrel close by so, she wrapped the bird with more binder paper. There were some pretty flowers growing on a bush close to the trash barrel and she pulled some off. She slipped them in the wrapped paper with the dead bird, making sure she didn't touch it. She would wash her hands really well at school, just in case. Her bus came and, as she climbed in, a gorgeous collie ran up to her, sniffing. "No boy, you can't get on the bus." She pushed the dog back and hoped it would find its way home. As she moved into her seat, she saw the dog sniffing around the ground and the trash barrel. Then the dog took off running back in the direction it came.

The first day back to her school was wonderful. All her friends and teachers were so glad to see her. She felt like a celebrity. She was able to continue her studies since the tutoring at the Hall had kept her on the same curriculum as the school's. Pagne was so thankful that she could finish her final weeks with her class. School during the day and the Masters in the evening; life was good and getting better.

Pagne woke up Friday morning with the anticipation of a child on Christmas morning. She and Lenny had been able to talk on the phone several times but, it wasn't the same as being with someone you love. He only had short blocks of time that he could use the phone, so it was always rushed, unlike the leisurely discussions they were used to. She labored over what she would wear. Pam was picking her up at school, so she couldn't come home and change. She finally decided on a cotton, peasant-style top that was deep teal and complimented her hair. She also put on jean shorts with sandals. She remembered they would probably climb their tree, so she changed again, to jeans and tennis shoes. Her skin was tender and scraping the bark was not a comfortable experience. She brushed her hair back into a ponytail, added a matching, teal scrunchie, and applied some pink lip gloss. She was very pleased with her reflection.

Pagne could hardly focus in class. She watched the minutes drag by on the clocks. At lunch, she ate quickly, hoping it would speed up the lunch hour. It didn't. She just endured the rest of the break, not able to concentrate on her friends' conversations around her. The afternoon was even worse! She was a little burpy from eating so fast and from the excitement. She was hoping that any gas in her system would work its way out before seeing Lenny. Her biggest fear was to burp or fart in front of him. He would never let her live it down.

Boys thought it was hilarious, but girls were so embarrassed. It was just a man-thing for them and, the louder or smellier, the better, which was not fair!

Finally, it was three o'clock! Pagne ran out front and watched for Pam's silver mini-van. *Why couldn't she have a more distinctive color?* thought Pagne. So many silver mini-vans came and went and Pagne was now sure Pam had forgotten. It was already 3:05. Where was she? By the time Pam pulled up at 3:08, Pagne was worked into a frenzy. "I'm so glad to see you, I thought you might have forgotten me!" exclaimed Pagne.

"Never," said Pam, trying to keep a straight face. The drive only took fifteen minutes, but to Pagne it was an eternity. She reapplied her lip-gloss three times, patted her hair smooth, and repeatedly checked her blouse for hair or lint. Pagne caught Pam watching her and blushed.

"So," Pam started, "does Lenny know you're coming or are you surprising him?"

"Oh, he knows. Visitors have to get the office's permission and the kids get to say yes or no. That's how it's supposed to be, anyway," Pagne added, remembering her mother's surprise visit.

"Well, I know that this is a special time for both of you." Pam pulled up to the front of the Hall. "Have fun, and I'll be back here in four hours. Brent will keep dinner hot for you."

"I got permission to eat with Lenny if that's okay?"

"Sure, I'll let Brent know."

"You're going back home? I thought you would stay with the twins."

"Oh, no. She needs her time with them. Might be confusing for the babies if I'm there, too. I'm going to head back home and I'll be back to pick you up at 7:15. I get the twins at 7:30, sharp."

"Oh, please pick them up first," begged Pagne.

Pam smiled. "Sure, hon. I'll be here at 7:45. Be ready to go. The twins will be ready for bed."

"Okay, Mom." Pagne said as she leaned toward Pam to give a hug. Pam grinned at her.

"Okay, my love, have fun." Pagne jumped out of the car and ran to the front entrance. Pagne didn't know why "Mom" had slipped out. She thought it a lot but hadn't intended to say it.

Lenny was waiting for her just inside the doors. They didn't yell, scream, or say a word. They just held on to each other. This feels so good, thought Pagne. She hoped these arms would always hold her. She signed in and they made a mad dash for their tree. Lenny teased her about taking so long to climb up. Her face burned with embarrassment. The jeans were a good idea, but not such tight jeans. She thought at one point that Lenny might have to push or pull her up. She finally made it to their spot, smack in the center of the tree.

"You look incredible," he finally said after minutes of grinning at each other.

"Thank you. You're awfully cute yourself. I like your hair." He had gelled the grown out buzz into short spikes. It made him look much older than she remembered. He even had a few hairs sprouting on his face. She thought about teasing him but didn't want to ruin the mood by making him self-conscious. He wanted Pagne to start, so she shared her stories about Bree, Richie, the twins, Pam, and Brent. She realized she she was smiling the whole time. She talked about church and the shopping spree and Lenny said he was looking forward to a fashion show, too. "You would look good in anything, Pagne," Lenny said with such conviction. Pagne grinned.

Next, it was Lenny's turn. Lenny was cautious, but said that he and his mom were working through things. He didn't know how it would play out, but they were starting counseling together. He wouldn't be moving back home any time soon, though. She admitted that she hadn't handled things right and was willing to find out why. Pagne touched Lenny's face while he sat quietly for a few minutes. "I know she hurt you terribly," said Pagne, "but at least she admitted it and is willing to try and fix it. My mom never admitted that she did anything wrong. I hope you and your mom can find a way to work this out."

"You think it would be good?" asked Lenny.

"Oh, yes. She's your mom. You can never change that. She'll always be in your heart and mind. Better that it have a happy ending than a miserable one."

Lenny took Pagne's fingers in his and said those sweet loving words again, "Always, Pagne, Always." Pagne believed him. Lenny filled her in on some of the funny stories here at the Hall. He was a big goof-off and made life better for the other kids. After Lenny had covered everything that he wanted to share, they heard the call for dinner and made their way down the tree. It was a little easier getting down but, Lenny went first to help her if she needed it. Once on the ground, Lenny turned in close and whispered, "How you look in those tight jeans was worth being patient while you struggled getting up and down the tree. I'm so glad I went down first and could appreciate the view from below!" He flashed a sly grin as Pagne playfully tried to slap his arm. He turned quickly, laughing and acting like his pants were too tight when he ran. She ran after him, pretending to be angry by yelling at him to knock it off. They had a romantic dinner in a cafeteria of one-hundred clamoring kids.

After dinner, Pagne got to see some of the other kids she knew. They shared and hugged until Lenny walked Pagne to the front entrance. 7:45 came too soon. He couldn't go outside, so they stayed in the foyer with the door open where Pagne would be able see Pam's car. "I miss you, Pagne," Lenny said softly.

"I miss you, too but, I'll be able to come next week."

"Not sure if I'll still be here," he admitted. "Might be going into a group-home."

"Here in town, right?"

"Yep, I insisted on that. My mom is trying to kiss my butt. She offered to get me a phone. I wouldn't take anything from her but, if it lets me talk to you more, I'll take it. Maybe you can get one too?"

"I'll ask and, if not, I'm sure I can use the house phone."

"I'll call you when I get it," promised Lenny. Pagne's heart dropped when she saw Pam pull up.

"Gotta go, Lenny." She turned back to face him and suddenly felt his lips on hers. It was a small, gentle kiss but, she felt it course through her body into her toes. He immediately turned every shade of red. "I love you," he said softly as she stumbled out the door. When she climbed into the car, she looked up at the door and saw him slowly closing it. She knew she was grinning from ear to ear but, she couldn't help it. She was glad that Pam was watching the road ahead.

"How was your visit?" Pam asked.

"It was wonderful," Pagne said, dreamily. Pam smiled as she reminisced. Pagne just let the emotions swallow her up for a few minutes. "Pam, if I do some extra chores, do you think I could get a cell phone? I'd be really careful with it and you can tell me when and how much I could use it." Pam said that she would need to discuss it with Brent but thought that it might be a good idea.

A few days later, Bree was on her bed and Pagne was in the closet. They were trying out their new phones. "This is so cool," Pagne said to Bree as she opened the closet door to talk.

"Say it on the phone, you dork," said Bree, laughing.

"Oh yeah, this is so cool," said Pagne to the phone at her ear. The girls were so excited to have their own phones. Pam and Brent thought it would be a good way to stay in contact with the girls. They had unlimited text messages, which Pagne thought was dumb. *Why not just talk?* Bree said that everyone was texting, no one talked anymore. Pagne hoped that Lenny wanted to talk on his phone because she loved the sound of his voice. He did. Once he got his phone, they spent many long hours talking and laughing.

Chapter 9

The girls had become very connected to their church and the youth group. They never missed a Sunday. Pam hadn't been thrilled but, she didn't discourage them. This particular Sunday, Bree and Pagne raced each other home. They burst into the front door, laughing, faces flushed. Richie was waiting for them. "When are you going to tell Mom to let me go?" he demanded.

"Richie, we can't make Mom let you go, but I'll talk to her today and we'll see what happens. But don't bug me. I gotta find a good time," Bree explained.

"Okay," Richie said reluctantly.

The girls asked in unison as they moved into the kitchen, "What's for lunch? We're starving."

Pam looked up and shushed the girls. The babies were asleep, passed out on the floor. "I was afraid they would wake up if I moved them." The girls looked over and saw that both babies were curled around the toys, sound asleep.

"Where's Dad?" Bree whispered.

"He had to run to the office for a few hours to meet with a new client. Why don't you girls go get out of your good clothes? We thought we'd go to the park for a picnic."

"Sure thing, Mom," Bree responded. The girls quietly moved up to their room.

Once changed, they headed back to the kitchen as Pam was finishing up with the lunch. "Try to wake the twins gently, Pagne. They are stirring, but not quite awake. Bree, can you help me take the food, blankets and chairs out to the car?" As Pam and Bree left through the French doors, Pagne moved over to the babies. She began cooing quietly, calling their names as she rubbed Matt's belly and Mattie's leg. They started grinning in their sleep and then their eyes started to blink open. Both of them focused on Pagne's face and reached for her with wide smiles. Pagne pulled them up to sit on her lap. They were so cuddly and let her hold them. Pagne could tell they needed a diaper change. One or both had the unmistakable odor of poop.

Pam and Bree came back in and Bree picked up Matt. "Will you help me change them? Mom is going to get Richie ready," she said to Pagne.

The girls took the twins upstairs and changed them into clean diapers and play clothes suitable for an afternoon at the park. Pagne was getting better at changing diapers but she was relieved she didn't get the poopy one. They were now ready to go. On the drive over, Pam said, "Daddy is going to meet us there. Richie, you wanna go fishing?"

"Yeah!" Richie yelled.

"I packed your pole and your Dad's pole."

"The park has a lake?" Pagne asked.

"Oh, yes. You will love it. This isn't a city park. This is a state park with a forest and trails," explained Bree. Pagne was excited to get there and, after a short drive, they pulled into a parking lot. They unloaded the food and blankets and put the twins in a double stroller with big, rubbery wheels designed to roll on rougher terrain. They made the short hike to a grassy, tree sprinkled area. There were picnic tables but they were taken by other families. Pam and the kids continued for some distance and, as they came around some large trees, they arrived at their usual place by the water. The lake glistened in the sun, and no one was around. "We always grab this spot," Bree told Pagne. Richie ran immediately to the water's edge, throwing rocks in with loud splashes. Pam reminded him, "Richie, you'll scare away all the fish."

"Oh yeah," he said as he dropped a big rock he was about to hurl. Pam and Bree had a system of setting up their picnic area so they asked Pagne to entertain the twins while they threw the blankets out on the soft grass and got the lunch items set up.

Next thing they heard was someone crashing through the trees. Pagne whirled around just as Richie was screaming, "Daddy!" Brent had taken the shortcut through the trees and had his arms full of baby equipment, including a collapsible playpen and a big bag of toys. He had put them in his car before he left for the office. Pagne helped him set the playpen up and then dumped the toys into it. They fed the twins first and set them into the playpen where they couldn't crawl away. The rest of the family filled their paper plates with sandwiches, chips, and fresh fruit salad. There was a small ice-chest filled with juices and water. Lunch was delicious and Pagne ate until she thought she would pop.

"Save some room," Pam advised. "I brought German Chocolate cupcakes."

Pagne groaned, "Why did you let me eat so much? I can't fit another bite!

"Once you do some hiking, it'll all squish down and you can squeeze one in," Bree teased.

Brent took Richie down by the water to fish and Pam settled in with her book near the twins. "Bree, show Pagne around but, be careful. There are some wild animals in the park. Keep your distance from any strangers, too."

"Okay Mom," yelled Bree as they moved along a path that winded through an opening in the forest trees. Bree was familiar with this park so, she moved through it with confidence and clearly had a destination in mind. They had only been on the trail for fifteen minutes but, it felt like they had hiked for an hour. Pagne was surprised how out of shape she was compared to Bree. They rounded a corner and Pagne saw a piece of Heaven, a gurgling stream running down to join the lake, ferns everywhere, wild flowers blooming in the sunny areas, and trees that made a ceiling for shade.

"This is beautiful!"

"I thought you'd love it," said Bree. "This is my favorite spot. Sometimes I see deer coming through here and, last spring, there was a doe with two little fawns. I wish I had my camera." They found a mossy area under the trees and plopped down.

Pagne and Bree began to daydream together and share their plans for the future. Bree told more stories and Pagne shared her feelings about Lenny. The afternoon was drifting lazily. The sounds of the stream were so soothing. As Pagne dozed while listening to one of Bree's extensive recounts of the mean girl who tormented her at school, she caught the scent of something sweet and familiar. It was her angel, and Pagne smiled. "I've missed you," she whispered.

"You say something?" asked Bree.

"No," Pagne lied, savoring the visit from her angel.

The scent continued and became incredibly strong. Not like a whisper, but a scream. Pagne realized they were in danger and jumped up. She heard something coming toward them through the shrubbery nearby. Bree heard it also and turned to look behind them, afraid that it might be a wild animal. There were mountain lions, skunks, and wild pigs in this forest but, this was worse, much worse.

Almost immediately they heard cursing and laughing and it sounded like several people heading over to them, drunk and loud. Bree jumped up, ready to run. The voices cleared the last cover of forest and Pagne almost collapsed when she saw a man and a young woman, about twenty-five, trying to keep her balance. It was Adam and he was cursing about where she was taking him. He saw the girls, flashed his too-white, capped smile, and made a crude comment about what he could do with three young women. Pagne could see that he was drunk. She moved closer to Bree and started to herd her toward the path they had come up on. As the couple got closer and Adam was able to focus, he started laughing, a disgusting laugh.

"I know you," he said. "You're that deformed kid of what's-her-name, Leah. Yeah, Leah." The young woman with him looked clueless and dropped to her knees on the ground, struggling to stay conscious. "Wow, what a small world, a very small world. How you doing, Gimp? What was your name again?" Pagne didn't answer. "You got a real cute friend there. Maybe you girls wanna party with me and Lucy here." He giggled, "*Loooosie,* good name for her." He patted her on the head and winked that disgusting wink.

Bree and Pagne reached the path and Bree ran back to her parents. Pagne was moving slower, scared but unexplainably curious. "Hey, don't go, kid. We got some catching up to do. You still need a daddy?" Adam moved onto the path, his arms outstretched, offering himself up while blocking her. Pagne froze. He grinned at her and continued to speak. "Saw your mom few weeks back. She's still working the streets, screwing anyone that's got five bucks. Maybe you two should offer a special: Worn-out hag and a freak tag-team. Won't get rich, but it'll keep your mom stocked in champagne." Pagne felt the hot tears of humiliation rolling down her cheeks. She forced herself to run toward him, pushing Adam off his feet as she slipped past him. The last thing she heard Adam say was "Champagne, I remember now. Pagne, you're that pathetic, deformed kid, Pagne," and then a horrible, howling laugh. The tears were blinding Pagne and she couldn't see the path clearly. She tripped over an upraised root and, as she began to fall, she felt arms grab her. She looked up, frantic that Adam had somehow gotten around to the front of her, but instead she saw Brent and she let herself crumble in his arms, sobbing.

After a few moments of just holding her, Brent whispered, "Did he touch you?"

"No," she lied. It wasn't the kind of touch Brent was worried about but, he had touched her heart, deep inside, and then viciously twisted it and ripped it out.

Brent scooped Pagne up into his arms and carried her back to Pam and the kids. Pam saw them coming and sensed the devastation in Pagne's limp body so, she instructed Bree to quickly pack things up.

Richie ran up, concerned. "You okay, Pagne? Did you fall down? Sometimes I fall down. Are you bleeding?"

Pagne lied again when she said, "No, I'm fine." The ride back was quiet. No one said much. Richie kept asking what was wrong and what had happened, but Bree told him to be quiet, that everyone was just tired. When they got back to the house, Pam suggested that Pagne go up and take a long, hot shower. While Pagne was in the shower, the family unpacked the car, put the twins down for a nap, and Brent took Bree and Richie to the store as suggested by Pam.

When Pagne got out of the shower and had put on some loose, comfortable clothes, she grabbed her pillow and blanket and curled up in the closet. She heard Pam come in and quietly knock on the closet door. "Pagne, can I come in?"

"Sure," said Pagne, not really wanting to see anyone. Pam stepped into the closet with some of the cupcakes and milk.

"Thought maybe you'd like a snack."

Pagne shook her head. "Thank you though."

"Maybe later," Pam suggested as she set the tray on one of the closet shelves. "Pagne, I'd like to talk with you. Would that be okay?"

"Don't have much to say but, you can if you want." Pam sat on the closet floor with her legs crossed and looked sadly at Pagne, not sure where to start. "That had to be very scary to see this Adam guy in the park." Pagne didn't respond. "He is the man you're mother dated that tried to touch you?"

Pagne looked shocked. "How did you know? Did Bree tell you?"

"No, Pagne, anything you have told Bree is private. Bree doesn't discuss what you two talk about. She is very trustworthy. When you came here, they gave us a file that has some of your history in it. That way we know better how to protect you and how to understand what might be upsetting for you. I don't know everything that happened, just that there was an investigation about possible abuse. When Bree ran back to us, she just yelled that a bad man you knew was there and he was saying bad things. Brent ran up immediately to keep him from hurting you." Pagne appreciated Brent's attempt to protect her.

Pam reached over and touched Pagne's leg. Pagne jumped slightly and Pam pulled back. Pam paused a few minutes before starting to speak, "Pagne, I know how you feel, hon." Pagne shot a look that clearly said, "How dare you think you know how I feel." Pam took a deep breath and began again. "I have been wanting to explain some things to you and maybe this is a good time. Okay with you?" Pagne nodded. "I'll be right back." Pam jumped up, went over to the window seat, and grabbed a bunch of the pillows. She came back into the closet and padded the floor and the wall. She sat down and leaned against the pillows. "Much better," she murmured. Pagne had mixed feelings, part of her just wanted to be alone and feel like the Gimp she was and part of her was so thankful that Pam was here.

"I think I'll just start at the beginning. My mother, her name is Grace, or was, not sure if she is still alive, got pregnant with my older brother, Peter, when she was fourteen. I call her Grace since I have a difficult time referring to her as mom. Her parents sent her to live with my great-grandmother, who was much too old to be raising a teen, especially one that was as wild as my mom. After she had my brother, things got worse. She would sneak out and meet up with older guys who provided her with alcohol and drugs. My mother eventually worked her way up to heroin. My great-grandmother didn't realize what was going on and, when my mom told her she was pregnant again, my grandmother kicked her out.

"She was seventeen by then and she and my brother moved in with my father. He was a working drug-addict. He was thirty-two when I was born. I had some real health issues from my mother's drug use while she was pregnant but, I survived. Not sure how but, I did. Grace and Luis, my dad, partied harder and harder until my dad overdosed and died. He died in our apartment and my mom didn't report it for four days. Because of her high and her fear, she left him laying where he fell. It affected my brother more than me. I was still very young. She finally called the police but, we had moved out of the apartment with one of her druggie friends. I never knew any of my relatives on my mom's side, because they had disowned her, and I never met anyone on my dad's side. I was three when my dad died." While listening to Pam, Pagne remembered that she knew nothing about her father or his family either. This added to her feelings of abandonment but also connected her to Pam.

"We lived with my mom's friend Sarah for almost two years. She partied like my mom but not as bad. She made sure my brother and I ate and bathed now and then. Sometimes, she'd bring us second-hand toys. We never even knew when our birthdays were, let alone celebrated them." Pam paused. Pagne reached for Pam's hand to comfort her. Pagne knew how badly the disregard felt. "I'm not sure how they paid the rent but, I think Sarah bartended and I figured out later that my mom was prostituting herself. When we lived with Sarah, no men were ever around so it was a good time for me and my brother. That lasted until my mom stole money from her and then Sarah was done with her. She kicked us all out.

"My mom was able to get us a room in a disgusting hotel and, without Sarah there to have some say, things got bad. Some nights my mom would be gone all night and, quite a few times, she'd come home all beat up. During the day, she would either sleep or scream at my brother and me. We weren't in school and seemed to be invisible. Eventually, she started to bring men back to the room. We didn't know what was going on but, we knew it was bad. She told us to stay in the bathroom while she entertained her guests. Mom was going downhill fast because of her drug addiction. She had a harder and harder time getting men to pay her for sex. She had lost most of her teeth and rarely bathed.

"One evening, she came home with a stranger." Pam became quiet and struggled to continue. "We were heading to the bathroom, our usual routine but, she kneeled down and pulled us both up to her. She told us that the nice man was giving her a lot of money to spend time with us so, she wanted us to do what he said. She promised us a toy and ice cream and then she left. We had no idea what was to come." Pagne looked up at Pam's face and saw tears rolling down her cheeks.

Pagne squeezed her hand, "You don't have to do this," Pagne said.

"I know, hon, but I need to." Pam blew her nose on some tissue she had brought with her and took a deep breath.

"The next day, my brother and I were so ashamed. We couldn't even look at each other. My mother slept all day. She had brought home a few groceries and a coloring book with a box of crayons. This was our reward for the horror we endured. The next night we heard the key but, mom didn't even bother to come with the man. This was my life for eighteen months. Our tender bodies were used to support us and to support my mom's drug addiction. During this time, I was sexually brutalized, developed infections, and suffered injuries. Some of the men just wanted to hurt us. I can't tell you what was worse. These assaults on my young body resulted in the internal damage that doesn't allow me to have children." She stopped and Pagne knew she was trying to get her composure back as she blew her nose again. "When my brother was nine, she left us alone for several days and there was nothing to eat. He went to the small grocery store a few blocks away to steal some food and he got caught. The store owner called the police and my brother finally told them about me and where we lived. The police came and took us both into protective custody. They treated us for several diseases that the men had given us and I had to have my arm rebroken and set. I didn't know that my arm had been broken and healed badly. I just knew it hurt all the time. My mother was located and arrested for abuse and all sorts of other charges. She ended up serving seven years in prison. My brother and I were eventually put into foster-care homes. They tried to keep us together…" Pam paused and sat, biting her lip, then she continued, "But we had become so physically dependent on each other and we found comfort with each other in ways that were not good. This created a lot of issues in the homes and we had to be separated." A long deep sigh escaped from Pam.

"We could speak fairly well but could barely read. Thank goodness for Sesame Street. We had to have special education to catch up to where we were supposed to be and it took many years. My brother and I could have supervised visits, talk on the phone, and write. We kept in touch a lot at first but it became less and less because I started to pull away. I had the chance to be someone else. I could be anyone that I wanted to be. I wanted to reinvent myself so I eventually refused his calls and visits. When I was sixteen, they told me my brother had killed himself. We hadn't spoken for six months so, I don't know if something happened or just the weight of his life was too much." Pam stopped there and Pagne thought she might not be able to go on. "Excuse me, hon." Pam jumped up with her hand over her mouth. Pagne heard her throw up in the bathroom next door. She heard a flush and then the water running. Pagne heard her leave the bathroom and then more water running. Pam came back in smelling of mint. She sat back down and sighed again, very deeply. "I don't know if I could have helped him. I wish I had stayed in closer contact but I just didn't want to be that girl anymore. He was a reminder of who I had been. Make sense?" Pagne nodded. She, also, wanted to be someone else. She, also, wanted another life.

"I was in a lot of foster-homes. Some very good, some very bad, but most were just okay. Most families didn't know how to deal with my issues. They had to remind me constantly to bathe and to brush my teeth. I would wake up screaming in the night with terrible nightmares. I was afraid of men and couldn't be alone with them. I was a challenge. My last family had me for three years and I was living there when I found out about my brother. Luckily, they were loving and supportive. They helped me deal with Peter's death and made sure I got counseling. After I graduated from high school, I received several scholarships. The Burton's covered what the scholarships didn't. I was able to go to college and that is where I met Brent. I never saw or spoke to my mother again after the day that the police found my brother and me."

Pagne looked into Pam's eyes and felt hers tearing up. "Thank you, Pam. I've never known an adult that could understand what I feel." Pam slid over and held Pagne. "This is why Brent and I do foster-care. We want to provide a home that is a place to heal and to be valued. My foster-parents gave me the chance to have a good life and they loved me. If I can give that back, then my life was worth living. If you ever want to talk, Pagne, I'm here for you."

"Would it be okay if not today? I have a lot of thoughts moving around and don't think I can say the words."

"I totally understand," Pam said. "When, and if, you're ready."

"Think I could have one of those cupcakes?" Pagne asked.

"Sure, I'll have one, too." They sat there, eating cupcakes and listing all the foods they loved. When Pagne had only eaten half, she set it down, and lay with her head on Pam's lap. Pam rubbed Pagne's head, wrapping her curls around her fingers. Her breathing aligned with Pagne's and they both drifted into sleep.

This is how Brent found them. Brent gently touched Pam's shoulder, and she awakened. "Hey, doll, the kids are watching a movie and the twins have been fed."

"What time is it?" she asked.

"About five-thirty."

Pam tried to shift without waking Pagne and realized her body was seizing up. She carefully slid Pagne onto the pillows and Brent helped her get up.

"Should we wake her? asked Brent.

"Let me get dinner ready, then I'll send Bree up. She can use the rest."

"Okay, but let me cook. You can keep me company," he insisted.

"Okay," she said softly. She felt exhausted.

Pagne lay in the closet, so cozy. She dreamed about running through fields of flowers, the sun shining, and other children with her, laughing. She then grew wings and flew up toward the clouds, looking down and waving at the kids on the ground. Angels zipped past her, then swirled and dipped. She looked for her angel. She was sure she would recognize her. Then there was the wonderful, familiar smell that she knew so well! Lasagna. Pagne was starving. She opened her eyes and only knew it was still the same day because they would never cook lasagna for breakfast. She went into the bathroom, used the toilet, and washed her hands and face. She looked at herself in the mirror, a long studying look. She was not a freak. Adam could say whatever he wanted, but it didn't make it so. She did know that he was telling the truth about her mom. Something had broken in Leah that last night and all of her self-worth poured out; she was empty.

Pagne came downstairs to find a loving family in the process of living and cherishing each other. Would she ever have this? Everyone looked over when they heard Pagne come in. Mattie crawled over to be picked up and Bree smiled at her as she pushed Matt in the swing. Richie just said, "Finally!" and turned back to his game.

Pam smiled and said, "Hey sleepy head. You get to set the table," which she did with great appreciation. She claimed this family. In this moment, she could pretend.

Brent was adding fresh grated cheese to the top of the hot bubbling pasta. "Dinner is ready," he announced with a wave of his oven mitts. They put the twins in their chairs and gave them bread to gnaw while the rest of the family took their seats. They were a family, discarded people that found each other and mended together to make a new family, a strong family. Their scars made them tough and courageous. They were badges of honor. Pagne wore some of hers on the outside but she shared scars of the heart with the rest. She cherished this family, even if it wasn't hers.

Once alone in their room, Pagne told Bree what Adam had said about her and her mother. "Oh, Pagne, I'm so sorry. He is such a sleazy, old creep. Do you think he really saw her? You know, like he said?"

"It wouldn't surprise me," said Pagne. "I think she had a brain meltdown that night and, if she is on the street, she'll do whatever she has to so she can drink."

"Well, maybe she found someone nice and is doing okay" Bree pretended.

"Yeah, maybe," Pagne pretended right back. Once they had their clothes laid out, they went into their closet. All the pillows from earlier were still in there. They plopped down and got comfortable. They read the Bible together for about fifteen minutes and then they then faced each other holding hands and prayed for their family and friends. It had become a nightly ritual for these two friends, these sisters. They would meet in their closet before bed, sometimes for a few minutes, sometimes for hours. It depended on what was going on and how much they needed God.

~

They eventually placed Lenny into a group-home for boys. The Masters' assured Pagne they would include Lenny in as many summer activities as possible. The next few months were filled with camping, swimming, movies, and picnics in the park. Lenny and Brent kept an eye on Pagne and were aware of who was around at all times when at the park. Pagne was flattered with Lenny's protectiveness of her but she was also concerned about his anger when he heard about Adam in the park. She was very glad he had not been there.

Some of the best times were at the old drive-in theatre where they played older movies. They loaded up chairs, blankets, and coolers and go with several other neighboring families. They parked their cars in a semi-circle and set up an outside viewing area in the center of the cars, turning on all the drive-in speakers full blast. It was loads of fun, sitting under the stars watching movies and it seemed like every time they went, their group got bigger and bigger.

They were three weeks into summer break when the girls woke to sirens, flashing lights, and yelling. They looked out their bedroom window and saw that a house one street over was on fire. They heard Pam and Brent talking in the hall. Bree called out, "Come in here! You can see the fire from our window." Pam and Brent pressed in with them at the window. A lovely home was in flames and water sprayed over the house like a thunderstorm. The firemen were also spraying the roofs of the surrounding homes. The Masters and Pagne watched as they slowly put the fire out. Pam put an arm around Pagne's shoulder, not knowing how the fire was affecting her. Pagne had strong memories about her fire but she also had a sense of peace. She knew that this fire could not touch her. She prayed that the family in the burning house was safe as well. She continued to watch until all the vehicles pulled away and the sun was coming up. The fire had taken nearly the whole house. Only part of the first floor was standing. Partial walls that darkened to black charcoal were all that was left of the second floor and roof. Pagne felt exhausted, physically and emotionally. The others had gone to bed earlier, when it was clear that the fire was under control and the surrounding houses were safe. Once Pagne curled up under her blankets, an overwhelming sense of joy came over her. A powerful whiff of Chantal lingered for a few moments and then faded away. She drifted off to sleep with a smile firmly planted on her face.

That evening, when Brent came in from work, he had the day's paper. "Come check this out!" he yelled as he set down his briefcase. It was an article about the fire. Everyone had gotten out safely because the family's dog had warned the family members, who were all asleep on the second floor. The dog was a hero and had saved the family from serious injury or death. The parents hadn't smelled anything and knew the batteries in the smoke alarms needed replacing, but had kept putting it off. The Humane Society was going to honor their dog, Chance, with an award. Pagne smiled, as she wondered if the dog would even care. She remembered feeling very special when she was honored. She decided that Chance would, too.

At dinner that night, Brent said the fire had started him thinking. He decided to make sure all the smoke alarms had fresh batteries and would check the fire extinguishers, too. They already had an emergency exit plan that Pam had shared with Pagne on her first day in the house, but they reviewed it again, all together. Brent ordered rope ladders that would be in each bedroom so they could escape through the windows if fire and smoke blocked the stairs. Pagne liked the idea that they would be better prepared because she never wanted to experience the panic she had at felt at Grandma Buttonhook's again.

The twins returned to their birth mother shortly after school ended for the summer and Pam had an open invitation to visit them as much as she wanted. She had developed a close friendship with their mother, Annie. Pam enjoyed playing the big sister. Annie was doing very well and was in her own little apartment. Brent and Pam loved garage sales and found everything she needed to set up her new place. Annie was thrilled with her new start. Pam also decided to take a break from taking in more babies for a while. Pagne figured she wanted to make sure Annie was successful, just in case the twins needed to come back. Pam was very attached to Matt and Mattie, but it seemed that Annie, with the help of friends and family, was doing very well.

Chapter 10

Lenny and his mother went to counseling every week. At first, he was indifferent and had agreed to go because of Pagne's urging. Lenny was very surprised by how much his mother, Suzanne, was trying. She was direct and honest in their sessions, and she applied the skills the counselor was teaching her. It was too soon but Lenny was beginning to soften to her efforts. He refused to see his father though. Suzanne would go once a month, but didn't discuss it with Lenny, which is how he wanted it. He still struggled with her visiting him at all.

What Lenny didn't realize was that his father, Len, had met some men in prison that were truly good men. One was a pastor that came to visit every week and held meetings. In these meetings, the men could talk, get anger management skills, share their lives, and talk about why they had the anger and substance abuse issues. They learned a lot about abuse and about how to end it. Len was beginning to see the destruction he had brought to himself and his family. He knew Lenny might never forgive him or believe that he was changing. He knew that it would take time, if it would happen at all. Len began keeping a journal and wrote about his childhood, the abuse, beatings, and neglect that had shaped his life. He described the physical fights to defend his youngest sister from his brutal father, including the fight that left his father in a coma for months and eventually killed him. Len could remember the feel of the heavy hammer in his hand and the dull thuds in his ears with each blow that made contact with his father's flesh. His father was so strong, so angry. Len couldn't remember how many blows it took before his father stopped beating his sister and turned his wrath on him. The hammer was his only hope of survival. He painfully recalled his mother forcing him to quit school to support her and his three younger siblings, even though he was only in his freshman year, all the while loathing him for killing her husband. He wrote of his attempts to numb the memories of all the pain, blood, dreams lost, and hatred with drugs and alcohol. He had mixed emotions of rage and guilt. Len wrote it all down and the result was a purging that led to healing. The pastor, Pastor Mike, was loving and patient. He created a safe environment where these men could reveal their pain, open their hearts and minds to God, and find redemption through God's grace. This group of men became brothers, fathers, and friends to Len, something he had never known in his life.

The girls continued their prayers and reading the Bible and soon they began to see changes in their priorities and their choices. They finally approached Pam and Brent about the Wednesday night youth program and Pam reluctantly gave in. She still had a hardness about her position, but knew these girls needed all the hope and support they could find in life. Also, Richie was able to start attending Sunday church with them and he loved it. His difficulties were graciously accepted and he was blossoming in the church environment. He actually joined the children's choir and decided he wanted to be more and more involved with activities and events. Brent or the girls took him to these activities but Richie was getting irritated with Pam never coming to watch him practice or sing. Pam could feel the noose tightening. One Sunday, at the end of August, the church was having an end-of-summer program and a picnic for the congregation. The kids' choir would be performing and Richie had a solo. He brought the permission slip home for Pam and Brent to sign because the parents had to commit to having their child at rehearsals. After Brent signed it, Richie walked over to Pam and said very clearly, "Mom, you will be there to hear me sing my solo, right?" Pam looked at the girls and they could see her irritation with the dilemma. She took a deep breath and said, "Of course, dear, wouldn't miss it." Richie ran past the girls and said, "I said it just like you told me and she's coming." Bree and Pagne ducked out of the room as quickly as they could but they didn't miss Pam's glare.

Lenny also started attending church and youth with the girls. The group home he was in was supportive of their kids having a normal life. They encouraged them to attend church and to be involved in activities with friends. Lenny was uncomfortable at first, but once he got to know some of the kids and the youth pastor, he really felt a connection to the youth group. Bree had prayed the prayer of salvation and took her new life as a Christian very seriously, but Lenny, on the other hand, was still testing the waters and had lots of questions that seemed unanswerable. He still took part in the youth's outreach efforts with Pagne and Bree. Bree had a big heart for the elderly, the homeless, and the needy and Pagne saw her thrive at these events. Bree also began to look at community-supported programs. She was filling her spare time more and more and sometimes Pagne felt little pangs. She just wasn't motivated the way Bree was and Bree started doing things without Pagne. This was the beginning of their personal paths.

It was August tenth, and when Pagne entered her room to put clean laundry away and she heard quiet crying in the closet. She tapped on the door lightly. "Bree? You okay?"

"Yeah, I'm fine, be out in a minute." Pagne hesitated and leaned against the door to listen. Silence.

"Can I come in? I have laundry to put away." Silence. Pagne opened the door and saw Bree sitting cross-legged on the floor of the closet, in the dark, her face flushed, her eyes swollen, and a pile of tissues lying next to her. "Bree, what's wrong?" Pagne whispered, as she dropped to her knees. Bree looked into Pagne's face, and the tears rolled down her cheeks. She started hesitantly, "You know I love all of you, right?"

"Yes, of course."

"And I'm very happy here, right?"

"Yes." Pagne couldn't imagine where this was going.

"Today is my mom's birthday."

Pagne looked at Bree, confused. No one had told her it was Pam's birthday. Bree understood immediately. "No, not Pam. My real mom, Linda."

"Ohhhh," now Pagne got it.

"I miss her so much, Pagne. I miss all of them. I don't want Pam and Brent to see me upset. They are such good parents and I don't want to hurt them."

Pagne moved down and sat next to Bree. "Oh, Bree. They don't expect you to forget about your family and your life before. You loved them." Bree leaned into Pagne and wiped her eyes and nose.

"I'm starting to forget, Pagne. I can hardly picture them or remember what my life was like. It feels like I'm losing them again." Pagne hugged her and tried to think of what would help.

"Do you have pictures of them?"

"Yes, a big box here in the closet. I haven't put pictures out because it would upset me every time I looked at them."

Pagne had an idea and she smelled a hint of Chantal, which confirmed that it was a good idea. "Give me five minutes and come downstairs with your box."

"What? I don't think that's a good idea at all."

"Please trust me, Bree."

Bree looked long into Pagne's face. "Okay, but this could be all bad." Pagne squeezed Bree's hand and headed downstairs. She found Pam and Brent in the family room. Richie was outside in his tree fort. Pagne asked Richie to come inside and she stood before all three of them. She tried to choose her words carefully because she wasn't sure that Pam and Brent wouldn't be hurt if they knew Bree still missed her family so much. "Mom, Brent."

They saw the seriousness on her face. "Everything okay?" Pam asked.

"Bree is upstairs pretty upset. Today would have been her mom's birthday and she really misses her and her family." Pam moved to go up to her. "Please wait." Pam reluctantly stopped. "I figured we could let her share her family and her memories. She has a box of pictures and I thought we all could go through them with her, to hear her stories." Pam and Brent were touched by Pagne's ability to see into the heart of things.

"That sounds like a great idea," Brent confirmed. They all turned to the doorway when they heard Bree come into the family room, clutching the big box. "Need some help with that, hon?"

"No, Dad, I've got it." Pagne's heart ached at the pain she saw in Bree's eyes. Bree stood there, scared to reveal her loss but knew she needed to speak. "Today would be my mother, Linda's, birthday," started Bree. "I miss her." She couldn't say anything else. Brent took the box from her and set it down in the center of the room. Pam and the others sat around the box.

"Bree, we would love it if you would share your family with us," Pam said softly. Bree sat down in front of the box and opened it. On top was a family portrait. Bree began to cry again, as all the loss, fear, pain, and regret gushed out of her. Pam and Pagne moved to each side of her, their bodies close for support. Pam took the picture out of the box and looked lovingly at the family. "Your mother was beautiful, Bree. Such a sweet face." She passed the photo to Pagne. "You look like her," Pagne added. Brent reached to take the framed photo and searched the faces of these people, the life that Bree had before them. He couldn't imagine the loss Bree must feel. The pictures started circling within the group. Bree said little at first, just identifying each event and their ages but, as they got deeper into the box, the stories began.

"This one was our first camping trips. Dad built the fire too close and our tent caught on fire." Bree began to giggle. "He stomped on the tent to put it out and broke all the tent supports. We had to go get a motel room." It was like a sixth sense, the others knew when they could laugh and ask questions. They watched Bree begin the healing right before their eyes. Richie's questions were so direct and silly, they all began crying from laughter. They were on the floor for hours. Pagne noticed that Bree had pulled out a folded piece of paper and stuck it in her pocket and she was curious. The mood was much lighter now and everyone had a better picture of Bree's life with these wonderful people. When they finished, Bree started to put the pictures back into the box and Pam looked into her lovely face and asked if she would select some of the pictures to be displayed in the family room. Bree looked at Pam, confused.

"Bree, these photos are part of your life. This home is about all of us, not just about now, but about our histories and our memories. I think we should honor that part of your life by remembering it every day. Let's honor your family." Pagne loved this woman. Bree and Pam set the framed family portrait aside and found six others that were special to Bree. Pam had some extra frames and they placed Bree's precious pictures on the shelves that surrounded the fireplace. They made room by tightening up the existing pictures. Bree stepped back and saw her old family mixed in with her new family. She packed up the rest of the pictures and closed the box. Brent offered to take the box upstairs for her. As they walked up the stairs, everyone could hear Brent telling Bree that he would pick up some photo albums so that she could protect these treasures. He also told her that he was sorry that she had lost her family. He wished he could thank them for having such an incredible daughter for him to love. The others didn't see what happened next but could guess that it involved some serious hugging.

Pam stretched and rubbed her neck and knees. "Oh, Pagne, don't get old... parts just don't work the same." Pagne grinned.

"You think the alternative is better?" asked Pagne.

Pam grinned, "Well, I guess not. Pagne, I think you are wise beyond your years. Your idea is just what Bree needed! I asked her when she first moved in if she had things she wanted to display but she said no. I knew about the box but didn't want to push. I figured that it would need to be her timing. You were the perfect person to help her open up. It has been an intense afternoon and I think we all could use a night out. Richie, want some pizza?"

"YEAH! Can we go where they have the playground and games?"

"Of course. What's pizza without games? Can you go tell Bree and Brent our plans?" asked Pam as Pagne headed upstairs.

Pagne met Brent in the hall, "Pam says we're going out for pizza."

"Sounds good to me," Brent said. "I'll be down in a few," and he headed into their bedroom. Pagne heard him dial the phone, then say, "Hey Mom, just wanted to call and say hi." Pagne went into her room and saw Bree sitting in the window seat, looking out at the sky filled with a beautiful sunset.

"We are going out for pizza."

"Mmmm," said Bree, "I'm starving." Bree turned and looked at her best friend. "Thanks Pagne."

"You're welcome."

Bree got up from the seat and pulled the paper from her pocket. She laid it on the bed and then picked it back up. "Pagne, I want you to read something." She handed Pagne the paper.

Pagne looked at her, "What's this?"

"My mom lived a few days after the accident. She told a nurse to write down her words for me. She couldn't write it herself." Pagne touched the paper with her fingertips and got it. The brief note that her own mother had left her was important to Pagne, even though she wasn't sure why. She didn't know if she would ever see her again. This letter had to be a treasure to Bree. She opened it cautiously, with respect.

My Dearest Bree:

I am so sorry that you have lost your brother and your daddy so suddenly. I know that I will be joining them in Heaven very soon. You will feel very alone, but know this, my love, we are with you. Always. We will be watching over you and will rejoice when we are all united in Heaven, our family together again.

I wanted to tell you how thrilled your daddy and I were when you were born. We looked into the face of an angel. You were the best present God could ever have given us. It is important that you remember this. You belong to God, you are his precious child. He gave you to us so we could learn how to love deeply, completely. You were such a good sister to your brother. So loving and patient with him. You made us very proud to be your parents.

I pray that you find yourself in a loving family again, a family that you can love. That is my wish for you. I don't want you to think that you will betray us if you love others. God built us with an expanding heart. We can never fill it up. We can fit there with your new family.

I am so sorry that I will not be there with you for the big things and the little things. I am so sorry that I was not strong enough to survive the accident. I tried Bree. I tried so hard, but my time here is done. Yours is not. You have mysteries to solve, emotions to feel, accomplishments to complete and people to love.

I will be watching, sweetheart, excited to see the person you become.

All my love, your Mom

Pagne didn't have words. She ached for this kind of love. She wanted to have a mother that was proud and thankful to have her. Pagne laid the letter on Bree's bed. "That was beautiful, Bree," is all she could say. Bree picked up the letter and slipped it under her pillow. Bree hesitated for a moment, breathed a deep sigh, then they heard Richie yelling.

"Come on you guys! You're taking too long!"

Pagne headed toward the door, "You heard him. Let's get going." The family headed out to the car and looked forward to an evening of fun. They were determined not to think about loss, pain, tears, or regret this evening. They were going to enjoy each other and laugh!

The summer was ending too soon but Pagne was excited that school was starting. She would be at Bree's school this year. They had become very close and it was scary how they could finish each other's sentences. It felt like they were wired together, the way identical twins sometimes were. Lenny had agreed to move back with his mom before school started as they were doing very well and a lot of healing had occurred. Lenny still did not want to have anything to do with his dad but, he secretly read the letters he received every week. These letters told Lenny about his father's life in prison and how God was changing him. Being forced to be clean and sober revealed the reality of what a monster he had become. He shared how sorry he was for hurting Lenny and his mother for all those years. Lenny longed to believe the letters but he couldn't risk his heart and make himself vulnerable. He knew what his father was and he was convinced his father was manipulating them again. At the same time, Lenny couldn't explain why the letters were tucked under his mattress, worn from his repeated reading.

Lenny would be able to continue at his previous school and life became joyful to some extent. He spent most of his free time with the Masters family and Pagne. Brent Masters was like a big brother, only because he dare not think of him as a father. Lenny cherished the relationship they were building. Their time spent together created a natural bond that allowed Lenny to trust an adult for the first time.

Richie could hardly sleep. It was the night before his big solo. He had fussed over his costume and practiced his song over and over in his fort. He had insisted that no one come out back and listen. He wanted to surprise them. They all went, including Pam, as a family to support him. When he came out on stage and saw Pam, Brent, and the rest of them in the front row, he grinned and glowed. The girls could see Pam's uneasiness but when the room darkened and the show started, she got swept up in the passion that Richie oozed out of every pore. She was a proud mom, watching her son blossom before her eyes. She had to admit that the church experience and support he received had made a big impact on him. After the show, they all went out to his favorite restaurant for lunch. They decided not to press for the church picnic because Pam had already made a real effort to be there for Richie. Richie basked in the glory of being a celebrity.

Chapter 11

Several days later, Pam had an appointment with her gynecologist. She had always had painful, irregular menstrual cycles. The scarring of the uterine walls made the natural contractions much more difficult. The doctor had advised Pam on several occasions that she should consider a hysterectomy. Pam just could not lose another part of herself but her menstrual complications were getting worse each year. She suffered even more this last month, and none of her medications helped. She had decided that the surgery might not be avoidable any longer. The appointment was to discuss and, probably, arrange her surgery. Pam dreaded the stirrups and didn't understand why an exam was necessary if they were just going to remove everything, but the doctor insisted. She was lying on the examining table and she heard her doctor say, "Hmmm." *Odd response,* she thought.

"Everything okay?" she asked.

"Well, I'm not sure. I want to run some tests. I'm feeling an enlarging of the uterus and I want to do a sonogram. If there is a tumor, we'll need to consult an oncologist before we do the surgery." Pam felt her throat tighten. She wished now that Brent had come with her.

The doctor ran her tests and asked Pam to wait in the waiting room. It would take a little while to get and review the test results. Pam considered calling Brent but thought it would be better if she had all the facts first. *She found herself cursing God, asking him why this was happening to her. Hadn't she endured enough?* The nurse came out and asked Pam to follow her into the doctor's office. Dr. Wilson came in shaking her head. She sat at her desk, peered into Pam's file again, and then closed it. "I don't want you to get excited but, Pam, you are pregnant." Pam thought she would pass out. *What, did she hear her right?*

"I'm pregnant? How can that be? I was told that I would never be able to have children."

"The scarring was significant in your fallopian tubes and the chances of fertilization were very low, apparently not totally impossible, however." The doctor became quiet and seemed to struggle to begin again. "Your uterus does not have enough viable surface to support a baby." Pam's head was still reeling. "The chance of this pregnancy coming to term is nearly impossible. Your uterus is compromised and the lining is unlikely to retain enough blood supply to support a baby to term. A bigger concern is whether the uterus can expand without hemorrhaging. That would cause termination of the pregnancy and a very real risk of death for you." Pam didn't know how to respond. She could hear her doctor but she was still absorbing the previous statements. "We need to schedule your hysterectomy right away." This pulled Pam back to clarity.

"But, the baby."

"Pam, it's much too risky for you to continue the pregnancy."

Pam felt her whole world falling out from under her. She kept thinking… *God, how can you be so cruel? To give me a child I can't carry.* "I need to think," Pam said. "I don't want to kill my baby."

"Pam, you have to understand. You run a very high risk of not surviving this pregnancy. If your uterus hemorrhages, you will bleed out in just a few minutes."

"I want to call Brent," she said. She really needed him with her. Dr. Wilson asked the nurse to put in the call to Brent. "Doctor, if I want to continue the pregnancy, what would I have to do?" Pam asked. Dr. Wilson sighed.

"Pam, I really can't support that decision. It is too risky. I have never seen a pregnancy come to term with the amount of tissue damage you have. I can't allow you to risk your life."

Pam quietly sat in the doctor's office with both hands on her abdomen. Brent must have flown to the doctor's office. It seemed like only moments after they called that he ran into the waiting room. "Pam," he called. "Where's my wife?" They showed Brent to the doctor's office. He saw the pale, blood drained face of his Pam. She looked as though her mind was a million miles away. "Pam, are you okay? What's going on?" Pam stood and crumbled in his arms. The doctor asked them to have a seat. "Doctor, please tell me what's going on." The doctor explained Pam's condition and the extreme complications she faced if they did not do the surgery.

"Brent, we need to schedule the surgery. It needs to be done this week." Brent's heart was aching so badly. He looked at Pam and saw the detachment in her face. Brent took her hand. She was cold and clammy.

"I want to take Pam home so we can talk and wrap our heads around this," he said. "Will she be at risk if we take twenty-four hours to make a decision?" He already knew what they had to do but he also knew Pam. He knew she had to work through this.

"I don't want to delay any longer; we must talk by this time tomorrow. She needs bed rest and absolutely no lifting," the doctor instructed.

Brent helped Pam up and led her out like a shell-shocked soldier coming out of a war zone. They drove home in silence. Brent felt this was beyond his capabilities. He didn't know what to say. When they got home, Brent half-carried, half-walked Pam up to their room. He got her undressed and into her pjs. He felt as though he was dressing a child. She moved when he needed her to but, she had checked out. She lay down and he crawled in bed next to her. Wrapping himself around her, trying to protect her and their baby. "We'll figure this out, Pam. Just give me some time to think." He felt her body begin to shake. The tears began to fall and her quiet sobs tore out what heart he had left. Pam finally drifted off to a fitful doze. Brent heard the kids coming in from school. He slipped out of their bed, closing the door as he left their room. He quickly made it down the stairs before the girls could make their usual run to their room. "Shhh" he said. "Your mom isn't feeling well and just fell asleep." The girls saw his drawn face and knew something was up. "Can you guys fix yourselves some dinner and help Richie with his homework? I want your mom to get some rest. I'll be in the room with her."

"Sure," they both said, giving each other a panicked look. "Come on, Richie, let's get you a snack before we hit the homework," said Pagne.

"But, what's wrong with Mom?"

"She has a really bad headache," said Brent. "You gotta keep quiet, okay?"

"Okay. Give her a kiss for me."

"Okay, buddy. Be good and mind the girls." Richie ran off to the kitchen for cookies and milk. Brent looked at Bree and saw her concern. "Bree, it's going to be okay. We'll explain tomorrow but we gotta figure some things out first."

"Okay, Dad. You sure she'll be okay?"

"Yes, hon. I won't let anything happen to Mom."

The girls attempted to keep the mood light, especially for Richie's sake but, there was such a darkness over them that night. After dinner was done and the kitchen cleaned, Bree got Richie ready for bed and met Pagne in their closet. "Oh, Pagne, I just know something awful is happening."

"I feel it, too," said Pagne. "Let's pray and ask God to come and keep Mom safe." The girls knelt, held hands, and poured their hearts out to God. Brent had come out of the room to check on the girls and, when he stepped inside their room, he heard them praying. He sat on the floor outside the closet, put his head on his knees, letting the tears roll, and joined them in prayer. They needed a miracle. He slipped out of their room when he heard them finish.

He went downstairs and grabbed some fresh fruit, crackers and cheese. He hoped that when Pam woke, he could convince her to eat a little. When he went back into the room, Pam was sitting up. She looked so tiny and frail. "Hey, sweetheart," he said. "I brought us something to snack on. Can you eat?" She shook her head. He set the tray down on the dresser and moved onto the bed next to her. She laid her head in his lap and he stroked her head, feeling her body relax. "Pam, I know this is difficult but, we have to talk. You know that I can't lose you. We need to schedule the surgery." Pam didn't comment. "Pam, I need you to help me with this."

"I had a dream," she said. "A wonderful dream. I was walking through the woods and I heard Richie yelling Mommy! Mommy! I turned, and he was running up to me. I felt so blessed to have this child in my life. I couldn't love anyone more than I love him." Brent was relieved. It sounded like Pam was accepting that her motherhood for Richie could be enough. "Then you came up through the trees, with a tiny little girl on your shoulders, our little girl. She was beautiful, my dark hair but your eyes. The grin on your face said it all. You adored this little creature. You came up to me and we held each other, all four of us. Bree and Pagne came running up with Lenny and we all moved on through the forest. Brent I can't give up on her yet."

Brent was speechless. He wanted this dream, too. He'd always desired to have a child with Pam, their child together. He took her hand and held it softly, inspecting each fingernail and each line in her palm. "I think we need to look at this objectively. We both want this baby but, the kids and I need you. None of them needs any more loss in their lives, Pam. I think we need to look at this in a different way. If you had something you wanted to keep and it was broken, what would you do?" After a pause, Pam answered thoughtfully.

"I would call a professional to inspect and evaluate. Once I knew if it could be fixed and what the cost would be to fix it, I would make an educated decision."

"Exactly!" agreed Brent. "Tomorrow morning we will find the best specialist in the area and get an evaluation." Pam held onto Brent as though her life depended on it because it did. They drifted off in each other's arms, dreaming about their family, their four children.

Early the next morning, Brent was online, searching for doctors that specialized in risky pregnancies. He found several impressive doctors; the closest was in Los Angeles, only a few hours from where they lived. Brent called the office at seven a.m. and left a message that it was urgent. He described the circumstances briefly, and asked them to return his call as soon as possible. The girls were up getting dressed for school when Brent went in and explained that he may be taking Pam into LA to get some more tests done. They would explain everything as soon as they had more information. He warned them that they wouldn't be back in time to pick up Richie. He gave Bree twenty dollars and told her to order them a pizza. He hugged them both and headed to the kitchen. He made Pam and himself a cup of coffee, grabbed some muffins, and went upstairs to let her know what he had found out. By nine o'clock, he was on the phone with Dr. Olsen's nurse. They said they could see Pam that afternoon. Brent would need to request Pam's medical records and a referral from her primary doctor be sent to their office as soon as possible. Brent called Dr. Wilson's office and explained to the nurse what he needed. She put him on hold and Dr. Wilson picked up the line. Brent didn't care if she was insulted or not, this was his family. Surprisingly, Dr. Wilson was supportive and said she would cooperate in any way she could. She admitted that she hadn't been able to sleep last night, because she knew how much this baby meant to Pam and Brent. She reminded Brent that it was a long shot and that he should prepare himself and Pam for the worst.

The doctor's facility in LA was impressive and beautifully decorated. Brent found a seat for Pam and let the front desk know they were there. They told Brent there would be a short wait and to have a seat. When he joined Pam, she was looking at all the baby portraits on the walls. Wooden letters above one large grouping said Our Miracle Babies. They were adorable. Within ten minutes, they were taken back to an examination room. They took Pam's temperature, blood pressure, and weight. Brent helped her disrobe and put on the gown they provided. She was still not herself. He could see how her fear was pulling her into a child-like state and this problem was too big for her to cope with right now. He helped her onto the exam table. They were prepared to wait some more but Dr. Olsen came right in. "Hello Mr. and Mrs. Masters. May I call you Brent and Pam?"

"Yes, please," Brent said.

"Okay then. I've reviewed your file and I have to admit that your case is very difficult, at best. I can make a better evaluation after examining you." Pam assumed the position on the examination table. Brent saw Pam's face tighten with a low groan as the doctor invaded her cervix and womb. He pressed and pushed. "I want to get another sonogram. We have superior capability with our equipment and I can get a very clear picture of the damaged tissue and the thickness of the uterine walls. Pam, you can take your feet out of the stirrups, but don't sit up. We'll take you in for the sonogram right away."

He left the office and several nurses immediately came in. They rolled Pam out and told Brent they would bring her back shortly. He could wait in the exam room. Brent took a seat and breathed. He liked the doctor, no nonsense but passionate. He believed this doctor would provide their best chance, if there was one. The twenty minutes felt like hours and Brent realized he hated waiting. Pam was rolled back in and told to stay flat. She was quiet, but not detached like before. "You doing okay, babe?" he asked.

"Yes, trying not to think too much."

"Yeah, me, too." He slid the chair over by her head and leaned in to kiss her. "We got each other, no matter what," Brent whispered. She smiled that goofy "I love you" smile that warmed his heart.

The doctor came back in with a very serious expression. He sat down looking at both of them, not speaking. "Okay, here it is," he started. "All logic would say that this pregnancy cannot succeed. You should get the hysterectomy and play it as safe as possible." They looked at each other, hearts breaking in unison. "But, I would guess that you two are fighters and are capable of not playing it safe." They both nodded their heads. "I must tell you that attempting what I am proposing has real risks. We can be very careful but, we cannot promise that everything will be fine. Pam, you must know that this pregnancy will put your life at risk. With that said, I am going to explain the procedure and then you and Brent will need to make a decision. You will need to be on medications that will build up the healthy uterine tissue. There are side effects. You will have swelling and headaches and you will be on complete bed rest, only getting up to use restroom. Move your bed as close as possible to the bathroom. You will need a shower chair, no standing for any length of time. No baths. Climbing in and out of tub is too risky. You will have a lot of abdominal pain as the baby grows. The strain on the scar tissue will be intense. I read in your chart that you are already experiencing pain; it will get much worse. We can help with some pain medication but, it will not be as strong as you'd like. We can't put the baby at risk." Pam nodded in agreement.

"I can bear anything to save this baby," she whispered.

"A specially-trained RN will give you weekly exams at home to monitor the stress on your uterus. If your uterus does not fail, you can remain home until the beginning of your seventh month. You will then need to come to the facility and finish out your pregnancy under our supervision. You will be here for remaining months of your pregnancy. If the uterus is compromised, we will do an emergency cesarean delivery. Your survival is primary and we will not be able to delay to protect your baby." He paused at this point to allow the information to sink in. "If you carry through your eighth month, we will deliver through cesarean, because your uterus will not be able to endure the strain from the ninth month, labor, or vaginal delivery. The baby will be premature but this is a very viable age with assistance from our excellent staff. We cannot risk allowing you to go to term; your uterus will not expand that much without tearing. Now, you must realize, this is best-case scenario. If there is any bleeding, we must do a cesarean, even if the baby is not viable. You both must sign a release that the mother's life is primary. We will also need permission to perform a hysterectomy at the time of the cesarean, as the uterus will be compromised after this pregnancy. If you have an issue with any of these conditions, we cannot provide our services." Dr. Olsen took a moment to breathe. "Now, this is a lot to take in and you have some time, but not a lot. We need to start the medications right away or the baby will not have enough blood supply to survive. Again, I must warn you this is not a logical choice. It requires a lot of self-sacrifice, a strong desire to beat the odds, sheer will, and it can't hurt to have faith in something bigger than you. I'll give you both some time to discuss it." Dr. Olsen left them alone in the exam room.

Brent didn't know what to do. He didn't want to risk losing Pam but he also knew that the loss of this baby would be heartbreaking for her. He looked at her, knowing it had to be her decision. Pam lay there with her eyes closed, barely breathing. "You know, Brent, when I was a little girl and I had to live through all those months of humiliation and pain, I made it. I survived. If I can survive that hell, I can do this for our precious child."

Brent squeezed her hand and kissed her forehead softly. "Difference is, I'm here with you," assured Brent. She squeezed his hand back.

"Yes, you are." They arranged to begin the treatment.

When they got home, Brent warned the girls they would have a family meeting shortly but, first, he had to get Pam up to their room and into bed. He would call the kids in when they were ready. They heard furniture being moved across the floor and looked at each other. After about thirty-minutes, Brent called them all upstairs. He motioned for them to sit at the foot of the bed. Pam was actually grinning. "Well, it appears that I'm having a baby" Pam announced. The girls were dumbfounded.

"What? How Mom? You said you couldn't have a baby," asked Bree.

"I know. I didn't think I could either but, there is a little baby growing inside of me." Brent put his hand on her shoulder to unite them for the tough part.

"The thing is, this is going to be a very difficult pregnancy for your mom." Brent continued "She has to stay in bed, except to shower and use the toilet. She has to get lots of rest and she can't go to school functions, the grocery store, or anywhere else. She can't drive. When she's closer to having the baby, she will have to stay in the hospital in Los Angeles."

"But we can talk on the phone," Pam assured them, looking at Richie's panicked face.

"What that means for all of us is that we will be doing all the cooking, shopping, housework, laundry, everything. We also need to keep the house quieter than normal, so Mom can rest. Mom might be grouchy some days because she's hurting but, we have to be nice to her. She's working hard to keep our baby safe and needs our help so she doesn't worry about us or the house. Can we all handle this?" Pagne and Bree quickly agreed but Richie was quiet. Brent scooped him up and suggested they go downstairs and have some ice cream. Brent wanted some time alone with Richie to see how he was handling things. The girls stayed with Pam.

"Oh, Mom. How exciting. Our own little baby. It's a miracle."

Pam looked at the girls very closely, "Yes, I do believe it is a miracle," she said quietly, but Pagne sensed that there was more.

"Mom," Pagne hesitated, "Mom, is this dangerous for you?"

"Yes, there is some risk but the doctors are watching me very closely. I know that my doctor is very good and he knows what he is doing. It's not going to be easy and I'll probably have times that I'm in pain and crying but, we are choosing to give our baby a chance to have a life with us. I'm willing to do what it takes, so be patient with me and remember that I love you both very much."

"We can handle the house, Mom," said Bree.

"I want you both to know there will be times that I need to rest but that doesn't mean we can't hang out in here together. We can watch movies and maybe you guys can read to me. I can help Richie with his homework, at least for a while. Brent is putting a big-screen TV in here so we can make this a family room." They discussed lots of ideas to make the new arrangement work. They could see that Pam was fighting sleep so they kissed her, told her again how excited they were about the baby, and left her to rest.

~

Brent and Richie had gone into the family room. Brent lay on his back on the floor and Richie sat on his stomach. "Okay, buddy, what are you thinking?" Richie looked away.

"You'll think I'm a baby if I say."

"No I won't, Richie. I want to know."

"I don't know if I want this baby. What if you and Mom like it better than me?"

"That's not possible, Richie. Parents have special magic that lets them love each child the same. They don't run out of love. We've had babies here before and you weren't worried."

"Yeah but they weren't here forever. I knew that I was your real kid." Brent saw how fragile he was.

"We are nutso about you. Nothing is going to change that. You will have a special job when the baby is here, so I hope we can count on you."

"Special job? Me?"

"Yep, only you can do it."

Richie grinned, "What's this special job?"

"You have to be the big brother. Bree and Pagne can't do it" Richie started to puff up.

"Oh yeah, I'm the only boy kid."

"That's right. You know what big brothers get to do?"

"No, what?"

"They get to teach the little ones things, important things. They get to be like policemen. They protect them. Little kids love their big brothers and want to be just like them." Richie grinned. Brent and Richie spent the next hour wrestling, tickling and laughing.

The girls came down to join them. They worked as a team, making soup and salad for dinner. After watching a movie, Brent had Richie get his PJs on and get in bed. He could read for half an hour but then lights out. "Remember Richie, Mom needs to sleep so I need you on mute, okay?"

"Sure, Dad." Richie tiptoed out of the room. Brent's attention then turned to the girls.

"A lot of the burden is going to be put on you two. Think you can handle it or should I bring in some help?"

"Let us try, Dad," insisted Bree. "If we all pick up after ourselves, it shouldn't be bad."

"Okay, I know Mom would be more comfortable with just the family if we can do it. But, be honest with me, if it becomes too much and starts affecting your schoolwork or your sanity, tell me."

"Okay," they both agreed.

"Now, I was thinking that we could come up with a schedule. One week, one of us cooks and cleans the kitchen, another cleans the house, and the last one does laundry. Then we rotate. We can have Richie help with making sure Pam has what she needs. I'll take care of the shopping so just give me a list of what you need for the week, but let's keep meals simple. Did Mom tell you we're setting up our room so we can all spend time with her in there?"

"Yes, she said you were putting a big-screen TV in there."

"Yep, but this needs to be the rule: if she gets tired, we clear out and finish the movie or our visiting later. There will be no complaining and no bringing problems to her. Run them through me first and I'll decide if she needs to be involved. Her health comes first. I'm also getting intercoms so she can call us when we're downstairs. I'm moving in a larger table by the bed so we can keep some things within her reach. I want water there, tissues, a phone, and whichever books she wants at all times. Her nature is not to stay still so we need to make sure we're all there for her."

"Got it," they both agreed.

"This is not going to be easy," Brent said with dread. "Not so much the house and taking care of her but, she is going to be miserable and in pain. We'll need a lot of grace. I'm taking a few days off to get us organized but, I'm relying on both of you to work out the schedule. We all need to make time for Richie, too. This is going to be more difficult for him." Brent spoke with a quiet seriousness, "Girls, you need to know that there is a real risk for Pam. If you see bleeding, I don't care how little, call 911. Got it? Her uterus can tear and she could bleed to death very quickly, so no hesitation. Call 911 first and then me."

"Okay, Dad," Bree said with understanding.

The girls somberly went up to their room. They waited for the other to suggest prayer in the closet but both were emotionally exhausted. Instead, they said goodnight, murmured a prayer for Pam and the baby, and fell into a deep, but troubled sleep. They both had dreams about everything from flashing red lights, to smiling babies, to blood. They tossed and turned all night.

The family soon became a well, oiled machine. After a week or so, they had all the kinks worked out. Brent was right, Pam staying in bed and remaining sane was the biggest hurdle. Each of the kids had their "Pam-Time." They would talk or read to her, because Pam loved to be read to. Each one picked out a book and would read a portion during their time. Brent got a hospital tray table on casters that they could use to play board games. They could roll it over Pam's lap when it was her turn, then back out for theirs. Pam found just the right configuration of pillows to lift her up enough to be comfortable but still remain lying down. It frustrated her that she tired easily and needed to lay flat on and off throughout the day. "Wish we had gotten the adjustable bed instead of this number bed, it would make it so much easier," she complained. Brent came home that night with a device that went under the mattress. She had a remote that filled an air bag wedge that raised her up. When she wanted to lie down, a release button let the air out slowly. It was perfect. Brent was able to find several other items that made Pam's life in bed more comfortable. Lenny spent a lot of time with the family. He helped with the yard-work and some of the cooking. He was getting good and Pagne loved sharing the kitchen with him. He didn't participate in the family time in Pam's room because it seemed too personal, her bedroom and the presence of her pain hovering.

They all cherished the family time. They moved the pillows from the window seat into the room so the kids could lie comfortably on the floor because not all of them could fit on the bed. They started a ritual of movie selection. They did rock, paper, scissors, until one man was standing. Everyone groaned when it was Richie. He only chose from two movies: Superman and Batman. They quickly became sick of these movies and decided to make a game out of it. They each selected a character and said the lines along with them. The one who did the best each night got the honorary possession of a canned ham and Pam was the judge. It was funny because they truly coveted the ownership of the ham. Everyone but Richie understood that a dramatic person was called a Ham. Richie just accepted it as the trophy for beating out the others.

They built many wonderful memories during the months of Pam's pregnancy, but there were also sad ones. Pam had pain from the beginning, but each month it increased dramatically. She would whimper at times and cry. The girls took turns sitting with her, refreshing the cool, wet cloth she used on her face. They would pray silently, asking God to give her the strength to endure and to bless her and the baby. Sometimes, Pam would cry out for Brent and he would have the girls take Richie to the park, anything to get the kids out of the house. Pam needed privacy to let go and scream, curse, and let Brent hold her. Pam was a person that complained very little so, when she did, you knew it was bad.

The weekly exams showed that Pam was doing well and the baby was strong. They increased her pain meds gradually but couldn't give her anything strong enough to eliminate all the pain. The pain and the pregnancy were draining on Pam's body and the nurse decided she needed more nutrients. They inserted an intravenous drip and had her drink fortified liquids to replenish her system.

They began to see the wear on Brent's face. He was struggling to work, sleep, and keep the family functioning. The girls kept a beeper on them at all times, especially during the day while at school in case Pam needed them. The school had given them permission to leave campus if she paged.

One afternoon, a car they didn't recognize was in the driveway. They ran in, thinking the worst. Sitting in the living room was Brent and an attractive, older woman. Bree ran up and hugged her while calling out "Grandma!" She squeezed and held Bree.

"My, Child, you have gotten so tall and pretty. Let me look at you." She stepped back from Bree while holding her hands. "Lovely, just lovely."

"When did you get back?" Bree asked.

"Just last week. I took care of some things at the house and headed down." Maxine worked with Physicians Without Boundaries. She was a retired nurse and spent most of her time traveling the world, assisting doctors that volunteered their services for the needy. This grand woman then turned her attention toward Pagne. She grinned, "I know who you are. You're Pagne. I'm Brent's mother and you can call me Grandma." Pagne reached out to shake her hand. "Oh no, you don't get past my hug, young lady." Grandma Maxine grabbed Pagne and hugged her firmly. Pagne loved the scent of her.

"Have a seat girls," Brent instructed, "Richie is in with Mom." The girls weren't sure what was going on but sat down and focused on Brent. "I'm concerned about Pam being here alone while you kids are in school and I want to be with Pam when she is in the hospital. I called my mom last week and she said she could stay with us until the baby is born," Brent explained.

Grandma Maxine cleared her throat. "You are all doing an incredible job and I won't interfere. I'll be here to help care for Pam during the day so please assign me the chores that will lighten your burdens when you're home. I can take a week of cooking if you'd like. I'm a good cook." The girls relaxed. While the girls welcomed the help, they had become the women of the house and didn't want to be reduced to kids again, not until Pam was back in her rightful reign. They both had become very protective of their home and family.

For the next several months, Grandma Maxine supported the family and took the burden off the girls. They were able to attend after-school functions, attend their church's youth events, and focus on school and homework. She did this with such grace and allowed the girls to feel that they were critical in the functioning of the household. Pam adored Grandma Maxine and they spent a lot of time chatting and laughing. When the pain was severe and Brent wasn't there, Grandma Maxine would hold her and soothe her like a small child in her mother's arms. Pam needed this surrogate mother. She appeared to be weaker and weaker as the pregnancy progressed. The family spent fewer evenings in the room due to Pam's exhaustion and her need for sleep. Even the frustration of being bed-bound left her and she cherished any sleep she could manage.

Grandma Maxine was a churchgoer. She and the girls would get up early on Sunday mornings, make a wonderful breakfast for everyone, and leave Pam in Brent's care while they attended services. Grandma Maxine was bold about her love for Jesus and the girls pumped her for understanding of the Bible and God's plan for mankind. They would sit in the backyard for hours and, while Grandma Maxine didn't have answers for every question, she was incredibly knowledgeable. Pagne loved the conversations that sometimes turned into debates. What they didn't consider was that Pam's window overlooked the deck and she could hear the sharing, the explanations, and the joy of their conversations. She heard their prayers for her and the baby and, strangely, found some peace.

One evening, Pagne looked in to check on Pam and found her awake and feeling decent. She was rubbing her belly and talking to the baby. "Pagne, come here, quick!" Pagne moved over next to her. "Put your hand here. Feel that?" Pagne almost jumped.

"I do. Is that the baby?"

Pam grinned, "Yep, trying to make more room I think. I imagine that it has to be very crowded in there." Pagne left her hand on Pam's stomach and thrilled with each wave of movement that she felt. Pagne sat on the edge of the bed, sharing this miracle with Pam. "How you holding up, hon? Guess you didn't bargain on this drama when you moved in." Pagne looked at Pam with affection.

"I'm fine. I just pray that you and the baby will be okay." Pam put her hand on Pagne's and they shared the excitement of the baby's life together. After a few minutes of silence, Pagne began to speak. "Remember that day in the closet when you told me about your life?"

"Yes," acknowledged Pam.

"I really wanted to talk to you about mine but, I just didn't think I could without totally losing it. I felt like I was just barely hanging on."

"I know, Pagne, I have felt those feeling so often." Pam squeezed her hand.

"I don't want you to think I didn't trust you."

"Hon, pain is tough and we all work through it in our own time. I just hope you know that you can talk to me whenever you're ready."

"Would now be a good time?" asked Pagne. Pam patted the bed next to her. Pagne slipped off her shoes and laid down on her side facing Pam. Pagne poured out her heart and shared every terrible detail. Pam listened quietly, nodding when appropriate, and tenderly touching Pagne when she saw the pain in her eyes. It felt like hours but it was only forty minutes. *How could so much pain be described in such a short time?* thought Pagne.

"Pagne, you are a survivor, like me. You have a strong spirit and heart. It is important that you hear me. Others do not determine your value, especially your mom. She is broken, and what she thinks is affected by her brokenness. You are a lovely young woman, inside and out. I know you will accomplish many wonderful things in your life. Who you are and will be is not controlled by who your family was. Understand?" Pagne believed her and trusted her.

Pam had bad days and tolerable days. The family loved on her, fretted over her, and prayed. Brent secretly talked to God, promising him everything and anything to save his wife and child. He remained strong for Pam and the girls but, at times, couldn't contain his tears when he heard his wife's pain. He would hold her for hours, rubbing her head and her belly, soothing her with his touch and his words. He would urge her to hold on as she was only a week away from going to the hospital. They were close. "Soon. We will have our precious baby, soon," he would whisper softly in her ear.

Saturday morning, Pagne tapped on Pam's bedroom door. She had breakfast for her. Pam wasn't eating much so they tried tempting her with the foods she loved. This morning, Grandma Maxine had made Belgian waffles with fresh berries and whipped cream. Pam's favorite. Pagne didn't hear a response to her knock so she quietly opened the door and slipped in. The drapes were closed and the room was very dark and oppressive. Pagne noticed the scent immediately; she hadn't smelled her angel in months. "Mom, I have your breakfast," she said. Pam did not acknowledge her presence in the room and Pagne became alarmed. She set down the tray, moved closer to Pam, and heard her breathing. Pagne would have felt a sense of relief but the scent of her angel was getting stronger. She knew that the angel was preparing her. She nervously turned on the light and looked at Pam. She was so drawn, so pale. The pregnancy and pain were definitely taking their toll on Pam's body. "Mom? You awake?" Pagne touched her shoulder and Pam still didn't respond. Pagne began to panic. She pulled the blanket away from Pam's full, round belly and barely remembered hitting the floor as Brent and the others raced into the room in response to her screams. There was blood, lots of blood.

The rest of the morning was a blur. She remembered Grandma Maxine pulling her out of the room, speaking in soothing tones, trying to get her to calm down. Bree grabbed Richie, half-dragging and half-carrying him into the girls' room. Brent was on the phone, frantically talking to the emergency operator. Then flashing lights were out front and people were pushing their way into Pam's room. She was swept away and howling down the street before clarity could even surface. Brent was in the ambulance with Pam. They wanted him to meet them at the hospital but he wouldn't leave Pam alone. The EMT's could see the determination in his set jaw and eyes.

Grandma Maxine kept her arm around Pagne once they were in the bedroom with Richie and Bree. They both looked like scared deer, facing the end of a hunter's gun. Grandma Maxine motioned for them to follow her into the closet. The girls had shared the intimacy of their closet with Grandma Maxine. The four of them sat in the closet, snuggled together. Only Pagne was aware of her angel. The lovely, ominous smell remained. They started crying as they held on to each other. Grandma Maxine started praying first. Her voice was low and struggling. Pagne joined her, then Bree, and then Richie. They poured out their hearts and their fears to God in that closet.

They took Pam to the closest emergency room. Dr. Olsen raced to meet them there. The EMT's had called ahead and the surgery room was being prepared. They would need to be a quick and organized if Pam and the baby were to survive. Pam was not conscious of her world. She was elsewhere. Brent could feel her body, hear her breathing, hear the baby's heartbeat on the monitor, but he was alone. He was unable to bring them to him and unable to protect them. Once they reached the emergency area, They took Pam directly to surgery for prep. They led Brent to a private room and assigned him his own nurse. Molly Ambrose. She would be his connection to Pam and keep him updated on her progress. Brent felt very small and very ineffective. He should have said no. He should have made Pam understand that he could not risk her, not even for their child, but that was a long time ago and he now had the reality of their decision to survive.

Pam was in surgery for two hours. They did a cesarean and immediately did a complete hysterectomy. She had lost a lot of blood and they were doing everything they could to stabilize her. She survived the surgery but struggled to remain alive. They immediately took the premature baby, Amanda, to the ICU for infants and placed her in an incubator. The doctors could not give Brent a prognosis because Amanda was much too early and they could not predict her outcome. They were making every effort to keep this baby alive. They finally took Brent to view Amanda once she was stabilized. He was struck by how small his beautiful daughter was and how serious a struggle she had ahead of her. Brent loved her instantly but found himself wanting to guard his heart. Loving her and losing her would be more than he or Pam could endure.

Molly came to get him and took him to the ICU to be with Pam. He saw the sparkle in her eyes when he came into the room. She was weak and her words came with difficulty. "Did you see her yet? Is she beautiful?"

"Yes, my love, she is so precious."

"I wish we could hold her."

"Soon, Pam, soon," Brent whispered with a hollow promise. He sat next to her and held her hand in his, then he broke as the aching sobs rolled out of his heart. "I thought you were gone; I thought I had lost you." He laid his head down on the bed, and sobbed as she hushed him softly and stroked his head with her free hand. The nurses stepped into the doorway and pulled back when they realized he was calming down. They had seen this anguish so many times. They knew that, in most cases, it gushed and slowed just as quickly as it had begun. They left them with their privacy for as long as they could.

Pam drifted off to sleep. The doctor came in and motioned Brent to the hallway. "Well, we were very lucky that Pam and the baby survived. She hadn't been bleeding long, thank goodness. There was a major tear in the uterine wall and, if she hadn't been discovered when she was, she would not have survived. However, we are very concerned about her general health. The strain from the pregnancy has compromised her heart and liver, so we will be watching her very closely. I don't want to discourage you but, I think it would be wise to have everything in order. In case..."

Brent looked at the doctor in disbelief. "But it's over. Pam lived. The baby is alive."

"Yes but Pam is very weak and your baby is in critical condition. We are doing everything possible to keep them both alive, Brent."

Brent went out to the hospital gardens and walked in silence, trying to get the depth of their circumstances to sink in. He knew he needed to call the family but didn't know what to say. Brent dialed his mom and briefly explained what he knew. She assured him that they were all right. Brent hung up and went back to the nursery and watched Amanda. He then headed back to Pam's room to stand watch through the next chapter of his life with her. She didn't stir when he came in. He settled in the chair and was amazed that he was so tired. He drifted off.

"Brent, you awake, baby?" Brent opened his eyes to see Pam looking at him.

"Yeah, yeah, I'm awake. How you feeling?"

"Kinda odd I guess, almost like I'm water logged. My arms and legs feel so heavy."

"Are you in any pain?"

"No, these drugs must be strong. I'm not feeling anything. Have you heard any more about Amanda?"

"Amanda is stable but she's got a struggle ahead of her."

"Did you call the kids?"

"Yes, hon, I talked to my mom when you got out of surgery. The kids were scared but are doing much better. They're excited to come see you and Amanda."

"Those girls are going to spoil her rotten! You're going to have to get a second job to pay for all the shopping!" Brent smiled. He sure hoped it would play out that way. "Am I going to be okay?" Pam asked quietly.

Brent touched Pam's nose with his finger. "You'll be fine. You're not leaving me with all these kids! You gotta get well quick. Lots of mothering to do!"

Pam smiled a very content smile. "Sounds good to me," she agreed.

The doctor came in and explained the tests they would be performing. "Brent, she is going to be tied up for several hours. Why don't you go home, get a shower and some hot food, and spend some time with your kids. You can stay all evening and all night when you come back." Brent reluctantly agreed. He gave Pam a loving kiss on her lips, then her nose, then her forehead.

"Check on Amanda before you leave," whispered Pam. He nodded and stepped out of the room so the aids could get in. He watched them roll Pam out, down the hall, and through the double doors. He went by the nursery and watched Amanda moving and kicking. She appeared to be very strong for being so tiny. He headed home.

When Brent walked in the door, he smelled something wonderful coming from the kitchen. He had called his mom from the parking lot and she had gotten everyone helping in the kitchen. Brent realized that he was hungry when he smelled the food but, he didn't know how much he could actually eat. His stomach was in a huge knot, coiled in his gut. He had taken some pictures of the baby with his cell phone. They girls ohhhed and ahhhhed when he showed them. Richie was very quiet and just wanted to sit on his lap.

Brent was able to eat more than he expected. There was grilled steak, mashed potatoes, and fresh pea pods. His mom was a great cook and he enjoyed the flavors and the warmth the food brought to his belly. He took a long, hot shower, letting the water roll over his head and back. He turned the showerhead to a hard massage setting and let it pound on his neck and shoulders, trying to work out some of the tension. He allowed himself to cry, knowing that no one could hear him. After shaving, brushing his teeth, and putting on some fresh clothes, he headed into the bedroom. Everyone was piled on the bed, watching Batman. Richie had drifted off but the rest kept watching the movie anyway. As Brent got ready to leave, he assured them he would call as soon as he knew anything. They surrounded him with hugs and kisses for Pam.

Before he reached his car, he heard his name called. "Brent," it was Pagne.

"Yes, sweetheart?"

"Can you give this to Mom for me?" It was a folded piece of paper. He looked into her blue eyes, so full of concern.

"Yes, of course." He placed the note in his pocket and patted it. "Just as soon as I see her."

"Thanks, Dad," Pagne said as she turned back to the house. Brent smiled a sad smile. How long he had hoped to hear her call him dad but now he didn't know if it was wise.

When Brent got back to the hospital, the sky was darkening. A storm was coming their way. Brent shivered and tried not to take it as an omen. He entered the hospital and sat with Amanda for a short time, memorizing every detail. He had brought his camera this time and took several pictures to share with Pam. He made his way back to Pam's room, feeling anxious and full of dread.

She was awake, but very groggy. *She must really be getting some good drugs,* he thought. Brent was thankful that her pain was gone. She grinned at him and told him how good he cleaned up. "Mmmm, you smell good too."

"Nothing but the best for my babies." He sat down and showed her the pictures of Amanda while they waited for the doctor to meet with them. "Oh yeah, Pagne wanted me to give you this." He handed Pam the paper. As she started to open it, Dr. Olsen walked into the room and Pam set the note on the table so she could focus on what the doctor was going to say.

Brent and Pam were hit hard by the severity of her complications. The doctor tried to be encouraging, but the pregnancy and the blood loss had ravished her. There was permanent heart damage and the blood transfusions were not as effective as they hoped. Brent and Pam shared that quiet moment when there are no words. The doctor had been brutally honest and Brent knew that, if he spoke, he wouldn't be able to contain himself. He didn't want Pam to think he had lost hope. The doctor said they would know more in the next forty-eight hours. Pam drifted into a fitful sleep, while Brent watched her, wanting her home with him, in their bed, making love, with no pain or fear. He tried watching some TV but nothing held his attention. He took several walks to look at Amanda and go to the vending machines for something to stuff down the screams with. At about one a.m., he finally fell asleep with Pam's hand nestled in his.

~

The nurse came in about two o'clock and woke Pam up while checking her vitals and drip levels. The nurse asked if she needed anything. "Maybe some water, if that's okay."

"How about some ice chips. They want to limit fluids until tomorrow because they could upset your stomach."

"That would be fine," said Pam, feeling lightheaded and relaxed. She saw Brent sleeping soundly in the chair. She knew his back would be killing him tomorrow, but she needed him there. Pam remembered the note, so she opened it quietly so as not to wake Brent.

Dear Mom,

I was so scared when I found you today. I thought that I had lost you. I know that you are very sick and I am praying for you, very hard. I hope that doesn't make you mad. I know you think God doesn't care and maybe isn't real, but I just wanted to share something with you. I so needed to be loved. I knew God loved me, but I needed a real person. A mom who could hug me. God gave me you and Brent, Dad. Oh yeah, I decided to call him Dad today. I hope he doesn't poop his pants or anything like that. I've been wanting to say it for a long time, but just didn't know how to start.

I don't know how to say this so I apologize if it sounds bad. I realized today that any of us could die. A car wreck, sickness, and what scared me more about you maybe being dead today was that I didn't know if I would get to be with you again in Heaven. Remember how I told you about the cartoon and the movie. I love you so much and want you in the movie too. I want to run around Heaven and do all the wonderful things there with you. I can live with losing you for a little while but not forever.

Your daughter, Pagne

PS: If you want to be in the movie, just ask Jesus in your heart and ask him to forgive all your sins. I don't know of any sins because you're wonderful, but just in case.

Pam realized that tears were rolling down her cheeks. She read and reread Pagne's note, feeling surprisingly peaceful. She found the pen by her bed and managed to write a few lines, hopefully legible. She closed her eyes, trying to picture Heaven with her family. She drifted off, muttering, feeling light, and smelling the most incredible smell. *Was it Pagne's angel?* It was her last conscious thought before she fell into a deep sleep, dreaming of a beautiful place with her family.

~

Brent woke up with a start when the obnoxious beeping finally punctured his dreams. They told him to move back as nurses and doctors surrounded Pam. He had known Pam would not survive.

Chapter 12

It would be several months before Amanda could come home. She was doing better each day but her lungs and several other organs were just not ready to be independent of Pam. Brent tried to look at the positives of having a child of his own but, it felt hollow without Pam. They were attending her memorial service today. The hours and days following Pam's death were a blur but, he did all the required things, signed all the necessary papers, and informed all the necessary people. He wanted to be strong for all of them, especially Richie but he was on autopilot. He knew he was breathing, talking, eating some, and dozing but nothing felt real. The kids were just now able to hold back the tears. Brent was sure there just weren't any left. They were all cried out and the numbness had taken control. Nature kept them functioning.

Bree and Pagne helped Richie with the finishing touches. He normally would have been excited to have a man suit but even he knew this was the result of pain and sorrow. Brent noticed the kids were kind to each other but each was isolated in their own pain, unable to comfort the others. They had all decided to accept Pam's wishes to be cremated. None of them wanted her remembered the way she was when she died, so drawn and so much of a shadow of herself. Instead, they filled the raised platform in the large banquet room with picture after picture of Pam. Some were of her alone but many more were of her with the family. Sadly, there was nothing prior to her college years except one picture of her with her brother. It must have been taken during one of their supervised meetings. They were both in their very early teens. Pam and Peter stood stiffly next to each other, an emptiness in their eyes.

Lenny positioned himself between Pagne and Bree during the memorial. He needed to be there for each of them. Brent focused his support on Richie.

Brent's extended family flew in to give Brent their support.

Pastor Tim and Eddie were there. Pagne knew they didn't have the answer to the big question: Why? It made no sense. But, having them there meant a lot to her. At least they didn't forsake her as God had. Pagne hoped that her angel didn't reveal herself. She didn't think she could feel anything but anger toward Chantal right now.

Several of Pam's friends and associates from the foster agency spoke about Pam's capacity for love and selflessness. Matt and Mattie's mother shyly shared the support Pam had given them. She would always be grateful for the love Pam had shown her and her children and the continued support once she had her children back. Once everyone had spoken, there was not a dry eye in the room. Brent and the girls wanted to share their Pam at the memorial but the intensity of their loss would not allow them to speak. Amanda was still in the hospital and, sadly, the family was relieved she was not there. It was as if the pain and anger needed to be flushed away before she was brought into the family. They all loved her but, right now, she was a reminder of their loss. However, they didn't hold her responsible because they all knew that Pam had made the choice to give Amanda a chance. Amanda was an innocent bystander, just like the rest of them. They needed Pam's memorial to be the family core, the unit that knew and loved Pam so deeply. Amanda would never know her and that thought added to the ache in Pagne's heart. After the last person left the memorial, the family stood there, not really knowing what to do next. They hadn't planned to serve food, because they could not deal with the requirements of an ongoing event, being polite, not falling apart, and the sadness in everyone's faces. Brent finally took the lead and guided his grieving family to their car. They drove home in silence.

Brent's mother decided to stay permanently and help with the baby. Brent hadn't thought out all the details yet, but he knew he couldn't work all day and expect the girls to be Amanda and Richie's mother. They had their schooling and lives of their own but, Brent didn't want a stranger raising Amanda either. His mother was the perfect solution and she was willing to love and care for her grandchild. She would go back to Washington in the morning, close up the house, and get things situated up there. She would be back before they released Amanda from the hospital. Brent wasn't sure how they would all fit in their home but he knew it was the only way to survive the nightmare.

The kids had been excused from school after Pam's death. Brent knew they needed to get back to their routines and lives but, he also needed Pagne and Bree to have an extra day off after Richie went back to school. They needed to work out the details of the house. The home was spacious but not suited for so many people of different ages. Richie had his room, the nursery was ready for the baby, and the girls had their room. Grandma Maxine would be moving out of her temporary room in the nursery and into the master bedroom, because

Brent couldn't sleep in there anymore, not without Pam. Brent and the girls needed to move Brent's clothes to their closet so Grandma Maxine could move her things in. They would also have to pack up Pam's things. Brent knew that they could only get through that together.

Brent wandered the house at night until he finally passed out on the couch from exhaustion or slept on Richie's floor, next to his bed when Richie cried at night. Having Brent in his room calmed Richie down and allowed him to go to sleep. The floor was uncomfortable, but Brent found some peace in listening to the rhythm of Richie's breathing. Brent felt displaced in his own home, lost and abandoned. Why did he let her take the risk? He didn't think he could ever forgive himself.

Several days after the memorial, Brent's mother and the rest of his family left for the airport. Grandma Maxine would be returning in a few days with the rest of her belongings. Brent drove Richie to school and spoke briefly with his teacher. "Please call me if there are any issues," he instructed. "I don't know how he'll adapt to being back at school."

"Don't worry, Mr. Masters, we'll be sensitive to his situation." Brent went back to the car and saw Richie at the cyclone fence, fingers wrapped around the wire with such a sad expression. Brent realized that Richie would be changed forever.

When he reached the house, a car pulled up in the driveway; it was Pagne's social worker. Brent walked over and opened the door for her. The social worker stepped out of the car and Miss Renee climbed out of the other side. Both ladies looked heartbroken and expressed their sorrow at Brent's loss. Brent had forgotten that a routine meeting had been scheduled for this morning. "Please come in," he invited. "Pagne and Bree are staying home today to help me pack up Pam's things and prepare for my mom to move in. She'll be living with us to help care for the baby."

Mrs. Locke and Miss Renee followed Brent into the living room. Pagne and Bree walked into the room and realized Brent was not alone. Miss Renee hugged both of the girls and squeezed them tightly. "So sorry" is all she could say. Mrs. Locke looked uncomfortably at Brent and asked him if they could speak privately with him.

"Of course. Girls, can you start organizing your closet while we talk?" Pagne sensed that something serious was up. She followed Bree up the stairs while looking at Miss Renee. Miss Renee did not make eye contact. Pagne felt a knot starting in her stomach.

Brent invited the ladies to have a seat and asked if they would like something to drink. "No thank you," Mrs. Locke said. Miss Renee declined also and sat down. "Mr. Masters, we have a situation that does not have a simple solution. The death of your wife has affected the licensing you have as a foster-parent." Brent's face dropped.

"Excuse me?"

"The county restrictions do not allow Pagne to be placed in an unlicensed home." Miss Renee just kept looking down at her feet, wishing the floor could swallow her up. She didn't approve of Mrs. Locke's approach but she didn't know of a better way to break the news.

"I don't understand. We love her."

"I understand that but your licensing is based on your wife being the primary caregiver since you work full-time. As a single father..."

"You mean widowed father," he cut in angrily.

"Yes, I'm sorry, widowed father. The county does not license widowed men as foster-parents for female teenagers." Brent thought he might take all the pain and anger out on this woman. *What was she suggesting?* He loved Pagne like his own daughter. The worker continued. "I am not suggesting any inappropriate behavior on your part but it is the procedure we use to protect these young ladies."

"What about Bree and Richie?"

"Mr. Masters, they are your legal children. You have adopted them and the county has no jurisdiction." Brent's heart sank. He looked at Miss Renee. Pam and Brent had requested the paperwork and started the process to adopt Pagne through Miss Renee but the pregnancy complications had put the plans on hold.

"Couldn't I adopt Pagne? On my own?" Neither ladies could bring themselves to answer him.

"Brent," Miss Renee finally spoke. "I know that you love Pagne very much. Please know that I am working with the county to make sure she stays within city limits so that she can continue a relationship with all of you but you have a lot to deal with once the baby comes home. Richie is going to need a lot of your energy to recover from such a terrible loss."

"But what about losing a sister? Don't you think that will hurt him even more?" Miss Renee remained quiet as she searched his eyes.

Mrs. Locke interjected, "Mr. Masters, this is not our decision. This is the county's policy and it is not to punish your family. Your circumstances are tragic and we are all very sorry that our obligations will add to your loss." Brent knew from her tone that there probably was no point arguing with her but he had to try.

"What about my mother? She'll be living here," Brent pressed.

"That was considered in their decision. Your mother's age and the obligations of caring for a premature baby and Richie will disqualify her from becoming licensed in this county."

"Brent," Miss Renee spoke softly. "I know this is very confusing. Our county has not adopted the tolerant perspective that some other counties have accepted. We are restricted to the limitations of a very established process and a conservative judge."

After a very uncomfortable pause, Mrs. Locke suggested that Pagne be asked to join them.

"No, please, not this way. Give me today. Let me talk to her. You can do what you have to tomorrow." He turned to Miss Renee. "Please, you have to give us this. We can't take much more." Miss Renee looked questioningly at Mrs. Locke. Mrs. Locke bit her lip.

"I can't give you until tomorrow. We have to have her at Langston Hall by this evening. I can give you until six o'clock tonight. I will be back then to collect Pagne and her belongings. Mr. Masters, I know you are a good man but don't think you can resolve this matter rashly. The police will be brought in to intervene. It can create a very difficult situation for you and your children." Mrs. Locke rose and headed to the door. "Again, Mr. Masters, I am very sorry for your loss." She let herself out. Miss Renee also stood up.

"Brent, I will do everything in my power to keep her close. She needs all of you." Miss Renee touched his arm, and when he felt the warmth, he was reminded of Pam. He pulled his arm away and glared.

"You better. She can't take much more."

"I know," Miss Renee whispered. "Are you sure you want to do this alone?"

"Yes, right now, for today, I am her dad."

~

Miss Renee moved out to the porch and he quickly shut the door behind her. She moved down the steps and opened the car door. Mrs. Locke just sat there, not saying a word. Miss Renee looked up and saw Bree and Pagne looking down at her from their bedroom window, a sad resign on their faces. Miss Renee climbed in and closed the door. She had no clue how to process the emotions. Mrs. Locke started the car, pulled away from the curb, and made it around the corner when she suddenly pulled over to the side of the road, turned off the engine, and sat there. Miss Renee was a bit alarmed. She looked at Mrs. Locke face and saw such disgust and frustration. Miss Renee reached over and touched her hand. The physical contact sparked an electrical current that threw the switch and Mrs. Locke began to rock while sobbing. "How do we do this to them? How do I look at my husband and my children tonight, knowing I tore a family apart today?" Miss Renee squeezed her hand.

"It is beyond us. We have to do the best we can for these kids with the limitations we have. The perfect solution would be two parents who love and adore their children but when we have parents with no regard for these young lives, they will be forced to deal with institutions and rules that have no emotion. Pagne is strong. We will be there for her and do everything we can to get her through, okay? We're a team, right?" Mrs. Locke looked at her with such softness in her eyes, something Renee hadn't seen before.

"Yes, we're a team." She pulled a tissue from her purse, wiped her eyes, and blew her nose. She then started the car and headed back to the job that made her the emotionless enforcer she needed to be.

~

The girls slowly came down to the living room. Brent was sitting on one of the chairs, his face in his hands. He looked up when he heard the girls come in. His eyes were red and swollen, tears still flowing, and he couldn't speak. Bree rushed to his side. "Dad, what's wrong?" Pagne stood where she was, not wanting to get any closer. She knew what was coming. Pagne had seen Miss Renee's face when she looked at the house before climbing into the car, a look that clearly said... "You're screwed, Pagne, and there's nothing anyone can do about it." She knew that she would be leaving. Pagne stayed back from them, her family. She had to break the connection. It was too painful to do it slowly. Instead, it had to be a quick, hard pull, like a band-aid. Brent finally made eye contact with her.

"I'm so sorry, Pagne. They have pulled my licensing for foster-care." Pagne heard Bree gasp. Pagne knew what he was going to say before he said it. She would have to leave.

"How long before I go?" asked Pagne.

"They will back at six o'clock this evening. Pagne, I..." Pagne couldn't hear his apologies. Pagne needed to get out of that room... to breath. She ran out back and climbed up into Richie's clubhouse. She curled up in the small area and held herself. Not crying, just holding herself. She realized that her mother's words were true. Pagne would always be her daughter and she wouldn't get another life, no matter how much she wanted it.

Only minutes later, Bree was at the base of the clubhouse. "Pagne, please come down."

"Just go away," Pagne hurled at her. "You have your family. You aren't a part of this."

"Pagne, I am your sister and I will always be your sister. Now get down here so we can figure this out. Otherwise, I'm coming up and you know I can drag you down if I need to." Pagne lay for a moment longer but really did need Bree. She slowly maneuvered her way down the ladder and stood in front of her. Bree grabbed her with both arms and wrapped them around her. Pagne melted into her and let the anger rush out of her with a flood of tears and cursing, which surprised Pagne even more than it did Bree.

Brent was inside watching this display of raw emotion. "Why didn't we make her future a priority when we had the chance?" he uttered with painful guilt.

Once Pagne was worn out from the emotional outburst, they sat down with Brent to brainstorm. Rather than focusing on what he didn't do, Brent became committed to what he could do now. Brent assured her that Miss Renee was going to do everything possible to keep Pagne local. They would have visitation and she would still be part of their family. After they had developed a plan, they hugged and the girls went upstairs to pack Pagne's belongings. Brent made two calls after the girls were gone. First, he called Lenny's school principal and explained the circumstances. Mr. Adams agreed to excuse Lenny so that he could be there for Pagne. When Lenny burst through the front door, Brent hugged him and said, "Go on up. The girls will explain."

Lenny darted up the stairs and Brent heard him yelling "Pagne, what's going on?"

"Oh Lenny, you're here," and then the sweet mutterings of two people in love. Brent had also called Miss Renee. He asked that she come back over to the house, alone. He knew that the social worker was only doing her job but they needed a friend right now, someone invested in Pagne on a personal level. She would be there at five o'clock.

Brent went upstairs and asked Bree to meet him in his bedroom. He thought that Pagne and Lenny could use some time alone. While Pagne and Lenny started packing, Pagne realized that she had come to the house with nothing and her small duffle bag wouldn't even hold a fraction of what she now owned. Lenny knocked softly on the open door to Brent's room and explained the dilemna. Brent opened his closet and pulled out Pam's luggage. "Here, Lenny, tell Pagne that I want her to have these." The set was black with a soft pattern of vines and lavender flowers. There was an overnight bag, a very large suitcase, a smaller suitcase, and a wardrobe bag for hanging clothes. "Lenny, tell her that she doesn't have to pack her summer clothes. We will keep whatever she doesn't need right now here in her room for her."

"I'll tell her, Mr. Masters," Lenny responded as he rolled the luggage down the hall.

Bree had started going through Pam's drawers, filling the storage boxes that Brent's family had gotten while they were there. They thought it would make it a little easier for Brent and the girls because packing up Pam's belongings would be painful enough. The family appreciated the small gesture. The girls had already gone though Pam's clothing and jewelry and taken what they wanted and Brent had saved some jewelry pieces for Amanda when she was older. Richie had selected Pam's favorite sweater, which he slept with, and a watch. It had a leather band and could pass for a boy's watch. Brent had stored Pam's wedding rings in the same box they had come in. He wasn't sure what would become of them but he had them safe until he knew. Brent had started on the closet items.

Bree opened a dresser drawer that the girls had not sorted through yet. It held Pam's bras and both girls knew the bras would not fit them. Bree found a group of DVDs wrapped with a ribbon. There was an envelope on top with Pam's beautiful writing "For My Family." Bree stared in shock. Brent came out of the closet and saw the look of shock on Bree's face. She lifted the DVDs out of the drawer and handed them to Brent. He looked at Bree with the same shock. He suddenly yelled, "Pagne, Lenny, get in here." As they ran into the room, Brent untied the ribbon and opened the envelope. There was a note from Pam. Brent began reading softly.

My Dearest Family ...

If you are reading this, then my suspicions were correct and I am no longer with you. I hope that Amanda survives so that you still have a part of me to hug and hold. I asked Maxine to record these dvd's to each of you. She promised to keep it my secret.

I am so sorry that these are my last words to you. I was so blessed to have a family that was so loving. You all made my life worthwhile.

All my love, Me

Brent looked at the DVDs in his hand and saw that there were six. They were labeled My Family, My Sweet Husband, Richie, Bree, Pagne, and Amanda. He looked up at the others, not sure what to do next. He handed the girls their DVDs and sat on the bed holding the others. Lenny saw their shock and thought they needed a jumpstart to continue. "Mr. Masters, I have a suggestion." Brent looked up, thankful for the prompt.

"Yes Lenny?"

"Why don't we finish the packing. Pagne and I are almost done. We can help you finish up in here. Between the computers and TVs, you can each watch your DVD alone before Richie comes home. Then you can all watch the family one together before Miss Renee gets here." Brent nodded in agreement.

"I think this evening would be a good time for me and Richie to watch his together," said Brent quietly. They all focused and the packing was finished up quickly. They lingered over a few items but were so anxious to see their beloved Pam again, even if on a DVD, they didn't spend a lot of time reminiscing. Once Pam's things were packed, they moved them to the garage. Pam had always made it clear that in the event of her death, after the girls had selected what they wanted, she wanted the rest of her belongings given to the children's shelter for the teen girls who were living there. Pam had wonderful taste in clothing and the girls would love her beautiful clothes. Brent had some friends with a truck that would be taking the boxes over that weekend. Brent was thankful that his part was done.

Once everyone was back inside, Bree ran up to her room to put the DVD into her computer. Brent went into his bedroom to watch his. It was odd how he had avoided the room but now it felt like the most natural place to be with Pam's DVD. Pagne slipped hers into the DVD player in the family room. Lenny awkwardly stood there, not sure if he should leave. Pagne sat on the couch and patted, indicating for him to sit next to her. He moved next to her but didn't touch her. He wanted this to be about her and Pam.

The beginning would have been comical except for the seriousness of the circumstances. Grandma Maxine and Pam were fussing about how close the camera should be and how much lighting was needed. The room was lit, but softly so that it was hard to see Pam clearly. Suddenly, there was a bright flash of light and Pam put her arms in front of her face. "Nooo, too much!" The light quickly went off. Apparently, Grandma Maxine had tried to use Brent's spotlight from the garage. Grandma Maxine finally opened the drapes and Pam was bathed in lovely golden sunlight. Pagne's heart tightened. She could see just how worn out Pam was. It was so odd to see her alive, talking, and giggling with Grandma Maxine. Then Pam seemed to remember the purpose of the camera. She focused her look at the camera. "Ahhh, my dear Pagne. I haven't written any notes on what I'm going to say so I might ramble. I wanted this to be from my heart and in the moment. I am making your DVD first. That's why there was all the confusion. I won't erase it since this is about life and confusion will always be a part of life." She paused. "First thing I want to tell you is that you are my hero. I am amazed at your grace and ability to love. You fit into our family as though you have always been here. I don't know about this whole God thing, but if you are a result of his love for me, then He's looking better and better every day," Pam continued sharing memories, sometimes laughing and other times struggling not to cry. Pagne had never felt so valued by another living person as she did by Pam. Pam saw everything; she knew the secret of Pagne's self-worth. Pam kept assuring Pagne that she was beautiful and that she was so lucky to have Pagne in her life.

At several points, Pagne reached for Lenny's hand, holding it tight. Then she would let go again and it was just her and Pam. Lenny had come prepared and handed Pagne tissues when he heard her sniffling. Pam was sounding very tired and Pagne knew the DVD would be ending soon. She didn't want it to end. She loved how close this brought Pam to her again.

"Well, sweetie, I'm getting a little sleepy. I'm going to finish this up and get some rest. I want to close by telling you that I hope you are right about Heaven. I want to see all of you again in a world filled with love and beauty. Until we're all together, please help take care of Bree, Richie, and Brent. You will need each other and if Amanda is there with you, please love her the way you love me. You are precious, Pagne."

The DVD ended abruptly. Pagne sat motionless, speechless. She leaned into Lenny as he brought his arms around her. It had been wonderful to see Pam and to remember their life together but something disturbed her. Pam talked about seeing her in Heaven. How could that be if she didn't accept Jesus Christ? She didn't want to think about it. She just savored the loving words of Pam and the idea of seeing her again. She felt the heat from Lenny surrounding her, his strong body holding her. She loved Lenny and knew he loved her. It mattered so much to her, especially now.

Lenny and Pagne heard Bree enter the room. Her eyes were red and swollen, but there was a glow in her face. She sat down next to Pagne and the sisters just were. No words were needed. Brent came down a short time later. He was obviously emotional but, he was trying to sound normal and suggested they all deserved lunch. Friends and neighbors had brought over casseroles, desserts, and salads over the last week. The fridge was stuffed. Brent started pulling everything out onto the counter and they all piled their plates full of the delicious food. They focused on taste, living, and having each other in that next hour. They laughed and teased but didn't talk about the DVDs or share what was on them, at least for now. It was their time with Pam.

Once they were gorged, the girls started to clean up. Lenny and Brent went up to Richie's room to put together a second twin bed. This would be where Brent could sleep if he wanted a real bed. Pagne asked Bree if she thought Brent and Richie would move into the girl's room and Bree would move into Richie's room. "No way. Dad already said that our room is our room. You'll be here more than you aren't." Pagne hoped she was right. After they put the bed up and the master bedroom was ready for Brent's mom, Brent left to get Richie. They planned to sit and watch the family DVD together. Pagne wasn't sure how Richie would handle the news that she would be leaving today.

A short time later, Richie and Brent came in and Richie ran up to Pagne. He threw his arms around her. "You can't go Pagne! I won't let them take you!" he cried. Pagne's heart broke. She held him while he dumped his frustration and pain out with tears. When he calmed down a little, Pagne smoothed his hair back from his face and looked into his eyes.

"You are my little brother; no one can change that. We are going to make sure that I'm here so much you won't even notice a difference. We'll still go to church together, the park together, and watch your dumb movies together."

Richie hugged her and sadly said, "I don't want to watch my movies without Mom." It reminded Pagne again how much they had all lost.

"I agree," she said, "we'll find some new stupid movies you can torture us with." Richie actually giggled. "Did Dad tell you we're going to watch a movie that Mom made for us?" Richie nodded. "Well, let's go sit on the couch together, okay?" Richie took Pagne's hand and led her to the couch. Once she sat down, he curled up next to her, almost in her lap. The others found a spot to see the TV screen. Brent moved in close to Richie and brought his arm around the back of the couch so he could stroke Pagne's head.

Lenny did the honors of taking out Pagne's DVD and carefully putting it back into the case. Pagne reached for it when he seemed confused about where to put it. He inserted the family DVD and started it then sat on the other side of Pagne. When the movie started, Pagne smiled to herself. The lighting and the camera position were perfect. She was flattered that her DVD had been the first one made. Pam had even thought to apply a little makeup for this one and Grandma Maxine had set the stage a little nicer. There were lots of pillows behind Pam and she was wearing her lovely blue robe. She had twister her hair up and out of her face. Pagne took a moment and looked at the faces of her family, which appeared to be a mixture of adoration and longing. Love is a powerful emotion. Pam smiled and welcomed them to the premiere of her sixth film. They grinned at her playfulness.

There is no way to describe the depth of regret, compassion, affection, and total adoration contained in the movie Pam made, but, everyone in that room had no doubt about how important they were as a family to Pam. How this group of misfits had changed the existence of her fragile spirit. Pam then went on to share her faith in them as a strong unit who would continue to be the family she had relied on. She pleaded that if Amanda was alive, they were never to blame her for their loss. She needed them to be her arms, ears, eyes, and love so Amanda could know who her mother was.

Time stopped while they watched Pam. They had left the present and had stepped into another dimension, one that allowed them all to be together. Once the DVD had finished, they sat there in silence. No one wanted to acknowledge that their journey with Pam was over, that everything from this time on was memories. It hurt so much and they couldn't go there. These DVDs had given them one more chance to share the unknown with Pam. As if timed in a stage play, the doorbell rang. Brent looked at the clock on the wall and saw that it was five o'clock. Not enough time to savor; He wanted more. He needed more. Brent slowly got up and moved to the front living room to greet their guest. Lenny shut off the TV and left the DVD in the player. He was sure they would view it many more times before they put it away in a safe place. He reached for Richie and asked if he could play in the clubhouse with him. Richie reluctantly followed Lenny to the back yard. They had made these plans earlier in the day to distract Richie.

Bree had insisted that she be included in the meeting with Miss Renee. The girls moved into the front living room and each took a seat on the ends of the couch. Brent sat between them to present a united front for Miss Renee, which was one of Bree's contributions to their master plan. Brent escorted Miss Renee in and motioned to the high back chair facing the couch. He then moved into position with the girls. Brent took each girl's hand in his. Their protectiveness of each other touched Miss Renee. "We want to discuss your plans for Pagne," Brent said directly. "We need your help to keep our family together." Renee knew they viewed her right now as the enemy, part of the organization that was heartless when it came to children. It was so far from the truth, but she understood their fear. They felt helpless to control their future as a family.

Miss Renee began, "Brent, the rules are very rigid regarding licensing. I wish there was a way to work around them. You know that I love Pagne and I, too, want her to be safe and happy. I know that her time here has been such a blessing for her. I do not want her to lose you. There are several ways that we can approach the county on this. Pagne can reside at Langston Hall until she is 18. You would have visitation but extended visits would be limited. Overnight visits would be difficult to arrange. The second option is a local group-home but there would still be restrictions. The third option, which I think would work best for all of you, is if we place Pagne in another local home as soon as one is available. The foster-home environment does not have the group-home restrictions. You could work with the foster-parents regarding weekends, vacations, and other time spent with your family. I would play a big role in selecting a family that would be cooperative with Pagne's desire to remain connected to this community, your family, her school, and her church."

They looked at each other. "What do you think, Pagne?" asked Brent. "Think you could adjust to another household?" Pagne certainly did not want to leave or try to fit in with another family. She had a family already but, she knew how tight the rules were at Langston Hall. She really didn't have much choice.

"I will do whatever I have to," she whispered. They held each other's hands tightly.

"Can you girls go spend some time with Richie? I know he could use all the "Pagne-time" he can get right now." The girls looked at Brent oddly. "I have some things to discuss with Miss Renee privately." They moved out of the room looking suspiciously at each other.

~

Once Brent heard them go out the back door, he turned to Miss Renee and began to discuss the long-term plans. He knew that Miss Renee's position and her heart for Pagne were the perfect combination to help him succeed. He pulled out his laptop and shared a portion of Pam's DVD to him with Miss Renee. Pam spoke from her heart regarding Pagne and her future. Miss Renee understood the wonderful life and love Pagne had found here with these people. She left after assuring Brent that she would begin the groundwork immediately. He thanked her and joined his children in the backyard. Six o'clock would come much too soon and he wanted to cherish every moment they had left. His heart lifted when he heard their laughter as he closed the French doors behind him.

Mrs. Locke was there promptly at six o'clock. Brent didn't see any police, but figured she had a police car waiting around the corner in case they put up a fight. Lenny and Bree loaded Pagne's bags into the car while Brent and the social worker finalized some paperwork. Pagne sat holding Richie on her lap, whispering that things would be fine and sharing her ideas for the next family outing. Then it was time. Brent suddenly remembered he wanted to give Pagne some spending money in case she needed something while at Langston Hall. He opened his wallet and saw the note that Pagne had given Pam. He hesitated, not knowing if it would help or make things harder for her. He felt a strong sense that he needed to give it to her. Along with the cash, he handed her the note. Pagne looked down, confused at first. He smiled at her. "She did get it, Pagne, and she read it."

~

Pagne saw a scribbled note written on the outside. "Doesn't make sense to me," he added. Pagne opened the first fold, which revealed the whole note.

"I would love to go to the movie with you. I prayed for a ticket!" was all it said. Pagne felt a tug in her heart and such joy. She smelled her angel, strong and powerful, surrounding her. She held Brent and sobbed. He thought she was crying from sadness but it was from sheer joy and relief. She ran to share the news with Bree. Brent walked out to the porch to see the girls screaming, jumping, and laughing joyfully. Pagne saw the shock on Brent's face and whispered to Bree.

"Will you explain it to him?" she asked.

"It will be my honor," Bree said. Pagne hugged and kissed Lenny and Richie and then slid into the car next to Mrs. Locke. She looked over at Brent and blew him a kiss then shouted, "LOVE YA, DAD! I'LL SEE YOU SOON!"

When they lost sight of Mrs. Locke's car, Bree shared the reason for their celebration. Once Brent understood the meaning of Pam's scrawled note, he dropped to his knees and prayed for his ticket, too. He would be with Pam again for eternity.

Chapter 13

Pagne settled into her dorm room and made the rounds to see if she knew anyone there. Some of the staff was familiar, but none of the other inmates, which was their name for each other, were anyone she knew. She met the girls she would be sharing a room with and they seemed nice enough. Pagne had already decided this was a brief stay. She had a family and she didn't plan on getting close to any of these new faces. She would be kind and polite but not close. She still had her cell phone and Lenny and Bree texted her almost to the point of exhaustion. Bree let Pagne know that Richie saw his DVD that evening. Unlike the rest of them, Richie wanted to share every detail with Bree. She finally suggested that she watch it with him after church on Sunday. Pagne so wished she could be there with them. She had two texted conversations going most of the evening and well into the night. She hoped that none of the girls in the dorm would report her as they were supposed to shut off their phones at nine o'clock. Pagne wasn't thrilled about being there but this connection with her outside life made it tolerable. She knew that Miss Renee was working quickly to get her a family close to the Masters but, the wait would be agonizing.

The next morning, Pagne was disoriented when she woke up. Her surroundings looked familiar, but it wasn't her bedroom. Then, the memory of yesterday sunk in. She wasn't in her room, not this morning. Pagne knew the drill. She got up, got dressed, and straightened her belongings. She thought about texting Bree but knew she'd still be asleep. Between their emotional day yesterday and being up so late, Bree would probably sleep until at least noon. Pagne went out to the dining area and ate some breakfast: toast, fruit, and hot tea. She could pack away food but her stomach felt a little queasy and she didn't want to make herself sick. She tried Lenny but his message was clear... *Arggg, still asleep*. I'll call you later. Wanna talk, no text. He really did prefer to talk and Pagne liked that.

After eating, Pagne went outside to her glorious tree. She looked at it across the grounds; it was magnificent. She walked over to the lowest branch and began her climb. She heard a sharp voice above her. "Hey, this tree is mine, go find somewhere else to park your butt." Pagne was shocked.

"Your tree? I don't see your name on it," she muttered. It sounded childish after she said it. Pagne looked up, but the shadows made it hard to see any details.

"Look right there. Your hand is on it." Pagne looked down and saw the carving in the tree bark. "Climb and die! Macey."

"Macey? Macey Willows?" Pagne asked, remembering her old family at Mrs. Buttonhook's.

"Yeah, what about it?"

"It's me, Pagne."

"Holy crap. Pagne? Is it really you?" Pagne climbed up as Macey was descended. They met and hugged.

"Please don't kill me now," teased Pagne. Macey looked embarrassed.

"That's just to keep the losers out." Both girls climbed up into the upper branches and settled in. "When did you get here?" Macey asked.

"Last night. You?"

"I've been here on and off after Mrs. Buttonhook. Lots of foster-homes but all of them lousy. I've been here six months this time. Guess they're having a hard time placing me. It's fine with me if nobody wants me. They all just want the money anyway." Pagne saw a very different Macey than she remembered. Her soft, sweet face was hardened with dark goth makeup. Her hair was died an unnatural faded black. "I wondered what happened to you and the twins."

"They came by the hospital once. Said they were in a good home," Pagne shared.

"They haven't been back here since I've been here. Why are you back?" Macey asked.

"Well, my mom abandoned me after I went back to live with her and I was put in a wonderful home. My foster mom died after she had a baby and they brought me back here."

"That really sucks, Pagne. If anyone deserves a good home, it's you."

"Us, Macey. We both deserve a good home."

The girls spent several hours catching up. Pagne's heart went out to Macey when she described her homes, the indifference, and the painful existence. Pagne could also see that Macey had contributed to the issues. She was very angry and really hadn't given these families much of a chance. Macey expected them to send her back so she behaved as if it was only a matter of time. She wasn't going to let anyone get close to her again. Pagne didn't bring up her observations because she knew that Macey needed a loyal friend in that moment. They heard the announcement for lunch. Pagne was hungry after her light breakfast. "Gonna go eat… you coming?" Macey looked like it was a huge decision to make.

"I guess. I usually skip most meals."

The girls climbed down out of the tree. When they stepped into the sunlight, Pagne tried not to react to the red lines spaced perfectly apart running up the inside of both of Macey's arms. Pagne had seen cutting before but nothing this extreme. Macey had not had any cuts when she knew her at Mrs. Buttonhook's. She tried not to stare but Macey caught her look of concern before she could look away. "You looking at these?" She didn't wait for Pagne to respond. "These are my battle scars. I figure I might as well let my pain show on the outside, too." Pagne didn't have a response for her. They walked silently into the dining room. Pagne was relieved since she had no idea what to say.

While they were filling a tray with their choices, Lenny called Pagne. "Hey, can I call you back this afternoon? Remember Macey from Mrs. Buttonhook's? She's here at Langston and we're still catching up."

"Sure, Mom's got some stuff for me to do anyway."

She hesitated, "Lenny?"

"Yeah?" he responded.

"Are you my boyfriend?" There was silence and she grimaced, very awkward.

"Ummm…" was all Lenny said in response to her question.

Now she was irritated. "Talk to you later," Pagne said abruptly and hung up. She turned around and saw that Macey had selected a table in the far corner away from everyone. Pagne gratefully sat with her, still bugged. *Ummm that's all he could say? Maybe he didn't feel that way about her. Maybe he thought of her as a friend or a sister.* She realized Macey was talking to her.

"Your boyfriend?" asked Macey.

Pagne looked at her, confused, "Huh?" Macey pointed to the phone.

"Oh, not sure. His name is Lenny."

Macey grinned. "You're not sure?"

"Well, I hope so."

Macey shared that she also had a boyfriend. He was older, twenty. He was going to take her away from all of this soon. Pagne was impressed but she also got the creeps. Macey began sharing the details of their relationship. She went on about how cute and grown up he was. He was showing Macey what love was all about and what you did when you were in love. He didn't mind that she was young. He said he liked that about her. Pagne was getting uncomfortable with the conversation but didn't want to hurt Macey's feelings. After all, Macey sat through her stories about the Masters family and Lenny.

Macey's boyfriend wasn't allowed to visit her here at the Hall and Pagne instinctively knew that was a good thing. Macey, sadly, said that she missed him and the kissing and touching. "I dream about him almost every night," she said. "I'll be with him soon. We have plans," Macey whispered. Pagne was pulled back to the conversation after she had drifted off thinking about Lenny.

"Huh?"

Macey looked angry. "So sorry I'm boring you."

"No, I'm sorry. What did you say?" asked Pagne.

"Later, maybe," she threw back as she got up to throw away her uneaten food. Pagne knew she had hurt her feelings. Pagne grabbed a few bites of the mac and cheese, snagged the fruit and milk, and followed Macey.

"Macey, I'm so sorry. Please forgive me for being so ditzy. A lot has happened in the last few days and my brain is on overload." Macey looked at her and then grinned.

"Okay, you're forgiven, but stay outta my tree," she laughed, as she ran down to the rec room. When Pagne caught up, Macey had two pool sticks and challenged Pagne to a game. They were good.

As the days came and went, Macey and Pagne began to rebuild their friendship. Brent, Bree, Richie, and Lenny came to visit every Sunday afternoon as well as on Wednesday and Friday evenings. It was bittersweet. Amanda was doing well but she was not out of the hospital yet. They all seemed to be surviving but they were still wounded and it showed. There was sadness in their eyes, the laughter was forced, and Richie became sullen and angry when it was time to leave. On one of their visits, Pagne introduced them all to Macey. She behaved oddly. She was sarcastic and made comments that made her look cheap and hard. Pagne could see the wall she was creating. She was apparently afraid that they would judge her so she made it her choice. They wouldn't like her because she decided, not them.

She was this way with all of the adults and most of the kids. Only a few got to see Macey's true heart, Pagne and two others. They were much younger and Macey was very protective of them. She was kind to them, like a big sister would be. She only tolerated everyone else. If pressed, she made it very clear she had no time or energy for them. *What had happened to her?* Pagne wondered. This wasn't the Macey she remembered. Sometimes it was so bad, Pagne was embarrassed to be seen with her.

Miss Renee met weekly with Pagne, giving her updates. The only option open so far was a group-home but, Miss Renee was concerned about placing her there. The girls were all in high school and had behavioralissues. Visitation with her family would be limited, too. Pagne agreed to hold out for a foster-home. Besides, Macey needed her and Pagne didn't feel right leaving her alone.

When an opening came up in Macey's dorm, Pagne asked to switch rooms.

Macey didn't say much but, the way she fussed helping Pagne get moved in, made it very clear she was pleased. Pagne was in a very precarious position. She knew Macey needed to trust someone but, she also knew she was leaving soon. Pagne wanted to help her but didn't want to set her up. Pagne kept reminding herself that God was in control and she could only pray for his will since she didn't know what the solution was. With each day, the girls became closer.

Lenny came to visit her alone one Wednesday evening. He told Pagne that he had asked the Masters to give him some time with her. Pagne was flattered and a little curious. They were allowed to go onto the grounds so they headed for their tree. When they got there, Pagne realized Macey was up in the branches. Lenny looked disappointed, and Pagne wanted this time, their spot, with just him. "Macey, could you give me and Lenny some time with the tree? This was a special place for us." Macey looked at Pagne, shrugged her shoulders, and started to climb down. When she reached them, she glared at Lenny and slowly walked away from the tree. Pagne could read her body language very well by this time and knew she was pissed. Lenny felt the chill as Macey moved past him.

"What the…?" he asked. Pagne didn't know what to say.

"Guess we're not the only ones that claim this tree as theirs," he said. They climbed into the tree, and soon forgot about Macey. Lenny and Pagne were together, alone. It felt wonderful and the conversation was comfortable and familiar as they brought each other up to speed. Things were still going well with Lenny and his mom and he finally admitted to reading the letters that his father was sending him. He hadn't answered any, but just reading them was a good step toward healing. Lenny shared some of his father's thoughts and experiences in prison. Pagne had to admit that his dad seemed to be changing even though they couldn't see it since he was locked away. *Maybe Lenny and his father could work through all the hurt,* thought Pagne.

Lenny took a deep breath and blurted, "Will you be my girlfriend?"

It caught Pagne off guard. She looked at him in shock, grinning ear to ear. "Yes, yes I will!" she answered. He leaned in close and kissed her lightly on the lips. His lips felt like velvet on hers. She felt her body tingle. Every nerve was alive. Lenny pulled back, reached into his pocket, and pulled out a small box. It contained a gold ring with a heart-shaped amethyst set in it. There was a small diamond on each side of the heart. It was beautiful. Lenny slipped it on her left ring finger.

"Someday, I plan on replacing this ring with a wedding ring." Pagne looked at the ring and savored all it implied. Lenny kissed her again, much firmer this time. Pagne's head was spinning.

"Why did you leave me hanging when I asked if I was your girlfriend?" she asked. Lenny gave her an evil grin.

"Cuz, I knew it would drive you crazy and I wanted to give you the ring, in our tree, alone." She rotated her hand and admired the ring. It was well worth the torture, she thought, but would never admit it out loud. Her hands looked balanced now. She'd been wearing one of Pam's rings on the center finger of her right hand. Now both hands displayed deep, enduring love, love she never thought would be hers. Their time was running out for the night so, they climbed out of the tree and headed toward the main entrance. Lenny reached over and lightly touched Pagne's hand. She took his hand and held it firmly. They said their goodbyes and Lenny gave her a tender peck on the check and mouthed "I love you" as he slipped through the door. His mother was there to pick him up. As Pagne headed toward her room, she got a text from him. She smiled. He was still there, right next to her, both in mind and electronically. They texted well into the night.

Pagne was back into the routine. Langston Hall wasn't a bad place but the need for places like Langston Hall was sad. There was no news about her mother. Leah had literally dropped off the face of the world. Pagne wasn't sure how she felt about that. She was barely coping with the loss of Pam so, she tried not to think about her mom. It pushed her to an edge she didn't want to fall over. Usually God and Chantal brought her peace but, she felt removed from both of them. She struggled with why God hadn't saved Pam. He knew how much Pagne needed her. It really was His fault that she was back at Langston Hall. While entering the dining area, one of the office staff approached her. "Pagne, we've been advised that you are abusing the use of your personal phone. Have you been texting past the nine o'clock curfew?" Pagne's first impulse was to lie but, she realized they could review the calls on her phone.

"Yes, Ma'am. I did."

"The rules are very clear. We will hold your phone for a week for the first infraction." Pagne turned off her phone and gave it to the lady. "You're allowed one call in the office to let your family know that you have lost your phone privileges," the lady said. *A week was going to be a very long time,* thought Pagne angrily. As she continued to the breakfast line, she saw Macey ahead of her. Macey filled her plate and sat at a table. Pagne looked over at Macey and they made eye contact. Macey quickly looked away without acknowledging Pagne. Odd, she thought. Pagne looked over the food choices and glanced back at her. Macey was looking at her with a sinister twist of a smile. Pagne now knew who'd reported her.

After breakfast, Pagne found Macey in the rec room and confronted her. "Why did you report my phone calls to Lenny?"

"It's against the rules. You say you're this goody-two-shoes now but you broke the rules." She was right but Pagne wasn't going to give her the satisfaction of hearing that.

"I thought you were my friend?" Pagne asked, her anger building. *How could she have done this to her?* she thought.

"You don't need me. You have Lenny and the Masters," Macey shot back hatefully. She got up and shoved past Pagne. Macey's anger surprised Pagne.

The next couple of days were very tense. There was a negative energy between her and Macey. Pagne tried to talk to her but she would either ignore her or make a sarcastic remark. Since Macey was not open to talking, Pagne decided to give her some space.

Pagne went to take a shower and laid her jewelry on the sink counter, including the two rings she wore every day. Pagne felt a shudder of cool air while letting the hot water beat down on her. She listened but didn't hear anything. When she came out of the shower and finished drying off, she moved to the counter to brush out her red curls. She realized then that her rings were missing, but her earrings and the cross she always wore were still there. She looked on the floor and in the sink but the drain was too small for them to slip down. She quickly got dressed and went into the adjoining dorm room, but no one was there. Pagne felt sick inside. These rings meant the world to her.

She looked down the hall and saw no one acting suspicious. She knew several of the kids a few doors down. "Did you see anyone come out of my room a few minutes ago?" she asked.

"No," they responded. They had just entered the hall themselves. Pagne was panicking. She didn't want to think that Macey had taken them but it was her first instinct. She moved into the shared living area and looked around. Macey was sitting alone, reading one of her science fiction books.

"Macey, my rings are missing. Did you take them?" Pagne was surprised by her directness. Macey looked up slowly, not responding at first.

"Why would I want that garbage? Not my style." She held up both hands, displaying gothic silber jewelry, designed with dragons and skulls. "You should take better care of your things." Macey gave her a smirk and then looked down again, pretending to read. She and Pagne both knew this was not over. Pagne grabbed the book and tossed it next to her on the floor.

"You are the only one mean enough to do this. I know you are jealous of Lenny and my family." Macey stood up, a full six inches taller than Pagne. She used her height to try to intimidate Pagne. Pagne thought she smelled Chantal but dismissed it, too caught up in the heat of the moment.

"Jealous of Lenny? You're nuts. He is as lame as you are. You two deserve each other. And your family, the Masters? If they love you so much, why are you here? They could've adopted you, but they didn't. You're just a deformed kid that no one wants." Anger had been simmering in Pagne since Pam's death, anger over returning to Langston Hall, losing Bree, Lenny, and everyone she loved. As Macey's words cut deeper and deeper, the scent of Chantal got stronger but Pagne didn't want to love. She didn't want to show grace. She was mad and she wanted to hurt someone. She heard Chantal scream in her head.

"Noooooooo, walk away!"

Pagne lunged at Macey, hitting her square in the body, and knocked the breath out of her. They both fell into the chair as Pagne began to pound on Macey. Pagne's fists made contact with her chest, her arms, and her face. She didn't care where she hit.

Macey could have easily protected herself from Pagne because of her size but the fury of Pagne's blows and the emotions that gushed out in anger had shocked her. Once she realized what was happening, she did her best to block the attack while trying to push Pagne away from her. Macey's mouth stung and she tasted hot, salty blood. She felt a hard fist hit her eye.

Pagne heard yelling but couldn't make out the words. She felt several pairs of hands grabbing at her, pulling her off of Macey. Pagne grabbed one of Macey's many piercings and ripped them free from her flesh. Then there were adults holding her tightly, her arms trapped at her sides. As her breathing slowed down and the anger began to slip away, Pagne saw Macey trying to pull herself up out of the chair. Her face was bloody and scratched, one eye swollen and turning bright red. Blood flowed from her ripped earlobe.

The voices cleared into scolding threats, and disbelief at her behavior. They took her out of the room and placed her in a cool-down area, patting her down for weapons, she supposed. One of the staff explained that she would remain there until they were sure she was calm and not a threat to herself or others. The lady left the room and Pagne heard the door lock. The room was empty except for a mattress on the floor. There was nothing on the walls and no furniture, nothing but a single light above with a wire mesh cover. On one wall was a large window that faced into an office of sorts. Pagne could see other rooms like hers connected to this central office. Apparently, the staff could view the surrounding rooms and monitor the kids placed here. A woman entered the room and sat at the desk to watch Pagne in her cage.

Pagne went over and sat on the mattress. She felt both entitled and ashamed at the same time. *What would Lenny think of her? Brent and Bree would be so ashamed of her behavior. They had shown her so much love. Didn't this look as if she didn't trust them, allowing Macey to get to her like this? Was it Macey calling her deformed?* Pagne wasn't sure what had flipped her switch. She just knew that it had felt so good in the moment. But, now she was afraid to find out what the consequences would be.

Pagne lay down and soon felt herself relax, as if she melted into the mattress. Until someone came in, she wouldn't have to deal with her behavior. She drifted off to sleep.

Pagne woke to someone stroking her head and whispering her name. Her angel? The angel had tried to warn her before she attacked Macey. She felt ashamed that she now wanted her soothing. She didn't deserve it. It took a few moments for Pagne to realize that it wasn't her angel. It was a real person. She opened her eyes and saw Miss Renee's face above her. Pagne couldn't read it. Was she angry? Disappointed? Pagne tried not to cry but she couldn't stop the tears from rolling down her cheeks. Miss Renee sat on the edge of the mattress as Pagne sat up. Curious adults peered through the window at them.

"What happened, Pagne? Why would you hurt Macey?" Pagne looked down, the full weight of her shame hitting her.

"I'm not sure. She was saying mean things. She called me deformed and my rings are missing. I know she took them."

"Well, you are being taken to a higher security section of the facility. You" have to speak with the counselors there to talk about why you chose to resolve this situation with force. I know this is not who you are Pagne but a lot is going on inside and we need to resolve it. They'll pack your things and take you to your new dorm. We'll be heading over there shortly. Are you hurt?"

"No, I'm okay. She didn't hit me."

"Okay, I'll be back in a few minutes," Miss Renee said, as she stood up and moved toward the door.

"Miss Renee?"

"Yes, Pagne?"

"Is Macey okay?"

"She'll be okay in a few days I think. You knocked out a tooth, her eye is swollen shut, her ear is swollen, and she has some serious bruising on her arms and chest."

Pagne felt the lowest she had ever felt. She was disgusted with herself, knowing she was capable of hurting someone. Her entitlement was gone. She cringed at joining the ranks of Lenny's father and other people who resorted to physical violence to process their pain. She paced the room until Miss Renee returned and then they took her to her new room. She slipped one arm around Pagne's shoulder and gave her a squeeze.

"You'll see a counselor tomorrow and discuss what happens now. You've lost all phone and visitor privileges." She said. Pagne was horrified.

"What? No, Miss Renee, please. I'm so sorry."

"I know, Pagne, but I can't change the rules." Miss Renee left Pagne standing next to the bed in her new room, alone.

How stupid she felt, knowing Macey would love this. She'd lost everything that meant anything to her again. She was glad Macey was hurting; Macey ruined everything. Her entitlement was returning and she blamed Macey for the fight. Macey had asked for it. Pagne aggressively unpacked her belongings. Several of her new roommates walked in, saw the rage in Pagne's face, and decided to come back later. After her area was neatly organized, everything folded and smoothed, Pagne threw herself on the bed. "You're such a witch, Macey," she said under her breath. Pagne stewed until she heard the call for dinner. She wasn't going to go. She'd show all of them and starve herself. They would have to summon Lenny and the Masters to try to save her life. She would force them to let them visit. Her stomach was churning. She hadn't eaten anything since early that morning. She decided to go eat just enough to keep her strength up. When she entered the dining area, she smelled lasagna, her favorite. Well, she'd eat good tonight and then start her hunger strike in the morning, better to start a new plan first thing in the morning.

By breakfast, Pagne had forgotten about the hunger strike. Instead, she had a meeting with a counselor she had never met her before. Her name was Mrs. Corning. She seemed nice enough, kind of a no-nonsense person, but not mean. Pagne wanted to be in her good graces figuring it was the key to getting time with Lenny and the Masters. She would be a remorseful, sweet, crippled kid. She would play up the abandonment issues and her feelings of suppressed anger from the scars and the pain she had endured. She entered the office with an expression of shame plastered on her face. Mrs. Corning introduced herself and explained how her assault on Macey would change her experience there and that it could affect her placement in a foster-home. It would definitely delay any placements and the attack would be a permanent part of her file. Prospective foster parents would be aware of the assault. Pagne felt her anger building. Damn Macey, she thought. Let her go to hell. Pagne knew this was not how she should be thinking, not a child of Jesus, but she didn't care! Macey ruined her life on purpose.

"Do you understand the repercussions of your choice to physically assault Macey?"

"Yes," Pagne said through clenched teeth.

Mrs. Corning knew all the behaviors. Pagne wasn't fooling her. She knew this was the first step to resolving Pagne's anger, to let her feel the impact of her actions. She knew Pagne's anger wasn't limited to Macey. It was her whole life. Mrs. Corning had reviewed Pagne's file the night before and was surprised that Pagne hadn't acted out sooner. Even though the counselor could understand why, she still needed to help Pagne learn better ways to cope with the pain. If she didn't, this young woman did not have good odds for a positive life.

"Please tell me what led up to your assault on Macey."

Pagne hated that she kept referring to their fight as an assault. It sounded so much worse but Macey had never hit Pagne so, was it a fight? Don't both people have to hit each other to be a real fight? Macey asked for it though. Well, not asked, but deserved it. How much was Pagne supposed to endure? Didn't she have feelings? Didn't she bleed? She tried to remember where she had heard that. Sounded good, but she knew it wasn't hers. Pagne started with the cell phone incident. As she told the counselor the details, several things came to mind. She did break the rules with the phone. She didn't see Macey take her rings and Macey only used words to hurt her, not her fists. Pagne began to see her role in the events. She thought about how she talked on and on to Macey about Lenny and the Masters. Pagne also remembered how jealous she was about Bree being adopted. *Wait, I have a right to be mad,* she told herself. *I don't have to be the nice person this time.*

The counselor asked Pagne a few questions about how hitting Macey made her feel. Did she know of any other ways to process her anger? Mrs. Corning thanked her for being cooperative and said that they would meet again tomorrow. She handed Pagne a journal.

"I would like for you to start writing your thoughts, anything that comes to mind, about your mother, your life, your scars, and Macey. You can decide to share all, parts, or nothing. It is your journal. The only rule is that you have to write six sentences or more each day." Pagne took the journal and politely thanked her for taking the time to see her. As Pagne left the office, she thought ... *how lame was that*. She has to see me. But, deep inside, Pagne felt that Mrs. Corning really cared and Pagne was thankful that she did.

Pagne's six sentences that first day were the thoughts she'd had in the meeting about her responsibility in the ASSAULT. Her last line was ... I want my rings back. They are my link to their hearts. She counted six lines. That was all she was going to do, just what she had to. Her day went on as all the rest for the next two months.

Miss Renee was allowed to meet with her once a week. Pagne was concerned about Lenny and the Masters and wondered if they still loved her. Miss Renee had contacted Brent the day of the assault and explained the situation. If he was mad at her, Miss Renee didn't reveal it. She only shared that they loved her and would be there just as soon as it was allowed. Pagne's heart ached when she fully realized what her assault had cost her. It seemed so foolish now. She asked Miss Renee about letters and Miss Renee said that she would find out and get her some writing supplies and stamps if it was allowed. Pagne prayed that it would be. She missed them all so much.

One afternoon in the "Berserk Ward," the name the kids had given this division, Pagne was called into the counselors office.

"I have something for you, Pagne." The counselor handed her an envelope. In the envelope were her rings. Pagne was shocked.

"How? Who?"

"Well, Macey was responsible for the return of these." Pagne knew it. Macey had probably felt guilty and admitted to stealing them.

"Is she in a lot of trouble?" Pagne asked, hoping that Macey's fate was as bad as her own.

"Well, no. She noticed one of the girls in your dorm room wearing them yesterday. She told the girl that if she didn't turn them into the office immediately, she would report her." Pagne felt her jaw drop open but didn't catch it quick enough.

"Thank you, Mrs. Corning." She slipped on her rings and savored the moment of reunion. "Do you think I could write a note to Macey?"

"I think that would be a wonderful idea. Under the circumstances, I'll need to read it first."

"Okay," Pagne agreed.

Dear Macey:

I feel so stupid thinking you took my rings. I knew you were mad at me, and I thought you were trying to get back at me. I hope that are feeling better. I am so sorry for hurting you. Some of the things you said made me so crazy mad and I just wanted to hurt you. My counselor said I'm like a teapot boiling on the stove; I was ready to blow off the steam, and you were in the wrong place at the right time. Instead of screaming like a teapot, I hit instead. We're figuring out how to make sure that I don't do that again.

I wanted to blame you for the trouble I'm in, but it is my fault. You didn't even hit me back and I know you could have.

I hope that you can forgive me. I don't know if you will ever want to be friends again, but I hope you do. Thank you for getting my rings back, they mean a lot.

Pagne

After two months of counseling sessions and restricted living, Pagne was able to return to the open dorms. She had not been able to write letters to Lenny or the Masters. Mrs. Corning wanted this to be Pagne's last and only stay in Berserk Ward. Mrs. Corning smiled to herself every time she thought of the name the kids had come up with. Pagne had not resolved everything, no one could, but she better understood how to control her reactions and how to resolve conflict.

Pagne carried her belongings into a new dorm room. She had mixed feelings about not sharing a dorm with Macey any longer. She had gotten a short note from Macey saying she understood why Pagne had beaten the crap out of her and apologizing for the mean things she said. Pagne didn't know about their friendship yet. After Pagne put her items away, she headed into the shared living area. A lot of the kids were focused on games, ping pong, or the TV. Pagne saw Macey sitting in the same chair Pagne had assaulted her in. As Pagne walked over to her, Macey looked up with a serious expression that melted into a smile. To Pagne's dismay, one of Macey's front teeth was missing. There was a gap in her smile. Pagne felt sick to her stomach. She had thought that Macey's tooth would be fixed by now. Macey started laughing hysterically.

"You should see your face!" she howled. Macey reached into her mouth and wiped off what looked like black paint on her tooth. Pagne felt such a relief that there was a white tooth under it. Macey jumped up and grabbed Pagne, hugging her long and hard. "I missed you, Pagne." Pagne felt an even stronger sense of relief.

'Did I knock out your front tooth?"

"Nahhh, you hit hard but not that hard. You knocked out a loose baby tooth that I still had. Didn't have to have the dentist pull it after all."

Pagne was relieved, but also a little disappointed. The story sounded much better if she could say she knocked out a permanent front tooth. A baby tooth was hardly impressive.

"Macey, I am so sorry."

"Stop, Pagne. I knew I was pushing all your buttons. I was trying to. I was jealous and angry that I didn't have people to love me the way you did. I'm sorry for hurting you so bad. I knew I acted horribly and regretted it right away but you shocked me when you jumped on me like you did. I have to say, for a short chick, you can kick some butt!" Pagne tried not to smile but it slipped out.

"So, we okay?" asked Pagne.

"Yes, we're good. I think two months in the Berserk Ward makes us more than even. Guess it was hard not to see Lenny or your family."

"Yeah. It was really tough but, I made that happen, not you."

"Well, let's just say we both made it happen," Macey insisted.

"Wish I was in your dorm."

"You are," Macey confirmed. "When I found out where they were putting you, I asked to be switched. The girl that stole your rings was glad I moved. I would stare at her every night before lights out and do that stupid finger thing to my eyes to let her know I was watching her. Nobody has missed any of their stuff since." Pagne giggled at the thought of Macey's description. "When do you get visitors again?"

"I don't know yet but, hopefully, soon."

The girls headed out to the tree and made the climb into another world, their world.

"Oh, Pagne."

"Yeah?" Pagne responded.

"I'm really sorry about how I acted when Lenny was here last time. Anytime you want the tree to share with him, just say so. He's not lame and he's actually cute, too cute for you." Pagne started to act as if she was going to hit Macey playfully and then thought better of it.

"I know, he's dreamy," Pagne said.

Once settled in, Macey wanted to know about Pagne's stay in the Berserk Ward. She still felt guilty knowing she had pushed Pagne to the point of exploding.

"It was actually okay except for not being able to see the people I care about. I don't know what Lenny or the Masters think about what I did and that drives me crazy. Maybe they decided I'm not who they thought and they won't love me anymore." Pagne picked at the bark.

"No, Pagne. They will love you just the same."

"Maybe the Masters will, but Lenny? Who wants a crazed girlfriend? He might just say forget it. He might be afraid that I'll come after him if he ever made me mad." Silence fell over them for a time.

"The counseling was really good," Pagne finally said. "Mrs. Corning explained a lot of things to me. There was so much pain smashed down inside of me and, when Pam died, it was just too much to keep inside. She said what I did wasn't surprising but I couldn't let my feelings take over and ruin my life. We worked out some things for me to think about and do if I ever feel that angry again."

"Like what?" Macey asked.

"First, I'm supposed to step back and try to walk away. If I can't, then I remember what the other person is saying or thinking is just what they think, not the truth." She giggled, "She said something really gross."

Macey's ears perked up. "What? What?"

"She said that it can help if you pretend they are three years old having a tantrum or they are in their underwear." They laughed as Macey tried to picture an adult saying that.

"I've used that one before," Macey said. "When I get bored in class, but they were naked!"

"Ewww " said Pagne, "that's sick." They both laughed. It felt good to laugh.

"Know what's sad?" Pagne asked. Macey waited. "My angel tried to warn me. I was so angry though. I ignored her."

"Oh yeah, that's right. You have an angel. I forgot about that."

"I smelled her and she actually told me to walk away. I should have listened but I just wanted to hurt someone." Pagne blushed and cautiously looked at Macey. Macey looked at her but didn't say anything.

"Well, if we're ever in a fight, I want you on my side," Macey finally teased. Pagne relaxed. "You serious about this angel, Pagne? How do I know if I have one?" Pagne tried to find the best way to answer.

"Well, each one is different, like your friends are all different. Mine likes to smell," Pagne said and they both laughed. "And she does speak sometimes but not often. I don't hear her with my ears like I hear you. It's almost like a wild thought that crosses my brain and I know that it's not mine. Make sense?"

"Kinda."

"I've met some people who know how to hear their angels but they don't smell anything. They just get the voice thoughts and sense things, like they just know. Sometimes it's warnings about danger but, mostly, it tells us we're are doing the right thing. We get a sense of peace, like we know we're not alone and we can be strong."

"Wow, that sounds cool."

Pagne didn't want to push Macey but thought this was a good time to continue. "I don't know if you have to be a follower of Jesus to have an angel but everyone says they feel them stronger and more often when they give their heart to Jesus."

"I thought about doing that when we lived with Mrs. Buttonhook," Macey admitted, "I wasn't sure if it was all real or not. Then, when the fire happened, I sorta figured it was all pretend, ya know? Why would God let you get burned and Mrs. Buttonhook hurt? Then she lost her mind and that sorta proved it to me. But, you figured out it's real?"

"Yes, it's very real and, remember, my angel probably saved all of us that night."

They had many talks in that tree. They talked about angels, God, and their pasts. Pagne felt a bond with Macey because their stories were similar. Macey's mom and dad had drug abuse issues, her dad bailed, and then her mom got worse. Boyfriends were in and out and there was no structure, no one looking out for her. Luckily, she had not been sexually abused, but the neglect and the verbal and physical abuse had bruised her heart and soul. Neighbors finally reported their concerns and Macey had ended up at Mrs. Buttonhook's. They reminisced about their time there and wondered what had happened to the twins, then Pagne brought up Mrs. Buttonhook. Macey had heard she passed away a few months ago but wasn't sure if it was true.

Chapter 14

Thankfully, Pagne only had to wait a couple of days before her visitation was reinstated. She was relieved when she saw Lenny, Brent, Bree, Richie, and Amanda on her scheduled visit list. She was so excited because she had never seen Amanda other than in pictures. Amanda was two months old but should be no months old, since she should have been in Pam's stomach these last two months. She should have just now been born. Pagne preened and prepared herself for her reunion. She wanted to look her very best. She changed clothes many times, then styled and restyled her hair just to end up with loose, flowing red curls. It was how Lenny liked her hair best. She had gotten her phone back earlier that day but she didn't want to speak to them on the phone. She needed to see their faces and read their eyes to see how much damage she had done.

She made the long walk to the visiting area and squealed with delight when Bree and Lenny ran to her, squealing just as loud. Oh God, how she loved these people. How badly she needed them! She let the tears roll as they hugged and laughed. Brent stayed back a short distance, holding Amanda. He knew a small baby would get squished in a reunion this powerful. They made their way over to Brent. Pagne wasn't sure what to do. She felt so ashamed before Brent. Brent handed Bree the baby and wrapped his arms around Pagne. He brought his mouth to her ear and whispered… "It's okay, sweetheart. We all mess up. Doesn't change how much I love you one bit." Pagne released all her tension and leaned into his strong, warm chest. She let herself be held while Brent breathed in rhythm with her those few minutes and then he kissed the top of her head. "Hey, I want you to meet your sister. Pagne this is Amanda. Amanda, this is Pagne." Pagne released her hold on Brent and turned to the pink bundle in Bree's arms. Oh my, do they see it too? She looked just like Pam. Amanda had her eyes, her nose, her coloring, and her lovely hair. Pagne touched her soft cheek.

"Want to hold her?" asked Bree.

"Yes but give me a minute. I just want to look at her." Bree shifted the blanket to reveal more of Amanda. Pagne ached for Pam and felt so much regret that this baby would not know Pam the way they had and Pam did not get to cherish this new life, the life she had died for. Pagne reached for her and Amanda squirmed and cooed. Pagne's heart melted for this precious baby.

Pagne felt a tug on her sleeve. "Pagne?" She hadn't realized that Richie was there until that moment.

"Oh Richie. Where were you hiding? I didn't see you 'til now."

"I was behind my dad," he announced. "I wanted to see if you were going to hit anyone first." Pagne's felt a stab to her heart. She handed the baby back to Bree while giving her a confused look.

"He must have overheard dad and I talking," she whispered.

Pagne then focused on Richie. "Oh, Richie, I'm so sorry I worried you. I did a very stupid thing and it won't happen again. I could never hit you." She reached for Richie and he hesitated a minute. Pagne hadn't even thought about how Richie would process her violent lash out. He looked into her eyes as he stepped in close for a hug. Pagne just held on, whispering how sorry she was that she scared him.

Brent suggested they grab one of the sitting areas before they filled up. They chose an area with a couch and several chairs. As they settled in, Pagne smelled her angel, lightly at first, just enough to know she was there. Pagne sensed that she wanted to share the reunion with her, to be there for the joy in her life not just the drama. There wasn't enough sitting area and Pagne opted to sit on the floor in front of them. She smiled while her angel settled in around her, softly bathing her in the Heavenly scent.

"I have a few things I want to say to all of you. First, I'm so sorry that I disappointed you with how I acted. I'm ashamed that I got into a fight but my biggest regret is that I did something that kept me from all of you for so long. I didn't think about what my actions would cost me and I hope you can all forgive me." Pagne continued, "I'm working with my counselor to make sure I handle myself much better in the future." Pagne waited to see what they had to say. Lenny looked at Bree and then they looked at Brent.

"We've had a long time to think about this," Lenny said. "We were shocked, dismayed and all that stuff. We came to a unanimous decision." They all shouted out, "LOVE YA ANYWAY AND YOU'RE NOT GETTING RID OF US THAT EASY!" Lenny, Bree, and Richie piled onto Pagne, knocking her flat on the floor. They started a tickle-fest and everyone laughed and squealed. Pagne felt such joy and love. The smell of her angel increased to such intensity that Lenny, Bree, and Richie stopped and looked at Pagne. "Is that her?" Lenny asked.

"You can smell her?"

"I think so," Bree said, "very soft and sweet." To Pagne, the smell was intense but they could barely smell her. The giggling and tickling started again until Brent noticed the staff's disapproving glances.

"Hey guys, that's enough for now. They're going to kick us out if we keep this up," Brent said, grinning from ear to ear. The kids climbed up off the floor and found their seats. They started sharing stories to catch Pagne up on what she had missed over the last two months. They saw the incredible likeness of Pam in Amanda. Brent's mom was working out well and they had a system that worked for all of them but, they were missing a very important part of the team and that was Pagne.

Visiting time ended and Brent asked the others to meet him in the car. He wanted a few minutes with Pagne. Pagne said her goodbyes and let them know she had her phone again but there would be no texting after nine o'clock. She would have to shut the phone off at nine so she wasn't tempted. She looked directly at Lenny as she said this. He nodded and pouted. *He is just too cute,* Pagne thought.

After the others left, Brent leaned in close to Pagne. "I wanted to explain some things to you and ask a few questions."

"Okay," Pagne responded, not sure if she should be alarmed.

"The incident you had will be in your file. It's going to make placement in a foster-home harder than before. You won't have as many options to move closer to us." Pagne looked down at her hands. The shame began to build again. "Pagne, I'm not saying that to upset you, but you need to know what is going on."

"Okay," she said quietly.

"We still have the group-home option. That could happen much sooner." Pagne nodded. She was realizing how badly she had messed things up. Brent was quiet for a moment. He set his hand on her shoulder. "Pagne." Pagne looked up at him, into those soft, kind eyes. "Do you want to be part of our family permanently?" Pagne's heart leapt in her chest.

"Oh yes, more than anything."

"I am working with Miss Renee about getting legal guardianship for you to begin with. Then we would work on adoption. Pam and I talked about adopting you before she got pregnant. I am so sorry that we let her health delay our plans. This whole mess could have been avoided if we had known how little time we had." Pagne saw the regret in Brent's eyes, regret for her and for Pam.

"Dad, I knew that you both loved me and that is enough for now." Brent squeezed her shoulder for a brief second and then exhaled deeply.

"Okay, I will ask Miss Renee to proceed. It might be a real battle. My being a widower makes it a lot harder. The foster-care system isn't budging on their position so, we have to approach this a different way. The courts will determine guardianship and Miss Renee and I will get everything in order. You'll be interviewed by the judge, the counselors, and whoever else the court decides. Miss Renee will keep you posted on what's happening and when. You need to think about what you want to do while this plays out. Here or a group-home closer to the house. Whatever you decide is okay with me." Pagne wanted to think it through but she knew Macey needed her right now. Unless they went to a group-home together, she would stay here but, she didn't want to tell Brent yet. Brent gave her a long hug and then held her face in both of his hands. "Pagne, I will do whatever I need to so we have you back with us. Please be patient and don't discuss this with Lenny or Bree yet. I don't want to have all of us crazy while this process is going on. I've only told them that I'm looking into our options."

"Okay, Dad. I won't say anything till you say I can."

"Love you, sweetheart. We'll be back soon. Lenny is pushing for the next visit alone." Pagne grinned and then snatched it back, thinking she was revealing too much. Brent winked at her and headed out to the others. Life was good and Pagne skipped back to her room, unaware of the soft, translucent shimmering of wings skipping behind her.

Macey was waiting for Pagne in their room. "How did it go?"

"They love me," Pagne said, as she wrapped her arms around herself and fell back onto her bed.

"I told you," Macey laid back on the bed next to her.

"Macey, you think you'll go into another foster-home?"

"Doubt it. My record scares them off. Guess I didn't think things through any better than you did. Kinda screwed myself up."

"What about a group-home?"

"Never been in one. Think I'd be nervous about it. I know what it's like here and what to expect. Why?"

"No reason really. Just wondering."

"What do you think will happen to you, Pagne?"

"No idea right now. Dad, Brent, said that he was looking into our options."

"That's cool," Macey said. Both girls drifted off to sleep without changing into their PJs or even brushing their teeth. Pagne even missed Lenny's text at 8:58, telling her how much he loved her and how beautiful she is!

The days seemed to drag. Pagne was still having weekly appointments with her counselor and Miss Renee would pop in now and then to keep Pagne filled in. Pagne figured she could call her instead but she realized Miss Renee enjoyed their visits too. She had become a good friend to Pagne. Pagne asked her about the group-homes and if she thought Macey could be considered. Miss Renee wasn't familiar with Macey's current situation and said she would check into it. Pagne was still on probation and would be for another three weeks according to the rules. Everyone remained at the hall for four months after an altercation. The visits became Pagne's lifeline. Lenny and her family divided the schedule. Lenny got Wednesday evenings and the Masters got Friday evenings. Sunday afternoons, Pagne got them all unless someone had to be somewhere else. Grandma Maxine would come when Brent couldn't make it on Sundays but he always made it on Friday evenings. Pagne appreciated their commitment to her and she knew that Bree was missing school functions and church activities to visit her. When the girls were texting Thursday evening, Bree mentioned the school dance. Pagne asked her if she was going. "No, of course not, it's Friday night. I'll be with you silly." Pagne decided Bree's life couldn't be on hold just because Pagne was locked up.

"Bree, I want you to go. You can give me all the details of what I'm missing on Sunday."

"Pagne, I would feel guilty because you can't go."

"That's silly. We have stuff here that you can't come to and I don't feel guilty. It's usually lame but that's not the point.

Bree texted back. "You sure?" Pagne felt relieved.

"Yes. Go, dance, kiss a boy. I want all the gory details!"

"You're nuts, Pagne. You know I'm saving myself for Mr. Wonderful."

"Maybe he will be at the dance," teased Pagne. "Seriously, Bree, go to the dance!"

"Okay, I'll go if you're sure," agreed Bree.

"I am sure! Gotta go. Need a shower real bad," said Pagne.

"Okay, Pagne, I'll text you tomorrow and tell you what I'm wearing."

"Cool, send me a pic when you're ready."

"Okay. Love ya. Scrub all the crevices Pagne!"

"Gross," Pagne replied.

~

Miss Renee was here to see her, which was very unusual on a Tuesday morning. Pagne usually saw Miss Renee in the afternoons. Maybe this was a good sign? Pagne went into one of the small visiting rooms, the same one she had shared with her mom years ago. Odd, she hadn't thought of her mom for a long time. Leah would come up sometimes in her counseling sessions but Pagne never dwelled on her. Miss Renee looked excited to see Pagne. "Hi, sweetie. Come have a seat." Pagne joined her at the table. "Well, we have a court date but it's several months off." Pagne groaned. "I know, hon, but these things take time. You'll be meeting with a court-appointed psychologist on the twenty-eighth. They'll make a recommendation to the judge. Just be yourself and be honest, Pagne. Don't try to guess what they want you to say. If you contradict yourself or get caught up in lies, it won't work in your favor."

"Okay, I understand," Pagne agreed.

"The psychologist has your case file and knows everything we know," she said. Pagne nodded, realizing she had nothing to lie about anyway. Pagne had a question to ask, but dreaded the answer.

"Could my mom stop this?" Pagne held her breath.

"No, Pagne. Her parental rights were terminated quite some time ago. The system takes physical abandonment quite seriously. She got consideration the first time because she left you in a courtroom where you were safe. Leaving you alone for days at your residence fell into a whole other category," Miss Renee assured her. Pagne was relieved. "And no, Pagne, we have had no leads or contact with your mother." Again, Pagne was relieved, which made her sad in one respect but still relieved. Pagne had been having nightmares that just as the judge was starting to pound his gavel giving Brent guardianship, her mother would burst into the courtroom screaming that she belonged to her and no one could give her a different life.

The twenty-eighth came quicker than Pagne expected. Miss Renee drove her to a large office complex with lots of doctor's names on the directory. When it was time for Pagne to go in, Miss Renee kissed her on the head and assured her she would do fine. Pagne followed the nurse down a short corridor and entered Dr. Swenson's office. He was a large man, tall and wide, with a full, curly beard and piercing, blue eyes. "Have a seat Miss Crenshaw. May I call you Pagne?"

"Yes, please, Sir."

"Do you know why you're here today, Pagne?"

"Absolutely, Sir. I'm here to help get my family back." Dr. Swenson smiled at her.

"Well, sounds like we can get started. I assume then that you are in favor of Mr. Masters having legal guardianship over you?"

"Oh yes. Mr. Masters is my dad, not my real dad, you know, but it's better really. Dads get stuck with you but Mr. Masters wants me." Pagne scooted back a little further in her chair.

"You lived with him and his wife for quite a while?" Pagne nodded. "And you were happy there?"

"Very much so, Sir. It was the first place I really knew I was loved and safe. We shared the chores and took care of each other."

"Took care of each other?"

"Well, Mom, Pam fostered drug babies. When I came, we had the twins, Matt and Mattie. We all helped take care of them."

"I see. Would you say your role in the family was as a babysitter?"

"Oh, no. I was their sister. We were all family. We did lots of stuff together. Then Mom got pregnant and it was very hard for her. So, we all took care of her the way she took care of us."

Pagne shared her memories of that time: all the evenings in Pam's room, talking and reading to her, watching movies and lip-syncing to win the canned ham. Dr. Swenson seemed to want to hear it all. He asked a lot of questions about Pam and Brent's relationship, how they dealt with problems, who was the one who punished, and how they were punished if they did something wrong. He asked about Brent's habits, such as, did he drink alcohol? Most of the questions Pagne didn't like, especially when he asked if Brent ever did anything that made her uncomfortable. Did he ever stare at her or touch her oddly? Brent was not Adam. This, Pagne knew for sure.

After several hours, Pagne had answered all of Dr. Swenson's questions honestly. Dr. Swenson had made a lot of notes and Pagne didn't know if this was good or bad. "So just a few more questions and we'll be done for today." For today? Pagne wondered how many times she would be in this office before she got her family back. "I would like to cover the assault in your files briefly. I read your counselor's notes and believe I have a clear understating of what happened. How do you feel about your behavior now?" Pagne cleared her throat. She knew this would come up.

"I feel bad about attacking Macey. I was so angry about a lot of things and it felt like I just exploded. It cost me a lot but I think that's good. I understand now. Everything I do affects me and the people around me. I want to bring good things, not bad."

"Last question, I promise. If the judge decides that you can live with the Masters, what would this mean to you?" Pagne thought hard for a few moments.

"It would mean that I'm where I am supposed to be, that I'll be with everyone who has really loved me, that I'll have my family and my life back. I want to be home and living my life, not in storage."

"Okay, Pagne. You did very well, my dear. It was a pleasure to meet you and I look forward to seeing you again." Dr. Swenson stood and reached out to shake Pagne's hand. When she extended her hand, her scarred arm was visible below her sleeve. She knew the doctor notices, but he didn't coment. Pagne rejoined Miss Renee in the waiting room. Miss Renee gave her a questioning look and Pagne shrugged her shoulders to indicate she didn't know. On the drive back, Pagne filled her in.

The next few months were stressful with several more meetings with court-appointed people. Pagne wasn't sure what they did, exactly. There were lots of questions and most were the same questions over and over again. Pagne figured they didn't care about the answers as much as observing her as she answered them. She only met with Dr. Swenson once more. They talked briefly and it seemed to be about how she was dealing with the process. Pagne looked forward to her visits with Lenny and the family. They tried to make the visits feel personal. One evening, Brent brought his laptop and showed Pagne movies of Amanda cooing and smiling. She appreciated the opportunity to see her awake and active. There were a lot of children at Langston Hall, which meant a lot of colds and germs. They didn't want to expose Amanda due to her fragile health. When she did come, it was early evening and she was usually asleep. Pagne wished she was home with them. She wanted Amanda to know her like she knew Bree and the others.

Pagne and Brent discussed Pagne's plans and agreed that she should stay where she was. There was no point in settling into a new place, and possibly influencing Macey to move, when the court date was so close. Pagne knew that going home to her family would affect Macey and she didn't want to make it worse by uprooting her.

It was the morning of their court date and Pagne dressed to impress. Miss Renee and her social worker would take her to the courthouse. They would meet Brent there. When Pagne saw Brent, she ran to him and he held her snugly. "Sweetheart, we're gonna give it a good fight, okay?"

"Okay," she agreed. They walked into the courtroom hand in hand.

Everything seemed to go well. Dr. Swenson was very positive about the relationship that Pagne had with the Masters and recommended consideration for Brent's petition. Miss Renee and her social worker also encouraged the court to grant guardianship. Pagne was feeling very hopeful and wondered if her angel would make an appearance as she silently prayed during the entire process. They called Brent up and he presented himself as a loving father who wanted to be reunited with his daughter. Pagne could hardly believe that he felt so strongly about her and she felt grateful. When Brent was finished, they called Grandma Maxine to come forward. She explained her commitment to Brent and to raising the children and they asked a lot of questions about her health.

Miss Renee and Brent had really worked hard to stack his case in his favor. The teachers she had while at the Masters were brought in and Pastor Tim spoke on their behalf. Pagne was feeling more and more confident that everyone would see how much she belonged to this family. Finally, they asked Pagne to step up. They allowed Miss Renee to question her and then the court-appointed attorney for the county approached her. This man had been very kind to each person he had questioned but, Pagne was leery of him. He had a very serious personality and she knew that he was a "by-the-book" person. Once he had finished questioning her, they asked her to take her seat.

The judge asked if there were any more witnesses or questions by Miss Renee. She indicated that there were not but asked that she be allowed to share a video provided by Pam Masters before her death. She had made this portion of the video just for the purpose of Pagne's custody. The judge hesitated but then agreed to allow the video. They pulled down a screen on the left side of the judge. Pagne saw her precious Pam come up on the screen and felt a lump in her throat. She reached for Brent's hand, just as he was reaching for hers. Pam was not made up and the room was not staged. This was raw footage, similar to Pagne's DVD. It was obvious that Pam was in a lot of pain. Her face and voice showed the weariness she felt. She had added her comments to Brent's DVD, near the end, just before she went to the hospital.

"Hello. I have asked my sweet husband, Brent, to share this with the court." Pam shifted a little, trying to get comfortable and cleared her throat. "We had every intention of petitioning the court to adopt Champagne Crenshaw. My pregnancy and health were compromised, and we delayed the procedure until after the birth of our baby. I believed that I would survive my pregnancy and would be there with you, in person, to fulfill our dream of being Pagne's parents." Pam became visibly emotional. "Obviously, that is not how things worked out. I know that my death changes things and will make it more difficult for Brent to be able to adopt Pagne. But, it doesn't change the most important thing. Pagne is our daughter. We function as a complete family with her here. If Pagne had been our biological daughter or we had completed the adoption process before my death, you wouldn't be in court, determining Pagne's fate." Pagne fought the wave of emotion that was building inside.

"Brent loved a broken person, me. He brought stability and self-worth to my life and Pagne deserves to know that kind of love. He has more compassion and sense of honor than any person I have ever known. We watched Pagne transition into a loving part of our family and a big part of that is due to Brent's ability to love unconditionally." Pam smiled so sweetly, Pagne knew it was for Brent. "Pagne, Bree, and Richie have a relationship no less than any siblings. Please allow them to continue as brother and sisters." Pam hesitated and Pagne felt that Pam was looking directly at her. She saw the tenderness and compassion once again in her eyes. "My sweet Pagne, we will always be your family and no one can take that from you. I am so sorry that we waited." Pam's eyes teared up and she tried to wipe the tears away but they continued to fall. Pam looked heartbroken and spoke in a whisper. "We thought we had more time."

The video stopped at that point. Pagne looked at Brent through tear-filled eyes as he fought to hold back his own tears. He squeezed her hand.

Next up was the attorney for the county. He seemed to be struggling to clear his throat. "Your honor, we do not deny that this is a nurturing home nor do we intend to discredit Mr. Masters' intentions. However, the conditions for guardianship are very clear and have been established in the interest of the child. I know Mr. Masters' intent is honorable and I believe they do love each other as much as any family could. We must consider the impact of Mrs. Masters death and the responsibility of the existing three children in the home. Mr. Masters has an infant, which may or may not have health complications due to premature birth. He currently has assistance from his family, but that could be affected if his mother suffers any health issues. We recommend to the court that this is not a suitable situation for guardianship." The attorney, Mr. Andrews, looked over at Pagne and Brent sadly as he sat down. Pagne felt her heart in her throat.

"It's not over yet," Brent whispered. Miss Renee stood up. She had prepared for this.

"Your Honor, Mr. Masters would like to address the court."

"Please come forward, Mr. Masters," the judge instructed.

Brent moved up to the front seat next to the judge.

Pagne held her breath as Brent started, "Your Honor. Mr. Andrews presents some valid concerns. I had to review my circumstances carefully before beginning my petition. This is what I know. My daughter Amanda has no indication of any complications and her doctors have provided medical statements for the courts review. Also, my mother is only in her late fifties and her health is excellent. My business is quite successful and provides a substantial income that would allow for in-home care for my younger children if my mother's health should deteriorate suddenly. Pagne is fourteen, very self sufficient, and does not require assistance as a small child would require. My wife had a substantial life insurance policy and has requested that it be earmarked for the care and financial needs of our children, including Pagne. Your Honor, we are not looking to add to our family. We are asking to reunite our existing family. Pagne is my daughter. Please allow me to finish raising her."

The judge looked at Brent for a long time. "I believe I have everything I need to make a determination. Court is adjourned." The judge rose and focused on Pagne, seeing the affection she had for Brent. He would be breaking some long-established and rigid rules if he ruled in their favor.

~

That evening, after dinner, Pagne's judge was reviewing the court transcript and Pagne's case file. His wife stepped in with a fresh cup of coffee. "Looks like you'll be up for a while."

"Hon," he said as he laid down Pagne's file. "Do you love Jamie any less than Sammy?" She looked at him surprised.

"Of course not." Jamie was an adopted daughter. They thought they could never have children but, once they adopted Jamie, she found out that she was pregnant with their son, Sammy.

"Do you think adopting her caused you to love her?" he continued.

"Jamie made me love her, not the act of legally being responsible for her. Why all these questions?" she asked.

"I'm just trying to decide when the connection happens."

"It's different for different people," his wife explained. "Sometimes it is the instant they meet," she put her hand on his shoulder and grinned at him, "sometimes it requires more time."

"If a man is loving but alone and struggling to raise his children, would it be fair to place another child in that home?" he asked quietly.

"I am assuming there is history with this man and child?" she asked.

"Yes, they seem to love each other very much and insist they are family. The teenager lived with the family for over a year. The foster mother died recently in childbirth and the teenager was removed when the father lost his foster-care licensing."

"Oh my goodness, how sad," she said.

"They had planned to adopt her but the mother's complications took priority and then she passed. I just don't know if it's enough, if stretching the rules is warranted here."

She pulled back and looked at him in disbelief. "That would be like asking if I died, would Jamie be better off staying with you and Sammy or getting sent to Langston Hall? Carl, you are struggling with man's rules, rules that try to make sense of broken families. Sounds like this is a matter of the heart. What does your heart say?"

"It's just not that simple, dear!"

"Isn't it?" she asked as she left his office. She knew he took his job seriously and he trusted the laws. They gave him order in a chaotic world. She would pray that he could see past man's legislation and into the heart of this family.

~

Each day that passed, Pagne felt her optimism diminish. It was so obvious that she should go home. Why were they taking so long? She hadn't heard from Miss Renee and when she talked to Brent, he was just as clueless as she. He kept telling her it would work out… somehow. Brent told her she needed to believe and pray.

They had been to court on a Monday. That Friday, the called Pagne into Mr. Phillips' office. She didn't know what to expect. As she came through the door, there sat Miss Renee and Brent. Their faces were beaming! Pagne crumbled in their arms. She felt such a sense of joy that it overwhelmed her. "How soon can you be packed up?" Brent asked her. Pagne jumped up with energy that surprised her.

"About three seconds. I've been packed since Monday."

Brent chuckled and said, "Well go get your stuff. We're going home." Pagne ran to her room, laughing in utter joy. She skidded through the doorway and slid up to her bed. Macey sat on the bed staring into her hands.

"Macey, I'm going home!" Macey looked up with a sad smile on her face.

"I'm so happy for you, Pagne. I really am. I'm going to miss you." Pagne hugged Macey and tried to think of what to say.

"Macey, I have something for you." She reached into her nightstand drawer and handed her the phone and charger. "You keep this so we can stay in touch."

"Won't your dad get mad?"

"Let me worry about that. I'll call you when I get home." Macey fingered the phone gently.

"Please don't forget about me, Pagne," she said in a sad whisper.

"Never, Macey. I love you. I'll come see you so much you won't know I'm gone"

"You better," Macey said, sadly.

"You know, Macey, Jesus Christ is here with you always." Macey looked doubtful.

"I know you believe that Pagne but why would he want me?"

"Oh, Macey, you are his daughter. He loves you."

Pagne stood there, frozen, not knowing how to walk out of the room. Macey saw her struggle and stood up.

"Let me help you carry your things," she offered as she grabbed one of Pagne's bags and started out the door. Pagne was grateful for her bravery.

Once at the house, Pagne ran up to her room and just stood there, still shocked that she was home. She was really home, and no one could change that now. She threw her bags on her bed and looked for Grandma Maxine and Amanda. Grandma Maxine was grinning when Pagne came into the nursery. "You're just in time. Wanna help me give her a bath?" Pagne couldn't think of anything that she would rather do in that moment. Grandma Maxine handed her Amanda, and then Grandma Maxine wrapped her arms around both of them, holding tightly while she cried with joy. Pagne was soon overcome with emotion, and joined in the blubbering.

Chapter 15

When they go to the house, Pagne ran up to her room and stood there, still shocked that she was home. She was really home and no one could change that. She threw her bags on her bed and looked for Grandma Maxine and Amanda. Grandma Maxine was grinning when Pagne came into the nursery. "You're just in time. Wanna help me give her a bath?" Pagne couldn't think of anything she would rather do in that moment. Grandma Maxine handed her Amanda and then wrapped her arms around both of them, holding tightly while she cried with joy. Pagne, overcome with emotion, joined in the blubbering.

When it was time for Bree and Richie to get home from school, Brent told Pagne to hide in the closet and play along. Pagne made sure her bags were out of sight. They didn't know about the court hearing or the outcome because Brent knew they couldn't deal with the disappointment if it didn't work out. When Bree and Richie walked in, Brent had a very stern look on his face. "I thought I told you two no pets without a family discussion. Have you hidden a hamster or rat in your room young lady?"

"No, Dad, what are you talking about?"

"Well, I keep hearing a scratching noise and it sounds like it's coming from somewhere in your room, Bree. I looked but couldn't find anything." Bree and Richie were immediately up to the adventure.

"We'll find it, Dad," they called as they ran into Bree's room. They looked under the beds and checked behind the furniture. Then they heard a scratching noise coming from inside the closet.

"It's in there," Richie said in a quiet voice.

Richie picked up a shoe and Bree grabbed one of her books. She slowly opened the door and Pagne jumped out at them. Bree and Richie jumped back, clinging onto each other, screaming. After a few seconds of terror, they recognized Pagne grinning at them, but they were too confused to think straight. They were still screaming as Brent stood in the doorway, laughing hysterically. As their screams began to fade, Pagne could see the shock on their faces. "I'm home! I'm home to stay!" she explained. Then Bree and Richie squealed with delight and grabbed her. The three of them fell to the floor holding each other, crying and laughing. I'm home, thought Pagne. The words gave her such warmth and peace. That evening was a mad, crazy reunion. Brent and Pagne explained what had been going on and Bree was upset that she hadn't been included, but understood why Brent kept it a secret. Brent assured them that adoption was the next step to securing their family.

After a huge, delicious dinner filled with laughing and excitement, they were exhausted. Everyone decided to get some sleep. Pagne had already put her things away and settled into her room. As she headed upstairs, she stopped by Brent in his recliner. "Thanks for letting Macey keep the phone. I promise I'll get a part-time job to pay for the monthly fees."

"Pagne, it's fine. One more phone on our plan isn't much at all. I'm glad to keep the connection there for you and Macey. You're a good friend. I still have Pam's phone so you can use that one, okay?" Pagne kissed him on the top of his head.

"I love you, Dad." She paused and then spoke, "I really miss Mom. It was so good to see her in court."

"She truly loved you, sweetheart." Pagne went to bed feeling perfectly complete for the first time in her life. Lenny would be there tomorrow. She smiled to herself in anticipation of his reaction when he found out she was home. He thought he was coming over because Brent needed help cleaning the garage. As she drifted off to sleep, she felt herself floating up into the skies. She was flying with powerful wings, flying to Pam, who waited for her in her tree. "Thank you, God, for loving me!" she whispered and fell asleep.

~

When Pagne looked back over the next four years, her high school years, she cherished her life. Lenny became a serious part of her plans for the future. Bree, Amanda, and Richie were embedded into the very fibers of her heart. Bree and Pagne began to define their priorities and the direction of their lives. Bree had made the commitment to a missionary career. Pastor Tim was helping her to connect with the right organizations and people. Pagne was feeling a strong push to deal with kids in the system. She, Bree, and Lenny visited Macey on a regular basis. If they couldn't all go, at least one of them was there every week. They began to feel led to reach out to the other kids that had no family or visitors and they convinced the administration to let them set up a peer outreach program at Langston Hall. They planned activities every other Saturday afternoon. Lenny would sometimes hold readings in the big tree and read his short stories. Bree brought her art talent to the group by holding art classes for the kids. Pagne's contribution was games. She would invent crazy games and have prizes for the kids. They called their group the Kennel Kids Club. To outsiders it may have sounded derogatory but that's how the kids referred to themselves. Brent funded as much as he could for supplies and prizes but, as it grew, the kids realized they needed to get more financial help. They began approaching local churches and businesses for donations. They got a wonderful response for their endeavor and Pastor Tim encouraged the church body to support them. The church voted to give them a monthly allotment to help cover the costs.

The county didn't approve of them coming in as a Christian group but they had opportunities to share their love of Christ as relationships developed. They started to get local publicity and letters were coming to Langston Hall from previous system kids for advice on how to start a similar program in their area or thanking them for the inspiration to "pay-it-forward." Pagne was amazed at how much their small outreach was generating interest in the kids and it brought her great delight to think that fewer and fewer kids would be forgotten. Kennel Kids Club began a wave of outreach programs that spread from their state throughout the nation. Brent helped the kids set up a website and they received emails daily from former system kids who were now adults as well as current kids. They started a blog to provide the kids with a way to share their stories. Grandma Maxine took on the responsibility of answering mail and emails, flagging the ones the kids needed to respond to. It was a life-changing experience for Pagne and Lenny; they had found their calling.

Bree graduated from high school during Pagne's junior year. She decided to join a missionary group of young adults that traveled in Africa. The family was excited for Bree but they dreaded the day she would leave. They thought they would have the summer with Bree but she decided to leave with the first group in mid-June. The tears were obnoxious and the hugging was desperate. The drive back from the airport was silent. When they got home, Pagne went to her room and felt the emptiness there. She sat in their closet and truly felt her heart ache. Chantal knew that she needed her company and Pagne drew in her smell.

Macey became a vital part of the club and helped fill the gap Bree left. She wasn't as good an artist as Bree but she had a passion for it. Lenny and Pagne considered Macey their sister and their bond grew strong. Macey had been right, no one wanted to deal with her past issues. She was okay though; she had the club and she was making a difference. She earned a level of respect from the staff and the other kids adored her. Brent looked into becoming a licensed foster-parent again so Macey could live with them but he was turned down.

The next year flew by. They got regular updates from Bree and she loved her life of serving God. She sent incredible pictures of the places she traveled to and the beautiful children she ministered to. The people there were excited to learn about God and Jesus Christ's salvation. She saw hundreds of souls saved at a time. Bree was being trained to assist the doctors who traveled with them and she loved it, except giving the kids shots. She always made sure she had candy in her pocket to help with the tears. Lenny and Pagne would graduate together, and they were both impressed with how well they had done in school. Lenny carried a 3.8 and had several scholarships he qualified for while Pagne had her scholarship from the city. They were both trying to coordinate which college would work for both of them.

Richie was getting by but he had periods of deep sadness. They would find him watching Pam's video and it was obvious that he still missed her very much. He had turned out to be quite a good singer and continued with the church choir and the school's glee club. Music became his life. He convinced Brent that a guitar would be a good investment and he was right. Richie was an awesome guitar player. He had an ear and could pick up a tune just by listening to it. They knew there was a somber side to Richie. He would keep to himself sometimes and pull away from the family. They would try to tease and tempt him out but learned that he would come around when he was ready. Brent was keeping a watchful eye. Richie was getting to the age where more and more options were available to him, many unhealthy. As Richie got older, Brent became more concerned about the frequency of his dark moods. The circus began with counselors, doctors, diagnosis, and medications, but nothing seemed to help. Richie wouldn't cooperate with the specialists and seemed most comfortable living in the shadows.

It was prom night and Pagne had gone shopping with several friends from school and found the perfect dress. It fit her like a glove and it was girly but not fancy. The dress was white with an opalescent shimmer to the fabric. It had spaghetti straps but it also had a filmy wrap to conceal her arm. She'd accepted the scars on her arm but she still tried to camouflage them when she wanted to be especially pretty. She had purple accessories and shoes that complimented the fabric shimmer as well as her hair. She applied her makeup lightly. She had learned that a lot of makeup didn't compliment her porcelain, freckled skin. She'd hated her freckles when she was young but she now realized that they set her apart. Lenny loved to take a washable marker and connect the dots, and he found some crazy things on her extremities. She let him do her face once but the marker had left a hint of color for several days. She looked in the mirror one last time and was finally ready. She admired her almost-adult frame. She was still small compared to most of her friends but perfectly proportioned. She wore her hair down and pulled up on the sides. The shorter hair around her face hung in soft tendrils. She was wearing Pam's amethyst jewelry and she felt like a princess. Brent had come into the hallway and tapped the bathroom door. "Lenny's here," he announced. Pagne opened the door and started to step out. Brent froze as this lovely creature mesmerized him. "Oh, Pagne, you look exquisite!" She shot him an excited smile as she floated past him and down the stairs. Lenny was also smitten when he saw the angel coming toward him.

"I, ahhh, I, ahhh got you some flowers, I mean a corsage."

Pagne giggled, "Lenny, it's just me."

"I know but it's an incredible you." She giggled again. Brent took way too many pictures and Richie stood back and took in the scene. Amanda, now four, wanted to know where her flowers were and kept touching Pagne's dress in awe as it shimmered. Finally, they were out the door and on their way for a night to remember.

Lenny had gotten a part-time job and had been saving everything he could for this night. He had more than enough for a limo, tickets for the dance, photos, and a very elegant dinner. He fawned over her as if she was royalty. At dinner, she pretended they were adults and the magic continued when they arrived at the prom. After several fast dances and then several slow, sensual songs, they were both very warm. Lenny took Pagne out to the balcony while everyone else stayed inside to watch the crowning of the prom king and queen. The balcony was decorated beautifully with twinkling lights everywhere. Several large, white gazebos were outlined with tiny, glowing lights. They looked out over the lake and watched the moon shimmering on the surface of the water.

Pagne felt Lenny pull her close as he turned her to face him. He leaned in to her and found her mouth with his. They kissed with such longing and passion. Pagne could feel her body responding. She trusted Lenny and knew that in this public place, nothing more would happen. She gave herself over to the emotions and the incredible sensations her body was creating. Lenny stopped and looked into her eyes. "I love you so much, Pagne. I want to be with you forever, in every way. You drive me crazy every time you brush against me." Pagne grinned because she also knew that feeling. She had been feeling it more and more. "I know we need to focus on college, but not having you," he looked down at her body, "will make it so much harder." Pagne pulled back, not sure she understood. She knew that some girls lost their virginity on prom night. Was that what he wanted from her? Pagne and Bree had taken a vow of chastity. Lenny knew immediately what Pagne was thinking. "No, baby, I don't want you to give yourself to me tonight but I do want you to accept this ring and marry me as soon as possible." Pagne looked down at Lenny's hand and saw a beautiful engagement ring. It was a heart-shaped diamond with tiny amethysts surrounding it. She loved it.

"Oh, Lenny. Yes! Yes!" He scooped her up and twirled with her in his arms, showering her with kisses. She wanted him. She wanted him now.

They had the limo pull over a block from Lenny's house. Pagne waited in the limo while Lenny slipped into his car and pulled around in front. Pagne jumped out of the limo and climbed in next to Lenny. As the limo pulled away, Lenny looked at Pagne intently. "Are you sure, Pagne? Tonight?"

"Yes, we can get to Vegas and back without anyone knowing. We have our driver licenses. That should be all we need, right? We are eighteen," justified Pagne. She knew he was second-guessing their decision so she slid over closer to him and laid her hand on his upper thigh. Pagne felt his leg jerk as he shifted the car into drive and headed east. They didn't say much on the drive, afraid they would convince themselves it was crazy. Pagne knew she wanted Lenny forever and had no doubts but she wasn't sure how her dad and her family would react. Where would they live? Lenny didn't make enough to support them and Pagne only worked part-time at a fast food restaurant on the weekends. Maybe she could get more hours but she didn't think it would be enough. Lenny's apartment with his mom was so small, he slept on a fold-out couch. Pagne didn't think she could ask Brent to let them live there. Lenny must have been thinking the same thoughts when he finally said something. "Maybe we shouldn't tell anyone right away, just pretend everything is the same." Pagne thought it might work. They saw each other all the time and they would be graduating in several months. They had both volunteered for a missionary trip to the Mexico in the summer and then they had college in the fall. They would only have to pretend for a while. She felt they could do that.

When they reached Las Vegas, they were shocked at how easy it was to get married. They firmly agreed on no drive-thrus and no having Elvis anywhere in the building. They found a cute chapel despite the flashing, neon cupid shooting an arrow on the roof. Since Pagne already had flowers, she removed the corsage and carried it as a bridal bouquet. The regular justice-of-the-peace was on vacation and his replacement was a man of foreign descent who wore his hair bound up in coils of bright red fabric. They had a very difficult time following his direction as he struggled to speak English. The witness was a stranger provided by the chapel. They opted for the bridal package that included pictures. It was odd posing with these unknown people on such a special day. Pagne felt a flutter of regret but focused on Lenny. They posed for several more pictures alone, their love for each other pouring out all around them. It was finished; they were married. If they had known each other intimately prior to the ceremony, it would have been tacky and anticlimactic. They saw it only as the permission they needed to explore each other. They didn't have a lot of time as the drive back would take several hours but they were going to have their honeymoon. On their way out of the chapel, they saw a vending machine with condoms. Pagne immediately turned red and Lenny threw her the keys. "I'll be right out." As she left the chapel, she heard the distinctive sound of a metal knob being turned.

They found an inexpensive motel that was plain and stark, but clean. The physical anticipation built to a frantic exploration and ended very quickly. They lay in each other's arms and felt the connection that had been created between them. Lenny saw that Pagne had teared up. "Oh, Pagne, did I hurt you?" Pagne shook her head, "Just a little," she admitted. "That's not why I'm crying."

"It was too quick? Not romantic enough? You didn't enjoy it?"

"Oh, Lenny, not any of those things. It was exciting, sexy and wonderful. It's just that I will never be the same. I crossed into a whole other world. I'm joyful Lenny, so thankful it was with you and not someone like Adam." He loved this girl and vowed to himself to never hurt her or let anyone else hurt her. After a few minutes, Pagne felt stirring on Lenny. "Oh my, you can again? So soon?"

"Oh yeah but, this time, much slower my love, much slower and it's all about you." She giggled and submitted herself to her husband.

~

They took a few minutes for a quick shower and tried to look like they had been dancing all night and not making love. On the drive home, Pagne curled up next to Lenny and dozed in a blissful sleep. It was so natural and comfortable between them. Lenny shut off the engine a few houses down from Pagne's house so Brent would not see that they arrived in his car instead of the limo if they woke him. Pagne woke up to soft kisses and Lenny's hands on her. They continued to kiss and fondle each other's bodies until Lenny couldn't take it anymore. "You gotta go Pagne or I'm going to drive away with you." Pagne wanted to stay, to tease, to see if he would take off with her but it wasn't the way she wanted her family to find out.

Pagne would have been very late if she hadn't gotten permission to join friends after the dance for breakfast at a all night cafe. They decided she should quietly walk to the porch without Lenny coming up with her. She could slip in easier if she was alone. Pagne made it in without disturbing anyone. She tiptoed to her room and out of her clothes for the second time that night, then crawled into her bed. How she ached to have Lenny lying next to her but they knew they had to be patient and lay low. She replayed the night over and over in her head and finally drifted off with a satisfied smile on her face.

Pagne didn't wake up until noon the next day. *Where is everyone,* she thought? She looked down at her ring and kissed it. She had hidden the marriage license and the photos in her nightstand. She pulled them out just to confirm that she hadn't been dreaming and was pleased to see that she really was married. She gently put the photos back into the drawer. When she got up, she found that she was tender in areas that had never been tender before. She quickly slipped into the bathroom to check for any visible marks on her neck but it was all clear. She had reminded Lenny several times that she bruised easily and he had to refrain from sucking on her neck. Each time, he willingly stopped and moved to less exposed areas. She tingled at the thought of his mouth on her body. She felt very sexy when she saw his love bites where only undressing would reveal. She touched them longingly.

Pagne showered, dressed, and headed back to her bedroom. She noticed that her phone was beeping with messages. The first one was from Brent. He had taken Richie and Amanda up to the lake and Grandma Maxine had taken off for the day to visit friends. Lenny had left ten messages, most only saying WOW. She smiled and deleted them. She didn't want any evidence of last night. The last message from Lenny read, "Call ASAP, I have to have you." Pagne had never felt sexy before but now she blushed with her thoughts. She called Lenny and they shared their undying love and told each other how much they missed each other. Pagne felt like she had a limb floating out there somewhere. Lenny was going to come over to the house and Pagne would make lunch. Brent had never really said anything about Lenny being there with her alone. It had never really come up because there was always someone at home. She didn't want to call and ask Brent. He would probably say to wait until they got back. She wanted to be alone with Lenny, even if only for a short time. She decided to risk it.

Lenny was over in a matter of minutes. As Pagne prepared sandwiches, Lenny pressed up behind her, touching her and kissing her neck. Pagne giggled but then got serious. "Lenny, we have to be careful. You can't be this personal with me here at the house or around your mom. They will know something is up. I want to pick the right time to tell them." Lenny acted rejected and sat on one of the barstools. Pagne shot glances at him while she finished making their lunch. At one point, he was rubbing his nipples through his shirt and she grinned. Next, he flexed his arms and puckered his lips. She felt herself responding to his lame attempts at seducing her. When she brought the food over, he pointed to his swollen groin and gave her a sad, puppy look. "Knock it off," Pagne said while laughing. "Eat your food and be good." Lenny grabbed her hand to bring it to his crotch when they heard Richie burst in through the French doors. They both jumped and tried not to look embarrassed.

"Hey, you're awake. Dad said you'd probably sleep all day. Did you make enough food for yourself?" Richie asked as he swooped in and grabbed Pagne's plate. "Thanks, sis!" Richie smacked Lenny's back. "You looked cute in a monkey suit, Lenny."

"Thank you, but I think I looked totally hot."

"Yeah right," grinned Richie. Amanda and Brent came in behind Richie.

"Well, if it isn't the promers. How was the dance?" he asked.

"Just wonderful," they both said in unison.

"Wasn't sure when you guys would be back. Let me make more sandwiches," offered Pagne.

"Thanks, hon. Amanda, let's go wash our hands. Richie, I'll assume you did before you handled that stolen sandwich."

"Yeah, sure Dad," Richie lied.

"Hope you like the taste of fish and snake," Brent shot back. Richie's face scrunched up. He had forgotten that he'd handled fish and a snake. He ran into the bathroom and scrubbed the gunk from his hands.

Pagne moved about the kitchen so smoothly, Brent thought she looked like she was floating. She prepared more sandwiches, pulled out fresh fruit and grabbed a bag of chips. Brent couldn't get past this feeling that Pagne was different. He saw the tender way Pagne would lean into Lenny when she laughed and how Lenny followed her every move with his eyes. Brent knew they were crossing the line into intimacy. He didn't know how he was going to deal with this.

After lunch, Pagne told the family about Lenny proposing and showed them her ring. Amanda loved it and wanted one, too. Brent was congratulatory but concerned about them moving too fast and Richie didn't say a word.

Lenny left about three o'clock to take care of some chores for his mom and return his tux before work that evening. Pagne walked him to the door and gave him a quick peck on the cheek. Lenny looked at her with a demand for more. She grinned and shooed him out the door.

Brent had come into the living room and asked Pagne to sit down. "Pagne, I really sense that things are moving very quickly with you and Lenny. Don't get me wrong, Lenny is a great kid. But that's the point. You two are kids." Pagne felt so bad agreeing with Brent, knowing she had gotten married the night before, but it was not the right time to tell Brent. They had too many things to work out first. But, if Pagne was honest, she just didn't know how to tell him. "You and Bree took chastity vows until marriage. I was very proud of both of you but I know it's your decision to honor that vow. Please believe me when I tell you that sexual intimacy will change your life and your relationships forever." Pagne did believe him. All she thought about was when she could be with her husband again. "If you decide to become sexually active, you need to be prepared and protect yourself." Brent sat looking at Pagne intently, waiting for her to react. Pagne tried not to look mortified but failed miserably. Brent was visibly uncomfortable. This would have been Pam's area to cover with the girls. "I'm not comfortable with Lenny here with you when no one else is home." Pagne felt herself flush with the awkwardness of the conversation and the guilt of her secret. She had to pull herself together. She took a deep breath and exhaled.

"I have plans for my life, Dad. I want a family some day but not now. I want to go to college and make a difference for the kids. I can do that best by getting an education." Brent looked relieved and smiled.

"I love you and Lenny very much. I know that you two plan to have a future together some day. If you and Lenny are truly meant to be together, I will be honored to walk you down the aisle when the time is right," Brent said, as he stood up. "You know, after college."

Pagne didn't know what to do other than nod in agreement. She didn't regret marrying Lenny but she realized they had created a situation that would hurt the people she loved.

"I love you, sweetheart!" Brent said as he hugged Pagne.

"I love you, too, Dad."

Pagne went to her room and called Lenny. "I got the refrain and safe-sex talk just now." Lenny began laughing. "It wasn't funny. I was so embarrassed and I had to lie to Dad."

"I'm sorry, Pagne. I think we need to figure out our plans and tell them soon. I feel bad about my mom. She kept asking me all about the prom. I couldn't even tell her who won king and queen."

"We better find out," said Pagne. "That won't look good at all."

"Changing the subject now. I was thinking about you naked again for the hundredth time today."

"Oh Lenny, you are disgusting!" she teased.

"But you love it," he stated and Pagne agreed.

"I'm going to go by the clinic and get on the pill this week. I want your babies some day but not in nine months."

"Good idea. I hate condoms." Pagne giggled at the picture of Lenny trying to master the art of applying them.

"Oh, by the way, Dad says you can't be here when no one is home. He can tell you have the hots for me."

"The man is very wise."

For the next month, Pagne and Lenny would steal moments. Lenny's car became their place for lovemaking. They were trying to save everything they earned so they didn't rent motel rooms. One evening while bunched up in the back seat, Lenny told Pagne to be sure to have Saturday night off from work. He had a surprise for her. She dressed especially sexy and, when he picked her up, they drove back to his mother's apartment. "What are we doing here? I thought you were springing for a big night out."

"Just wait," he said. He had Pagne shut her eyes at the front door. He walked her in, then closed and locked the door behind them. "Open your eyes," he demanded. Pagne opened her eyes and almost cried. The room was dark with candles lit everywhere. Rose petals were scattered around and a table was set with wine glasses, sparkling apple cider, and more candles. "Mom is away for two days visiting her sister in Sacramento."

"Oh Lenny, I Love You!" They wasted no time taking advantage of their privacy. Several hours later, Lenny ordered pizza and they picnicked naked on the floor. Lenny began smearing pizza sauce on Pagne's throat and the frenzy began again. Exhausted, they laid on the floor, watching the ceiling fan spin.

"I have something for you." Lenny pulled out a gift box from behind the couch.

"A gift for me?" she squealed. "It's not my birthday."

"You forgot, didn't you?" he said, obviously hurt.

"Forgot? Me? Forget our one month anniversary?" she grinned.

"You're such a brat!"

Pagne laughed as she reached into her purse for her gift box and handed it to him. Lenny loved his watch. Pagne had it engraved with their wedding date and 143 Pagne, which was short for "I Love You, Pagne" When Pagne opened her gift, she laughed uncontrollably. It was flimsy lingerie.

"This was supposed to be for me, not you!" Pagne teased. Lenny grinned.

"Dig deeper," he said. Pagne found a smaller box and inside was a gold locket. When she opened it, one side had a picture of her family. It was an older picture, taken when Pam was alive. Lenny had taken the picture at the lake. The other side had a picture of Lenny, shirtless and flexing his muscles. She laughed. "Just a reminder of the husband you have waiting for you, in case you forget." She kissed her finger and touched both of the pictures.

"I could never forget, Lenny. Thank you. I love it." She hugged him. She felt his hands slipping down to her bottom.

"Now, please, put on that nightie." Pagne slipped the filmy, lacey fabric over her head. She felt like a woman. She grinned at Lenny when she saw the lust in his eyes.

"Now, you gotta catch me." She took off running with Lenny closing in fast.

~

Later in the week, Pagne and Lenny were at Langston Hall going over the last of the details with Macey for the Kennel Kids Club. They would be stepping down for a while at the end of the school year when they left for their Mexico mission trip. Pagne and Lenny were so excited to be on their own as adults for the first time. This trip, however, also created anxiety. They knew they would have to tell their parents they were married before they left.

Macey was a year older, nineteen, and had moved out on her own with several other girls last year. Macey was the only person that knew Pagne and Lenny were married. She felt honored that they trusted her. Langston Hall had hired her as the activity director. She was thrilled with her job and excited about continuing the Kennel Kids Club. They had several new volunteers who had spent many years at Langston Hall. They had decided to limit volunteers to previous system kids because they had an understanding that the average person could not offer.

"Have you told your families about being married yet?"

"No, I thought it would get easier with time, but it's harder. The lie is getting bigger and bigger. We've had to tell so many little lies. It would have been a shock if we told them on our wedding night but now it will be even harder. Making the decision was one thing but keeping it from them has been next to impossible," explained Pagne.

"Why don't you just tell them and get it over with?"

"We're being selfish, I guess. We thought we'd wait closer to when we leave. That way everyone will have space to recover," offered Lenny.

"You guys just don't want to suffer the consequences," said Macey.

"Guess you're right," admitted Lenny. He looked at Pagne and saw the shared shame. They said their goodbyes and left Macey in charge.

That night, Lenny couldn't stand it. He had to have Pagne and not in a car. He slipped out of the apartment and drove over to the Masters' house. Lenny had figured out how to climb up to Pagne's window. He got to the window without any complications and tapped on the glass. He tried several times but Pagne didn't stir. He texted her. Pagne woke to the phone beeping and looked at the time. It was three a.m. She checked the message and it just said "Open your window." Pagne looked over and saw Lenny leering at her.

"You idiot," she texted. She got up and slid the window open. "What are you doing?"

"I just have to have you. I can't stand it Pagne, I'm hurtn' here!" She grinned but knew they were treading on thin ice.

"You can't come in. Dad will kill us."

"We'll be quiet and it won't take long, then I'll go."

"So just service you?" She teased.

"You'd only be servicing me if you didn't want it, too!" Good point, she thought. She did want him. He climbed quietly into the room. They were very cautious and quiet at first, but eventually got lost in the passion of being with each other. Suddenly, Pagne's door flew open and Brent ran in with a bat raised high in the air.

"Pagne, I heard you scream," yelled Brent. Lenny rolled off of Pagne and brought his arms over his head to block the blow of the bat. Brent froze in shock. As the realization of what was happening became clear, he boomed,"Get your clothes on and meet me downstairs, both of you." Brent stormed out of the room and stomped downstairs.

Lenny pulled on his pants and Pagne put on her robe as Grandma Maxine showed up in the doorway. "Oh my," she said.

"Please protect us, Grandma," Pagne begged.

"Oh, my dear. I think this is your mess to clean up. I'll make sure there is no bloodshed but, other than that, you're on your own."

Luckily, Richie and Amanda did not wake up.

Grandma Maxine went downstairs and tried to calm Brent down but he was furious and would not be calmed. Lenny headed down first while Pagne grabbed the papers from the nightstand. She knew they had to come clean and regretted that it had happened this way. Lenny had forgotten to zip his pants and Grandma Maxine discreetly pointed to his zipper. Lenny looked down, blushed, and turned his back slightly to zip up. He obviously did not want to lose sight of Brent with the bat.

"Sir, I can explain," Lenny squeaked.

"You shut up, Lenny. I don't want to hear from you. I know you're type, taking advantage of my daughter. You were in her room. She was not in yours."

Pagne pushed in front of Lenny and said "Dad, stop! We have something to tell you."

"You're pregnant? That doesn't make it okay… only worse. I should..."

"No, Dad, I'm not pregnant. We're married. We got married on prom night." She held out the paperwork to him. Brent was not processing quick enough.

"You're what?"

"Married, Dad. We got married over a month ago." Brent took the papers from Pagne and half-sat, half-fell back into the chair. Grandma Maxine turned on the light and stepped over to see the papers.

"What are you talking about, Pagne? This makes no sense."

Grandma Maxine grabbed Lenny and pulled him to the kitchen, "Give them a few minutes," she whispered. Lenny sat down at the counter, head in his hands.

"This is so bad!" he kept saying over and over.

Grandma Maxine slipped her arm around Lenny's shoulders. "He loves both of you. It will be okay. He just needs to process all of this. It's a lot to deal with at three o'clock in the morning." She stepped back, picked up a dishtowel, and slapped Lenny on the head. "You idiot. What were you thinking? Oh that's right, boys don't think with their brain!"

Pagne kneeled down in front of Brent and waited for him to speak. "Pagne, why didn't you tell me? Why would you get married in secret? You're not pregnant?"

"No, Dad. Lenny and I were virgins until our wedding night. That's one reason we got married. We knew we would be together forever and we wanted forever to start now. It was impulsive but we're so happy. We wanted to tell everyone when the time was right but it was never the right time. The lie just got bigger and bigger. We didn't want to hurt anyone but this was for us. It was what we wanted, what we needed."

"I thought I would give you away someday… to Lenny but, I thought I would be there."

"I am sorry, Dad. I thought about that after but it was too late."

"I need a drink," Brent admitted. He walked into the kitchen and saw the scared look on Lenny's face as he grabbed the dishtowel. "You idiot," he said, as he smacked Lenny in the head. "I could have killed you. What if I had a gun?" Pagne was standing behind Brent, shaking her head to tell Lenny to keep quiet. Brent opened the fridge door and poured himself a glass of apple juice. He downed it, breathed deep for a few breaths, and turned around.

"Lenny, you need to go home but be back here at ten o'clock, not a minute before and not a minute after. We have some things to settle. Now go, I don't want to do or say anything I'll regret." Lenny jumped up and moved to kiss Pagne. "Don't touch her… you've done enough touching tonight. Go, go now!" Lenny backed out of the kitchen and ran out the front door. "Pagne, you and I will talk at nine o'clock. I need you to go to bed and let me wrap my head around all of this."

"Yes, Sir," she said as she slipped out of the kitchen and ran upstairs.

Brent looked at Grandma Maxine and said, "How did this happen?"

"Now, Brent, I know this is a shock."

"I thought there would be a wedding. All our family, friends. I would be able to walk her down the aisle."

"Yes, son, I know you are disappointed. I was, too, when you and Pam eloped." Brent looked at his mother. He had forgotten that they had also eloped. They had only known each other for six months. They were nineteen, only a year older than Pagne and Lenny. He sat down, worn out. "When I asked you why, you said it was the right thing for you and Pam. You were sorry but you were ready to start your lives together. Remember that, son?"

"Yes," he said dully.

"Now, I know they are young, but you've known for a long time that they are each other's half, just like you and Pam were."

"I hate it that you're right, mom." He began to chuckle and then howl.

"You should have seen his face, Mom. I must have scared him into next week!"

Grandma Maxine sat down next to him and stroked his hair. "They'll be fine, son. We can't make it easy on them but we do need to be supportive. They have a long road ahead of them. To be honest, I'm glad Lenny will be with her on her journey. He's a good boy, man, no, manboy. Oh crap, what are they at this age?"

"Got me, Mom. Let's get some sleep. I'm not letting Lenny off the hook just yet. I'm gonna enjoy tomorrow." Grandma Maxine laughed as she headed upstairs. "Mom?"

She turned to Brent, "Yes, son?"

"I'm sorry you got cheated out of a wedding."

She smiled. "I'm just glad you gave me Pam."

"Thanks for being here. I couldn't have made it alone these last four years."

"You would have, son, but I'm glad I was here to help."

~

The next morning, Brent was sitting in the family room waiting for Pagne. She came in and he motioned for her to have a seat. He had a tray on the coffee table with toasted English muffins and fruit. Pagne's stomach was in knots and she decided to pass on eating. "Well, Mrs. Lenny Wilson."

"No, Mrs. Pagne Wilson," she corrected. Brent smiled slightly.

"My mother reminded me last night that I also got caught up in love and eloped with your mother." Pagne relaxed just a bit and thought about how much she loved Grandma Maxine. "But we didn't lie about it or keep it a secret. We were proud of our love and wanted everyone to know."

"We're proud, too. We just didn't know how mad you might get and wanted to..."

"Avoid the consequences?" Brent finished. Pagne hated that observation.

"Well, yes."

"You know marriage is for adults and if you don't behave as adults, it won't be a successful relationship." Pagne felt her face warming. "You've decided you are a grown woman and ready for marriage and I cannot legally do anything. I will honor your decision but I am not comfortable with Lenny living here with you. So... you can each stay where you're at or you can move in with Lenny."

"Dad, there isn't room there."

"Then fine, you can continue to live here. You need to inform the mission organizer that you two are married so they can make appropriate arrangements. You certainly don't want to live separately for the summer." Pagne grinned and then caught his stern look. The smile immediately melted. "I had planned on an allowance to help you while you were in college but that was for you as a single, young woman working part-time. I have decided to assist you for the first year but, after that, you and Lenny will need to support yourselves. After all, you are adults."

Pagne picked up a muffin and began to pick at it. "Dad, I'm really sorry that you weren't at the wedding."

"Was Elvis there?" Pagne shyly looked up and saw Brent smiling and grinned.

"No, we both agreed that Elvis was not invited. But the justice-of-the- peace did have a turban." Brent looked amused.

"Seriously?"

"Oh yeah, you should've seen the neon Cupid!" She caught herself and looked at him, hoping her words didn't sting.

"It's okay, Pagne. I want to hear all about it." Pagne told him all the gory details, not the honeymoon, but everything else. They laughed and Brent shared his own Vegas horror story while they ate muffins and fruit. "This is personal, Pagne, but are you two taking precautions so you don't get pregnant before you're ready?" Pagne didn't know how he would feel about it but, she wasn't going to lie to him anymore.

"Yes, Dad. I went to the clinic and got started on birth control."

"Good girl, hon. Don't get me wrong. I will love being a grandpa but not yet, okay? Give me some time to adjust to Lenny as my son." Pagne looked into his eyes and was thankful for him.

"You got it, Dad."

They heard the doorbell ring. It was ten o'clock on the dot. "Head upstairs, Pagne. I get a little satisfaction before we let him off the hook."

"Okay, Dad, but remember, I do love him and he will be the father of your grandchildren."

"When you put it that way, okay," agreed Brent, reluctantly.

Brent extended his hand as he opened the door. "Mr. Wilson, lovely to see you again, with your pants on," said Brent as he jerked Lenny into the house, closing the door behind him. Lenny saw Pagne at the top of the stairs and gave her a pleading look.

"Good luck," she mouthed and slipped into her room, shutting the door behind her. Brent escorted Lenny to a chair and helped him sit with a firm hand.

~

"So you are man enough to be married to my daughter? Let's talk, son, man to man." Brent left Lenny hanging as he stared him in the eyes. When Lenny had squirmed sufficiently for Brent, he was angry but not cruel, he continued. "How are you going to provide for my daughter? I'm really interested in your plans."

For the next hour or so, Pagne paced in her room. She couldn't hear anything coming up from the living room. That could be good, no screaming, crashing, or banging. Or, it could be bad. She cracked open the door and could hear laughing. She ventured out on the landing.

"It's okay, hon, you can come down. We've cleaned up the blood." As she made her way down the stairs, she saw two men she dearly loved waiting for her.

Grandma Maxine and the kids arrived back from errands as Pagne reached the living room.

"I've got pizza," Grandma Maxine announced.

Brent kissed Pagne on the head and shouted, "Who's hungry? I'm starving. Here's a tasty morsel." He swooped Amanda up and gave her belly-boppers, which made her to laugh. Pagne looked at Lenny, "You okay?" She asked.

"Fine, you've got a great dad."

"Yep, I do. We'll talk later, okay?" Lenny nodded in agreement. They all moved into the kitchen.

Brent held up a piece of pizza and said, "We are celebrating today. Lenny is now part of the family. He and Pagne are married." Richie looked dumbfounded, Amanda was happy to celebrate anything, and Pagne could breathe again.

Between school and living at home while being married, the next few weeks were surreal. Lenny spent every free moment he could at the Masters. His mother had come for dinner to celebrate their marriage. She was happy for them but she was also concerned about how young they were.

One evening, they were all sprawled on the family-room floor, watching movies. It was almost one o'clock in the morning when the last movie was over. Lenny had fallen asleep on the floor, his head in Pagne's lap. Brent looked at the time and suggested that Pagne wake Lenny and have him head home. Lenny was groggy but he obediently got up. Pagne walked him to the front door where they held each other. Brent could hear Pagne assuring Lenny. "Soon, baby, soon! We'll be together soon." Brent remembered his passion for Pam and the ache he felt when they were apart. How much it meant to wake up next to her.

"Okay, you guys, Lenny can stay tonight, but no… no nothing. I better not hear anything." Pagne looked at her dad in surprise. "Get going before I change my mind. Lenny, call your mom so she doesn't worry where you are." Pagne and Lenny ran up the stairs to her room.

"I don't believe it," Pagne said as she shut the door. Lenny seemed to be in shock as well.

"He's not going to come in and check on us is he?"

Pagne giggled, "I don't think so, but keep your boxers on just in case." Pagne changed into discreet pjs and they curled up next to each other on the twin bed. It was cramped, but cozy. "We should just go to sleep. It feels weird with dad knowing you're in here."

"Oh, trust me, Pagne. The last thing I'm feeling is romantic." They spooned each other and quickly fell asleep. Brent tried not to listen but found it difficult not to. He finally drifted off to a fitful sleep. In his dreams, he was trying to find Pam; he could hear her calling him, but he couldn't find her.

There was only one week left of school and then another week before they left for Mexico. The pastor was disappointed that they had not been married in the church but he congratulated the young couple. They changed their room accommodations for Mexico to accommodate their marital status. Brent and Grandma Maxine decided to give them a romantic honeymoon the weekend before they left as a wedding/graduation gift. They reserved a gorgeous room in Monterey. They would graduate on Thursday and then head to Monterey on Friday morning. In the card, they had tickets for the aquarium and a whale-watching cruise. Lenny's mom had contributed some spending cash. Pagne and Lenny were thrilled with their gift. The weekend would be heavenly but it was more important that their parents had honored their marriage. The next two weeks flew by and Brent decided to let Lenny stay with them. They moved the two twin beds together and put a foam pad on top. It was wonderful having Lenny with her. They learned to be very discreet if they did enjoy each other physically. No one was embarrassed or uncomfortable, not even Brent.

They finally got a call from Bree. She managed to call for Pagne's graduation and was blown away when they told her about the marriage. Pagne and Bree talked privately for a few minutes and Pagne came back wiping away tears. "You okay?" asked Lenny and Brent at the same moment. They looked at each other as if challenging each other for possession of Pagne. Brent decided to back down and Lenny put his hand on Pagne's shoulder.

"Yeah, she's happy for us but very disappointed that she wasn't here. I think she is missing home really bad and feels left out of everything."

"It's hard," Grandma Maxine admitted. "Moving away from home is a big change."

The morning they were to leave, Brent found it difficult to say goodbye to another daughter. "You guys need to get to the church," Grandma Maxine prodded.

"We'll be back soon, Dad. We can call and email." Pagne said.

"Okay, let's go," Lenny urged. They were leaving Lenny's car at the house so Brent drove them and their luggage to the church. The buses were getting ready to leave and they had to load up and say a quick goodbye. Pagne watched Brent waving until he was a tiny speck.

Chapter 17

The bus ride down to Mexico was so much fun. They sang and told jokes and played the humming game. One person hummed part of a song and everyone else tried to guess what it was. They lovingly teased Pagne when it was her turn. She just could not hum. The vibration tickled her lips so bad, she would start laughing and wasn't able to get enough of the melody hummed for the others to make a guess.

Pagne was excited to be heading into Mexico. She wanted to make a difference and knew this was a journey she would never forget. Most of them thought Pagne and Lenny were kidding about being married and it took Pastor Tim to convince them it was true. They all congratulated them and wanted to know the details. Pagne and Lenny were the center of attention as they described their infamous wedding night in Vegas. They crossed the border into Mexico after six hours of driving but it would take several more hours before they reached the orphanage where they would be helping out. The group had brought tents and camping gear because the facility didn't have any extra space for them.

It was early evening when they pulled in. It was the first mission trip for many of the team and they were not sure what to expect. The buses came to a stop at an open field area, which was where they would set up camp. The guys piled out and started the process of erecting a small village. Pagne and the other ladies pulled out the food and kitchen gear. They had brought a large tent for the kitchen and dining area and it was the first tent to be set up. It had screened panels to let in the breeze but keep out the bugs. Pagne was impressed with how organized everything was. In two hours, they were pretty much done and ready to move into their assigned tents. Pagne and Lenny were thrilled to see that a small tent had been designated just for them. Lenny had a goofy grin when he inflated their full-sized airbed. After everyone had settled in, they met in the center of their community and Pastor Tim explained the basics for the first-timers. There was a shower and bathroom building by the orphanage that they could use. He restated the clothing restrictions for the women. It was a different culture and what was normal back home had different meanings in this remote part of Mexico. There would be no shorts. Capris were okay. No exposed tummies, no bra straps showing and no low-cut tanks. Modest attire was required at all times.

They were served a simple dinner of sandwiches, chips, and fruit. After everyone had eaten and cleaned up, they were escorted to the orphanage. Pagne was excited to meet the kids. The caretaker of the orphanage was a short, stout man with a full head of black, curly hair and he reminded Pagne of a circus ringmaster. He was very animated and had a big white smile. She liked him instantly. His name was Mr. Jose Sanchez. He gave them a short history of the facility and his history as the caretaker. He and his wife, Lucinda, had been there for ten years. She was assisting the staff with the smaller children's showers but would meet with them shortly.

Mr. Sanchez began the tour by showing them the community areas where the children had tables and bookcases holding games, books, and paper for drawing. Pagne hadn't expected everything to be so worn and used. There was peeling paint, broken chairs, and rickety tables piled in a corner. The room was dingy and hardly a place you would expect to see children. The tour continued to the dining area, which was much brighter and more recently painted. There were several murals on the walls of angels and Jesus, which brought charm to the room. The kitchen was clean but Pagne could see that everything was old and needed to be replaced. They went outside into a partially enclosed play area but there hadn't been enough money to finish so the remaining fence was a combination of scrap plywood, cyclone wire, and anything else they could find. There were a few toys in the yard but the playground was pitifully stark. There weren't any plants, just gravel mixed with dirt. While the men made notes about the yard project, Lucinda joined them and Jose introduced her. Lucinda explained the needs of the children and then everyone left the orphanage to go back to their area. Pagne was disappointed that they didn't get to meet the kids but, it was after nine o'clock and the children were in bed.

Back at the camp, they sat around a fire pit that burned brightly. Pastor Tim explained the schedule of projects that they would need to address. One team would finish the fencing and the play area, which they would furnish with donated riding toys and a gym set. Another group would paint the common area and repair the furniture. Several of the members of this team were wonderful artists and they would do a large mural in that area, something fun and colorful.

Each year, the mission group tackled new projects for the facility. They had completed the dining area and the roof the year before. This year, they brought an electrician to inspect and repair some wiring issues. Pagne's group would be working directly with the children. They planned a program full of arts and crafts, music, and Bible classes. Dr. Paul Martin had come with them to assist with shots, exams, and general medical needs. He would only be there for the first week. Pagne was impressed that he donated a week of his time and supplies every year. The group had also brought boxes of donated clothing, shoes, and personal items for the children. Jose and Lucinda ran the facility on the generosity of churches because they received very little funding through the government in their area. The community was extremely poor and many children were abandoned at the orphanage to ensure they had a warm bed and food. Pagne thought it was sad that parents had to make such a painful decision.

After several songs of worship under the stars and by the crackling fire, Pastor Tim prayed for their safety and that God would give them the ability to accomplish much. It was time to get some sleep. They would be starting early in the morning. Pagne checked the schedule for kitchen duty on the way to her tent. She was relieved that she wasn't scheduled until Wednesday breakfast. The breakfast crew had to be up an hour earlier than everyone else. Lenny and Pagne crawled onto the airbed and were surprised at how comfortable it was. They curled up and Pagne drifted off to sleep. She could feel Lenny getting familiar with her but soon he was snoring. She was relieved. Sleep was all she had on her mind.

The next morning, Lenny and Pagne were up early and headed over to the breakfast tent. They grabbed a plateful of delicious food and ate quickly. Lenny was working with the playground team and, because he was such a big kid, Pagne knew he would love it. Pagne found her group and they used a cart to bring all the art supplies into the biggest tent, filled with lots of tables and kid-sized chairs borrowed from the facility. Because they would be painting the children's common room, they had decided it would be easier than trying to keep the kids away from the wet walls. Besides, they wanted the mural to be a surprise. Pagne was excited to be here and laying out the materials for their first day.

Their program was supposed to start at nine o'clock but, when she stepped outside at eight thirty, there was already a long line of children. She was impressed by how polite they were as they stood quietly in a straight line. The youngest children were first, then the girls, then the boys. Jose insisted on this order out of respect. When it was time to begin, Lucinda joined them to help with translation. Several other members of their group could speak fluent Spanish but most, like Pagne, understood very little. The children filed in and quietly found a seat. Pagne could feel the energy. They were ready to burst with excitement, but maintained themselves. Lucinda introduced Pagne's team and explained the day's activities. They would begin with crafts, then lunch, followed by Bible study and then games. The kids clapped with joy, which made Pagne feel very welcomed and appreciated.

Every day was a blessing and Pagne didn't know who was having more fun, the kids or her team. Lenny was buffing out, which Pagne really liked and his body was lean, muscular, and tan. Pagne had to be very careful with her fair skin but she did manage a golden glow. They worked hard through the week and played even harder with the kids on Saturday. Sunday mornings they went to Jose's local church and Sunday evenings the teams had their own service under the stars. Pagne loved the evenings because she felt like the Heavens were open and looking down on them. Several members of their group had brought musical instruments, which made their worship time sweet and intimate.

Lenny and Pagne shared many private moments but exhaustion from the day's work usually meant snuggling, giggling, and short back scratches and massages. They didn't mind because they were together and felt no pressure from each other to perform.

Pagne soon realized that some of the kids were drawn to her. Several had deformities and they would touch Pagne's arm and then their own bodies. They had developed a kinship with her and they would follow Pagne wherever she went. On Saturday mornings, they would sit in view of her tent, waiting for her come out. She frequently had one child on each side, holding her hands. Sophie and Elanna were their names. Sophie was five and Elanna was seven. Elanna was very small for her age and had a deformed leg that was shorter than the other. The difference caused a twist in her spine. Pagne asked Jose about lifts but they had nothing available except for a wooden block attached to the shorter leg. It was very cumbersome and Elanna would remove it as soon as no one was watching. They had eventually stopped forcing her to wear it. Sophie had been burned. She had an alcoholic father who passed out while smoking in bed. He was lost in the fire and Sophie had been burned on the right side of her head and face, down her shoulder, and onto her upper arm. Her hair had grown back in patches on her burned scalp. She had not received the appropriate medical treatment and the scarring was lumpy, much worse than Pagne's rippled arm. Pagne fell in love with these little girls. Lenny gave them turns riding on his shoulders and spinning with them until they were dizzy. They giggled and begged for more.

As the summer progressed, they completed their projects and took on other, smaller ones that needed done. They planted fruit trees around the buildings so the kids would have fresh fruit and shade on hot afternoons. On a particularly hot day, several of the team members went into the larger town close by and rented a water truck. They attached hoses and the kids played in the sprays of cold water. The adults and teens soon found themselves running and getting soaked with the kids. It was a special treat because water was expensive and usually not available for play.

The trip was nearing the end and Pagne was not looking forward to leaving the kids, especially her two little shadows, Sophie and Elanna. The playground, the common room, and the mural were done. The volunteers were blessed by the excitement and joy of the children and the staff. Their last week was a mixture of sightseeing and free time with the kids. Payne missed her family and the conveniences of her life in California but a part of her would remain here in Mexico when she left.

The day came when it was time to pack up. Elanna and Sophie sat off under some brush and watched as the tents came down and the suitcases and supplies were loaded into the vehicles. There were only three buses sitting in the clearing when they had finished. Pagne came over and sat between the girls. While sightseeing, she had bought each of the little girls a silver locket. Inside each locket was a picture of her on one side and a picture she had taken of each one of them on the other side. They were thrilled with their gifts and, when it was time to go, Pagne kissed each one on the cheek and stood up. She had taken a few steps away when she felt them come up behind her and wrap their little arms around her legs. How am I going to walk away from them? she thought. Lenny came to her rescue. He smiled at the girls and offered Elanna a ride on his shoulders. She reached up for him and Pagne picked up Sophie. They carried them over to where Jose and Lucinda were saying goodbye to Pastor Tim. "Think you might want these," Lenny joked. "If not, we'll take them with us." They reached out and took the girls in their arms.

"We'll keep them here for you until next year," Jose said, with an appreciative smile. "Pagne, you have no idea how much your sweetness and compassion has meant to these girls."

Pastor Tim looked at Elanna's leg. "I'll let you know what I can find out."

"Thank you Pastor Tim. Do you have the measurements?" asked Lucinda.

"Yes, right here in my wallet," he responded as he patted his pocket.

"We're going to take the girls back to the facility now. I think that is best," Jose said.

"Okay," said Pagne. She kissed each girl once more and headed to the bus with Lenny and Pastor Tim.

"What was that about?" Lenny asked Pastor Tim.

"Oh, I'm going to see if I can get a doctor to donate a support shoe for Elanna. If she doesn't get her legs even, she may not be able to walk soon," he explained. Pagne slipped up next to Pastor Tim and hugged him.

"Thank you," she said.

"No problem."

The drive home was long and everyone was exhausted. The lull of driving made everyone sleepy. It had been a life-altering summer. Pagne knew she would not look at her life and her blessings the same way again. She curled into Lenny and started to drift off to sleep. "Oh yeah, Lucinda said if I write to the girls, she will translate."

"That's good, baby," he agreed sleepily. Soon they would be home. Pagne thought she knew what to expect when they returned, but she didn't have a clue.

They rolled into the church parking lot very late that night. They still had to unload the buses. Many of the parents were there to pick up their kids and help with the unloading. It went much quicker than the loading had. Brent was there with Amanda. Pagne was thrilled to see them but was disappointed that Richie wasn't with them. She had so much to tell him and she'd gotten him several items for his room. When Pagne asked about him, Brent made a vague excuse and Pagne felt strongly that something was up. She would wait to get her dad alone to ask. Pagne wasn't sure if Lenny was going home with them or if they were dropping him off at his mom's apartment. When Brent made a left on Pagne's street rather than a right, she knew she would be with Lenny. She found herself pulling him closer to her.

When they got to the house, Pagne and Lenny grabbed their bags and headed up to Pagne's room. Pagne looked toward Richie's room and saw that the door had been patched, which seemed odd. She looked at Lenny and he just shrugged. Brent was getting Amanda ready for bed and she literally passed out as he put her PJs on. Brent was heading downstairs when Pagne came into the hall. "What happened to Richie's door?" she asked. Brent hesitated and brought his hands to his head. A sure tell that he was upset. "Dad, what's wrong?"

"Richie got mad and punched it." Pagne looked at him in disbelief. "I'm really struggling with how to handle him, Pagne. His mood swings are getting worse and worse." Pagne took her dad by the hand, led him into his office, and shut the door.

"Is Richie in his room?" she asked.

"No, he went out with his friends and hasn't come back yet." Pagne was surprised.

"But, isn't it past his curfew?"

"Yes, I was just heading out with the car to look for him."

"Dad, why didn't you say anything when we talked over the summer?"

"Oh, hon, you were all the way down there. What were you going to do?"

"I could have talked to him, threatened him."

"Pagne, he has changed. I don't think you could have said or done anything more than what your grandma and I have done." Pagne sat down, trying to picture Richie as this belligerent kid. He was thirteen now and big for his age. He could present a physical challenge if he wanted to.

"Can I ride with you? I'd like to help look for him."

"Pagne, you've had a long day. You need to get some sleep." Suddenly, they heard a smashing sound in the family room. They ran in and found Richie sitting on the floor, laughing hysterically. He had come through the French doors and knocked the lamp off the end table. It lay shattered on the floor.

"Ooppps," he said and rolled onto his knees, trying to stand up. He realized that his dad was standing there. "Hey, Pop. Sorry about the lamp." He was on his hands and knees still trying to stand.

"Pagne, please go upstairs." Pagne saw anger in her dad's face that she had never seen before. It scared her to think what could happen if he unleashed it. He grabbed Richie by the back of his shirt and yanked him up with such force that Richie's feet cleared the floor for a minute. "Are you drunk, Richie, or high?" He asked with controlled rage.

"Well, Pops, I'd say a little of both, want some?" He pulled a baggie full of pills from his jean pocket. Brent snatched the bag with his free hand. "Hey, those are mine." Richie yelled. He swung and almost clipped Brent in the face. Brent threw him down on the couch and insisted that Pagne go up to her husband. By then, Lenny had heard the scuffle and was standing in the doorway to the family room.

"Mr. Masters, you can't reach him right now. He won't remember anything tomorrow."

"Guess you know more about this than I would," Brent said.

"Let me help you get him to bed, Mr. Masters. He needs to sleep it off." Brent moved to take one of Richie's arms and Lenny took the other. They lifted him and half-walked, half-dragged him across the room. When they reached Pagne, Richie focused enough to see her face. "Ohhh, Pagne, you're back. Missed you, sis," and then proceeded to throw up all over the front of her.

They got Richie wiped down and into bed while Pagne showered and changed and then they met downstairs. Brent had cleaned the vomit up off the floor. He was sitting with his elbows on his knees and his head in his hands. "When did this start?" Pagne asked.

"Almost as soon as you left. He started giving Mom a hard time and wouldn't do his chores or spend time with us. I'd talk to him, try to reason, reward, and then punish. He didn't care. He wanted to sleep all day and be up all night on the computer or out with his friends. I took away his phone and put blocks on the internet. He stopped bringing his friends over and he always wanted to go to their house. I found out these kids had parents that allowed them a lot more freedom than I was comfortable with. I suspected that he was drinking and maybe experimenting with pot, but never caught him."

Lenny picked up the bag of pills. The pills were different shapes and colors. Lenny explained, "These look like prescription pills. Kids go through the family's medicine cabinets and snatch whatever they can. They throw them in a bowl and divide them up. They just randomly take a few or a lot."

"But, that is so dangerous," said Brent. "They don't know what they are taking or combining. That's insane."

"Yep, but it's happening a lot. They just don't understand how certain pills can be deadly when combined with others. It's that 'I'm invincible' thing we kids have. Plus, they've usually been drinking, too, so their thinking is blurred and they want to fit in with the other kids that are doing it."

Pagne moved next to Brent and sat close to him. "Dad, Richie's not stupid. I think we can explain some things to him tomorrow." Brent looked at Pagne.

"I don't know, Pagne. It feels like we've lost him."

"He's not lost, Dad. He's just confused." Pagne was exhausted and it showed on her face. It was almost one a.m.

"Sweetheart," Lenny said, "go on up to bed. I'll be there shortly. I want to talk to your dad for a few minutes." Pagne didn't want to be left out but she saw Lenny urging her with his eyes.

"Okay," Pagne left the room and headed upstairs. She heard Lenny speaking softly, "Mr. Masters, there's some things you gotta understand…" She closed the door and fell onto the bed, asleep before she hit the pillow.

"… drugs and alcohol take over your mind. From what you're describing, I think Richie is in pretty deep. For him to be so cocky, he has a strong bond with those friends and feels very connected. Family isn't important. The high is first and his friends come second. I think you gotta do something quick, before it's too late."

"I'm not sure what to do," Brent admitted.

"Can't solve nothing tonight. We can figure it out in the morning. Trust me. We have time. Richie won't be awake before noon, if then. Mr. Masters, I think it really messed Richie up when Pam died. I think he stuffed a lot of garbage deep down. You might also want to get those pills checked out." Brent hadn't even thought about that. "You gotta lock up any pills or booze and lots of kids huff the propellant in canned whipped cream." The list was growing. Brent had never experimented with drugs and was naive about the threats in his own home.

"Lenny, did you do these things?" Lenny looked down, embarrassed to admit that he had.

"Yes, there was a time, before Pagne, that I wanted to be numb. I would take or try anything that was around. I didn't have money for street drugs so I experimented with what I could find. Kids share their ideas and pills they find; it grows from there. Parents trust their kids and leave pills and stuff lying around."

"Weren't you worried about dying?" Lenny looked into Mr. Masters eyes and thought back.

"No, I actually hoped I would die. My life was so screwed up, I would fanaticize that the other side could be incredible or maybe I'd come back to a better life or just not exist anymore at all. I really didn't have anything that tied me here but, Pagne changed that. She showed me the good things in life. This is not a phase that Richie's going through, sir. We have to deal with him now."

"Okay, let's try and sleep and we'll figure out a plan in the morning," Brent suggested. Lenny headed upstairs as Brent headed into his office and new bedroom. Because Richie was getting older, Brent had converted his office into a bedroom of sorts. He turned to catch Lenny before he went into their room.

"Lenny," Brent said quietly.

"Yes Sir?" Lenny responded.

"You think he's okay. Should we take him to the emergency room?" Lenny stepped up close to Richie's bedroom door and listened. He heard strong, steady snoring.

"He'll be fine. You might want to check on him now and then if you're worried. His throwing up was actually a good thing." Lenny turned again toward the bedroom and Pagne.

"Lenny, can you do me a favor?"

Lenny stopped and responded, "Sure."

"Please call me, Dad. After all, you are my son now."

Lenny grinned, "Sure, Sir. I'd like that. Goodnight Sir… Dad."

"Goodnight, son," Brent said with warmth and a deep sadness.

Brent couldn't sleep so he headed to the kitchen and opened the pantry. There was a box of medication on the shelf. They had cleared it out of the master bathroom when Grandma Maxine moved in. Brent had put all of the medicines in this box with the intention of going through them, but like so many things, it was forgotten. Pam had been on so many pills during the pregnancy and many were pain pills. Brent turned on the overhead kitchen light and set the bag of pills on the counter. He couldn't identify most of them, but quite a few matched the pills in the box. Pam's pain pill containers were empty and Brent saw the medications to thicken her uterine wall, pills for nausea, pre-natal vitamins, sleeping pills, and antibiotics in the plastic bag. Richie had been taking from everything in the box.

Brent sat down on a stool, overwhelmed by the dangerous behavior his son was engaging in. He realized they would need to check his mom's medications in the morning. Brent knew she had pain pills and blood-pressure pills and didn't even want to consider how dangerous her drugs could be to a young boy, especially if he was combining them with God-knows-what. Brent took all the pills and poured them in the garbage disposal, turned on the water, and annihilated them. He also checked the fridge for whipped cream cans. There was one partially empty can, which he also emptied in the sink. Brent could remember wondering why the propellant always ran out before the cream was gone and he cringed at his naivety.

They didn't keep much alcohol in the house, mainly wine for cooking. They liked a particular one and Brent would buy it by the case and store it on the bottom shelf of the pantry. He pulled the brand new case out, which had been purchased only a few weeks ago. *It should be full,* Brent calculated. His heart sank when it slid out easily and there were only a few bottles left, nine of the twelve were gone. Brent opened and poured the three remaining bottles out. As he watched the red wine run into the sink and down the drain, he ached for Pam. She would know what to do. He was tired of making all the decisions, dealing with the kids' problems and needs. He was drained and felt such anger. Feelings of abandonment began to swell up inside of him. Why did God let her die? He wanted to believe in this loving Father but, this Father had allowed the love of his life to be ripped from him. He sank to the floor and sobbed. He couldn't do this, not without her.

Brent felt aching in his back and hips. He opened his eyes and saw the kitchen island in front of him. He had fallen asleep on the kitchen floor and he didn't know how long he'd slept. He stood up and went to his office. He grabbed any pain pills and cold or cough medicines and locked them in the desk drawer. He would find a better way to store them tomorrow or this morning, whenever he got up. He collapsed on the twin bed and passed out. His dreams returned to Pam and he thought he could smell her or at least he smelled something.

Sunlight came too soon. Brent smelled coffee and knew his mother was up. He went into the kitchen and gave her a kiss on the cheek. "Morning, Mom."

She faced him with a perplexed look on her face. "What happened in here last night?" she asked. She indicated the empty bottles of wine and the whipped cream. "You guys had a party?"

"Definitely not a party."

"You sure?" she pointed to the front of the cabinets on the island. "I washed off vomit."

"Oh, Mom, sorry, I thought we cleaned everything up. Richie threw up last night, all over Pagne."

"Is he sick?" She looked up toward his room with concern.

"No, Mom, he was drunk." Grandma Maxine's face fell.

"Drunk, that can't be, not our Richie!"

"Worse than that, Mom. He's been stealing medications from the house and inhaling propellants. That's why I dumped out the last of the wine and whipped cream. There were only three bottles of wine left in a full case. Richie drank the other nine." Brent could see the color drain out of her face.

"We would have known."

"No, Mom, we wouldn't. Our thinking just didn't go there. He's been very careful until last night."

"Well, looking back, this explains some of his behavior."

"Yes, it does. Mom, I need you to check your medicines and see if any match the pills in this bag." He handed Richie's bag to her. She fingered the bag and stared in disbelief at all the different pills. "Some are Pam's medications. I think the others are from his friends' houses." Grandma Maxine was now turning angry.

"I'll be right back." She took the bag upstairs. She quickly came back down and slammed three bottles on the counter with the bag. "My pain pills, blood pressure pills, and hormone pills are in here. Most of my pain pills are gone and I just filled them three days ago." She handed him the bottle. "What is he thinking?"

"He's not, Mom." She sat down and Brent saw the confusion and fear on her face.

"We need to lock up all the medicines, including the over the counter stuff. No alcohol or whipped cream cans in the house."

"Okay, but I hate the frozen cream in a tub!" Brent was amazed that he was able to grin at her.

"Me too, Mom, me too."

"Okay, son. I'll see if there's anything I can flush." She took her coffee and the pill bottles back upstairs. Brent picked up the bag and slipped it into his pocket. He poured himself a cup of coffee and went to his computer to surf the web for information. Shortly, he heard Pagne, Lenny, and Amanda get up. Brent could hear Pagne giving Amanda some of the highlights of their trip while she poured cereal for the three of them. When he came in, they were all sitting at the counter with mouths full of popped grain and milk. When Lenny looked up, Brent nodded to the wine bottles and the whipped cream can. Lenny nodded and ate faster. Brent heard several flushes of the toilet in the master bathroom. His mother came back down.

"Mom, Mandy is going to start kindergarten soon and we haven't done any shopping for school clothes, you think you could take her? If she wants to that is." He looked at Amanda, now five, knowing that her favorite thing in the world was to shop.

"Of course, dear. Finish up, Mandy and then get dressed. Let's get an early start before all the cute stuff is gone!"

"Okay, Grandma." She gulped down the rest of her cereal and ran up to her room. Bree, Pagne, and Grandma Maxine had converted the nursery into a little girl's room several years ago. It was all pink and girlie, just like Mandy.

"Thanks, Mom. I think it could get intense here today and I don't want Mandy upset."

"You're right, dear. There's a new movie out. We can go see that after lunch. That should give you plenty of time to deal with Richie." He kissed the top of her head and handed her a credit card.

"There's still room on this one," he teased.

"Won't be for long," she teased back as she picked up her purse and keys.

Brent made some toast and took Mandy's seat while he crunched. "I went online earlier and there are so many opinions: counseling, hospitalization, and boot camp. How do we know what he needs?"

"Well, I think confrontation is first. He needs to know that we know and that he can't continue without interference."

"I really think this is a symptom of the pain he is stuffing down," said Brent, thoughtfully.

"Me too," agreed Pagne.

"His moods have become darker and longer. He's always had shifts but not like now. His music and his friends seem to be his only focus," shared Brent. "He is so talented but the songs he writes are very dark and sinister. I thought it was just what kids like now, like a fad, but I think it reveals more than I ever dreamed."

"Let's see what happens when he has to face the truth," offered Lenny. "That should give us an idea of how serious this is. It might just be a cry for help and he wants us to intervene or he has crossed into a very dangerous place and we'll have to get tough."

"You are too wise for your young age, son. I'm sorry your life has made it necessary."

"Thanks, Dad, but I'm kinda glad now, if it helps Richie." Pagne grinned at Lenny and her dad.

Brent realized he hadn't even asked the kids about their trip. As they were telling him about the kids and their summer, they heard Richie stirring in his room. They heard him trip and curse, then a toilet flush. "Want us to stay?" asked Pagne.

"Yes, I think we need to deal with this as a family." Brent didn't want to admit that he didn't want to be alone. He had no clue what to expect and he trusted Lenny's instincts. A few minutes later, they heard Richie coming down the stairs, belching as he came into the kitchen.

"Hey, Peeps," he dully said. He went over to Pagne and gave her a token hug. "You guys get in last night?" He went to the fridge and pulled out a jug of OJ and began to down it. He realized no one had said a word so he set the jug down and looked at the somber group. "Someone die?" he asked.

"Not quite, but almost," said Brent. "We need to talk." Richie closed the fridge and took a defensive stance, arms crossed over his chest, leaning against the counter.

"What's up, Pop?" Brent threw the bag of pills on the island counter in front of Richie.

"You tell me," he demanded.

"Oh, crap!" slipped from Richie before he could catch himself. "Hey, Dad, those aren't mine. I was holding them for a friend. He's got allergies and stuff. I forgot to give them back." Brent was fuming.

"Don't lie, Richie, most of those pills came from our house." Richie looked at each one of them, trying to size up how much they knew.

"Okay, you got me, but I didn't take any yet. I was curious and it was stupid." Brent shook his head, amazed at how easily Richie could lie to them while looking them in the eye.

"Do you remember last night?"

"No, I had a couple of beers with some friends. I'm not used to drinking so it hit me hard. I made it home okay though, woke up in my bed. Couldn't have been too drunk." He turned to make some toast. "You don't need to worry, Dad. I learned my lesson."

"Shut up, Richie, just shut up. Everything out of your mouth is a lie." Richie turned around sharply, looking shocked at the level of anger in Brent's voice. He stood there, frozen.

"Let me tell you what happened last night, son. You came in here stumbling drunk, knocked over a lamp, showed me these pills, and then threw up all over your sister. Your puke contained the distinct odor of scotch and half-dissolved pills. I know because I was on my knees cleaning up your vomit. Lenny and I drug your butt into the bathroom, washed the stench off of you, and put you in your bed. Now you want to tell me again how you had only two beers? Oh yeah, let's discuss all the missing pills and wine and why the whipped cream never has any gas." Richie flashed an angry glare at Lenny. He knew his dad wouldn't know all of this without Lenny's input. Lenny didn't react and kept a hard stare. Richie looked away.

"Dad, I don't know what you think you know, but..."

"Stop, Richie. I'm sure that what I know is just the tip of the iceberg. You've fooled me for a long time and it stops today."

Richie's anger was churning and boiling. He felt his face flush red and the rage overtook him. "Okay, okay, you know so much. Who are you to tell me what to do? This is my life and I'll do what I want. You have Mandy, Pagne has Lenny, and it's just me. It has always been just me. My friends get me. They let me be myself." He headed to the French doors. "I don't need this aggravation." Lenny jumped up and stood between Richie and the door.

"You're not leaving," Brent said firmly. "You're a minor and I say where you go."

"Fine, Dad. I've never done Langston Hall. Why don't we give that a shot. I hear it comes highly recommended." He shot a glaring look at Pagne.

Brent moved to Richie and spun him around. "That's crap, Richie. We've all been here for you. You're not putting this on us."

"Oh, Dad. I've screwed up so bad. I'm so sorry." Richie leaned against Brent and sobbed. Brent put his arms around Richie and looked at Lenny. Then the "dad" part of him kicked in and he soothed Richie. Pagne joined them in a hug but Lenny kept his distance while shaking his head in disbelief.

"I love you so much, Richie. You know we're here for you," Pagne said.

"I know. I really do. I just forgot."

Brent decided that counseling would be the place to start. He contacted Miss Renee and she recommended a counselor that dealt with teens and drug abuse. Mr. Ramsey had a cancellation for the next day. Brent bought into Richie's display of regret and dispair along with Pagne. They spent most of the afternoon and evening trying to cheer Richie up by displaying their love and affection for him. Pagne even suggested they watch Star Wars, which was Richie's replacement for Batman after Pam died. Richie put on a tender face and said he would really like that. They had a very lovely evening. Grandma Maxine and Mandy returned home with Chinese take-out for dinner. It was a lovely picture of a happy family. Richie even managed to cry when he apologized to Grandma Maxine for stealing from her. Lenny was the only one who refused to buy into Richie's performance.

When the movie was over, Mandy had fallen asleep and Brent carried her upstairs. Richie stretched and stood. "I'm exhausted. This has been a really emotional day. I'm sorry that I worried all of you", he lied. "I love you." With that, he headed up to his room, relieved that the act could come to an end. Brent met him on the stairs.

"Love you, son," he said as he hugged him.

"Love you too, Dad. I'm really sorry," he lied again.

"We can fix this, son. You're not alone." Brent came back downstairs, sat on the couch, and let himself sink in. Grandma Maxine said goodnight and headed upstairs. Brent grinned at Lenny and Pagne. "This is going much better than I thought. I think with some counseling and our love, Richie will snap out of this." Pagne shared her dad's optimism, but Lenny remained quiet. "Son, you got something to say?"

"It's bull, Dad. He is playing along until he can figure out what to do. He wants you to think you've solved the problem so that you'll move on and leave him to do what he wants."

"But, Lenny, you saw him. He broke down. I've never seen him that emotional before."

"You're right. That's one reason why it's so fishy. He didn't show that much emotion when Pam died. It's not how he's wired, Dad, and he knows that you are. It's okay to be hopeful but don't buy into his scam. I think he's in real trouble."

Brent felt all the loyalty for Richie rushing to his heart. "Lenny, I know you mean well but you don't know Richie like I do. I think he really wants to get help and my family can help him do that." Brent had just yanked Lenny out of the family core without realizing it.

"Okay, Mr. Masters, I'll trust you to know what he needs." He got up, "I'm going to bed. It's been a long day." He left the room, trying to fight the anger he felt.

Pagne moved next to Brent, "I think we need to be optimistic, Dad, but I agree with Lenny. Something isn't right. We need to be careful and not be naïve anymore." Brent patted Pagne's hand.

"You're right, dear. Hey, great watching the movie together, right? It felt good being a family again." Pagne looked at her father and realized that he needed his fantasy. She hoped he would be able to cope once he figured out the truth.

"Going to bed, Dad. See you in the morning." She headed for the stairs and almost bumped into Richie in the hall. He glared at her.

Under his breath, he whispered, "You and Lenny stay out of my business or you'll both be sorry."

"Good night, Richie. I'll be praying for a full recovery." She met his glare with her own. As she passed him, he bumped her hard with his shoulder. She felt a sinking feeling in her gut. Lenny was right. It was bad. When Pagne slipped into bed next to Lenny, he was already asleep. She prayed for as long as she could stay awake. No smell, no Chantal. "Where are you? Think we all need you!" She drifted off.

Richie continued into the kitchen. "Hey, Dad, I can't get to sleep. Would it be okay if I take a couple of the nighttime aspirin? I've got a real bad headache and I don't want to be tired for our meeting tomorrow." Brent looked at him and felt a check in his gut but he rationalized it away. It's over-the-counter and two pills wouldn't hurt. He did want Richie rested for their first session with the counselor.

"Okay, Richie, but only two. I have to get them out of my desk drawer." He felt a pang of guilt now that Richie would know he had locked them up.

"I understand," Richie said as he managed to look ashamed. Brent went into the office and opened the drawer. He removed the bottle and was going to give him just two but thought better of it. He saw the progress made today and he wanted Richie to know that he still trusted him. He handed him the bottle. Richie opened it and palmed six instead of two.

"Thanks, Dad, this will help a lot." Richie left the office grinning. He thought about what a schmuck his dad was and realized that this was going to be easy! Just roll with it, Richie, just roll, he thought. He popped the pills and waited for the effects of the sleep aid.

~

The next morning, Pagne was watching Lenny when he awoke. He grinned at her, "Good morning."

"Good morning yourself." She snuggled into him and felt the firmness of this muscular body. He had matured over the summer and Pagne liked the changes.

"I'm really worried about your dad, Pagne. He's being sucked into Richie's game."

"I know," she agreed. "Richie threatened us last night."

"What?" He sat up, body tensed.

"Shhhhh, I think he was just bluffing." She told him what happened and Lenny was pissed.

"Pagne, he could go off the deep end. I've seen it happen, up close and personal."

"I know, I know. I think he's just was reacting to getting cornered. He couldn't vent on Dad, I was safer."

"Well, you watch yourself and I'll be watching him! Brother or not, he'll deal with me if he ever hurts you." She liked his automatic reaction to protect her but she also loved her brother and couldn't imagine that he would ever hurt her. They snuggled closer again, and Pagne felt Lenny relax. She timed her breathing to match his. She loved this connection with him. He reached over and started the familiar pattern that led to their lovemaking. They weren't frantic. It was sweet and tender and seemed to bring their world back to a sane place. They dozed for a while afterward. Pagne woke to a light knocking on her door. "Yes?"

"It's me Mandy. You didn't see my school clothes yet." Pagne grinned. She remembered her fashion show.

"Give me a minute, sweetie. I want to see everything." She slipped out of bed, trying not to wake Lenny, and slipped into some jeans and a t-shirt. Mandy was waiting for her, wearing the first outfit. After the show, Pagne went down to the kitchen and found Lenny eating the breakfast Grandma Maxine had set aside for them. Pagne grabbed the last piece of bacon and gave Lenny a mock nasty look for eating the rest. She sat down next to him at the kitchen counter.

"We need to make some decisions about getting our own place," Lenny brought up unexpectedly. They had decided to attend the local community college for the first two years. This would extend their scholarship money much further. They knew that Pagne's dad was willing to help them out for the first year and, with part-time jobs, they could afford to go to school full-time and still swing a small apartment. "School starts in a few weeks and we haven't discussed where you want to live." They had Lenny's old clunker of a car but they knew it wouldn't last long. Pagne had tried to save money to buy a car but she hadn't built up much. Since they'd gotten married, they'd focused on getting the necessities for setting up their own household first.

Brent came in and heard them talking. "You know you guys can stay here for a while if you'd like."

Pagne and Lenny looked at each other, relieved, but both of them were anxious to have their own place.

"We appreciate that, Dad, but Bree will be home soon and it'll get crowded around here."

Brent smiled and commented, "I remember young love. You two want your own place, I get it. Bree won't be coming home as planned. They asked her to extend for two more years and she decided to stay. She'll be coming home for two weeks next month but then she heads back."

"Well, that works out good, Dad. You can take the open room and have your office back."

"Nice save, Pagne," he said.

"Bree had a request. She wants you to take the car, Pam's car. She said it was a wedding gift." Pagne was thrilled. Pam had a great car, good tires, and it looked brand new. Bree had taken very good care of it after her dad gave it to her.

"Really, Dad, she won't want it when she comes back?"

"Nahhh, I think she'll be in Africa a long time; it suits her. Plus, she wants to introduce us to a young doctor she's met over there when she comes home. I think they may be serious." Pagne looked forward to Bree's next letter. Her last letter had hinted at this doctor but that was some time ago.

Brent looked at the clock and asked, "Anyone see Richie this morning?"

"Not yet," they said. Brent went upstairs and they heard him trying to wake Richie up. Finally, they heard the shower going. Pagne was relieved that Richie hadn't slipped out while they were all asleep.

~

Lenny was heading into his room when Richie was coming out of the bathroom, and Lenny shot him a challenging look.

"What's your problem, Lenny?" That's all it took. Lenny was on Richie and had him against the wall. His voice was calm and quiet but menacing.

"I love you, Richie, but don't mistake that for weakness. I know what you're up to. I lived this crap my whole life. You play it out, boy, but it's going to cost you big time. And know this, if you ever threaten Pagne or touch her in anger again, I will be the last person you want to be alone with. Are we clear?"

Richie saw a side of Lenny that he'd suspected but hadn't seen before. He'd also noticed the maturing of Lenny's body and bulk. He was smart enough to know that he was no match for him.

"Yes," he said with clenched teeth. Lenny didn't break his glare and held the firmness of his grip on Richie's shoulders. Richie could feel the strength in Lenny's grip and the pain. Finally, Richie looked away, accepting defeat in the encounter. Lenny backed off and continued into Pagne's room.

~

Pagne entered the room moments later. "Pagne, we need to look for our own place. We've got enough saved for first and last. Do we have everything we need to get by?"

"Bare essentials. Why the urgency?" He turned and wrapped her in his arms.

"I miss your screams," he said in a deep, sexy voice as he nuzzled her neck.

Pagne searched his eyes for the truth, Lenny knew he hadn't fooled her, but she didn't push him. They separated the dirty clothes and Pagne headed down to the laundry room with the first load. Lenny sat on the bed, staring out the window. He had lived the nightmare of drugs and saw the damage they brought. He wasn't going to do it again, not with Pagne. They deserved better. He deserved better. This was their chance to control their environment, his opportunity to be the man in his home. They would be support for Brent, Mandy, and Richie but, they wouldn't live it with them. Lenny knew there was going to be a tough road ahead and he was going to watch from a safe distance.

~

When Brent and Richie returned from the counseling appointment, Brent was glowing. "It went really well," he whispered to Lenny and Pagne. "He likes the doctor and really opened up." Brent's whole physical appearance had relaxed. Lenny didn't know what to do because he knew Brent wouldn't believe his warnings.

"That's great. Hopefully this guy can help," he said. See through the crap was what he was really thinking. Maybe he wasn't giving the counselor enough credit. Lenny and Pagne headed out to drive their new car and look at a few places for rent they had found in the paper. They let Grandma Maxine know that they would not be home for dinner. It felt so good to be driving, alone, and on the adventure to start their new life. They enjoyed all the feelings that came with it and left the concerns for Richie at the house, or at least pretended to. After checking out several places and finding the perfect studio apartment, they went to their favorite pizza joint and celebrated with a hot, gooey pizza piled with meat and veggies. They savored their time alone, then headed back to the house.

They described the apartment to Brent. They had just enough for all the moving costs but, it would take everything they had. Brent handed Pagne $1,000.00 in cash. "Here, this is for the first month. We can see how this works out. If you need more, we can adjust."

Pagne was speechless and then managed to say, "Oh, Dad, this is too generous."

"Well, you have food, gas, and school needs." Lenny shook Brent's hand and thanked him over and over.

~

Pagne ran upstairs to put the money in with their stash. She pulled the metal box from her nightstand drawer and, when she opened it, it was empty. She just stood there in shock. She brought the box downstairs and looked at Lenny.

"Did you move our money?" she asked.

"No," Lenny said with confusion, then realization, "Richie!" Lenny ran upstairs with Brent and Pagne right behind him.

"You don't know it was Richie. Calm down, Lenny." Brent said. Lenny threw open Richie's door but his room was empty. The window was open and Lenny looked down. Richie had used the emergency rope ladder to slip out of the house.

"Lenny, calm down," Brent said with urgency.

Pagne could see the rage building in Lenny's clenched body.

"We'll figure this out." Brent took off in the car, looking for any sign of Richie. He went to the homes of Richie's friends and his usual hangouts. Several hours later, Brent came in, alone.

Lenny had explained to Pagne while Brent was looking that being out on the streets wasn't as tough as it sounded. Either friends would slip you in their room after their parents were asleep or their parents didn't question a friend showing up late at night. Richie had over $1,200.00, and he could find lots friends with that kind of cash.

"Lenny, I realize now that Richie did take your money. I saw him coming out of your room earlier this evening and, when I asked what he was doing, he said you had a load of clothes in the dryer and he brought them up for you. Richie would never think to do that. I'll replace what he took. You guys make your plans for the apartment. Guess I need to call the police and report him as a runaway." Brent slipped into his office and shut the door.

Several police officers came to the house and took their statements. They said that because Richie had that much cash, it would be difficult to locate him quickly. They asked Lenny and Pagne if they wanted to press criminal charges. Pagne looked at Lenny with desperate eyes. "No," Lenny said, "we'll deal with it in the family."

Several days went by and there was no word from the police or Richie. Brent was crazed. He spent every waking moment either calling or driving and no one had seen Richie. Lenny knew Richie's friends were hiding him; he was their cash cow. They would all benefit until the money was gone. Pagne and Lenny had the apartment locked in and they were supposed to move in next weekend. What should have been an exciting time for them was filled with anxiety and worry.

"I've got everyone praying for Richie but I know God allows us to suffer the consequences for our actions. I am afraid of what Richie's will be," Pagne confessed to Lenny.

The night before their move, Brent got a phone call. They'd found Richie and he was at Mercy hospital. Some kid called 911 and, when the ambulance got to Richie, he wasn't breathing. Lenny knew the boy had probably been partying with Richie and things went bad. Brent, Pagne, and Lenny rushed to the hospital and found his room. Richie was hooked up to all kinds of monitoring equipment. His coloring was pale and he looked like a breathing corpse. Brent sat next to his bed, dropped his head on the mattress, and cried. The doctors told them Richie was in a coma and they didn't know the extent of the damage yet. His body was full of alcohol and a mixture of drugs. The prognosis was serious. They gave Brent a Ziploc bag with Richie's belongings. There was about $45.00 dollars left. The nurse told them the police were holding the boy who called 911 in another room. He was not quite twelve and drunk, though not as severely as Richie.

Lenny went to find the officers and the boy to see what he could find out. He saw them in the doorway of the room two doors down. He went over and introduced himself, explaining that he was family to Richie Masters. One of the officers pulled him to the side. "Not much I can tell you. This boy was with Richie at a party. Richie started to behave irrationally and said he was going home. This kid here, Donny," the officer nodded into the examination room, "was worried about him and followed him. A block or so away, Richie collapsed. The kid had a cell phone with him and called for help. Richie had fallen on his back and was throwing up. Donny rolled him onto his side and stayed with him until the ambulance got there. His actions saved your kid's life." Lenny looked in and saw a little boy looking scared to death. It was tragic that substance abuse started so young. Lenny headed back to Richie's room.

Richie's doctor had come in and was explaining the test results. They were treating Richie for alcohol poisoning and a drug overdose. They needed to detox his system and it would take days. The doctors had no way of knowing how long Richie would be in a coma. There was a chance he might never regain consciousness. The officers down the hall came in and asked the doctor for an update. The doctor stepped out with the officer Lenny had spoken to. The second officer walked over to Brent and looked embarrassed. Brent was staring at Richie as the tears rolled down his face. "Mr. Masters, I'm sorry to have to bother you right now but we need to get some information for our report."

"I'm sorry, Officer. What do you need?"

"Can I have a few minutes? I need to get some information from you for our report." Brent didn't seem to comprehend the officers request. Pagne stepped up and asked if she could help him. The officer looked at Brent and focused on Pagne, "Sure, Miss," he said.

"Mrs." Lenny corrected. The officer gave him a nod and suggested they step into the hall. Lenny positioned himself to be able to assist Pagne with any questions and still keep an eye on Brent.

Pagne could supply most of what the officer needed but Brent would have to give him the details about Richie's behavior over the last few months. Pagne apologized for Brent and the officer waved it away. "We can talk to him tomorrow. We have his contact information. This is a lot for him to deal with right now." The officer left and Pagne and Lenny moved back into the room.

"I need to call Grandma Maxine," Pagne said. "I think Dad needs her here," and Lenny agreed.

Grandma Maxine would be there as soon as she could make arrangements for Mandy. They didn't want to upset her until they knew more. When Grandma Maxine arrived, she went to Brent and held him. Brent gave way to the fear and pain and let his mother engulf him with her emotional strength. Pagne respected his privacy and she left Richie's room with Lenny right behind her. They knew he would not want them to see him appear as weak. They could hear Grandma Maxine's sweet voice soothing him as they went out into the night air and breathed in deeply. Pagne reached for Lenny and let him hold her.

"Oh, Lenny, I don't think Dad can deal with this alone. Maybe we should stay until we know what is happening with Richie."

Lenny chose his words carefully. "Brent needs us to show him that life keeps moving, Pagne. This could be days or months. He can't put his life with Mandy and his work on hold either. I think we can be there for him, without living there."

Lenny hoped that Pagne wouldn't argue. He had endured a hard life and drugs had almost destroyed him. This was too much for him to deal with and he needed to have a place to pull back into.

"Okay," was all she could say.

Brent stepped out and looked at the stars above. "Mom is sitting with Richie. She thinks I need to get some fresh air." Pagne went to him and hugged him and neither of them knew what to say. "You guys need to get home and get some sleep. The doctors don't expect Richie to wake up tonight. You've got a big day tomorrow." Pagne looked at Lenny, waiting to see if he would offer to delay their moving, but he didn't.

"You gonna be okay?" asked Pagne.

"I don't know but I guess I'll find out. Mom is going to stay with me here for a while and then we'll figure out what to do next. Right now, I'm just trying to remember to breathe. Pagne, think you could make some calls and get the church folks praying for Richie?

"Yes, Dad. They won't mind if I wake them up."

"Okay, sweetheart. I'll see you at home. Got enough help to move?"

Pagne laughed sadly, "We don't have anything but our clothes. Everything we've bought is being delivered today at the apartment."

"If you don't mind, can I borrow your angel tonight?"

"Absolutely." She kissed him goodnight and Lenny leaned in to give him a hug.

"Son, I owe you an apology. You tried to tell me and I wouldn't listen."

Lenny squeezed him harder and said, "Dad, I didn't expect this and you couldn't have known." Brent slapped him on the back, the "man-slap" which indicated that the intimacy was becoming too emotional. Lenny released him.

"Get our girl home, okay?" Pagne sensed that Brent was only holding it together until they left.

"Sure thing." Lenny and Pagne left with such a feeling of helplessness, not knowing what to do for Brent or Richie. They would have to rely on their trust in God and prayer.

As Lenny drove, Pagne called Pastor Tim. He assured her that she did the right thing by calling him and he would get a prayer chain going. Pastor Tim also said he would head over to the hospital to see what he could do for Brent.

When they got home, they slipped into bed. Pagne didn't sleep but stared at the ceiling for hours until exhaustion pulled her under.

Lenny awoke shortly after Pagne went to sleep. He was surprised to hear how deeply she was breathing, almost snoring. He decided to load up his car with all their packed items and let her rest. He left a note, telling her to call him when she was up. He would be at the apartment waiting for the deliveries. Now that they had two cars, it was much easier for them to get around. He left with the car packed full. He noticed that Grandma Maxine's car was back from the hospital, yet he hadn't heard them come in.

~

It was almost one o'clock when Pagne woke up to find that she was being stared at. Mandy was quietly standing at the foot of the bed. Pagne looked at the time, sat up in a panic, and saw the note. Then she relaxed and settled back against the pillows. "Hey kiddo, you been watching me long?"

"Yes, everyone is really sad, Pagne. Nobody will tell me why. Daddy just got home and his eyes look scary. They're all red and puffy. He went into his office and I hear him snoring. Grandma keeps crying and blowing her nose. She wants me to wait until Daddy wakes up and then they will tell me what's wrong. Did something bad happen to Richie? Is he coming back?" Pagne wasn't sure how to handle this but knew that Mandy was worrying herself sick.

"Come here, sweetie. Curl up with me." Mandy quickly obeyed and cuddled next to Pagne. "We got a call last night and they found Richie."

"Where is he?" she blurted.

"He is very sick and the doctors are taking good care of him. He's sleeping and won't wake up until he gets enough rest."

"Is he at the hospital?"

"Yes, that's where they make sure he will get well."

"He must be really sick if Dad and Grandma are crying."

"Well, they are worried a little and they were already upset because he ran away from home. I think it is both things that are making them cry."

"Is he going to die like Mommy?" Mandy asked, unexpectedly.

"Why no, I don't believe so. Doctors are very smart and Richie is very strong." Mandy looked at Pagne with such sadness.

"You still moving today?"

"Yes, I am. Lenny is already at the new place."

"Can I go there with you today? I don't like it here when everyone is so sad." Pagne didn't know how Lenny would take having company their first day but she made the decision to bring Mandy anyway.

"Sure, sweetie, you can help us unpack."

"Yeah! I'll go get my shoes." Pagne got up and threw on the clothes she had on last night. Lenny had taken everything else with him. She packed up her bathroom items after she freshened up and was ready. She just had to make a quick call. She hoped that Lenny hadn't set out candles and petals for her arrival.

"Hey, Lenny. I'm bringing Mandy over with me." He didn't respond, "Lenny?"

"Oh sorry, hon, they just got here with the bed. Sure, I think that's a good idea. We'll put her to work."

"Thanks, Lenny. We're leaving now." When they passed through the kitchen, Grandma Maxine wasn't in sight. *She must have gone to bed when Mandy told her she was leaving with me,* thought Pagne. Pagne grabbed some fruit, left over fried chicken, and drinks. There was nothing at the apartment and she knew Lenny would be starving. Pagne left a brief note for Brent so he would know Mandy was with her if he woke up before Grandma Maxine.

Several weeks passed and Richie was still in a coma but the doctors were excited about the brain activity they were observing and actually seemed to be resting. His color was back and he looked peaceful. The family took turns sitting with him, reading and sharing stories from the past. Mandy would go with Brent for short visits and sing to Richie. She loved to sing. Richie would always tell her to be quiet when she sang at home so they figured he was her captive audience now. Whatever her motivations were, they knew she felt as if she was contributing and that was good for her.

Pagne and Lenny had started their classes and really enjoyed school. They had several classes together. Between school, work, Richie, and making time for Mandy, they didn't get to enjoy their apartment much. They spent many evenings at the house with Mandy and Brent but it was still nice to know they had their own place. They gradually added items that made the apartment feel cozy. Brent surprised them with a futon set for the living room area of their studio apartment because they'd been using their bed as a couch. It also gave them an extra sleeping surface if Mandy stayed over.

~

Bree came home for a visit in the midst of Richie's coma but was only able to stay for a week. Dr. William Johnson made the trip with her. The family was a little surprised that Bree had not mentioned that her doctor was of African descent and born in the village where their mission was. His father had been an Afro-American missionary who met his mother while assigned to serve in Africa. As a teenager, William's family had been reassigned to southern California. Once William completed his education to become a doctor, he felt the Lord led him to return to Africa. Pagne didn't know if Bree purposely didn't mention his ethnicity out of concern for their reaction or if she was just so comfortable with their relationship she just didn't think about it. He was a warm, loving man and tall, with beautiful semi-sweet chocolate skin. Grandma Maxine seemed a little uncomfortable at first but, after visiting with William for a short time, she adored him. "He's a very profound Christian man who loves God mightily," Grandma Maxine explained. He wore his hair full of soft curls. Pagne loved his hair. It was jet black and softer than she would have expected.

She only knew that part because Bree insisted she feel it when he was visiting. Pagne felt awkward, but William grinned a wide, warm smile that caused his eyes to twinkle when he placed her hand on his head. "This is why she loves me!" he laughed and Bree playfully smacked him.

"Not true, just one of the many reasons!"

You could see they adored each other. William had a strong sweetness about him that was complimented by Bree's wilder, carefree side. Mandy wasn't sure what to think and kept staring at them. Finally, she piped up during dinner and said they would make pretty salt and pepper shakers. Pagne's family wasn't sure how William would react to this comment regarding his color. He looked at Mandy and grinned. "Why thank you, Miss Amanda. I've never been called pretty before." Then he began to laugh, a loud, deep, infectious laugh. Bree followed suit and they all joined in. Mandy laughed but they could tell she had no clue what was funny. It was a sad departure when they had to return to Africa. Bree expressed her regret that she could not be there for them and Richie. She did, however, promise to pray as she hugged Grandma Maxine.

~

One afternoon, in the hospital, Mandy was singing her favorite song, "Somewhere Over the Rainbow." She was into her third chorus when Pagne and Lenny happened to stop by and heard a grumbling voice say, "Mandy, please, not again!" They jerked their attention to the bed. Richie still had his eyes closed but was moving around trying to identify the items connected to him.

Brent moved up by his head and said firmly, "Son, it's time to wake up." Richie's eyelids began to flutter as Lenny pulled the blinds closed. He didn't think the bright sunlight would be appreciated. Gradually, Richie opened his eyes, but seemed to have trouble focusing, "Dad?

"Yes, son, you're in the hospital. It's time to wake up."

"Hospital?"

"Yes son, wake up."

Richie was smacking his lips. His eyes kept slipping shut. Brent slipped an ice chip between his lips. Richie seemed to grasp that it was wet and sucked and rolled it around in his mouth. His eyes opened again and stayed focused on Brent's face above him. He looked around the room at the tear-streaked faces. "What's going on? Where am I?" he whispered with a hoarse voice.

"You're in the hospital. You've been asleep for a long time," Brent said. Richie looked confused and then his thoughts seemed to take shape.

"The hospital?"

"Yes, son."

"Am I okay?"

"We think you'll be just fine!" Richie's eyes closed again briefly and then reopened as they all held their breath. He looked around and the next words shocked them all.

"Well, quit gawking and get some food. I'm starving!"

Brent ran into the hall, yelling and laughing, telling the nurses to get the doctors because his son was awake! The nurses ran to the room and stuck their heads in to see a young man sitting up and hugging his family. They teased Mandy for the rest of her life that her singing could wake the dead.

Richie appeared to be fine but the doctors wanted to observe him for a few more days and run some last tests. They brought a psychiatrist in to determine if Richie had any indication of suicidal tendencies. Frequently, people overdose with drugs and alcohol hoping they will fall asleep and die. They don't realize that death usually comes from choking to death on their own vomit, not a peaceful exit. Richie seemed genuinely happy to be alive and admitted that the partying had gotten out of hand.

Lenny was kind to Richie but expressed his true feeling to Pagne. "You know that nothing has really changed. Richie had a bad scare but he'll eventually forget it. Everyone ignores that he stole our money. I am glad Richie is doing well but there is still a long, hard road ahead."

Richie was eventually released and scheduled for an out-patient rehabilitation program.

~

Pagne and Lenny were finally able to play house in their own apartment. They cooked cheap but romantic dinners and spent Saturday afternoons just enjoying each other. Saturday nights, they would entertain friends from school and church and Macey was a regular visitor. Pagne was beginning to feel like an adult. They spent afternoons and evenings during the week working on homework together and Pagne loved the exchanges they had. She felt they were on a shared journey together. They both were focusing on required general classes and taking one psychology elective. They had this class together and it really opened up their minds and observations about life. It also got a little irritating when they tried to analyze each other, something most new psychology students are guilty of. It was an exciting year.

They still visited their families but purposely tried to establish their independence. Usually, they spent Sunday afternoons at Brent's home after church. Richie rarely went to church anymore but Mandy loved it. Pagne enjoyed Mandy's enthusiasm for God and baby Jesus. They all continued to pray for Richie as it was obvious he still had his own ideas about what was good for him. He followed the rules and his grades were better but not great. He continued with the counseling but that also seemed superficial. He didn't have much to say except things were cool and they shouldn't worry about him.

Brent was ill prepared for this journey he was on and he had a hard time recognizing the deception that surrounded Richie. They saw less and less of Richie as the months went on. He either holed up in his room working on his music or worked at the job Brent had setup for him to pay back the money he stole. Richie was allowed to keep one third and the other two thirds went to the balance he owed Brent. Pagne had the sense that he was laying low; doing what they expected of him until they loosened the leash. When they did see him, he was detached and kept the conversation shallow. He apologized for stealing the money but it was obvious he didn't carry any guilt because Brent had paid them back and he was working to pay back Brent. Pagne encouraged Lenny to get closer, hoping he could influence Richie but, Richie made it obvious he was not interested to the point of hostility.

Sunday afternoons at the house came less often. Brent worked a lot of hours, avoidance Pagne guessed, and Richie would shut himself in his room. Pagne and Lenny would bring Mandy back to their place for pizza, movies, or swimming in the facility pool when the weather was hot. She needed them and they were more than happy to include her in their lives.

Pagne also had an ongoing pen pal relationship with Elanna and Sophie, the young girls from Mexico. Lucinda translated their letters but Pagne saw the girls were slipping in more and more English. She enjoyed their stories and the pictures they drew and she found herself bonding to these two sweethearts even more. Her letters were always positive, encouraging, and she would send little gifts, ribbons for their hair, sunglasses, or cute jewelry. They appreciated anything she sent and Lucinda sent her pictures with the girls all dolled up. Pagne sometimes wondered about trying to bring them to live with her and Lenny but she knew they weren't in a position to raise two small girls with school and work. Pagne asked Miss Renee about the process and she explained that is was complicated and expensive to adopt children from other countries. Pagne was thankful they were surrounded by loving people and were well taken care of. She had to be content with what she could provide.

Chapter 20

Bree called on a Sunday evening and informed Pagne that she was engaged and getting married at the beginning of June. Bree asked Pagne to get Lenny on the phone. Both of their ears wouldn't fit on Pagne's cell phone but Pagne remembered she had a speaker option on the phone. They sat the phone on the table and told her they could hear her fine. Bree told them they were coming back to California to have the wedding. She hoped Pagne could help her coordinate things there because it was hard to plan a wedding from Ethiopia. "I want you as my maid of honor, Pagne."

"Of course!" she squealed. Pagne was excited to be part of a real church wedding. She didn't regret marrying Lenny the way they did but she would've enjoyed a church wedding, too.

"We're planning on a few days in Monterey for our honeymoon and then back to Ethiopia."

"Sounds wonderful," they both agreed.

"Well, this is the big question! When we head back, we'd like you and Lenny to come for the summer. We think you would love it here and we can use the help from people with your faith and love. Several of our staff members are going home for the summer and we need your help."

Lenny and Pagne were shocked. They had never entertained the thought of going to Africa. Lenny's first response was, "Bree that would be incredible but, we can't afford the airfare let alone cover living expenses for ourselves over the summer."

"Don't be silly, the administration would cover your airfare and you're living expenses would be next to nothing. Pagne, you can earn college credit in our program and you could apply some of your scholarship funding if you needed to. I think Dad might be willing to help out some, too."

"I don't know about that," Pagne interjected, "He was very clear about his willingness to help financially the first year and that's it."

"Let me talk to him. If he sponsors you guys, it's a tax write-off for him. He might benefit too." They talked a little more about general details, and Bree asked them to pray about it. She then asked how Richie was doing. She had spoken to him about a month ago on the phone and felt the same distance that everyone else had. They were all worried but not sure what they could do other than to keep him in their prayers.

When they got off the phone, the suggestion of Africa began to simmer. They thought it was impossible but the excitement of consideration began the process of resolving. They knew they could store their things in Dad's three-car-garage for the few months they'd be gone. They would lose the apartment but it could easily be replaced. Ads were always running for studio and one-bedroom apartments in their area around the college. Pagne asked Pastor Tim to put it on the church's prayer chain and, within a short time, he told them the church and several of its members said they could help finance their trip. It was beginning to look more and more possible. Pagne and Lenny prayed together for God's direction and they tried hard not to get ahead of God's will. They were thrilled to learn that it was exactly what God had intended. He opened all the doors and they would be heading to Ethiopia in June of that year.

School, their jobs, and life went on as usual. Things got a little hectic with adding in wedding plans and the trip to Africa. Bree mailed Pagne multiple suggestions for every aspect of the wedding and told her she would be happy with any scenario Pagne could work out within those guidelines. She would find her dress there in Ethiopia. She wanted the colors to be cream and pale-pink, with touches of any accent color that Pagne liked. Pagne had free reign with her maid-of-honor dress and Mandy's flower-girl dress. Pagne leaned toward purples but went with deep pinks to compliment Bree's dress and flowers. The shopping was so much fun with Mandy. She was surprised at how similar their tastes were once Pagne vetoed the dress with big, pink carnations scattered all over it.

They were only weeks away from the wedding and everything was moving along great. Pastor Tim was going to marry them at the church and the reception would be at Brent's house. The yard was lovely in June and Grandma Maxine was in charge of decorating. She found places for flowers and candles and there were tiny white lights everywhere. The wedding was in the early evening, so the reception would be at night. The yard would be magical in the dark.

William had a college buddy that would be his best man. His guest list was short: his sister and only a few friends. His parents had died several years earlier. Other than the church members, Bree's list wasn't much longer. They were serving cake at the church for everyone but the reception at the house would be small and private.

The time flew and it was only days before the wedding. Bree and William flew into LAX and rented a car to drive up to the house. They wanted mobility while they were there. They pulled into the driveway and everyone ran out and started a hug-fest. William held back for a few minutes but Grandma Maxine pulled him into the center. "You might as well get used to it. We're a hugging bunch." William relaxed and was a terrific hugger. They brought their luggage in and took it to Bree's old room. William would be using this room and Bree would be staying in Mandy's room with her.

Everyone noticed that Richie hadn't come down to welcome them. Bree stuck her head into his room and saw him tuned out with his headset on. She tapped his shoulder. "Hey, Bree made it in one piece huh?" Richie said as he lifted one side of his headset, making no effort to stand up.

"Yep, missed you at the greet," Bree replied.

"Too mushy for me. Figured I'd let them go crazy and say hey later." Bree felt the chill in his body language. She hugged him and said she'd catch up later. She headed down to the kitchen where she could smell Grandma Maxine's cooking. *Bree looks so much older,* Pagne thought. *Maybe I do, too.* They giggled and grabbed several pieces of fried chicken, which was Bree's favorite. Pagne, Bree, and Grandma Maxine went outside to show Bree the layout for her reception. Bree approved and couldn't wait for dark so that they could turn on all the lights. William, Brent, and Lenny were in deep conversation about the events taking place in Africa. William had seen the drought, disease, and suffering first-hand. His recounts were chilling and Brent began to wonder if having two daughters there was wise.

Next was the revealing of the dress. Pagne noticed Richie had slammed his door shut when they came up the stairs. It saddened her to see him missing so much joy and love. The girls went in and watched while Bree unzipped the clothing bag. She pulled out the most beautiful dress Pagne had ever seen. The lines were simple but most of the dress was covered with delicate open-weaved ivory lace. The fabric underneath was soft swirls of cream and soft pinks. Pagne knew the dresses she picked out would be a perfect compliment. They had Bree slip it on and it was gorgeous, a perfect fit. Pagne pulled her dress from the closet and held it up against Bree's dress. Bree began to cry. "Oh, Pagne, I love it."

"Mine looks just like it, but littler," Mandy offered. Grandma Maxine said they couldn't start crying now because she would look terrible for the wedding if they kept her crying for three days. They all shook it off and decided to invade the men downstairs.

That evening, everyone but Richie waited for Brent to flip the switch for the lights in the yard. Bree gasped with sheer joy. She hugged William and smiled broadly. He grinned and thanked Grandma Maxine for the magic she had created. It was beautiful and Pagne felt a twinge of regret. She looked at Lenny, who seemed to read her mind. He came over to her with a sinister grin. "It's pretty, but it ain't no neon cupid!" She didn't want to give him the satisfaction of laughing but couldn't hold it in. He hugged her and whispered, "We'll do it right on our tenth. How's that sound?"

"If you live that long," she teased. *If you live that long,* she thought, and felt a chill of regret. She looked into his sweet face. "You will be with me on our tenth, right?"

"Of course, babe. Where else would I be?"

~

Richie watched the show from his room. He had turned out the lights so they couldn't see him watching. He was so angry with them but he wasn't sure why. They were so sure that life was good, that they had a future and they were loved. He knew it was crap. He knew if he wanted anything, he had to take it. If he wanted to feel good, he made it happen. Love and people leave you; they let you down. He didn't know these people any more, let alone feel anything for them. Let them pretend. They'll find out that being God's kid is all fake. It doesn't matter how much you wish or pray, God doesn't care.

~

It was the day of the wedding, and everything was in place. Bree, Grandma Maxine, Pagne, and Mandy went to the beauty shop early that morning to get their hair and nails done. They chatted, laughed, and enjoyed the day of preparation. The guys did whatever guys do to get ready for a wedding. Even Richie was in good spirits and Brent was eating it up. He would find every excuse to keep him close because he missed his son. They left the house before the ladies returned and went to the church. This would give the ladies privacy to get dressed and not let the guys see them before they walked down the aisle. They were beautiful. Their hair was twisted and swirled with beads and ribbons, and they had flowers worked in. Bree had decided against a veil, because she wanted her hair to be her crowning glory. The bouquets arrived and they were a mixture of pink roses, cream roses, green ferns, and coiled ivy tendrils cascading down. Mandy's basket was weaved with pink and cream ribbons, filled to the brim with pink and cream petals. Mandy had asked for lots of petals to throw. The blend of hair, dresses, and flowers was breathtaking. They headed to the limo and off to Bree's new beginning as "Mrs. Doctor Johnson," as Pagne called him.

"That's not why I'm marrying him," responded Bree while trying to hit Pagne.

"But it doesn't hurt," teased Pagne.

Bree grinned. "Wait until you see where he practices medicine. You'll know it's not for the prestige," she shared with Pagne.

The wedding decorations were perfect, and they made a grand entrance that made both William's and Lenny's jaws drop. They floated to the front of the church on a massive path of petals; Mandy took her job very seriously. Pagne found herself thinking about Lenny as they said the vows. Then, all-too-soon, it was over. They had a receiving line and a cake for the wedding guests. After an hour of fellowship and congratulations, the smaller party went to Brent's house. Several ladies they knew from church had gone over earlier to set up for dinner. Grandma Maxine had prepared all the food, and it was delicious. They toasted and it was the first time Bree or Pagne had tasted alcohol. Pagne was not impressed. The evening was turning into a lovely memory for all of them. Pagne looked for Richie several times, but didn't see him. She was frequently distracted and continued celebrating. The evening was dark enough to turn on the lights and light the candles. Everyone Ohhhed and ahhhhed, which made Grandma Maxine glow. They were getting ready to cut the family cake and take some family pictures when Brent asked Pagne to see if she could find Richie.

She checked the outside areas and the ground floor of the house, but couldn't find him anywhere. She thought he might have gone up to his room, so she climbed the stairs, being careful not to step on the hem of her dress. She saw that his door was closed, but when she knocked, there was no response. She figured he had his headset on so she opened the door slowly and looked in. All the lights were out except for a small black light on the wall. She looked over at his desk but didn't see him sitting there. As her eyes adjusted, she saw him sitting on the floor, leaning up against his bed. There was an empty champagne bottle on the floor and another almost-empty one tipped up to his mouth. He had that sloppy, grinning face of so many drunks. Pagne suddenly remembered her mother and Adam and she knew that he could be disgustingly emotional or mean-spirited. "Oh Richie, please not tonight," she muttered.

"Ohhhh Richieeee, not tonight," he mocked. "Then when, Pagne? It's a celebration, isn't it? Another one bites the dust and all that crap." Pagne sat on the bed next to his head.

"They want you downstairs for cake and pictures. Can you do that Richie, for Bree?"

"Sureee," he slurred as he struggled to get up. Pagne's face showed every disappointment she was thinking. He saw the judgment and became angry. "You are my sister, not my mother. My mother is dead." He stepped back and forced himself to stand straight. "In fact, Pagne, you're not even my sister. You're a stray they brought in. Your pitiful puppy eyes and the scars. Man, that sure works for you doesn't it?" As Pagne stood and brought her hand up to slap Richie, she heard Chantal screaming "Nooo." It was too late. Her hand made contact with Richie's cheek and she hit him hard. They both froze in shock. She quickly reached back up to touch his reddening cheek and apologize, but he grabbed both of her wrists.

Richie pushed her back onto his bed and straddled her. He released one of her wrists and smacked her hard across the face. She could feel the blood running from her mouth. He looked at her, almost stunned, and then sneered. Richie grabbed her wrist again and pressed his mouth on hers, forcing his tongue between her lips. She bit his tongue hard and he yelped. He became crazed at that point. He pulled back and then punched her in the face with all his strength. Pagne screamed out in pain. Richie shifted and used his shoulder to press on her chest, holding her down. He used his hands, now free, to rip at her dress. Pagne tried to scream again, but she couldn't even breathe. She felt his fingernails ripping into her thighs as the dress shredded off of her body. Pagne suddenly saw Lenny's face over Richie's shoulder. His look of sheer rage scared her even more than Richie's attack had. She felt Richie pulled up and off of her. Next, she heard fists hitting flesh, hard. Then her father screaming, "Stop, you'll kill him." The lights were suddenly on and Pagne saw her brother balled up on the floor, face bleeding, teeth missing, and both eyes swelling shut. Lenny stood over him, panting. Brent didn't know what to do first. He ran to Pagne and asked if she was okay.

"I'm alright, Dad. See about Richie." Brent pulled Lenny back and told him to help Pagne. Lenny looked at Pagne's beaten face, the ripped dress, and felt the rage building again.

Bree rushed into the room and quickly pulled Pagne off of the bed and pushed her out of the room. As she passed Lenny, she grabbed him by the arm. He jerked away and glared at her. "Your wife needs you, Lenny. Come with us." Lenny didn't move, his focus was still on Richie.

Brent looked up at Lenny from Richie's side. "Get out of here, Lenny. Now!" he said through clenched teeth. Lenny stepped into the hall and, once his rage began to subside, he followed Bree into her room. Pagne was sitting on the bed, trying to make sense of what had just happened. Lenny went over and sat next to her, not knowing what to do next. His mind was split between wanting to comfort and wanting to kill. Pagne leaned against him and began to cry uncontrollably. Lenny found himself automatically moving to hold her. His anger began to melt as he found himself crying with her. Bree left them and found William. She explained what was going on and asked if he could come up and examine Pagne and Richie. Bree asked Pastor Tim to end the reception. William took the stairs three at a time and reached Bree's room first. He looked in at Pagne and saw that she was not in immediate danger. He continued over to Richie's room. Brent was sitting on the floor holding Richie, mumbling to himself. William asked Brent to slide over so he could get to Richie and he saw that he was unconscious. William couldn't tell if it was due to the alcohol or to the beating. He took his pulse, which was strong, and examined the injuries to his face. He was badly beaten. "Brent, let's get him to the emergency room. He needs x-rays and stitches. I think all the blows were to his face. He doesn't seem to be hurt anywhere else. I think his nose is broken and possibly his jaw." Brent slowly got up and helped William carry Richie to his car. "I'll meet you at the hospital, Brent, I want to check on Pagne."

"Oh my God, Pagne, is she okay?"

"I think so, I'll know more when I examine her." William ran back upstairs as Brent drove Richie to the hospital.

William shot Bree a frustrated look when he came into the room. "Brent is taking Richie to the emergency room." Lenny jumped up and headed toward the door, "Whoaaa slugger, he's okay. You messed his face up good but he'll be fine. How's Pagne doing?" William asked as he moved in front of her. He turned her face into the light and saw one eye swelling. She would need stitches along her brow. Her lip was swollen and split open. He was glad to see that she had all of her teeth. Next, he checked her shoulder and arm movement and Pagne winced in pain. "Think your collar bone might be broken. Richie's a good-sized kid and his weight on you could easily break it." William saw bruises appearing on Pagne's shoulder and chest. She had deep scratches along her thighs where Richie had ripped at her dress. She seemed to have no other injuries but she would be hurting for several weeks. "Pagne, did he, ahhhh, did he hurt you?" He wasn't sure how to ask with Lenny sitting there. He brought his eyes down to her lap.

"Oh, noooo," she assured him. William could see Lenny relax slightly. "Okay, you need to go to the hospital to get that shoulder x-rayed and stitches over that eye."

"Can I shower and change first?"

"No, I'm sorry, Pagne. The police will be called in and they will need to see you as you are now," he said.

"But, he's my brother. I don't want him arrested."

"Yes, Pagne, I know, but Lenny needs for the police to see why he attacked Richie." Pagne was getting it now. Lenny could be in trouble for protecting her. Richie, almost fifteen, was a minor and Lenny was nineteen, an adult.

"Okay, William."

They helped her up and half-carried her downstairs. Grandma Maxine had taken Mandy into her room so she wouldn't see the devastation. "Bree, grab some cold packs or frozen-food bags. We need to get ice on Pagne's face right away." As they brought Pagne out to the car, William asked Lenny if he had any injuries. Other than a couple of scraped knuckles, he was fine, on the outside anyway.

There was a dark, brooding pain inside. He had become his father in that moment. Yes, he was protecting Pagne but, he knew he could have stopped Richie without beating him. It was as if he had been given the excuse he needed to pound someone, the way his father did. Lenny would only find redemption through God and the passage of time.

When they got to the ER, Richie was already in an examination room. The police had been called when Richie was admitted and two officers were just arriving. They saw Pagne and were told she was involved in the reported beating. When Lenny identified as Richie's attacker, they wanted to take him out to the squad car. He begged them to let him stay with Pagne until they knew the extent of her injuries. They took Pagne and Lenny into another exam room and Lenny was handcuffed to his chair. He was humiliated to have Pagne see him that way but at least he was with her. A doctor came in and examined Pagne while one of the officer's took Pagne's statement. When the doctor was finished, the officer took pictures from every angle, showing her battered face, the scratches, the extensive bruising, and the torn dress. Afterward, the nurses helped Pagne out of her dress and into a hospital gown. They cleaned and treated Pagne's injuries.

The officer then talked with Brent, Lenny, William, and Bree about what happened. The officer could sympathize with Lenny, knowing that anyone would go crazy to see his wife being assaulted and possibly raped. It was much worse that it was a family member. He also took into consideration Richie's size and the damage he'd inflicted on Pagne. Her collarbone was broken in two places and she had several cracked ribs as well. Richie had literally been crushing her. The officer uncuffed Lenny and said they would be talking to him again so he was not to leave town until this was resolved.

Brent came into Pagne's room while the nurse was stitching up her face and they could all see the despair on his face. He didn't speak to Lenny but he focused on Pagne. "The doctor told me about your injuries. Oh, my sweet Pagne, I am so sorry this happened."

"I know, Dad. None of us could have seen this coming." Pagne looked at Lenny knowing that she wasn't totally honest with Brent.

"Richie is awake, groggy, but awake. He doesn't remember much."

"How badly is he hurt?" Lenny asked.

Brent didn't respond right away.

Pagne realized what a horrible position Brent was in. He had to hate what Richie did, but also feel so much anger toward Lenny.

Brent finally said, "Richie will be fine in time. His nose is broken, his jaw isn't broken, but dislocated and you knocked out three of his teeth. He requires multiple stitches over his right eye and they are concerned about the retina in the left eye." Brent explained with restrained emotion.

Brent leaned over Pagne and kissed her on the head. "The police do not need you to press charges Pagne so, if you're worried about that, don't. They have enough evidence to charge Richie." Pagne didn't realize what a relief that was. She knew Lenny would not let it go and she didn't want to be the one to ruin Richie's life.

"You okay here with Lenny?"

"Yes, Dad. I think they are letting me leave soon. I've already signed the paperwork." When Brent looked over at her dress hanging on the door hook, Pagne's eyes followed. It looked like something from a horror movie, ripped and shredded. She saw where Richie had ripped the bodice, trying to expose her chest. The rage that it must have taken for that kind of attack was beyond her understanding.

"Okay, I'll talk to you tomorrow." Brent walked into the hall and Pagne could see him stand before Bree. She put her arms around him while he kept repeating that he was so sorry. He stepped away from her and went down the hall to Richie's room.

Bree came in with a change of clothes that Grandma Maxine had brought. She looked at Pagne's dress on the hook, "Curse the evil that could shatter such a magical night."

The nurses had slipped a sling onto Pagne's arm and over her shoulder. The pain meds blocked most of the pain, but she still knew where every blow and scratch was. Pagne swung her legs over the edge of the bed and Lenny helped her stand. He couldn't bear to look at her beaten body and left as Bree helped her dress. Bree carefully slid the loose cotton pants up over Pagne's bandaged legs and helped her put on the loose Tshirt and sandals. Pagne glanced into the metal, paper-towel holder and saw a distorted picture of herself. Her beautiful, twisted and braided hair was torn apart. Her eyelid was turning a deep shade of purple and her lip looked gnarled up like that of a mad dog. She looked away, not wanting to cry, and felt herself buckle at the knees. Bree caught her and called for the nurse to bring a wheelchair. Bree started to roll Pagne over to Lenny, who was waiting by the ER entrance, when Pagne put her feet on the floor to stop the chair. "Wait. I need to see Richie."

"It's not a good idea," said Bree. Lenny looked like he had taken a jab to the gut.

"I'm okay, I need to do this." Bree looked at Lenny and he nodded. Lenny remained in the hall and Bree pushed her to Richie's room. As they made the curve into the room, Brent jumped up with a warning look at Bree.

"She wouldn't take no for an answer, Dad." Bree didn't take her all the way in but Richie was awake and saw her. He saw the damage he had done.

"Pagne, I ..." he looked down and turned his face away. Pagne saw his body begin to shake and the pain in his cries was too much for Pagne to bear. She asked Bree to take her out of the room. Lenny stepped over and took the handles and slowly rolled Pagne out of the ER, into the night air.

William joined Bree in the hall and they followed Lenny and Pagne to the car. They sat in the car for a few minutes, trying to figure out what to do. They had already stored their belongings in Brent's garage and they were planning to stay there until they left for Ethiopia but that would be too awkward now. "Oh no, what about leaving the country? What will we do about that?" Pagne asked with concern.

William talked in a soothing voice. "We'll figure it all out, but not tonight. Let's get a room for you guys. Bree and I will go back to your dad's for tonight. We can talk tomorrow morning and figure out what to do next." They pulled into a nearby motel and William rented a room.

"We can bring you whatever you need in the morning. Just try to get some sleep tonight," Bree instructed as they left. "Call when you're awake." Pagne noticed her blood on Bree's beautiful gown for the first time. Bree realized what was making Pagne tear up and hugged her. "It'll be fine, sis. I'm just thankful that you and Richie weren't hurt worse."

~

For the first time in hours, Pagne and Lenny were alone. They both lay on the bed and didn't speak for a long time. Lenny finally had the nerve to speak. "Pagne, I'm so sorry. I didn't mean to hurt him like that. He was on you and I saw him clawing your legs. I lost it." She reached over and touched his trembling hand.

"I know Lenny. I saw your eyes when you grabbed him, you weren't in there."

She was concerned about who was there, in his mind, but remained quiet. They both drifted off to sleep out of sheer exhaustion. Pagne could feel herself floating up in her dream, in her beautiful dress, feeling such joy. Then, there was oppressing pressure on her, pushing her down into a deep hole, suffocating her. She saw a monster with glowing red eyes on the edge of the hole, staring down into her eyes. She suddenly jerked awake and saw that daylight had entered their room.

Bree and William came over when Pagne called. They had their luggage and personal items from the bathroom. Bree drove Pagne's car over so they would have transportation. "I paid for you to stay at the motel while we're in Monterey," William told them. "When we get back, we'll know more about what the police will want from Lenny. He may not be able to leave with us on Friday, but there's always Plan C."

"What would that be?" asked Lenny.

"No clue, still working on Plan B." Bree and William had decided to go to Monterey and try to salvage their honeymoon. William and Lenny walked outside, talking about what Lenny could do while they were gone. Pagne looked sadly at Bree.

"I'm so sorry your wedding was destroyed."

"My wedding wasn't destroyed. It was wonderful. The party after my wedding was a nightmare, but my wedding, mmm, everything I wanted, thanks to you. I had a gift for you but the drama started before I could give it to you." She handed Pagne a box. When Pagne opened it, she saw a beautiful frame. In the frame was a drawing that Bree had done of herself and Pagne, laying in the grass at the park, by the stream, daydreaming. Bree had used the perspective of hovering above them. It was beautiful! She had captured them perfectly.

After some tears and hugs, Bree and William left for Monterey. Lenny left for the police station and Pagne called Grandma Maxine to get an update. Maxine told her that Brent was at the hospital because the doctors had wanted to keep Richie over night. They were charging Richie with assault and attempted rape. She didn't know yet if they were letting him come home or if he would be taken to juvenile hall. Grandma Maxine said she would call Pagne when she knew more. "How is Dad?" Pagne asked.

"Oh, hon, I'm not sure, please pray for him. He's going through the motions. I don't know if he can get through this."

"Have you talked to Pastor Tim? Maybe he can help?"

"The church has put us all on the prayer chain but Brent asked me not to encourage anyone to come to the hospital. Richie is adamant about not seeing anyone and an officer has been there most of the time. Brent is mortified."

"We're thinking about not going to Africa. We need to be here for Dad and for Richie."

"Pagne, I know this. You are supposed to go to Africa. God made it clear that this was your and Lenny's destiny. Your father will be even more upset if you stay. He will feel responsible for that also." Pagne realized that Brent carried the burden of what happened last night.

"Well, Lenny may not be able to leave Friday. He went down to the police station."

"Have faith, Pagne. God didn't open all the doors for nothing." Grandma Maxine said and then prayed with Pagne over the phone. When they finished, Pagne told her how much she meant to her. She laid back on the bed and asked Chantal to let herself be known. Pagne felt the sensation of feathers on her arm and could smell the aroma of her. She drifted in and out of a fitful sleep. She didn't know if she dreamed it or heard it, but Chantal was whispering to her softly. "You will love Ethiopia, Pagne. You will do incredible things there. Be faithful, Pagne. There is a plan and you have purpose."

Lenny came into the room quietly so as not to wake Pagne. "Hey, hon, don't worry, I'm awake," she announced.

"How you feeling?" he moved to the edge of the bed and picked up her hand.

"Well, it only hurts when I breathe." She tried to smile but her swollen lip made it more of a lopsided grimace.

"You taking your pain pills?"

"I'm due for some." He brought her the pills and a glass of water. She gulped them down. She shared what Grandma Maxine had told her and Lenny filled her in on how the meeting with the police went. They weren't pressing charges and Brent was not pressing charges either. Unless something changed in the next few days, Lenny would be able to go to Africa. The district attorney still had to review the case and he would make the determination. Lenny heard Pagne groan when she shifted.

"I don't think I'm going to be the problem, Pagne. You may not be able to fly by Friday."

Pagne had a peace about her. "It will work out, Lenny. We're going to Africa."

In the plane, over the ocean, Pagne rearranged the pillow under her head. They were heading to Africa and Pagne was reviewing the last few days. They allowed Lenny to leave, she was mending nicely, and Richie was being held at the juvenile facility. He'd refused to see Pagne before she left. Brent was coping and Mandy was confused. Thank God Mandy had Grandma Maxine. Pagne's body was stiff and sore but none of the injuries prevented her from leaving on schedule. Bree and William arranged for Lenny and Pagne to stay with some friends of theirs in the city for the first week because they didn't want Pagne dealing with insects and the heat until she was stronger. But, she would be in Africa.

When Pagne was well enough, they joined Bree. Their journey and their love of Africa began. Pagne found beauty in the African landscape and the faces of its people. They worked long hours, loved, prayed, and enjoyed the time they spent with the adults and children of this hot, poverty-stricken area. They received the smallest gestures with such appreciation. The weekly church services were packed with familiar and new faces. Pagne was amazed at how many souls were saved at each service. They were searching and God was collecting his lost children.

They had been in Africa for a month when Pagne came across a young man who seemed to hide in the shadows. He was about twenty or so and lived outside the village, alone. She was on one of her early morning walks when she first noticed him. She felt a stirring in her heart although she knew nothing about him. She made a point of lingering and admiring a plant or the sunrise each morning, hoping to see him. As the weeks passed, she would see him more often and he would pause before disappearing into the rocky terrain. This young man was lovely, with dark ebony skin but he had such sadness on his face. One morning, he didn't disappear. He stood still and watched Pagne. She moved closer and smiled as broadly as she could. "Hello," she said nervously. She was afraid he might take off.

"Hello," he said back. Pagne was relieved that he could speak English because not all of the citizens could. She moved closer while asking him his name. He moved back slowly.

"It's okay, I'm Pagne. I work with the mission, Bree and William. You know them?"

"No, I live outside of the village, over there." Pagne followed his gesture and saw a shack, which was just wood and scrap materials propped to form a shelter of sorts. She had mistaken it for garbage. "My name is Joshua." Pagne began moving closer and smelled Chantal. The closer she came to Joshua, the stronger Chantal's scent became. Pagne knew this was an important encounter but she didn't know why. Joshua didn't move away from her. When Pagne was within a few feet, the smell of Chantal became intense, almost nauseating, and Pagne trusted that this was Chantal's encouragement and not a warning. There was no sense of danger, but Joshua seemed very uncomfortable, so Pagne decided not to push her visit.

"Maybe I'll see you tomorrow," she suggested. "I'll bring breakfast." Joshua nodded and quickly moved out of her view into the ridge of rocks.

Every morning, Pagne would meet with Joshua. She would bring muffins or breads of some kind. Joshua would eat slowly, savoring each bite. He began to relax and open up more and more with each visit. They talked about life in general, and Ethiopia, but he refused to talk about himself or why he lived away from the village. Pagne tried to bring up the subject, but he would shut down and the visit would be over. Pagne thought it was odd but Chantal remained with her each time and her scent was strong and reassuring. As their friendship developed, Pagne was able to share her life and the story of Jesus Christ and his love for Joshua. She found out that Joshua could read, so she brought him books and a Bible. Pagne didn't ask any of the villagers about Joshua because she wanted to hear his story from him, when he was ready. Joshua had endless questions about God and Jesus. They spent as many hours together as Pagne's schedule would allow. She thought about bringing Lenny with her but she sensed the time wasn't right. It had taken a long time for Joshua to become comfortable with her. Pagne was intrigued, yet confused by this young man. Their friendship grew and she cherished the broad, warm smiles that he now shared with her.

One particular morning, Pagne was heading back to the mission when she was approached by one of the young ladies from the village she had gotten to know. "What were you doing with Joshua?" Setta asked.

"Do you know him?" Pagne asked.

"Not really. Just what I've heard in the village," she said.

"He's very sweet," Pagne supplied. "You should get to know him. He is very cute, too!" Pagne winked at Setta and Setta looked at her in disbelief.

"You are kidding, right?"

"Why?" Pagne asked, confused.

"He might be cute but how would I get past the stench?"

"The stench?" Pagne was struggling to understand. "He doesn't smell bad."

"You are the only one that doesn't think so."

Pagne now understood why Chantal remained with her. God wanted her to see and love Joshua the way He sees him, beyond the physical.

The next morning, Pagne cautiously went to meet Joshua. She didn't know if Chantal would shield her or allow her to face Joshua's reality. It didn't matter. Pagne was ready for whatever was to be. As she moved closer, she was grateful to smell Chantal, not quite as strong, but she was there. Joshua didn't look into her face when she approached. "Good morning, Joshua."

"You came," he said with a downcast voice. "I didn't expect you."

"What would make you think I wouldn't meet you this morning? I even brought your favorite, banana nut muffins."

"I saw you talking with that young woman yesterday. She looked at me with such hatred."

"Yes, I did speak with her briefly, Joshua but she said she didn't know you. We are friends now. Please tell me what is going on." Pagne could smell urine as she got closer to Joshua. She saw tears welling up in Joshua's eyes. Pagne stopped her approach and sat on a large rock nearby.

Joshua nervously paced and wrung his hands. "I lived with my papa just north of here. We were driving into Baro for supplies." Pagne knew this was one of the larger cities in the area. Pagne could see how Joshua struggled with his words. "I was driving, and the front axle on the truck snapped. I lost control and we went into a steep ravine. My papa was thrown from the truck and was killed. I remained in the truck but I was badly hurt. We were there for several days before anyone found us. The doctors were able to mend my broken bones and I healed from most of my injuries." He paused for a while before continuing. "But, they could not fix my bladder. I cannot control my urine." Joshua searched for words appropriate for the sweet missionary. "My body releases urine all the time. I try to keep myself clean but there is always the smell." Pagne's heart broke for this young man. *How embarrassing and frustrating this had to be for him,* she thought.

"Have you talked with the doctors? Is there any treatment?" Joshua looked at her with such defeat.

"I do not have any money and the doctors already treated me free for my many injuries. They said that this condition would be inconvenient but, I should be thankful to be alive. I cannot get a job. No one can stand to be around me. That is why I live out here. I can hunt for food and I get by."

"Why did you leave your village? Surely you had friends and family that would help you."

"They tried for a while but I saw the disgust on their faces. I could not bear the humiliation."

Pagne did not know how to respond to Joshua other than with compassion. She moved closer and the urine smell became stronger. She thought, Dear God, let me love him the way you love him. Pagne moved next to him and struggled not to react to the overpowering smell of the urine. She wrapped her arms around him and felt his body melt into a shaking mass. It was the first time anyone had held him in two years. Pagne was relieved to smell Chantal, strong and glorious. She realized that she could not have understood the depth of Joshua's shame if she had not been allowed to smell him for those few moments. Pagne visited with Joshua for a while longer. They talked about his family and his papa. Pagne knew what she had to do. When she left, she didn't promise him anything, but she had a plan.

Back at the mission, Pagne found William and Bree. She told them Joshua's story through her tears. Bree said that she had heard some comments by the villagers about a young man in the wilderness but didn't realize it was true.

"I should have checked it out," William said. "I heard the stories, too."

"Don't beat yourselves up. It took me a very long time just to get him to talk to me. What can we do? Is there any funding for medical treatment?" William told Pagne that he would check with their board of directors to see what they could provide. William asked Pagne to take him to meet with Joshua. He wanted to examine him and see if there was anything he could do to help.

"What about food and shelter? We certainly can help him out that way," Bree asked with excitement.

Pagne was relieved that they were willing to help Joshua but she didn't know how Joshua would react to the attention and didn't want him to run away. "He is very shy and embarrassed. Let me go talk to him and see if he will meet with William. Once he sees that we truly want to help him and are not disgusted by him, we can bring in Bree and Lenny."

"I think that is wise," said William. "Pagne, here is some cream that doctors use to cover strong smells. You rub a little under your nostrils." Pagne grinned at him.

"I have Chantal. She is blessing me with her presence."

"Okay, I'll be here at the mission all day. See if we can do it today." Pagne ran from the building and headed over to their kitchen. She made large, overstuffed sandwiches and grabbed cold sodas and several pieces of cake.

She ran out to Joshua's shelter and called his name several times. At first, he did not respond. Finally, he came from behind the shelter. He had a sack over his shoulder. "I didn't expect you back here today," he said guiltily.

"What's going on, Joshua? Are you leaving?" Joshua looked at her with that sense of defeat again.

"I have to move on, Pagne. There is very little game here and I can't survive much longer."

"No, Joshua. Please don't leave. We have food. We can help you."

"I am not a charity case, Pagne. I can take care of myself." He started to turn away.

"Joshua, wait, please hear me out. I talked with my team at the mission and they want to help you. Help you live a life without hiding and being alone." Joshua looked at her with a flicker of hope and then anger.

"They cannot help me, Pagne. I am disgusting. I should have died in the crash. The stench is my punishment for killing my papa." Joshua stood there, so rigid and filled with self-loathing.

"No, Joshua. It's a medical problem from getting hurt, not a punishment. God wants us to be there for each other. He uses us to help each other and spread love for him."

"I've tried to understand this God but he cannot love me. I know that my stink offends him, too."

"That is not true, Joshua. I need to explain how God is using me to help you. Please, Joshua, sit and let's eat lunch and I'll tell you just how much God does love you." Pagne was praying in her mind. Please don't let him leave. Not now.

Joshua saw the box of food Pagne was carrying. "Is that chocolate cake?" he asked.

"Yes, it is and it's delicious." Joshua looked longingly at the cake.

"Okay but I leave after lunch."

They found some shade under the scrub brush and sat down to eat. As Joshua hungrily ate the lunch Pagne brought, she told him about her angel. Pagne explained how Chantal protected her from the smell so that she could build a friendship with him. Pagne poured out her heart to Joshua and pleaded with him to see William. She admitted that she didn't how much they could do about his medical issues but he should let them try. After Joshua had eaten both pieces of cake, he stood and threw the bag over his shoulder. Pagne's heart ached in her chest. He was still leaving. He looked down at her and grinned, "Well, you gonna sit there all day or you gonna take me to William?" Pagne squealed with delight as she jumped up and hugged him with all her might.

As they walked back to the mission, Pagne was curious. "What convinced you, Joshua? Most people think I'm crazy when I talk about smelling my angel." Joshua picked up a rock and threw it hard.

"Every time you came to visit me, I smelled your perfume. It was lovely, but I couldn't figure out why you wore so much! And this morning, I didn't understand how the scent faded away and then came back."

Pagne's jaw dropped, "But, I'm not wearing any perfume."

"I know that now," he said. "I can smell your angel, Pagne. If God would cover my smell so you could be my friend than I want to know this God and see what he can do to give me my life back." Pagne could not contain herself. She laughed and cried all the way to William's office.

Luckily, no one was waiting to see William. Bree saw them heading in and smeared the cream that William gave her under her nose. Bree was sweet and gracious and Pagne saw Joshua relax. William came out right away and Pagne introduced them. Joshua seemed to connect to William immediately. They went into Williams's office and shut the door. Pagne and Bree anxiously waited until William came out. "Okay, guys, this is the plan. Joshua is staying here with us."

Bree looked panicked, "But how will the other patients and staff deal with the smell?"

"Sadly, Joshua has suffered needlessly. I've heard back from the board and they will fund his medical bills. I'm taking him to the medical center tomorrow to meet with a specialist. But for now, he needs a hot shower, clean clothes, and adult diapers." Bree and Pagne both slapped their foreheads. How simple, they both realized. One of the elderly mission board members had left behind a partial box on their last visit. William would be able to get more from the specialist they met with. William personally assisted Joshua to minimize his embarrassment. They would meet up again at dinner. Pagne was anxious for Lenny to meet Joshua.

William brought Joshua into the dining area. Pagne was so happy to see him looking so confident. There wasn't a hint of urine smell. She introduced Lenny, who welcomed Joshua graciously. The conversation was fun and relaxed and no one spoke about Joshua's issues or his life in the wilderness. When they brought out dessert, Joshua sat, staring at the pie then at the faces around the table. He teared up and fought to keep his emotions from overwhelming him. Pagne, looked at him with concern, "Joshua, you okay?"

Joshua could finally speak. "I never dreamed that I would be sitting at a table with friends or family again. I am filled with such joy and appreciation." William, trying to lighten the mood, grinned at Joshua.

"Well, we're happy to have you but the way you can pack down food concerns me. Please leave enough pie for the rest of us." Everyone, including Joshua, began to laugh, the kind of laughter that fills hearts and rooms with love.

Chapter 22

Lenny and William traveled to the more remote villages once a week to bring medical assistance. Lenny's respect for William grew throughout their stay in Africa. He was a quiet giant and his love leaked out onto everyone they met. They pulled off the dirt road next to a natural spring on one of their weekly rounds. There was some vegetation and a grassy area. William and Lenny wiped their faces with the cool water and drank until they felt refreshed. William sat on the grass and stretched out, staring at the clouds above. Lenny sat next to him. "I'm afraid," Lenny said, out of the blue.

"Of?" William asked.

"Me," Lenny admitted. "I know my reaction to defend Pagne from Richie was justified but I wanted to hurt him. I didn't try to find another way to stop him. Pagne saw it, too. She knows there is an evil side to me and I'm afraid that it could come out again." William leaned toward Lenny and looked at him intently.

"I once was a sweet, young boy who grew up in a small, loving village," William began. "My family moved to America when I was fifteen and we lived in a very violent neighborhood. There was a lot of fighting, murder, robbery, and drugs. I grew to be a young man who wanted to be good and kind but, because I was big, the other young men pushed and tried to make me mad. They wanted to see if they could beat me in a fight. I stayed good for a long time and I walked away from the insults and did not fight." William was silent and seemed caught up in his memories. "Until one day. I was with a girl, a friend really. I thought I loved her but she didn't know.

"We were at the park and it was getting dark. I knew we needed to leave but I wanted more time with her. I didn't listen to my head and I chose my heart.

Before I realized what was happening, a group of young men came up to us and decided they wanted the girl. They thought I would not fight so four of the men jumped on me, while the fifth began to rape my friend. Their punches, the taunting, and her screams released the monster in me. I responded with a rage that gave me strength I never imagined and I threw them off of me, one at a time. They ran away and left their friend. In a matter of minutes, I had beaten the man who raped my friend. The attacker was only 19. I broke his back and permanently injured his brain. He will spend the rest of his life hospitalized and in a wheelchair. I didn't go to jail but I was changed. I understood what pure rage could make you become. Was it okay what I did? Maybe. But, I could have stopped him without beating him so badly that his body and mind were destroyed. I had to decide if my size and anger would be my strength, if this monster would be my way to cope with the injustices of life. I decided that I wanted a higher power to guide my life. I chose God. I accepted that I had this monster but, I chose to chain it with the love of Jesus Christ." William got up and stared out at the horizon. "Lenny, we all have our monster. You need to figure out what unleashed yours because you have all the power you need. You have found God." With that, he walked to the jeep and waited for Lenny to catch up in more ways than one.

That night, back at their hut, Lenny lay under the netting, watching the fan blades spin. He asked God to forgive him for his brutality against Richie. He closed his eyes and God revealed to him that not only had Lenny become his father in that moment of rage, so had Richie. There had been so much disgust building over the last year. Richie had a family who loved him but, he was tossing them away with his arrogance and his use of narcotics and alcohol. Lenny saw the increasing disrespect in his treatment of Grandma Maxine, Mandy, Pagne, and Brent. When Lenny saw Richie on top of Pagne, he saw his father on his mother, beating her, hurting her. Lenny cried quietly, trying not to wake Pagne.

~

The months went by so fast and it was already time to go home. School would be starting in a few weeks. The experience in Africa had been incredible. Pagne and Lenny hoped that they would return someday. They considered staying but knew that Pagne's family needed her and they had to be back in September for Richie's trial. Richie had been at juvenile hall the whole time. He was undergoing counseling and being evaluated for emotional disorders. The doctors couldn't agree and had suggested several different diagnosis and options. Mandy sounded miserable in her letters to Pagne and wanted to know when they would be home. Brent's letters were odd, distant but nice. Pagne didn't know how the attack and Lenny's reaction would affect their relationship with her dad. She imagined that it would be strained at first. Grandma Maxine had found them a nice apartment and they could move in next week when they returned. Lenny and Pagne cut back on their class load, so they could work more hours to support themselves. Brent had covered Pagne's hospital costs since she had lost her medical insurance when she got married. Pagne didn't expect any more financial help.

It was a tearful farewell when Pagne had to leave Bree. Lenny and William had also become close and their long talks and fellowship in God's word had strengthened Lenny. They were quite a sight: Bree and Pagne blubbering uncontrollably, Lenny and William trying not to. Joshua helped them pack the car for the long drive to the airport. The doctors in the city of Asosa had decided that surgery would be the best option for Joshua and his surgery was scheduled for next month. Pagne would miss him so much. They had become very close. William had convinced the board that he needed another assistant and Joshua now worked at the mission. He had accepted Jesus Christ the same week that he left his shelter in the wilderness. Pagne hugged him and didn't want to let go. He brought his mouth down to her ear and whispered, "Thank you. Thank you for loving me." Pagne struggled to keep from becoming an emotional mess. As they drove away, she watched Joshua shrink and then disappear in the distance.

They were on their way home. Pagne had mixed emotions. She missed her family in America but knew that the storm at home was far from over and the distance in Ethiopia had been a comfortable buffer. She tried to rest and not think too far ahead. As she talked to God and Chantal in her thoughts, Chantal settled in around her, giving her peace that she would get through this, too. She finally drifted to sleep.

The flight was long, but still too short. Lenny and Pagne weren't sure how their home-coming would be received. Brent, Mandy, and Grandma Maxine were there to meet them. Mandy went insane, ran to Pagne, and jumped into her arms. She covered Pagne's face with sticky kisses. "Yuck, what have you been eating?" Pagne asked as she pulled back.

"Cotton Candy," she exclaimed. "Daddy let me get some from that man over there." Pagne saw a vendor with all kinds of sweets displayed.

"Thanks, Dad," Pagne teased. Pagne licked her lips and agreed it tasted good. Grandma Maxine and Brent gave Mandy first shot and then moved in to hold their girl. Brent's eyes teared as he looked at Pagne's face. "It's okay, Dad. I'm fine," Pagne assured.

"You look beautiful, sweetheart. We missed you so much." He didn't say it but his tears were relief that she had healed without any scars from the blows she had taken. Brent looked at Lenny and nodded but that was it. Pagne took hold of Lenny's hand and squeezed. Grandma Maxine saw the exchange and moved to Lenny with a hug and a kiss.

"Give him time, Lenny. He's barely holding on," she whispered. Lenny smiled sadly and kissed her cheek.

They got their luggage and made the drive back to Brent's house. Everyone welcomed Mandy's endless questions so the ride back wasn't silent. It was a bittersweet homecoming. When they got to the house and unloaded the car, Brent explained that he had to go to his office. He was working with his associate on Richie's case. He pecked Pagne's cheek and climbed back into the car. They brought the luggage in and piled it in the family room. Pagne had packed smaller suitcases to get them by for the few days they would be here. It made no sense ito lug everything up to her room, just to bring it down again. She plopped down on the couch next to Lenny and breathed. Being there stirred up a lot of emotions. Mandy jumped on Pagne's lap and started to tickle Lenny's face while he pretended to sleep. He suddenly jumped at her with a roar. She squealed and pulled back. Pagne also jerked as the memory of Lenny's face over Richie's shoulder came to the surface. Lenny saw the fear in Pagne's face, the fear he'd seen that night. Silence. Mandy looked confused at the sudden energy that filled the room. Pagne pulled herself back and tickled Mandy. "Don't you want to see what I got you?"

"Yesss!" She squealed in the high pitch that only little girls can manage.

"Get that bag right there." Mandy quickly obeyed and sat the bag in front of Pagne. She plopped next to her on the couch. Pagne pulled out two packages. "Now, this one is from me and Lenny. This one is from Bree and William." Mandy opened Pagne's first. It was a beautiful ebony doll. The details were exquisite. The doll was dressed in the native clothing of William's tribe. She also had a headpiece covered with pearls and sequins. The body was stuffed fabric. "When you play with her, you need to be extra gentle with her okay? We can't easily replace her at the store."

"Okay Pagne." Mandy inspected her hair and clothing and decided she needed a name. "How about Bragne? That's your and Bree's name together."

Pagne smiled, "That will be a fine name for her." Mandy set the doll on the table next to the couch and then squeezed Pagne and Lenny tightly with her hugs. "I love her! Okay, what did Bree give me?" She looked anxiously at the second box.

"Well, open it." Mandy opened it slowly. Pagne realized that Mandy loved anticipation as much as the experience. She got the lid off and pulled back the tissue. On top was a picture of Bree and William, dressed in native clothes. Pagne thought they looked like something from a travel brochure. Bree had signed the picture, "Love ya Mandy, Salt and Peppa." They both giggled at that. Bree's dress matched the doll's. Mandy was excited by this discovery. She set the picture next to the doll and grinned.

"I'll have to put them in my room together."

"You're not done yet, there's more!" said Pagne.

Mandy found a matching empty frame and looked confused.

"I'll explain, keep digging," encouraged Pagne. Mandy pulled back the last tissue folds and saw a headdress that matched the doll and Bree's. She got it now and continued to pull out the rest of her outfit. She was so excited. "When you put on your outfit, I'll take a picture. Then we will put your picture in the frame. We'll send a copy of the picture to Bree, too. She has the same doll and picture of her and William. That way you both are connected every time you see the doll and pictures."

Mandy jumped up, "Can we do it now, Pagne?"

"Of course. Go get dressed." Pagne started to get up and Lenny took her hand.

"Pagne, we need to talk tonight, okay?" She looked into his eyes, full of pain and shame.

"Yes my love and I think it's a night for silent sex." She grinned at him and he smiled but not with his usual reaction to the mention of lovemaking.

Mandy came back looking adorable and she and Pagne went out to the backyard to get her picture in a garden setting. They took some serious portraits and then the silliness began. They took turns taking pictures of each other with silly faces, with Pagne wearing the headdress, and with both of them together. Mandy was so short, Pagne was sure that her shots would be a clear picture up her nose. On the way back into the house, Mandy asked, "Can I wear this to church tomorrow?"

"Yes, Bree would love that! In fact, I got a similar dress when I was there. Why don't I wear mine, too?" Mandy grinned in agreement.

Grandma Maxine prepared a wonderful dinner for their first night back. She timed it for six o'clock, when Brent said he would be home, but he called her about six-fifteen and apologized; he had grabbed a hamburger earlier and was going to stay and work late. Grandma Maxine gave them his excuses and they sat down to a delicious meal in silence.

They each thought they should start a conversation but everyone was emotionally exhausted and let the silence engulf them. Even Mandy ate quietly and they knew she also felt the weight in the room. After dinner, Grandma Maxine brought out a wonderful dessert, which they picked at. Mandy was the only one who still had room for a piece of German chocolate torte. Lenny and Pagne helped Grandma Maxine clean the kitchen while Mandy took her bath. They kissed Grandma Maxine goodnight, explaining that they were exhausted from the flight. She knew the evening had been strained for everyone and she welcomed an early bedtime. Pagne and Lenny popped in Mandy's room and kissed her goodnight.

"Would you read me a story, Pagne?"

"Sweetie, I'm very tired tonight. Let's make a special night tomorrow. We can build a nest in the closet like Bree and I used to do. We'll get some junk food and make it an event."

"Okay. Promise?" Mandy whispered as she drifted off to sleep.

"Yes, I promise."

Finally, alone in the room, Pagne and Lenny undressed and got ready for bed. The twin beds in the room had been replaced with a comfortable, queen-sized bed. When they were in bed, Pagne began to tease and explore. She knew that Lenny would share his thoughts and feelings easier after sex. "No, Pagne, we have to talk first." She pulled her hands away and realized this was going to be one of those discussions that would shape their relationship. She sat up and fluffed the pillows behind her.

"Okay, I'm listening." Lenny started slow, explaining what he and William had shared the afternoon by the spring. He also told her what God had revealed to him and how he had let his past shatter her family and their world. He assured her that he didn't want that life for him or for them and that he would be setting up some counseling appointments with Pastor Tim. He knew that hurting Richie was not necessary to stop him. It was an excuse to release the rage he suppressed in the darkest part of himself. Lenny admitted he had made things much worse by his actions. He sat quietly as he waited for her reaction.

She looked into his face and his fearful eyes. She leaned over and kissed his forehead, each eyelid, his nose, and then his mouth. It was tender and sweet. She pulled back and nestled under his arm, putting her head on his shoulder. She put her arm over him. He touched the scars lightly, the scars not as defined as before, but still present. "Lenny, I knew you came with a history of pain, just as I did. We are growing and healing every day. We are going to blow it sometimes, just like I did with Macey. You remembered who I was even though my actions showed you all the garbage I had stored up. I see you for who you are and who you can be. The fact that you can identify the garbage and you want to clean it up is enough for me. I love you. You are my heart. We will figure this out together." Lenny turned toward her and began kissing her softly, then with more emotion, until his body craved her.

"Dad's not here, Mandy sleeps like a log, and Grandma Maxine is almost deaf. We could have sorta loud sex," whispered Pagne. She was grinning at him and had already started to remove his briefs.

~

The girl's matching outfits and Mandy's doll were a big hit Sunday at church. Mandy ate up all of the attention. Pastor Tim asked Lenny and Pagne to speak at next week's service to share their experience in Africa. They were excited. Brent didn't attend church or have dinner with them. He said he was working again but, they knew he was avoiding the house while they were there. They would move into their new apartment Tuesday morning so everyone dealt with the awkwardness.

Sunday night happened as promised. Pagne created the environment in the closet that she and Bree had shared. She had to pull things out to make room because the closet had stored more and more items over the years. Pagne got fruit and more cake, which she intended to pig out on, pickles, and chips. She hoped her stomach could still handle the onslaught of sweet, sour, salty, and chocolate. Since Mandy's bedtime was at eight o'clock, they entered the closet sanctuary at six. It would give them time for a story and time to talk. The evening brought back so many memories for Pagne, all the giggling, crying, praying, and memories of Pam. They munched on the snacks and Mandy loved the pickles and chips. Pagne never did read a story because Mandy wanted to hear her story. They talked about Pagne's scars, her angel, Mandy's mom, and Pagne's life there with Bree. She had so many stories to share and she realized, at some point, that Mandy had fallen asleep. Pagne sat there with her for another half hour, remembering the time spent in this closet and savoring her time with Mandy. She decided to let Mandy sleep where she was since she was already in her PJs. Pagne slipped quietly out of the closet and found Lenny reading in bed. It was ten-thirty. "Wow, I had no idea that we were in there that long." Lenny grinned at her as she climbed into bed. "You hear all that?" she asked.

"Just the last hour or so. You have some wonderful memories, Pagne."

"Yes, I do. I had a good life here, Lenny."

"I'm sorry I helped ruin that."

"Stop it," she said sternly. "You did no such thing. It's called life and sometimes life just sucks. We'll all get through this. Dad is fighting for Richie right now. That's how it should be. This will soon be behind us and we will heal! There is too much love in this family for things to end this way." She snuggled in and said teasingly, "No ideas about sex tonight, not even silent sex. We got a kid in the closet."

He smiled. "Never crossed my mind," he lied.

They spent Monday sorting out items in the garage. They had accumulated a lot over the last year. Tuesday morning, some of their friends from church helped them move into their new one-bedroom apartment. Brent was noticeably absent. Pagne hated the tension but also knew it was a matter of time. The new place was bigger than the studio they had. Pagne liked the idea of a separate bedroom. It felt more like a home. By evening, they were settled in. They bought pizza for everyone and the last friend left at nine o'clock. Lenny chased Pagne around the apartment, telling her they had to initiate each room that first night, including the kitchen. Pagne let Lenny catch her and they created a memorable first night alone in their new apartment.

Chapter 23

School started again and Pagne and Lenny were back to their jobs. Life settled into a smooth routine. The only bump was Richie's coming court date. Brent asked them to meet with his associate, Mrs. Evans, to discuss the trial. They decided to meet her at a local coffeehouse. They weren't sure what the point of the meeting was. The district attorney's office had talked with them prior to their trip to Africa and several times after they returned. Mrs. Evans was young and very attractive. She had a winning smile that made them feel relaxed. "May I call you Pagne and Lenny?" They both nodded. "I just want to go over some details and ask you a few questions." Pagne wondered if this was standard. She didn't know if the district attorney would be upset that they met with her but this was her brother and she wanted him to get help, not to be punished. Pagne couldn't speak for Lenny.

Mrs. Evans went over the details of the attack. There were a few questions about Richie's behavior prior to that night. She asked if Pagne had been drinking, if Pagne and Richie ever discussed an intimate relationship, and if Lenny had tried to remove Richie without force. Pagne knew she had these details, but probably wanted to see how they presented themselves. Lenny explained the panic and his instant reaction. He was sickened by Richie's obvious sexual intentions and his violent response. She reviewed the police report, the photos, and the doctor's comments in Pagne's file. "This must have been very scary for you, Pagne."

"At first I didn't understand what was happening, it was so quick. Then I just felt sick that Richie could have those thoughts about me. I knew I had to stop him, but he was so strong and so angry."

"What do you think should happen to Richie?" she asked Pagne.

"I want him to get help. I love Richie and I don't think that this is who he is. I hope that medication and counseling will help him work through whatever is going on."

"I see that you didn't press charges."

"No, the police said it wasn't necessary since the evidence was so overwhelming and there were eye witnesses."

"How did you feel about that?"

"Relieved. I didn't want to put Richie in jail."

"If the police said you had to press charges, would you have?" Pagne thought for a minute and avoided looking at Lenny.

"Yes, he needs to get help. We've all tried talking to him and loving him and it wasn't working."

"Okay, I think I have everything I need. If we ask the court to release Richie with orders for counseling and medication as well as probation for four years, will you support that?"

"Yes," Pagne said.

"Lenny, what about you?" Miss Evans asked as she looked at him.

"Of course," he said, "I love Richie and want him with his family if he is getting help."

"Okay, thank you both very much. I may be able to arrange things with the court and avoid a trial, especially if you," she looked at Pagne, "don't challenge the conditions. If Richie is released, I will request a restraining order to keep distance between both of you and Richie. This is for everyone's safety." She gave Lenny a hard look. "Thank you for your time and compassion toward Richie. It's refreshing to see a family looking out for each other, even when there has been so much conflict." Lenny stood as she rose to leave and reached out to shake her hand.

"Thank you for representing Richie. I really do want the best for him.

~

Pagne and Lenny were relieved when they heard that the courts were cooperating and would release Richie with the conditions his lawyer had reviewed with them. Pagne knew the restraining order would dramatically affect her relationship with Brent and everyone else at the house. This saddened her. Brent had suggested dinners once a week with her, him, and Mandy. She felt a cold slap when he excluded Lenny. She realized it was going to take more time than she ever dreamed to resolve their issues.

Richie was following the rules and Brent said he saw a big improvement in his moods now that he was on the medications. They were at their weekly dinner and it had been three months. Richie was doing well in school and seemed much more relaxed. Grandma Maxine had joined them for dinner and had taken Mandy to the restroom. Pagne wanted to feel out Brent's position with Lenny. "Dad, Lenny really misses you. Would it be okay if he joined us next week for dinner?" Brent looked away and Pagne saw a slight tightening of his jaw.

"I don't know, Pagne. I still see him standing over Richie and Richie beaten so badly. I have such mixed emotions about that night. I was so angry that Richie hurt you... especially in that way. I think Lenny could have pulled him off and restrained him without the violence." Pagne looked at him and sighed.

"Yes, you're right, Dad. He knows that, too. I think the trigger for him was that it appeared to be sexual and he just wasn't able to process it. He didn't see my brother in that moment. He saw another man violating his wife." Pagne saw the pain in Brent's eyes and decided to change the subject. Grandma Maxine and Mandy were heading back to the table anyway. "Anyone got room for dessert?" Pagne asked. Mandy cheered.

They shared several dessert items since they all sounded so good. Grandma Maxine and Mandy said their goodnights and headed to the car. Brent walked Pagne to hers. "Pagne, you know I love you and I'm not condoning Richie's behavior in any way."

"I know, Dad. It's got to be an impossible place to be in."

"Ask Lenny if he will meet me for coffee tomorrow evening. I would like the freedom to talk to him without you sitting there." She looked at him with concern and he smiled, "Don't worry, I miss him, too. I want to see if we can start working through this but, I need to talk to him man to man. Alone."

"Okay, Dad. I'll ask him."

"Goodnight, sweetheart. You're in a tough spot, too. Please know that I see that. I appreciate you caring enough about Richie to work with the courts."

"I just want him to be safe and happy, Dad."

"Me too, me too," Brent agreed. He gave Pagne one last hug before she climbed in her car.

~

Lenny was relieved that Brent would meet with him but was tense when he walked in. Brent was already there and had a table way in the back where they would have some privacy. Lenny was overwhelmed with emotions when Brent ignored his effort to shake hands. Lenny sat down awkwardly. "Would you like to order something?" Brent asked. He already had coffee steaming in front of him.

"No thanks, my stomach is pretty much in knots." Lenny couldn't take the silence and began to unburden his shame and regret. They talked for several hours, first about that night and then about life, plans, Ethiopia, and Pagne. Lenny didn't ask much about Richie because he didn't want to ruin where they were going.

Brent, however, wanted Lenny's advice. "Richie is doing what he is supposed to but I see the emptiness in his eyes, almost as if he was robotic. Can you tell me more about your dad, what patterns I should be watching for?"

Lenny tried to give him hope. His dad would never admit there was a problem, let alone get help. At least Richie admitted there were issues. But, Lenny also told Brent that Richie was in a forced, controlled situation right now and there were no guarantees that these changes were heartfelt. Lenny explained some of the warning signs about his dad's behavior, and encouraged him to go by his gutt reactions. If something felt wrong, it probably was.

Brent thanked Lenny and stood to leave. There was an awkward moment and they did the classic handshake with a slap on the back. As Brent opened his car door, he called out to Lenny. "You going to be at dinner next week?"

Lenny grinned, "I wouldn't miss it for the world, Sir." It sounded odd to say sir but he didn't think he could call him dad.

Brent nodded, "Good, see you then."

~

The next year seemed to fly by. Pagne and Lenny received their AA degrees. They enrolled at the state university for fall classes and both decided to continue with psychology as their majors. Brent and Lenny's relationship had progressed but they kept it low key. Richie harbored a lot of anger for Lenny and Brent didn't want to agitate things even more. Richie didn't ask much about anything so it wasn't difficult to play it down.

They didn't see any indication that Brent was dating or spending time with friends. His whole life was dealing with Richie, Mandy, and work. Pagne had an idea and ran it past Lenny. "Why don't we invite Dad over for a dinner party?"

"Dinner party. How would us three be a party?" he asked. Pagne gave him a sly grin.

"Well, we have four chairs. I thought we could invite Renee." He smiled. They didn't see Miss Renee often but Pagne and Lenny stayed in touch with her through email. They had dropped the Miss some time ago, and she was now their friend, Renee. Lenny was seriously considering Renee's offer to work with her program to assist children as advocates. Lenny's degree in psychology would be an asset. "Dad and Renee always got along well. She just broke up with the fifth Mr. Wrong," Pagne continued. Lenny asked if she was going to warn him or just ambush him. "He won't come if he thinks it's a setup. Once he's here, what can he do but stay?"

"Mmmm Pagne, I never thought you were a meddler."

"Well, he needs some fun and he's been alone so long."

"Okay, but if it gets messy, I'm ducking out for ice."

"Thanks, Chicken."

The evening was a great success. Brent seemed genuinely happy to see Renee and to have an evening out. They had a lot of things in common and made plans to do dinner and a movie soon. After they left, Lenny bowed to Pagne with mock admiration. "Told ya," she said. They were cleaning up when they got a frantic call from Brent. Someone had robbed the house and the police were on their way. Grandma Maxine had taken Mandy up to her daughter's home in Oregon for a few days and Richie was home alone. "Is Richie okay? Was he there?" Pagne asked. Brent was silent for too long.

"Richie isn't here, Pagne. Someone knew where my coins were hidden and where my extra credit cards and emergency cash were kept. The medications we locked away are gone, too." Brent was quiet for a long time.

"Dad, you don't know that it was Richie." She said but they both knew. This was the beginning of another four-year nightmare for Brent and his family. Richie was in and out of juvenile hall and rehab facilities. He cut most of his classes and didn't have enough credits to graduate from high school. Brent never gave up on him but, when Richie turned eighteen, he left without any indication of where he was going. Brent was worried sick, yet he was also relieved that the tension was out of their home. The feeling of relief came with a heavy dose of guild. Brent got word that Richie had been arrested in a drug deal gone wrong. He had enough drugs in his possession for felony charges. He also had a gun in his possession, which was in violation of his probation conditions. His choices had caught up to him and he received a five-year sentence. Richie refused to use Brent as his attorney, and would not see any of the family or return letters. They never stopped trying, but realized they only had the power of prayer in this battle for Richie.

~

Lenny and Pagne were excited to be graduating from college with their BAs, finally! Lenny was going to work with Renee as one of her administrators. He would work with the volunteers, providing guidance and training. The pay wasn't great but they could get by. Renee and Brent had begun a serious relationship and Pagne was happy to see Brent laugh and enjoy life again.

Pagne wasn't sure what she wanted to do. She had gotten a degree in psychology and had an appointment with Mr. Phillips at Langston Hall. Macey was now in charge of all recreation for Langston Hall. The "Kennel Kids" had become a huge outreach success. Macey wanted Pagne to be a part of what she'd started. She knew that they, as a team, could affect so many young lives. Macey was excited that they might work together again.

The interview went well and they offered her a position working with the administration and with Macey. Pagne felt led to take the position but wanted to discuss it with Lenny first. He was thrilled for her and told her she was the perfect person for the job.

Pagne and Macey were a dynamic team and improved the quality of life for each child residing at Langston Hall.

~

Months became years and Payne embraced them with passion and dignity. Life was good and, while her marriage to Lenny wasn't perfect, they adored each other and worked through life's challenges with respect and patience. They decided to wait until their careers were secure before having their own children but, eventually, their family grew and their home was filled with love and laughter. Pammy was the first addition.

Chapter 24

Pagne put on the finishing touches on her makeup. She heard Pammy yell for her to hurry up. The limo was here. She looked in the mirror one last time. Her thirty-five year old face was beginning to show some age. She had faint crows-feet and she thought she saw some gray hairs popping up along her hairline. She didn't wear her hair long anymore. It was cut in a short, curly bob. Her gown for the evening was aqua blue. She'd learned many years ago this was her best color and it made her eyes jump out at her in the mirror. The last layer of mascara was dry and it lengthened and darkened her lashes to frame her eyes. She applied deep peach lipstick just as Pammy stuck her head in the bathroom. "Mom, everyone is waiting." Pagne looked at the lovely young girl, her daughter, not her biological daughter, but no less her daughter. Lenny and Pagne had adopted her nine years ago. Her teen mother had left her at the hospital, unable to cope with the challenges ahead. Pammy's real name was Pamela after Pagne's mom. Pammy was born with deformities, including blindness, heart disorders, fused fingers and toes, and missing vertebra, which shortened her torso. Some issues they corrected with surgery but others would be her burden for life. Pammy didn't allow her blindness or her physical limitations to diminish her life. Pagne and Lenny had given her a home that encouraged and enabled her to achieve more than any of the doctors had expected. As Pagne stepped out of the bathroom, Pammy touched her arm and said, "Wait, I want to look at you." Pagne stooped down to the nine-year-old and let her fingers read the details of her face and hair. "You are beautiful," she told her. Pagne smiled. She was sure Pammy felt the same face every time but Pammy wanted to participate in celebrating the events in their lives.

"Thank you, sweetheart. Is your daddy dressed?"

"Oh yes, he's been ready for a long time."

Pammy and Pagne headed down the stairs and, when they saw her, Pagne heard Lenny, Mandy, and Chez whistle and clap. Pagne grinned and felt very pretty that night. Chez was their six-year-old biological son. Unlike Pammy, he was healthy in every way. He was an exact duplicate of Lenny, in every facial feature and body structure. But, Pagne was also in the mix. Chez had red, curly hair, Pagne's freckles, and her blue eyes. They saw the magic of each of them blended in their young son.

Macey and her husband Ben were joining them for the celebration and Macey could not contain the grin on her face. She was so proud of Pagne and her accomplishments. Pagne felt awkward about the award she was receiving but thankful that "Kennel Kids" was benefiting from the process.

As they were leaving for the limo, Lenny turned to Mandy. "Now you know..."

"Yes," she interrupted. "I know where the medications and the oxygen are kept and I have every phone number I'll ever need on the fridge. Don't worry, Lenny, the kids will be fine. I'm not a little girl anymore."

"I know," he said softly. "It's just that Pammy has been so compromised this year."

"I know, Lenny. I'll take good care of her." He hugged her and joined the others. "Please don't worry and have a great time," she called out after him.

Pagne felt like a celebrity. The award foundation had provided the limo. The last time she was in a limo was at Bree's wedding. Bree wanted to be here but she was busy with their medical clinic in Ethiopia. When the limo arrived at the auditorium, Pagne exited in a flash of light from the news media. She knew she wasn't the main attraction but she enjoyed the excitement of feeling important. They made their way through the crowd, greeting people they knew. When they arrived at their reserved table, Renee was already seated. She stood and welcomed Pagne with a big hug and kiss. Pagne felt the sting again of losing Brent. It had only been two years since he died. As they took their seats, Pagne noticed one empty chair. She thought it was odd since the event organizers were so adamant about how many people were in her party. There was going to be a lovely dinner after the ceremonies so Pagne couldn't understand why. She looked at Lenny and saw the mischievous grin on his face. "What's going on?" she asked.

"You'll find out soon enough," he teased.

The house lights went down to a soft glow and the front stage filled with bright light. The Los Angeles symphony opened up in a lovely rendition of Moon River, one of Pagne's favorites. The served wine and appetizers while everyone enjoyed the music. Many people came to the table, mostly strangers, and congratulated Pagne. After several songs, the mayor announced the governor of California. The room boomed with applause. Governor Michaels was a very admired and respected man. He had turned the state of California around. Many programs were reinstated because of his success in resolving the financial crisis. He was the educators' hero. He began announcing the names of people he called "the real heros" that were receiving an award. He described their dedication and accomplishments in education and community outreach programs. Many of these people, Pagne and Lenny had worked with over the years. They were good, compassionate people and Pagne was happy their efforts were being honored.

It was finally her turn. She was going last. The house lights dimmed for dramatic effect. She hoped she'd be able to find her way to the stage. A spotlight centered at the podium, shining on the governor but the rest of the stage was dark. When the governor began his introduction speech, Pagne stood and began the walk up to the stage. They instructed her to move toward the governor at that point. After he made his opening comments, he turned to his left. "I would like to bring out someone very special to be our first recipient of the Walter Graham Award." Walter Graham had been a successful Californian raised in the system, a "Kennel Kid." He had become wealthy and, when he died last year, he set up an award with funding to honor programs designed to assist children in need. Pagne was the first recipient and could not be more appreciative of this kind man giving back.

A smaller spotlight was shining on the curtain and out walked Bree. Pagne was shocked and excited to see her sister. She'd had no idea \she was here. She looked at Lenny and saw the smile that warmed her heart each morning. Pagne was trying so hard not to cry. She didn't want to be under those bright lights with mascara running down her cheeks.

Bree walked over to the podium and greeted the governor. He stepped back into the darkness and left Bree at center stage, alone. "Hello, I am Brianna Johnson, Pagne's sister. When they asked me to come and present this award, I was so honored and proud. I cannot think of anyone more deserving than Pagne to receive the first Walter Graham Award. I remember our days at Langston Hall. We were children, alone and fearful of what life held for us. Even at a young age, Pagne had strength about her. She was physically broken and alone but she had enough hope and grace for all of us. It was painful when we had to separate but God had plans for our lives. We were reunited in a family that poured love and encouragement over us, allowing us to have the determination to fulfill our destinies. Pagne brought that strength back to Langston Hall. She began a healing of these broken hearts and spirits that has spread nationwide. The response from previous "Kennel Kids" getting involved and reaching out to their younger counterparts has been extraordinary and the number of adoptions has doubled in the last five years. If there ever was a champion for our forgotten children, it is Pagne. She started a small outreach twenty-one years ago that has grown into a national network of committed, loving, forgotten angels that refuse to let the indifference continue. I would like to introduce my sister, Champagne Mari Wilson." The room built into a deafening clamor of applause, whistles, and shouts. Pagne looked at Macey and Lenny as she started up the stairs to the stage. You both should be up there with me, she thought.

Another light encircled Pagne as she stepped onto the stage and she realized she had to do something besides looking like a deer caught in headlights. She forced a smile and continued to Bree's side. "You brat, I will deal with you later," Pagne whispered. Bree giggled and quietly told her how proud she was of her. Bree then stepped back into the darkness.

Governor Michaels and Mayor Stevens joined her at the podium, one on each side. "It is with great admiration that I give you the very first Walter Graham Award," the governor started. "You have accomplished so much with your passion and respect for our children. They are all our children and you have shown us as a nation how we can respond to their needs and challenges, how to love them. I thank God that he has sent souls like you to us to show us the way." Pagne was overwhelmed with the compliments and the acknowledgement. She hoped Brent and Pam were able to see her from Heaven. She suddenly smelled Chantal, strong and sweet. She knew that Heaven was also celebrating her life. The governor handed Pagne a lovely, crystal figurine of an adult walking and holding the hand of a skipping child. A mahogany base, carved with the commemorating details of the evening, supported the figure. It was gorgeous. As Mayor Stevens handed her a parchment envelope containing a check, he announced the award for one million dollars. Pagne could only imagine what this would mean to her kids. She knew there was a cash award but the amount had not been revealed until tonight. Pagne felt herself going faint. She grabbed onto the podium to support herself. The governor felt her shudder and put his hand under her elbow to support her. The crowd was going insane. It felt like a dream as she saw flashes of lights going off throughout the room.

The room quieted and Pagne knew that she had to speak. She'd tried writing out a speech many times but it sounded rehearsed and contrived. Pagne decided to wing it and speak from her heart in the moment. "I would like to thank Mr. Walter Graham for his generosity and his involvement with "Kennel Kids" over the last ten years. He was my friend and a friend to all of our forgotten children. We miss him terribly. I am praying that the publicity of this event will reach out to even more citizens and encourage them to take an active role in nurturing and loving our wonderful children. We need foster-homes. We also need volunteers, tutors, mentors, and adoptive parents. We need to be a society that protects and honors our children. This generous award will provide so many wonderful opportunities to do just that." Pagne paused. The emotions were overwhelming. "I also want to thank my family for accepting a scarred, frightened child into their hearts. To see in me what I could never have dreamed possible. I love you." The governor and mayor escorted Pagne to the left where Bree waited for her, eyes brimming with tears of joy. The audience's response was a thunderous wave of acclamation.

The symphony came back on stage and the house lights came back up, lit but soft. The servers began bringing out the first course. Bree and Pagne made it back to their table in time for the second course, which was quite an accomplishment considering every few feet another well-wisher would stop them. Pagne was surrounded by love and the memories of a legacy that was hers to cherish. Everyone at her table wanted to see the award but the event organizers suggested keeping it backstage because it was fragile. She was able to show them the check. Lenny whistled, "I've never seen so many zeros." The oversized check only represented the payment that would be transferred electronically to the "Kennel Kids" business account on Monday.

"Kennel Kids" had an official headquarters now. Six years earlier, Pagne left her position at Langston Hall to focus full-time on the national development of "Kennel Kids." Her outreach survived on the generosity of community donations. They had several small offices in the same building that Pagne and Lenny had run to, to find Miss Renee many years ago. Renee's advocacy program had grown and, between the two organizations, they occupied the whole building. Pagne had decided that the figurine would be displayed there.

Pagne wanted to visit with Bree but would be patient. She was going to be staying for several days. Pagne divided her attention between everyone at the table and the people who made their way over to say hello. Richie and Bree slipped out briefly because they had not seen each other since the attack. They had written and spoken on the phone several times since his reunion with Pagne but it was the first time they had come face to face.

While the dessert dishes were cleared, the governor appeared at Pagne's side. "I don't want to go into details now, but please call me next week." He handed Pagne a card. "I would like to discuss teaming up to publicize the efforts of my agenda for our children and Kennel Kids. I think we could increase the community's focus on our kids throughout the state."

Pagne was honored. "I would love that, Sir."

"Please call me Adam. This card has my personal number. I have watched you over the last eighteen years, Pagne. You have the ability to make people hear and respond. You have sparked a movement of compassion and ownership for our discarded children that has never been done in this state or in this country. I need your help to accomplish what needs to be done, what these kids deserve." He congratulated her again and left with his security officers. Pagne was relieved that the evening was wrapping up and she could relax and spend time with Bree. Lenny had called Mandy several times and confirmed the kids were still alive.

When Brent had died, Mandy was away at college and Grandma Maxine was living with Brent and Renee. Renee and Brent shared eight years of marriage and Renee was thankful to be part of this loving family. She decided to move into a small apartment closer to her offices, since she knew the house belonged to Pam, Brent, and the kids. After Brent's death, Renee remained part of the family. Lenny and Pagne moved back into the house with their children so that Grandma Maxine could remain in the house. It would have been difficult for her by herself. The house was paid for and Brent had wanted Grandma Maxine to stay in the home for as long as possible. When the time came, the house would be sold and the profits split between Bree, Pagne, Richie, and Mandy. It worked out well. Pagne and Lenny had the master bedroom. Mandy had her room waiting when she came home for holidays and school breaks. Grandma Maxine took Richie's old room and Pammy shared Pagne's old room with Chez. The room was so large, they had put in a wall to divide the space. Pagne started the tradition of closet nights and the kids loved it. It was tight, but the three of them shared their desires and fears together in that closet. Sometimes, Mandy would join them. Pickles and chips were always on the closet menu and, oddly enough, they never ate them at any other time.

Bree so excited to be back at the house. Richie had visited them there quite a few times over the last eighteen months. He was grown now, a man, but they could still see the boy they all adored. He had not aged well. His life had worn his body down, but his health was slowly improving now that he was taking care of himself. Lenny kissed Pagne good night. He was exhausted. Grandma Maxine had already gone up to bed. Lenny knew that Bree, Pagne, and Richie would be up all night. The girls changed into some of Pagne's sweats and Richie changed into some clothes he had brought with him. Once comfortable with big mugs of steaming hot chocolate, they moved into the familiar family room. Not much had changed except for updated electronics. The couch had been replaced; so many years had worn the old one out. It still was their home. They could still feel the love of Brent and Pam in that room. Some of the pictures from their childhood were still on the shelves but many were new, photos of Lenny and Pagne's family. Bree had taken her biological family pictures and some favorite family pictures when she got married. Renee had taken the pictures during her marriage with Brent. Pagne's life was on those shelves, the progression of changes, additions, and time.

Bree and Pagne excitedly filled each other in on their lives while Richie listened and remembered the bond his two sisters shared. After they caught up on the kids and the friends that they shared in Ethiopia, they started the memories. Richie began to join in. They laughed until they cried. Bree got very quiet, "I miss them," she said. "We lost Mom way too soon... and Dad, it just felt good knowing he was here."

"Yeah," Pagne agreed.

"I was so glad Dad and Renee got married. Good plan you had," Bree confirmed. The girls realized Richie was very quiet again. "You okay?" asked Bree.

"No," Richie admitted. "When I finally got my act together, Dad was gone and I never got to apologize. I never had the chance to let him see that I could change." Pagne and Bree could see his grief and shame.

"Richie, we can't give you back those years," Pagne spoke softly, "but know this, he always loved you. He never stopped praying for God to intervene and he never stopped thanking God for giving you to him." Richie broke and the tears rolled down his cheeks. Bree and Pagne immediately moved in close and held him. They knew these tears released so much pain and guilt. They didn't try to stop him, they were just with him through the process.

They didn't talk about Richie's past that evening. Everyone knew the details of his return to the family. They were just thankful that Pagne had gotten the call from a friend that worked at the county hospital and recognized Richie's name on his medical chart. He was in bad shape. He had hepatitis and required treatment for exposure and malnutrition, as well as many other complications due to a life of drug use on the streets. Pagne was relieved to find Richie. They had never stopped looking for him and she didn't want to lose him again.

Pagne would sit with him for hours, even though he was asleep or delirious. She prayed and read scripture over him and put him on the church's prayer list. Pastor Tim would visit as often as possible and they would pray together. Most days she could smell Chantal, slipping in and out, swirling. The scent was strongest when Pagne prayed. One afternoon, Pagne was praying and felt a soft brush on her cheek, the scent of Chantal surrounding her.

"It is time, contend," Chantal whispered. Pagne opened her eyes and looked into Richie's face as he looked at her, confused.

"Richie? Do you know me?" She saw recognition in his eyes, then rage.

"Get out, Pagne, I don't want you here." He turned away, his body clenched into a ball. She got up and left silently.

When she got home, she told Lenny about Chantal's message, Richie waking up, and his outburst. Lenny held her in a strong hug. "Pagne, this is going to be tough for both of you. Either he is still the victim and he blames you or he's filled with guilt and shame and can't face you. Try short visits and see what happens over time. If it is guilt, it will take your assurances that you have forgiven him. If your angel told you it was time to contend, trust her. You have to know this won't happen overnight. To contend is to fight, fight hard."

~

She loved Lenny. He had become a very wise, loving man. Her fears of his dark side filled with hate had died a slow death over the years. He followed through and did counseling with Pastor Tim. He prayed for God to heal his heart. Pagne saw a breakthrough when Lenny finally agreed to see his father. Leonard was released from prison and moved back in with Lenny's mom several years back. Lenny had sent a few letters to his dad while he was in prison but they were always short and indifferent. They stated that Lenny was praying for him and that he hoped in time they could get past all the pain. Lenny had to decide if he would shut his father out and try to see his mother separately, but God had been healing Lenny's brokenness and hatred for his father. Lenny decided to try for his mother's sake, or so he said.

Lenny went to his parent's home. The evening was strained and his mother kept trying to lighten the mood, which irritated Lenny even more. Lenny's father, Leonard Senior, politely asked her to take a drive for an hour, which would give him and Lenny some time alone. "I'll go get ice cream for us," she agreed, "both my boys love ice cream." She left with a smile and a purpose. Lenny was big enough and strong enough that he didn't physically fear his father anymore, but he still felt the twinge of abandonment when his mother left. Leonard crossed the room and sat in the far corner, leaving Lenny lots of space and access to the front door. Lenny sat on the arm of the couch in a defensive posture.

"Son, Lenny, I don't expect you to believe me when I say that I'm not the person you knew. I'll have to prove that to you. I just want you to know that I am proud of who you've become and I did nothing to encourage or support you. You have become an incredible man on your own. It shames me to know that I did not have the character that you have." Lenny could see the tears welling up in his father's eyes. "I am just so thankful that there were people who showed me grace and let me find God's place in my life, a life that has value now. My job is to take care of your mother, respect and love her, and to work at becoming the man you have always been. To say that I'm sorry for all the damage I've done is hollow." He became silent, then continued. "Thank you for agreeing to see me. I know that it was not easy for you." They sat staring at each other. Lenny didn't have words. He wasn't ready to release his anger and pain yet.

They heard a car pull up. "You're mother has no sense of time and is back with the ice cream already. I hope you'll stay. I'll follow your lead, Lenny, and I will not push."

Lenny did stay and felt motivated to give his father a quick hug when he left. It would be a long process for them because trust is always a difficult tear to mend. Over the next few years, Lenny was able to ask his questions, vent, and eventually forgive. They never would have the type of relationship he and Brent had shared, but it was theirs and it gave them both closure to a very painful time in their lives.

Pagne did as Lenny suggested and slipped into Richie's room for a few minutes at a time. Sometimes, Richie would ignore her and sometimes he would thank her, especially if she brought him his favorite snacks. Sometimes he would look at her with tear-filled eyes and insist she leave. Pagne could see that it was

Richie's guilt hindering their progress. One day, she sat in her car and prayed for a crack in Richie's wall, a chance to break through the hurt of the past. She went into his room and set a box of cookies on his tray. He was dozing and started to stir. She sat down and, when Richie was fully awake, their eyes met. Richie suddenly closed off. "Pagne, please leave, I don't want to see you."

She swallowed and found her determination. "I'll go, but first, I have a few things to say to you." He closed his eyes and Pagne could see him physically bracing himself. "Richie, I love you. I am your sister and that does not change when things get ugly. What you did was horrific and it was very painful. Not just physically, but you ripped away my brother from me, a brother I want back. I have forgiven you and you need to forgive yourself. It's going to take the mercy of God for you to do that. Now, I can leave and never come back or you can be a man and deal with what happened so we can move on. If I leave, you will have to seek me out. I will not come back in here again." She crossed her arms over her chest and made it clear she was serious.

Richie opened his eyes and looked at his sister, an incredible woman who was willing to love him. "Why would you forgive me, Pagne? That is pathetic. I was a monster and probably still am." *Thank you Jesus,* she thought, *a crack.*

"I don't know exactly. I just know that I didn't stop loving you when you hurt me. I don't believe you're a monster. I think you need to take responsibility for your life and what you're doing to yourself but you're not alone. You have a family that wants you back. We want Richie, our brother."

"Obviously, Dad doesn't want me back. He hasn't been here once. I've asked the nurses." Pagne looked down, knowing this next news was going to be painful for him and her.

"Richie, Dad died six months ago. He had a massive heart attack and died instantly. There wasn't anything anyone could do." Richie's face fell and the sobs broke loose. Pagne moved to his side and rocked him. He clung to her and let his anguish and regret pour out. It was the beginning of the rebuilding of their relationship. Pagne continued to visit alone until Richie was well enough to leave the hospital. He would be on treatment for hepatitis the rest of his life and he agreed to go straight into a rehab facility, which would be covered by Brent's life insurance policy. It wasn't until Lenny saw his commitment to the program that he went to visit. They discussed the attacks and Lenny explained why he had reacted so violently. A lot of pain and anger were brought to light that day.

Richie extended his time in rehab beyond the twenty eight days. He knew he was not ready to be on the street. Lenny and Pagne visited Richie as much as they could. Pastor Tim also spent many hours with Richie. He brought God's message of redemption to Richie in a way the family couldn't. Richie had accepted Jesus Christ as a young boy but recommitted himself while in the facility. When he finally felt he could cope with the real world, Lenny, Pastor

Tim, and several of Richie's childhood buddies from church found him a room to rent, a job, and a cheap car. They knew he would struggle but they made sure he had the support he needed. Richie was also blessed to have a strong, Christian sponsor through Narcotics Anonymous. Richie decided to be baptized. Pagne and Lenny had never made this decision so, as a family, Richie, Pagne, Lenny, Chez, Pammy, and Mandy, celebrated their baptisms together. It united them in a very profound way. When Richie came to the house to visit, Pagne would sometimes find him standing in the doorway of his old room. He would give her a sad smile and then head back downstairs. Richie hung out in the clubhouse with Chez. He was glad it still served the fantasies of a young boy. Every day, Richie was closer to being the man he was intended to be.

"Well guys, I'm exhausted," Bree announced. She was using the office for a room while visiting. They had put an airbed in there for her. "Love you sis," she hugged Pagne and kissed her softly. She grabbed Richie and hugged him tightly. "I am so thankful to have you back, Richie. I missed you so much!"

"Me too, sis. I love you." Bree released him and headed to bed. Pagne saw Richie putting on his jacket.

"Richie, won't you stay?"

"Nahhhh Pagne, I'll come back tomorrow. I need to step away from all the memories for a little while." She nodded to let him know that she understood.

"Okay, but call us when you wake up."

"I will," he kissed her on the cheek and headed for the door. He stopped, "Pagne?"

"Yes?"

"Thank you for not giving up on me."

She smiled and responded, "You are my brother and you never give up on family."

"All the same, thank you. I believe you saved my life!"

Chapter 25

Lenny and Pagne woke up to the front doorbell ringing. It had only been a few hours since Pagne had gone to bed. When Lenny opened the door, there were several police officers on the porch. "May we come in?" Pagne felt her chest tighten up as Lenny stepped aside for the officers to enter the house. The officers looked at each other with an expression of dread. Pagne leaned against Lenny when she felt herself feeling faint.

"What's going on, Officers?" asked Lenny cautiously.

"Do you know Richard Masters?" one of the officers asked. For a second, Pagne felt relief. The name Richard didn't sound familiar until her sub-conscious mind screamed Richie's name. Lenny quickly brought his arm around Pagne. He knew she was going to need his strength.

"Yes, Officer, he's our brother," responded Lenny. By this time, Bree had thrown on a robe and was standing behind Lenny and Pagne. They knew that this was serious and wanted to know what was wrong but knew that once they heard, it couldn't be taken back. Pagne was the most aware of the pending doom because Chantal's scent was surrounding her, pulsing, as if to remind her to breathe.

"Sir, maybe we should have the ladies sit down," the older officer suggested. Lenny led Pagne and Bree to the couch and sat between them. Pagne wanted to scream "What? What? Please, just tell us," but she couldn't say a word.

The older officer, the one with more experience, began to speak. Pagne heard him clearly but his words echoed, as if he was deep in a cave. "Your brother was murdered this morning. He helped a woman that was being attacked and he was killed." There they were. The words that could never be returned. Words that changed lives forever once released. Lenny sat with his head in his hands, repeating "No! No! No!" Bree slid off the couch onto her knees, wailing in anguish. Pagne sat there breathing, just breathing in and out as Chantal prompted her. It took every ounce of her will just to breathe. The officers didn't speak, just stood there, as if standing guard over them, protecting them while they were vulnerable and helpless.

A few days later, the young woman Richie rescued asked to meet with Richie's family and they agreed. Pagne, Bree, and Lenny weren't sure what she wanted to say and they were curious. She was the last person to see Richie alive. Her name was Angela and she stood to greet them when they entered the small room at the police station. They were startled to see the extent of her injuries. Her attackers had been vicious animals. Angela tried to speak but cried instead. Bree and Pagne moved to her sides and lightly held her. "I'm so sorry," she finally managed. "If it wasn't for my stupidity, your brother would still be alive!" Through her tears and sobs, Angela managed to explain what led up to the attack. She worked in a bar and when her shift was over, she stopped to talk to some friends and missed her bus. Instead of waiting half an hour for the next one, she decided to walk home. She took a shortcut through the alley when the two men jumped her.

Richie must have heard her muffled screams when he got out of his car, because he ran into the alley where the two men were attacking her. One was behind her, with his hand over her mouth, holding her captive in a crushing squeeze. The second man was trying to rip off her clothing. Richie came up quickly, grabbed the man in front around the neck, and pulled him off the woman while choking him. The second man was startled, loosened his grip over her mouth, and reached out with his other hand toward Richie, trying to grab him. Angela was able to scream and she began hitting and kicking with all her strength. The man punched her in the stomach and, while she was doubled over in pain, he punched her in the face, knocking her to the ground. Semiconscious and struggling to breathe, she watched Richie fight her two assailants. He fought like a lion and delivered some serious damage. One of the men realized that Richie was not an easy takedown and pulled out a knife. He stepped in while Richie wrestled with his partner and stabbed Richie in the throat. The two assailants staggered off when they heard the sirens getting close. One of the neighbors had called the police when they heard the woman's screams but help did not reach Richie in time.

Angela was able to drag herself to Richie and hold him while they waited for the ambulance to reach them. He could barely speak but struggled to make her understand his last message. "Tell Pagne, I see my angel," he gasped, "I'll be waiting for them in Heaven." With that, he closed his eyes and died in peace.

Angela had known her attackers. They were regulars at the bar. They must have followed her and decided the alley was the place to overtake her. She was able to give the police their names and a physical description. They were arrested at the county hospital shortly after the murder. Richie had beaten them so badly, they needed medical treatment and had been covered in blood, theirs and Richie's. Once in police custody, DNA and fingerprints linked them to a series of unsolved rapes and murders.

Pagne, Bree, and Lenny were thankful that Richie was not alone when he died and they found great comfort in hearing that he died peacefully. Pagne thanked her for giving them the message and Angela wanted to know what it meant. Pagne explained about angels, salvation, and how to get to Heaven. The Holy Spirit had already begun to work in Angela's heart, allowing her to trust what Pagne shared with her in the police station. Angela accepted Jesus Christ as Pagne and Lenny prayed with her. She wanted the assurance that death was not the end. She wanted what Richie had, the peace that surrounded him in death. She wanted to know that she would be in eternity with souls as brave and loving as Richie.

Richie's funeral was somber and the family was stunned at how quickly they'd lost him. Pagne expected a very small memorial because Richie had not been a very social person. When the family came into the room, they were amazed at the number of people that were there. Everyone was given the opportunity to honor Richie. The tears streamed down his family's faces as person after person came up and shared how Richie had touched their lives. Many of these people had been in rehab with him and they shared how he had encouraged them and shared his belief in love and hope with them. Pagne was surprised at how many people had found Jesus Christ through Richie. Some of the people knew Richie from his years on the street. He had gone back and shared what money he had for food, talking with them and encouraging them. Several were on the road to recovery due to Richie's grace and generosity. There were neighbors that wanted to share how helpful Richie was, how he would always lend a hand when they needed help. One elderly lady who lived across the street said that Richie checked on her every day, making sure her milk wasn't sour and other thoughtful things. Pagne and the rest of her family were touched by this side of Richie they hadn't know about. He didn't boast and brag, he just did.

Angela was the last person to speak. She told the story of Richie's bravery and selflessness to save her. She had gotten permission from the family to share Richie's last words. "I want to truly know Richie and I will in Heaven some day. I pray that each of you considers today what your eternity will be."

Other than some quiet crying and sniffling, everyone sat in silence for some time, as if, as a group, they still had a link to Richie, a link that would snap when they walked out of the church.

Chapter 26

It was only a week or so since Richie's death, when a woman showed up at the offices of Kennel Kids. She asked to speak with Pagne. The woman introduced herself a Maureen O'Brien and she wanted to confirm that Pagne's maiden name was Crenshaw. Pagne looked at her cautiously and said yes. She asked if she could speak with Pagne privately so Pagne led her to her office. The woman sat down and took on a very uncomfortable demeanor. Pagne sat behind her desk, across from the woman. "What brings you here today?" asked Pagne.

"Well, I saw you in the papers last week, the story about the award you won. When I saw your scars in the picture," Pagne winced, "and your unusual name, I figured you were the right person." Maureen hesitated and focused on her purse handle.

"Yes?" pressed Pagne. Maureen started to rethink her idea of just showing up. It was too late now. She just needed to dive in.

"Well, I knew your mother. I took care of her for a spell."

"My mother? Pam has been dead for many years and I don't believe you ever knew her." Maureen looked confused and then explained.

"Your mother, Leah Crenshaw, died in my home last year. Isn't she your mom?" The reality hit Pagne like a ton of bricks. She wasn't talking about Pam, she was talking about Leah. The dismay showed on Pagne's face. Maureen continued, "Your mom was real sick and she lived with me for four months. I have what little belongings she had and I thought you might want them."

"Well... Mrs. O'Brien right? Mrs. O'Brien, I haven't seen my mother since I was a child. She abandoned me and I certainly do not want anything that was hers." Mrs. O'Brien stood up, shifted her bra strap, and tugged at her panties.

"Okay, doll, I just thought since she was your mom and all..." she started to leave the office. Pagne wanted this woman out of her office yet also wanted some answers.

"Wait, please. Can you tell me how she died?" Maureen looked at her and realized that this young woman needed closure, even with all the pain. She sat back down.

"Well, the drinking killed her liver. She suffered terribly, and there was no one but me to take her in."

"How did you know her?" asked Pagne.

"Our church provides cots and hot meals for the homeless at night. Your mom," she saw Pagne stiffen, "Leah, would come in when times were tough. We would talk and we got to know each other some. One night, she came in real sick and we took her over to county hospital. They told her that her liver was shot and there wasn't nothing they could do. She needed a warm, safe place until..." Maureen paused, "until the end. I thought she had suffered enough, alone, having a tough life and all." Maureen was surprised to see the rage that filled this beautiful woman's eyes.

"Tough life? You mean the drinking and whoring around? She chose that. She chose that over me." Pagne was livid that this woman had sympathy for her mother. Maureen decided to be brave and push.

"Maybe, maybe not. I just know she was hurting about her life and felt real bad about letting you go. She cried and cried about that."

"Let me go? Dumped me, you mean." Pagne was about to throw this woman out of her office. Maureen realized the depth of Payne's pain. She paused and began to speak softly while looking into Pagne's eyes with compassion.

"She let you go so you'd have a better life. She knew she was a horrible mama."

"But she left me in our apartment for days," Pagne said, with such hatred.

Maureen sensed that this was the tip of the iceberg, that her extreme anger was the result of many years of devastating abandonment. "She was mighty upset about that, but she thought you'd call your lady friend right away. She knew you didn't want to be with her and she knew she would keep hurting you. She didn't know that you waited for her until the police told her in the hospital. She was figuring she'd drink herself to death and you'd get adopted by a nice family." Maureen paused to give Pagne time to absorb her words. "That's why she left the hospital. She didn't know how to say goodbye. When she didn't die and release you, she just decided to disappear."

Pagne sat there in disbelief. *My mother never considered me before, how can I believe that this woman is telling me the truth,* thought Pagne. Maureen spoke in a calming, sweet voice. "Sweetheart, your mama loved you. She just didn't know how to be a mama. Figuring what she endured, who could blame her?" Pagne found herself curious against her will.

"Do you know what she endured?" Pagne asked.

Maureen clicked her tongue. "Child, it was terrible. She talked about it a lot those last few months. She would have nightmares and wake up screaming. Think the drinking kept the memories locked away and when she couldn't drink no more, her demons would come out and torture her."

Pagne asked Maureen if she'd like some coffee. "Why sure. Lots of cream and sugar, if you don't mind." Pagne loaded up her cup in the coffee room and headed back to Maureen. "She was very proud of you. She would sit outside Langston Hall and watch you in the yard. Then she found out you was living with a real nice family. Leah would check in on you now and then. When you started getting in the papers for your kids club, it was all she talked about. She'd bring in the articles to show us at the church outreach. Leah figured you was doing real good and so she figured she should stay away. When the doctor told her she was dying, she still wouldn't let us call you. She said it wasn't fair to expect you to treat her like your mama after all she'd done." Pagne could feel her heart aching and fought if off.

"I didn't know anything about her family or life. Will you tell me what you know?"

"It's a terrible story. You sure you wanna know, dear?"

"Yes, it's very important to me."

Maureen looked at her intently for what felt like forever to Pagne and then she began "Well, your mama was born back in Tennessee. She was the baby girl in the family with four older brothers. Her mama died when she was six and her daddy expected Leah to take care of the house just like her mama did. Being a small child, it was a difficult life. She didn't go to school because her daddy told the county she was being home-schooled. They lived way out in the country, so I'm guessing no one from the county wanted to put the effort in, so she just slipped through the cracks.

"Her daddy and the boys liked to drink and would get real mean. Leah would cry like a child when she talked about what they did to her." Maureen's eyes teared up as she continued. "Her daddy would burn her with cigarettes for the fun of it and her brothers would..." Maureen saw the horror in Pagne's eyes. "Well, let's just say they were very cruel." Leah had shared most of the gory details but Maureen didn't think Pagne needed to hear any more. After a long pause, Payne asked Maureen to go on. She needed to know. "They were brutal. They used your mama for their sick entertainment and there was no one to protect her," continued Maureen with disgust.

"When she turned seven, her daddy started touching her and made her touch him. It got worse and worse the older she got. Couple of her brothers figured out what their daddy was doing and decided they could, too. She said your grandpa encouraged all the boys when he found out but two of them said no. By the time she was twelve, she was pregnant, not knowing which one was the daddy. Her daddy didn't want anyone to know they'd been raping her so he told everyone that she'd been whoring around and got herself knocked up. He threatened to kill the baby if she told anyone the truth. Leah had the baby, a little boy, but her daddy put it up for adoption. She was heartbroken but she figured the baby would be better off. She thought about telling someone what was going on but she was so afraid of him, just like her mama had been. She knew he was capable of making good on his threats.

"She was pregnant again before she was fifteen but she lost her baby at six months. The baby wasn't developed right and your grandpa was afraid the doctor or someone might get curious so he kicked her out for being a whore. The small town had small minds and everyone believed the lies about her. Her daddy's extended family wouldn't have nothing to do with her and her mama's folks died when Leah was real young.

"One of her brothers gave her enough money to take the bus to California. Leah planned on getting a job and being on her own, maybe an actress someday. Once she got to Los Angeles, no one would hire a kid that young so she ended up on the streets prostituting herself to survive. Between the whoring and drinking to forget, she fell into a dark downward spiral. She admitted that she had several abortions but when she got pregnant with you, she just couldn't abort you. She didn't know why but she had to have you. She convinced herself that you were going to bring her luck and a better life but a baby made her life even tougher and she started resenting you. Leah felt real bad about that because she knew it wasn't your fault." Pagne was trying to grasp the details as Maureen pushed on with her mother's story.

"When her boyfriend tried to hurt you, all the past rushed back to her and she just didn't know how to process it. She wanted him to love her, to finally have a man that she could have a life with. She blamed you, like you was the problem. You were supposed to make her life better, not repeat her old life." Pagne was quiet while she listened. She didn't want to empathize with her mom but God was making that impossible. So many things were making sense. Pagne always wondered about the circular scars on Leah's thighs and back. She asked once but Leah glared at her and drank even more that day.

"I've got some pictures and her belongings, if you'd like to have them." Pagne was pulled back into the present. She had drifted off in the memories, thinking about the clues she didn't know how to identify at the time.

"Why I don't think..." she paused realizing she was curious, "Yes, I'd like that very much." Maureen pulled a scrap of paper out of her purse and wrote down her address.

"I'm home during the day, except Sunday mornings when I go to church. In the evenings, I'm at the outreach." Maureen got up, "Well, Pagne, I hoped my rattling on helped. Your mom should've had a better beginning. She had a big heart but it just got trampled at such a young age." Maureen got up to leave and headed toward the door when Pagne stopped her.

"I have one question."

"Sure, hon."

"Do you know if my mom was saved before she died?" Pagne asked somberly.

"I don't know. Me and the others tried talking to her about God but she was very angry. She figured he was a fairytale. He didn't do nothing for her or so she would say. Right before she died, some of the ladies from church was praying over her while I held her. We never heard her say the words for salvation." Maureen took Pagne's hand and patted it gently while giving her an encouraging smile, "Don't mean she didn't think them." Pagne thanked her and walked her to the front entrance. She went back into her office, turned off the lights, and closed the door. She sat in the darkness and thought about this young child who became her mother and how horribly she had lived. Pagne hoped that her mother had found her way to a better life in Heaven. She put her head on the desk and cried for the woman she had hated so long and the guilt that she didn't try to find her mother, try to save her. She cringed that Adam's description of her mother was how she had also seen Leah. *Dear God, please forgive me for not seeing her as you did, your daughter,* Pagne prayed with an aching heart.

Pagne went by Maureen's home several days later to collect her mother's belongings. Pagne knocked on the door of the shabby house that had several kids playing in the fenced front yard. Maureen answered and hugged Pagne, which she didn't expect. "Yours?" Pagne asked, nodding toward the kids as she stepped in.

"Nahhhh, I'm too old. Those are my grandbabies. My girl is on the street, Meth. Rachael comes to the shelter sometimes but she ain't ready to get clean. Breaks my heart that she don't let God clean her up and give her a life back, so I just keep praying." Pagne could see back into the family room where there were several people on twin beds. Maureen followed her eyes. "We're kinda crowded right now. I got a couple of young ladies in the family way staying here and some of my folks from the shelter are sick. I let them stay till they are feeling better. They need bed rest and the church program and most shelters are just at night." Pagne was touched by this woman's willingness to help these people. Maureen was getting ready to serve lunch and asked Pagne if she'd like to join them. Pagne saw such compassion in this woman; she was Mrs. Buttonhook, Pam, and Bree all rolled into one.

"Yes, I'd like that." Pagne helped her serve the two ladies in the family room. They looked at Maureen with such appreciation. Then two young, pregnant ladies came downstairs and they sat outside with Maureen, Pagne, and the kids. The two little boys were only about a year apart, maybe two and three, and the girl was ten. The two young ladies, Laura and Becka, were barely eighteen, no families and no husbands. Pagne saw no judgment from Maureen, just love and encouragement. Laura was keeping her baby and Becka was arranging to put her child up for adoption.

After lunch, Maureen brought out two boxes for Pagne. The large box had been Leah's clothing and shoes and Pagne asked Maureen to give them to someone in need. She only kept the small box. After a lovely visit with Maureen's brood, Pagne made her way back to her office.

When Pagne returned to her office, she checked messages and emails, then closed the door and focused on the box. She pulled out several pictures. One was of her mom's family when Leah was a child, maybe four. She was smiling at the camera. There was a very sad woman holding her. Leah looked very much like her. This must have been Pagne's grandmother and next to her sat her grandfather. He was very stern and rigid looking. Pagne saw no hint of emotion or joy. Behind these three stood four young men, ranging in age from seven to fourteen or so, she would guess. She wondered which two of them had raped her mother and which had given her the money to leave. Pagne wondered if the gesture was intended to protect Leah, or to protect him, or the result of shame because he believed the lies. Pagne could see physical similarities between her grandfather and herself, which disturbed her. Her grandfather had deep, auburn hair and was covered in freckles. She could understand why Leah had reacted the way she did about her freckles. She wondered about her brother. There were no pictures honoring his existence. She turned the photo over and there were no names or dates.

The second picture was her mother, laughing and holding a beer while a young man kissed her cheek. She looked to be eighteen or so. She was beautiful but obviously drunk. *Was he someone who loved her? If so, where did he go?* Pagne wondered. When she turned this one over, it had writing, "Leah and Mark, Forever." Pagne wanted to believe that her mother had truly known love with Mark. Next, Pagne saw several pictures of herself. One was when she was maybe a year old. It looked like a photo taken at a kiddy studio in a discount store. The photo was worn and tattered. The second photo was taken from a distance, through a cyclone fence. Pagne was older and was walking with Lenny to her glorious tree at Langston Hall. A third picture was Pagne and Bree in front of their house. They were high school age with backpacks, so she assumed they were walking to school. These last two photos caused Pagne to wonder how often Leah had been watching her from a distance. She would have needed to borrow a camera, so Pagne knew these were planned photos and Leah had to know where she was. The thought of Leah going to that much effort confused Pagne but also brought her a sense of comfort that she couldn't explain.

Also in the box was the engagement ring. The fake promise of love and hope. How much this obviously meant to Leah caused Pagne's heart to ache for her. She slipped the ring on her finger but wasn't sure why. There were a few legal papers, Leah's expired driver's license, and her faded birth certificate. Pagne opened the birth certificate carefully. Her grandparents were Mari Alanna and Edward Allan Crenshaw.

When Pagne saw the garish flamingo pin that she had found as a child, she couldn't control the tears that rolled down her cheeks. She had given the pin to her mother. She fingered the pin, remembering the surprise on Leah's face when she handed it to her and told Leah that she loved her. Pagne never dreamed that it would mean enough to her to keep all these years. The last item in the box was a thick envelope and, as Pagne lifted it out of the box, a tiny blue bootie slipped out. Pagne picked up the bootie and saw that it was very old and worn in spots. *Her brother's,* she wondered. *Must have been.* Pagne felt the surge of empathy that only a mother can feel for another mother. Pagne could only assume that the bootie was worn from frequent handling since the baby had been adopted. There was such a sad legacy in this box. Pagne's attention went back to the envelope. She pulled out the contents and saw newspaper articles about the fire, Kennel Kids, and various articles where Pagne had spoken out for the forgotten children at fund-raisers. There was even a program from a public awareness presentation held at the city library and Leah had been there. Pagne felt her compassion for her mother growing in her spirit and she began the process of forgiveness.

She had so much to share with Lenny but, before she left the office that day, she put a five thousand dollar check in the mail to Maureen from their discretionary fund that supported local individuals or programs that assisted the unfortunate. She also told the office accountant to add her to their monthly roster for continued support. She was thankful that her mother died in the arms of this earthly angel. Pagne thought she felt a kiss on her cheek as she slid into her car for the drive home. Was it Chantal, or maybe her mother?

The years rolled past and Pagne's children were growing up. Pammy, now twenty-one, had surprised even Pagne and Lenny with her accomplishments. She had such a gift for music and, once she discovered electronics, she was able to compose beautiful melodies without writing a note. The technology allowed her to overcome her limitations. Her roommate, Chelsey, had a wonderful talent for lyrics that reached the depth of everyone's soul. Together these young women were beginning a successful business and their songs were sought after by local musicians and businesses that needed scores and lyrics for marketing and advertising. They did the commercial work and were thankful but their passion was Christian Alternative Pop. Pammy and Chelsey were able to support themselves with the money they earned. Experts had told Pagne that Pammy would always need assisted living and disability benefits to survive. She thanked God for his blessings on Pammy.

They had given their son an unusual name, Chezare, who was a character in one of Pagne's favorite, old movies. Lenny would only agree to her choice if they spelled it how it sounded and they used a manly Z. Pagne also had to promise that she would call him Chez.

Chez was a senior in high school and had fallen in love. Pagne liked his girlfriend Belinda but was concerned. Belinda had been saved as a child but hadn't really developed a relationship with Jesus Christ. She was like many people that were "Sunday Christians" and Belinda lived for worldly gratification. Pagne knew that Chez was convinced they were perfect for each other and she and Lenny realized they needed to let Chez make his own decisions. They'd been dating for a year when they both asked to speak to Lenny and Pagne about a serious matter. Pagne knew it was not going to be good news and she prayed for wisdom and peace. After dinner, they sat around the kitchen table, finishing off dessert. There was that awkward pause as they wondered who would start? Chez finally cleared his throat and reached for Belinda's hand. "I know you both will be disappointed but we are thrilled." Pagne now knew and she could only fight to hold back her tears. The sweet scent of Chantal began to churn around her. "Belinda and I are having a baby." The group around the table was silent. Pagne looked at Lenny for strength, but she saw such disappointment in his eyes. Pagne knew someone had to speak and Lenny was not going to volunteer.

"Well, we are surprised," Pagne started. "We thought you had both committed to abstinence until marriage." Chez blushed and Belinda looked defiant.

"We love each other, Mom, we just couldn't wait." There was another long silence. It was excruciatingly awkward. Lenny pushed back from the table without speaking and headed out to the back porch. Belinda jumped up and glared at Pagne.

"I knew they would react like this," she threw at Chez. She headed toward the front door, "You coming?" she asked. Chez looked panicked. He knew he needed to talk to his parents but he also knew that Belinda would be a nightmare to deal with if he let her leave alone.

"Sorry, Mom. I'll be back this evening. We can talk then." Chez kissed Pagne on the cheek and headed over to the irate Belinda. Pagne could hear them arguing all the way to the car.

Pagne ran out to Lenny and fell into his arms. She couldn't hold the tears back any longer. Lenny held her but he was rigid. Pagne looked up in his face and saw such anger. "This is her fault," he growled. "He is a good boy. We raised him to honor his family and God." Pagne pushed herself back. She was surprised at Lenny's words.

"Wait a minute, sweetheart, this was Chez's decision too. I don't think you remember our prom night. We did get married before we had sex but, you have to admit, that night it was passion that drove us to Vegas." Lenny had forgotten. He reached for Pagne and pulled her in tight, squeezing her.

"But why her? Pagne, she isn't the one. I never felt that she was the one."

"I know, me either, but it has been decided. Chez has decided that she is the one. We need to be supportive and help them get through this. I don't know how her mom will handle the news," Pagne said, knowing that Belinda's mom had never been supportive of their relationship. Pagne and Lenny sat and watched as the sun began to set. Lenny looked to the Heavens and murmered, "Dear Lord, give us strength." They sat silently as they watched the beautiful sky filled with oranges, reds, and deep purples above. A scattering of stars began to shine.

The night sky was dazzling but it was chilly. Pagne brought out sweaters and steaming cups of hot chocolate. They heard Chez's car pull up front and the door slam. One door, good, Chez was alone. Chez came around the side of the house and slowly walked up the stairs to the deck. "Okay to sit with you guys?" he asked meekly. Pagne smiled at him.

"Of course, want something to drink?"

"Nah, I'm good." Chez knew he had to pull up the courage to begin, to step up and be an adult. "I know you're both disappointed and worried. I wish I could have told you in a better way but I guess there isn't one. Believe me, I tried to think of it. This is not how I thought I would start a family but this baby is on the way and I am ready to be a father." Pagne heard Lenny let out a strained sigh.

"You don't know what it means to be a father. You're still a kid. What were you thinking, Chez? You want to go to college. This is going to change everything," Lenny said.

Pagne waited for Chez to get on the defensive and maybe lash back but she was impressed by his composure.

"I know I'm young, Dad, but I've had years of watching you. If I can be half the dad you were, then my kid will be very lucky." Pagne saw Lenny's stiffened posture soften a bit.

"I'm not saying you can't do it, Chez, I'm just concerned that you won't be able to do all the things you've dreamed about."

"Well, I've created a situation that requires new dreams. I am scared but also excited, Dad. I love Belinda and we will be good together, raising this baby."

Pagne knew that anything they felt or thought didn't matter. This baby was coming and they needed to get past the shock. She actually began to get excited about the idea of a grandchild. Chez was a good man. He was young but a man and Pagne knew that he would be a great dad. "Have you guys decided on a date yet?" Pagne asked.

"Date?" Chez looked at her, confused.

"For the wedding, or are you going to elope? That can be very romantic," Pagne grinned at Lenny.

"Ummmm, Mom, we're not getting married, not right now anyway." Pagne felt her heart drop in her chest.

"You're not? But with the baby and..."

"Belinda and I talked and we need to wait. Her scholarships are based on her being single and her current financial situation, living with her mom. If we get married, she won't be able to qualify." Lenny stiffened again.

"How long are you going to wait?" he asked, through a tight jaw.

"Maybe four years. Belinda wants to get through school and then we will decide what to do next."

"And the baby?" Pagne was still trying to make sense of the situation.

"If Belinda and the baby live with her mom, where will you live?" asked Lenny.

"We haven't figured all that out, Dad. We've only known for a week that Belinda is pregnant." Lenny stood and said a hollow goodnight. Pagne felt abandoned by Lenny but she knew he was struggling to stay civil. It was best if he stepped away until he could calm down.

Chez moved his chair up close to Pagne after Lenny went into the house. "Mom, I know you guys are hurt and I am so sorry. This wasn't planned. It just happened."

Pagne looked at him and chose her words carefully. "Chez, it didn't just happen. You decided to be alone with Belinda, you decided to remove her clothing, and you decided to drop your pants. Each step was decided upon and acted upon." Pagne reached over and took his hand. "Chez, you know I love you, you know your dad loves you?"

"Yes," he humbly answered.

"Now that you will have your own child, you will understand the hope you have for your child's future. You don't want them hurting, struggling, or stuck in tough situations. So we look at you, knowing all the dreams you've shared with us, all the plans you have for your life, and we see obstacles now. It doesn't mean that you can't succeed and fulfill your dreams but it is much more complicated when you are responsible for a child. You become secondary or at least you should. Give your dad some time. This is difficult for us but we know that this child is God's child. We already love this baby." She squeezed Chez's hand. "I'm uncomfortable with the fact that you are delaying marriage. I hope you know that in our home, you and Belinda will be regarded as single."

"I know, Mom. I wouldn't have expected anything different."

"Let's both try to get some sleep. This has been a very intense day." They stood and hugged. Pagne moved into the house and upstairs to Lenny, dreading the dark mood that would fill their room. She was relieved to hear his soft snoring and glad that he was able to sleep.

The next few weeks were difficult for Pagne to watch. Chez was trying so hard to pamper and humor Belinda but she was on the warpath. She was angry that Pagne and Lenny were not gushing over the fact that she was having a baby and she was outraged that they didn't approve of them waiting to get married. Pagne and Lenny avoided any conversation about the baby, marriage, or the lack there of, but whatever Chez shared with her set the ball in motion. Belinda complained and whined about everything and Chez was like a puppy, trying to console her at every turn. No decisions about Chez's living arrangements had been made so he was still at home. One evening, Belinda had come over for dinner. After dinner, Chez and Belinda watched a movie in Chez's room and, at eleven o'clock, Lenny knocked on the half-open door and suggested that Chez needed to get Belinda home. Pagne came up the stairs in time to see the fireworks go off. Belinda was standing in the open doorway and screaming, telling Lenny how stupid he was. She was already pregnant, why couldn't she stay over and sleep in Chez's room? She lashed out about how fanatic their family was and how it was time to join the rest of world and get a grip on reality. Pagne was frozen, scared of Lenny's reaction. Chez was behind Belinda, his hands in his hair, not knowing what to say or do. Lenny looked into her face and very calmly said, "This is my home and God dwells in my home. I will not dishonor God to please you or anyone else. When you have your own home, you can decide what is allowed and what isn't. Good-night and good-bye Belinda." With that, Lenny turned and stepped into their bedroom and quietly shut the door. Belinda stood there with her mouth gaping open. She focused on Pagne and Chez could see her winding up for another round. He realized he had to step in. Chez knew his father would not remain in his room if he heard Belinda go after his wife.

He took Belinda's arm firmly and said, "We are leaving now." Belinda turned her glare to Chez.

"That's right, mama's boy. Don't be a man and defend the mother of your baby." Chez did not respond but deliberately moved Belinda over to the top of the stairs. Pagne had stepped back to let them pass. Belinda locked her legs and looked at Pagne. Belinda gave Pagne a hard look and then smiled, almost like she'd won a challenge. She spoke quietly, but with venom. "You will regret tonight; you don't control me like you do Chez. I've decided my mom was right." She then allowed Chez to escort her out of the house. Pagne went to their room and was disappointed that she did not hear snoring. She knew it would be a long night. Pagne was thankful that Grandma Maxine had not woken to the drama. Even though Grandma Maxine was considered elderly, she still had strong opinions and didn't hesitate to share them.

Lenny finally went to sleep and Pagne dozed on and off. She heard Chez come in around three o'clock and she thought she heard him crying in his room. She didn't know if she should give him privacy or get up and go to him. She decided that he needed to resolve his relationship without her interference.

The next morning, Lenny left early for work. Pagne figured he was not ready to deal with Chez regarding the night before so she slept fitfully for a few more hours. She had taken the day off to take care of some errands and it was close to ten o'clock when she finally woke up and headed into the kitchen for a cup of coffee. She saw Chez sitting out on the deck. His shoulders were slumped. Pagne poured another cup for Chez and headed out to sit with him. When she saw his face, she became sick to her stomach. His face was scratched across his cheek and red and bruised from being struck. "Oh my Lord, Chez, what happened? Is Belinda okay?" Chez looked into his mother's face and broke, the tears just poured from his heart. Pagne moved to him and held him in her arms. She didn't ask anything because she knew he couldn't speak. She allowed him to cry. When Chez was able to get his emotions under control, he sat back and stared at the clouds. Pagne was frantic to know what was going on. Finally, Chez looked at his mother.

"She broke up with me. She said that I wasn't enough of a man for her." Pagne wasn't sure how to respond. She wanted to defend him and assure him but he needed her to listen.

"Did she do this to your face?" Chez looked down in embarrassment.

"Yes. I was pleading with her and trying to get her to understand how much she and the baby mean to me. When she tried to get out of the car, I wouldn't let go of her and she started hitting me and scratching me."

"Oh, son. You know you can't physically restrain someone if they want to leave. Maybe once she has time to think and calm down, you guys can work things out. I'm sure she doesn't want to raise a baby alone."

"It wasn't just about her staying with me, Mom. She told me she doesn't want my baby either. She's going to get an abortion." Pagne couldn't believe what he was saying.

"Chez, she is just mad right now. She loves this baby, too." Doesn't she? Pagne asked herself.

"I don't think she does." Chez stood and pulled his keys out of his pocket and kissed Pagne on the cheek. "Not sure when I'll be home," he said and headed out to his car. Pagne could hear him pull out of their driveway and drive down the street.

~

Several days later, things were no better between Belinda and Chez. If not for the baby, Pagne and Lenny would have been relieved that the relationship had dissolved but they knew the life of this child was of paramount importance. Pagne wanted to talk to Belinda, to try to counsel her, but Belinda wouldn't take Chez's calls, let alone Pagne's. Pagne decided to go over to Belinda's house and see if she would be willing to see her. Belinda's mom, Anna, answered the door. "Hi, Anna, I was wondering if I could speak with Belinda." Anna didn't invite her in.

"She's not here right now and I don't think she wants to see you. She's very hurt about the way she was treated by you and Lenny." Pagne bit her lip, trying to stay civil.

"I'm sorry that she's upset. I hoped that I might be able to calm this situation down and give the kids a chance to talk and sort things out, you know, the baby..." Pagne was interrupted.

"Ahhhh, that's it, right? You're not here about how badly you feel about what you did to Belinda. You just want her to have this baby. Well, I want grandkids too, some day, but now is not the time. Belinda is too young and has plans for her life. Being a mom just isn't the best thing for her. Besides, Chez showed his true loyalties. She needs a man that will support her, no matter what. She needs a man to be her baby's daddy, not a kid wanting to make mommy and daddy happy." Pagne could feel the blood rising into her cheeks.

She had intended to remain civil but her thoughts were fueled with anger. *You mean she needs someone to kiss her butt, no matter what, to put up with her crap, no matter what. She needs a sniveling coward with muscles that will be at her beck and call, no matter what.* Then, unexpectedly, Pagne smelled Chantal and she began to feel shame that she was reducing herself to this woman's level. She looked at Anna, pushed down the insults, and calmly asked her to give Belinda a message.

"Sure, but don't think it will change anything."

"Just please tell her that we love her and we love the baby. I am here if she wants to talk. Thanks for your time." Pagne turned to leave and heard Anna speak.

"Wait. Guess you have the right to know. Belinda has an appointment at the women's clinic this Thursday at three thirty." Pagne didn't respond or turn around. She continued to walk to her car with tears streaming down her face.

When Pagne got home, she called every prayer warrior she knew. She asked them to pray for Belinda to connect with this baby and change her mind about the abortion. Pagne didn't know how the relationship between Chez and Belinda would play out but, she didn't want her grandchild to be the ultimate victim. She wanted to know this child, love this child, and have a relationship with this child. So many people were praying for mercy for this child's life. Lenny was praying but Pagne could see him trying to detach emotionally. Chez made himself scarce because he couldn't face the pain in his parents faces while he struggled with his own.

Thursday morning came and Chez announced he was going up to the mountains with some friends and the youth pastor for the weekend. Pagne was glad that these friends were there for Chez, to support him and pray with him, because he was so sad and frustrated. Lenny headed into work as usual but paused at the door and held Pagne tightly when she kissed him goodbye. "Call me if you need me," he said softly and then he was gone. Pagne took the day off. She knew she wouldn't be able to work and she wanted to have this time to focus on God and pray. She spent most of the day praying, crying, and talking with close friends who were also praying. The support network truly helped. Pagne hesitated but then asked God to reveal the outcome to her, either way. She needed to know what was to become of her grandchild.

Pagne was heading into the kitchen to make some tea when she suddenly felt as if her heart was ripped out of her. The sense of loss overwhelmed her and she began to sob. Pagne dropped to her knees on the floor and screamed out, "No, she's gone! It's done!" She smelled Chantal and felt her wings wrapping around her, holding her. She saw the clock that read four o' clock. "Chantal, please look after my grandchild," she pleaded.

Pagne crawled into bed and drifted off to sleep, exhausted from sobbing. She began dreaming that she was on the shore of a beautiful lake, surrounded by trees, flowers, and wildlife. She walked along the water and saw fish jumping and glittering in the light. She looked ahead and there was a young girl, maybe four years old, ahead of her. She had bright, big green eyes and deep, chestnut curls. She was flicking rocks into the water and watching them skip. Each time she was successful, Pagne would hear her precious giggle. As Pagne stood next to her, she saw the child looked like Chez and like her. "Are you my granddaughter?" Pagne asked.

"Yes, I am," she responded.

"What's your name?"

"Don't have one yet. You wanna give me one?" the girl responded. Pagne looked at this lovely young face, full of anticipation.

"I would be honored. Do you like the name Ophelia?"

"It's pretty, but kinda old-fashioned."

"You want a modern name? Brittany maybe?"

"No, I like Ophelia. She was a very special person to you?"

"Yes, she was a lovely woman."

"Okay, Ophelia!" She tossed another rock and then stared into Pagne's face, into her eyes. "Did you know we are going to be best friends?"

"We are?" Pagne said while trying not to cry.

"Yes, it won't be on Earth, it'll be here, in Heaven." Pagne felt her heart aching, knowing she would miss out on so much. She would miss out on watching this beautiful soul grow into a woman and miss sharing a lifetime of experiences with her. "Don't be sad, Grandma. I would have loved to have Earth with you, too, but Heaven will be better. I heard we can swim to the bottom of the seas, we can ride dolphins, and we can fly." Her list went on and on. Pagne was so caught up in her conversation with Ophelia about Heaven that she didn't notice Ophelia was fading. Pagne woke with a jump and smiled at the thought of Ophelia's sweet face, full of excitement. Pagne was filled with a peace that soothed her aching heart.

The next few years were sad for Chez. He got a tattoo of a fetus to honor his child's existence. Belinda and Chez did not reconcile and he decided to join Bree in Ethiopia when he graduated from junior college. The healing and the ability to forgive Belinda was a long journey for Chez. In time, he was able to fall in love again. His friendship with one of the young interns in Africa grew into a strong, loving marriage. Chez and his wife, Noel, made their home in Ethiopia and raised three lovely children. Pagne understood the importance of their work but she missed having her son's family and her grandchildren, close by.

Chapter 28

At eighty-eight, Grandma Maxine passed in her sleep. Lenny found her the next morning with her Bible on her chest. The whole family mourned the loss of Grandma Maxine but they also knew she was waiting for them in Heaven.

Mandy married a successful young man she met in college. She moved to Los Angeles and had several children of her own. She also began caring for drug babies, just as Pam had done.

Bree and Mandy didn't want the house sold. They wanted to know it would remain in the family, so Lenny and Pagne remained in the house and filled the rooms with children. They adopted three more of their foster teens and fostered twelve more children through the years. Pagne and Lenny had such a capacity for love and patience for these children. Pagne was still on the board of directors for "Kennel Kids" but had stepped back from the day to day operations when she got older. There was a wonderful staff and plenty of volunteers in place that kept everything running smoothly.

~

Pagne and Lenny were able get away occasionally to a quaint bed-and-breakfast on the beach just south of Monterey. They liked to take chairs out on the sand and watch the sunsets. They decided to make the trip for their forty-fifth wedding anniversary. They were set up in their usual place, throws for their laps and hot chocolate. Pagne was feeling very nostalgic and talked about their lives together, their many children, and the pain and the joy they had shared. "Lenny, I am so thankful that I had you to share my life with. I love you so much." Lenny had quietly listened but offered no mutual adoration when Pagne finally stopped rambling. It annoyed her because she was sure he had dozed off while she poured out her heart. She reached over to wake him up, realizing he was tired and the evening had come to an end. He didn't respond. "Lenny, wake up, hon. It's time to go inside." There was still no response. Panic began to build inside of Pagne. She jumped up and began to shake him. He stared, unblinking, into the magnificent sunset. As Pagne felt herself go limp, she saw the fluttering of multiple wings in the filtered light. She smelled Chantal and heard her whisper, "He is with us. He waits for you." Pagne dropped to the sand and wept. Lenny was only sixty-three.

The doctors determined that Lenny had passed from an aneurysm. His death was instant. Pagne felt she should have bugged Lenny about check-ups more earnestly and was only relieved of her guilt when the doctors assured her that checkups would not have caught the aneurysm.

They had to have Lenny's memorial in the largest church in town to accommodate the many people that wanted to honor him. Pagne would have preferred that Pastor Tim officiate but he had passed a year earlier. Bree, William, and Chez had gotten in that morning from Africa and they were shocked at how well Pagne was dealing with Lenny's death. She explained to them what she saw and knew that Lenny was fine. He was more than fine. He was in Heaven with their loved ones.

Bree couldn't wait to tell Pagne they would be staying in California. Her husband had been asked to head up a mission program in Watts, Los Angeles. The harsh environment of Africa was affecting their health as they became older, so they agreed they should come home and that Bree should be close to Pagne. Bree would only be a few hours away and Pagne was thrilled to have Bree back in the country.

It turned out that only two years later, Bree would move back to the house with Pagne. William was diagnosed with pancreatic cancer and only survived for eight months. Pagne was sad about William but glad to have Bree back with her. They spent many evenings enjoying the gardens and the memories their old house held within its walls. Pagne did not continue fostering children once the last few became adults and moved on to jobs or college. She knew her age was becoming a factor and she really wanted to slow down and enjoy her time with Bree. When Macey lost her husband to a heart attack, she also moved in with Pagne and Bree. They were a loving group of women. Bree started feeding the stray cats in the neighborhood. The cats often lounged on the patio in the sun. Pagne teased her that they had crossed the line and turned into crazy old cat ladies.

One evening, Pagne called Bree and Macey upstairs. As they climbed the stairs, they grumbled about their knees. "Why would God design such a necessary part to wear out before the rest of us does?" Bree complained. Pagne giggled and handed them both several of her joint-pain relievers.

"Here, you'll need these." She pushed them into the room once shared by

Bree and Pagne, now a sewing and exercise room. They saw boxes in the middle of the floor. While looking at Pagne, she whipped open the closet door. The inside of the closet was piled with pillows, blankets, and munchies. "No way, Pagne," said Macey. "Are you nuts?"

"Yes, yes I am, I am certifiably crazy!" She pushed them in and then struggled to sit on the floor, blocking the door. "There's iced-tea right there. Take your pills and park your butts."

Pagne thought Bree was going to argue but instead she heard her speaking, "Just humor her Macey! I've seen that stubborn jaw clench before. We ain't getting out of here without a fight." Bree downed the pills and slowly slid down the wall to the floor. They heard her knees creaking all the way down. Macey decided to go along with them and swallowed the pills. As she lowered herself, she lost her balance and fell on top of Bree. As Bree struggled to set her upright, Bree farted. They all froze and then began to laugh hysterically. Once they were laughed out, the memories and stories began to flow. Pagne pulled out the chips and pickles. It took a lot of coaxing but they finally got Macey to try them. "These are actually very good," she shared.

Pagne looked into the wrinkled faces framed by thinning gray hair and felt such love. They were able to endure the floor for several hours, but then Bree got a painful look on her face. "Bree, you okay?" Pagne asked.

" Yeah, I just have to pee, really bad!" This started another wave of giggles. As Bree tried to get up, she realized she had waited too long. "I'm going to pee my pants," she said.

"Don't try to stand," Macey directed, "Just crawl."

"What? You're kidding, right? On these knees?"

"It really helps."

Pagne considered asking how often Macey had crawled to the toilet, but she was focused on Bree not leaking on the carpet. With that, Pagne rolled over to give Bree access to the door. Bree crawled through the closet and into the room. They couldn't control their laughing. Through her own giggling, Bree kept telling them to stop or she'd never make it to the bathroom. She had to stop several times and squeeze as tight as she could. She almost made it but just as she got inside the bathroom, she lost the battle and peed on the tile floor. Rather than getting angry, she lay on the floor and let out a deep sigh of relief. "You're cleaning this up, Pagne. It was your bright idea to lock me in a closet for two hours. You know, you're still living up to your name!" There were more peals of laughter.

"Okay, okay, I'll clean the floor but I'm not washing your butt."

"You sure?" Bree teased, "It's still a mighty cute butt!"

"Gross," Macey threw in. "I always suspected but, now I know, you're both lunatics. I'm going to bed." She grinned at them as she moved down the hall.

"You need help getting up?" asked Pagne as she looked down at Bree.

"Yeah, if you can help balance me, I can pull myself up using the toilet." As Bree pulled herself up, Pagne was by her side, both of them avoiding the puddle on the floor. They smiled and hugged each other. "Thank you. Tonight was wonderful. I forgot how special that closet was," Bree shared. Sadly, Pagne could not convince them to attempt the closet again. It would be their last night celebrating life in their sanctuary.

Chapter 29

Fifteen years had passed by when Pagne climbed into her warm, cozy bed. The party had been such a joy. Old friends, all of her children, grandchildren, great grandchildren and many of the foster-kids had been there. Pagne was touched deeply by their affection. Quite a few of the foster-children had broken the family chain of addiction, despair and abuse. Pagne knew that she had given these young people an opportunity to see another life, confirmation that they didn't have to accept what their parents had shown them as their legacy. Chez and his family had been secretly flown in for the celebration. Pammy and Chelsey had written a song for Pagne. It was sweet, but funny; Pagne loved it. Pammy had a graphic-designer create a beautiful framed picture with the song lyrics and a photo of Pagne and Pammy when she was a young child. Pagne had hung it on the wall in her bedroom with so many other photos of family, and memorabilia. Bree and Macey had planned the perfect surprise birthday party. Pagne looked at the picture of Lenny next to her bed. "Eighty years old, Lenny. How did I survive this long?" She asked him. Pagne could feel all the tight and aching joints as she shifted, trying to get comfortable. "I miss you so much, my darling. Dear Lord, when will you call me home to be with you and my Lenny?" Her breathing became deep, as she drifted to sleep and began to dream that she had beautiful wings.

She hadn't dreamed about flying for years. She was hesitant at first, her body was brittle and stiff. She felt the weight of the huge, white wings. As the weight became more bearable, she tried fluttering them. She hovered the ground at first, just barely flapping. As she built confidence, she flapped harder, and she began lifting and moving through the air. She leaned and flew around trees. She noticed the stiffness easing up, the higher she ventured. She aimed for the clouds and dove down when she got scared. The joy was building in her chest, as she became braver and braver. She saw a lovely lake below her; she swooped down and saw her reflection on the water's surface. She looked like she had in the photos taken prom night. She was young and beautiful. She looked at her arms, and there was no scarring.

Then, she heard Lenny calling her. She pulled up and hovered, searching the skies. There he was. She flapped her wings with such strength that she was up to him in what seemed like a blink of an eye. She screamed and literally flew into his arms. They floated, as if they were on water, with their wings encircling them. They kissed and touched each other's faces in wonder. "Come on, I have so much to show you," Lenny smiled. They flew beyond the lake and viewed such beauty that Pagne couldn't contain her tears. They dropped into a field full of purple flowers. Pagne was speechless at the intensity of the colors and aromas. Her wings melted away, and she felt a tap on her shoulder. As she turned, she realized that she was encircled by Pam, Brent and Richie. Pagne fell to the ground, sobbing as the emotions surrounded her and filled her mind and heart. Then she laughed; she hadn't laughed so freely in her whole life. They lifted her to her feet and all talked at the same time while they walked into a grove of trees filled with exotic fruits. They laid in the grass, sharing fruit and memories. Pam held Pagne so tightly. "Thank you, Pagne. You are why I am here. Your note …" Pam became overwhelmed with emotion.

"Oh, Mom, or Pam. What do I call you?"

"Whatever you want, sweetheart."

"So is the movie better than the cartoon?" asked Pagne.

Pam cooed softly, as she nuzzled against Pagne, "Oh yes!" Pagne watched how Brent looked at Pam, with even more love than he displayed while they were on earth. Pagne began to understand that this was not a dream. She was here with her loved ones. Bree would find her body in the morning, there on earth.

Pagne felt a tug on her arm, she looked over into the glowing face of her granddaughter, Ophelia. She looked just as she did on the lake's shore that day so long ago. Pagne raised to her knees before her and squeezed her as tight as she could. "You're still a little girl?" Pagne asked in confusion.

"Only in physical appearance, I waited for you, I wanted to grow up with you." Pagne was so excited that she didn't miss the chance to be Ophelia's grandma. "The anguish you felt the day I died showed me that I was loved and that I would be missed; I mattered to someone. I wanted to share all the magic of growing up with that kind of love." Pagne thanked God for his compassion for her and Ophelia. Pagne looked to Lenny and saw the delight in his face. Ophelia stepped over to him, and pointed behind Pagne. Pagne turned to look and saw people standing off in the distance. They seemed to be impatiently waiting.

"These are people that have been waiting for you too." Everyone seemed to know what Lenny was saying and floated to where they were sitting. Pagne jumped up to greet her friends. She saw Mrs. Buttonhook, young and vibrant, Maxine, Lenny's parents, Pastor Tim, Renee, and so many other people that she had missed and outlived. Bree's husband, William, swung her around in his strong arms, as his huge white smile beamed. His head was once again covered with soft, curly hair.

"Bree will be with us soon," he whispered in her ear. "I can hardly wait." Pagne weaved her fingers through his soft curls.

"Bree will love that you have hair again," she teased. She had no sense of time, she just relaxed and heard the stories of her friends and family. Once everyone was caught up, Pagne pulled Lenny aside. "So where's Jesus and our angels?" she asked. Lenny grinned at her.

"In due time, they give us "Earthlings" a chance to reconnect to our family, and to adjust to the changes. You will meet them soon." Pagne knew that grin, he had a secret.

As people began to drift away, Pagne saw several people way off on a nearby hill. "Who are they?" she asked.

" Why don't you find out?" he suggested. Pagne began walking toward the couple. She seemed to move in bursts rather than steps. She then realized that she could think herself forward. She focused on these strangers and was very quickly up on them, almost knocking them over. The woman was her mother, Leah. She was confused and looked into the face of the man next to her. *Father?*, she wondered.

"Hey, sis," he said, with a huge smile. This was her brother. Pagne didn't know how to respond. They asked her if they could walk with her.

"Sure," she managed. Leah didn't make eye contact and kept some space between herself and Pagne. Her brother's name was Joseph and he was funny and loving. It felt like they had known each other all their lives. She could see herself in his grin. Suddenly, there were three more young adults with them. Pagne found out that these were her other siblings that had not come to term. She had two sisters, Martha and Amy, and another brother named Andrew. She saw that Martha stayed close to Leah and seemed to protect her. Pagne wondered if she was the first daughter, the daughter who died permaturely. They came to a beautiful garden and started the connections that would link them for eternity. Pagne loved her new family. Eventually, they all got up to leave, except for Leah.

"We are so thrilled to have you with us, Pagne," said Joseph. Then they were gone. Pagne was still confused about how people could move in this new place. Pagne turned to Leah and expected to see guilt in her eyes, but instead she saw peace and joy.

"Pagne, I can't begin to express the regret that I had for how I was with you in our earthly lives. I so wish that I had been healthy and valued you, but God has forgiven me and gave me a place with him here. Is there anything you need to ask me or say?" Pagne looked at her beautiful, hopeful face. Any anger or judgment left Pagne, as she smiled and thanked God that she was there with her mother. She knew that there would be lots of time to know the real Leah. Pagne felt a transformation happening: all the human guilt, pain, and regrets melted away, and she was filled with such peace.

"No, Mother, I just want the chance to know you." She felt a hand on her shoulder and saw Lenny beside her.

"Leah, I'm going to take her on the tour."

She grinned at Pagne, "You picked a good one, Pagne." Leah touched Lenny's face so gently. A gesture that said so much about her appreciation for him and the love that he had brought to Pagne's life. She hugged Pagne and was gone.

"Where do they keep going?" Pagne asked.

Lenny laughed. "You'll catch on. We are not limited in any way. We can fly, we can walk, we can teleport."

"Teleport? you've got to be kidding."

"Nope, darling, you ain't seen nothing yet." Lenny gently pulled on Pagne's hand, and again they were flying, wings flapping. "Figured you could see more this way, and I know you love to fly!" She grinned, Lenny was still the same Lenny that knew her inside and out. Pagne was in awe of the beauty she saw below her. It would have taken her forever to describe. So many things were familiar, but just as much was new and unique. They came close to a large city, shimmering and majestic. They dropped into a lush garden full of flowers, animals and birds. There was a pond with fountains that were spraying water in pulsating patterns that mesmerized her. Pagne looked around. It was beautiful, but Pagne had so many questions.

"Lenny, do we get to know the point of everything? The purpose for our lives on earth? The purpose of all the hardships and pain?"

Lenny looked deeply into her eyes and whispered softly, "It will all become clear;" he grinned at her and spun around as he said ... "Catch ya later, doll; I'm only a thought away." And he was gone.

Pagne was startled to be all alone, but this place felt familiar. She began to pick up on the aroma of her angel. "Chantal!" she screamed, as she turned around. There were people moving about, and there were creatures of such beauty with powerful wings. They had an inner glow that glittered, as if diamond powder was embedded in their skin. They were human, but not. Pagne followed her nose, as the smell became stronger and stronger. She entered a cluster of trees, and she found her angel, but something was definitely wrong. This creature smelled like her angel, but it couldn't be.

"Hello, Pagne, my name is Ennett."

"But, but you're a boy." He laughed a full belly laugh.

"Yes, yes in a way I suppose I am." Ennett was tall and radiated with light that moved through and around him. His body was muscular, and powerful.

"You can't be my angel; I heard her, and she was a girl."

"I thought speaking to you with a woman's voice would be more comfortable for you .... especially since you were so convinced that I had to be a girl. You named me Chantal, remember?" he grinned. She felt herself relax then tense up.

"But if you were with me all the time," she blushed, "the bathroom, the shower?" Ennett continued to grin at her.

"Ever heard of doors or shower curtains? I can also close my eyes," Ennett teased.

"I am so sorry about giving you a girl's name," Pagne groaned.

He shrugged, "At least you gave me a name. That is very unusual for us angels. Thank you." She looked very closely at him; he had dark, thick curls, intensely violet eyes, and that smile; she knew him. Pagne looked around and realized that she also knew this place. She looked back at Ennett with complete confusion on her face.

"Come, it will make more sense as you get all the pieces." It was as if he could read her thoughts.

Ennett reached for her hand, "May I?" She nodded, and he took her hand in his and suddenly they were leaving the ground, lifted by his strong wings. They slipped into an opening at the top of a huge dome and dropped into a beautiful, magical room. It was all so familiar. Pagne couldn't shake the feeling that she had been here before.

Pagne looked deeply into his eyes and tried so hard to make sense of her feelings, thoughts, and memories? Ennett saluted her and flew up and out, grinning the same type of grin Lenny had. Like someone who knew a wonderful secret that they were excited for you to discover. Pagne sensed someone behind her. She turned around and was facing a very wise-looking man. "Draken?" she asked.

"Yes, Anessia." She was so confused; why did her call her Anessia? Nothing made sense, yet it was part of her, she felt it with every inch of her being. Draken pulled a golden scroll from behind his back and handed it to her. As she touched the scroll, it all came rushing back. She had been here, and she knew this person before her. Anessia looked at the scroll and all the confusion began to fade away. She began to remember, the quest, this room, Draken, Ennett. She felt dizzy as the memories flooded in.

She sat on the floor, with her legs under her, and her feet bent to the sides. She smoothed the scroll and began to read. It was her life, the people she would love, the moments of decision that would create ripples into other lives.

Anessia was delighted to see that her compassion for the sick bird kept the dog from finding it, eating it and getting sick, so sick he would die. The dog that saved his family in the fire. The family that cherished their lives, and made differences that only near death could inspire. She began a chain of events, a ripple, that impacted a family and everyone they touched.

Anessia saw how her difficult childhood inspired Miss Renee to begin her journey to protect so many of God's forgotten children. Saving Chad's life allowed him to become a doctor specializing in burn treatment and research. He was able to revolutionize the medical treatment, which saved many more lives, many that were given more time to come to know Jesus Christ. The souls and lives he touched were now part of her legacy.

The day she reached out for Lenny, preventing the madness of murder and suicide that was in motion, which allowed his life to glorify God and bring souls home. The scroll included her love for Macey, which began the healing of her broken heart, and allowed her to fulfill her own quest. The scroll revealed that it was God's compassion that allowed her to love and forgive Richie, which freed him to return to his path, to fulfill his destiny. Her simple request to go to church. The request that encouraged Bree to return to her own faith, which enabled her to reach the souls in Africa.

Anessia smiled when she saw that the little girls in Mexico were part of the scroll. That she helped them find the courage to change the world around them. Anessia had loved them and showed them that their physical body didn't have to be a barrier to loving others. Ahhhhhh, Pam and Brent, Joshua and Maureen. The ripples of her existence went on and on.

She was amazed how little gestures, sharing her beliefs, forgiveness, moments of grace, and love for others rippled into massive waves of joy, hope, love and salvation. Anessia saw the map of her life's maze, the journey she could not see while in the midst of it.

Draken touched her head of curly, red hair and asked her to join him. She stood and took his arm. In a moment they were up on a ridge. Anessia looked out over a sea of people. "These are the lives you have touched. Many of these souls are here as the result of your willingness to love and trust God. To accept his purpose for their life. There will be many more coming because of your faith in our Lord. You have fulfilled your quest my precious one, with courage and strength, but most of all faith." Anessia was overwhelmed by the impact of this revelation, this tangible display of the purpose of her life. She looked up at Draken to see his face beaming. He looked into her deep, blue eyes. "Come Anessia, there is someone you must meet. He is anxious to speak with you and to present you to His Father." With that, they moved into the brightest light she had ever seen and Anessia was bathed in joy beyond anything she could ever imagine.

The Beginning

Dedications

There were many people who encouraged me when I thought I was crazy for assuming I could write a book. You guys will never know how much your support and love kept me motivated and believing I could really do this.

Pam Rich - *my cheerleader*

Your faith and trust in God inspires and amazes me. Thank you for your suggestions and insight. Everyone should have you in their corner. Your enthusiasm is contagious and we can all use a cheerleader! Your encouragement truly got me through this.

Donald Arnpriester - *my gentle giant of a husband*

You are my hero. The smartest thing I ever did was let you catch me. Thank you for your patience and support of my endeavor to write a book. You own my heart.

Alanna Lefsaker - *my little sister*

Hey sis, did you ever think I'd be dedicating anything to you?

Not only have you been an incredible sister, you are my friend. I am so thankful you were given to me as my sister. Your strength in your faith has a powerful effect on my own walk with Jesus Christ. You were a dynamic force in bringing me back.

Jenn and Rob - *my children*

Any similarities to your lives is strictly coincidental. I would never take advantage of my life experience as your mother to help me write a book. ;o)

Thank you both for loving me and tolerating my ramblings about the book. You are both the greatest gifts I have ever received. Rob, you do have your cameo appearance, but you have to read the book to find it!

Brianna Schear - *my totally awesome granddaughter*

Your enthusiasm and assumption that I could write a book means the world to me. I strive to see myself through your eyes, and yes, you are in the book ... check out Bree.

Rainy and Kaithlyn - *my new kids*

The day I met you began a wonderful opportunity to fall in love all over again. You both bring such joy and purpose to my life. Thank you for being so patient while I finished my book. I look forward to a lifetime of hugs and kisses from both of you. You will always be in my heart.

Another inspiring novel written by

Karen Arnpriester

raidersvendetta.com

ISBN-10: 1466274743

karnpriester@gmail.com

RAIDER'S Vendetta

Charley knew what God wanted from her. She was willing to trust and obey as she protected the others in the bank. Then He would save her from her captor. There was no way she could have anticipated the rage that would be unleashed in response to her prayers and her faith in God.

Raider was desperate, hardened, and his past had set the stage for an insane game of survival and spiritual warfare. The vendetta was in motion and Charley discovered that she needed her God to provide extraordinary miracles to keep her alive.

FIRST SIX CHAPTERS FOLLOW:

Introduction

I am thrilled to present my second book. Only the Lord knows how I ended up on this journey of telling stories. Stories about the pain life presents and the healing that can come from Heaven's grace.

As the writer of this story, I was able to step into the heart and mind of a very angry, vindictive person. Raider could easily be the type of person that we throw away, but the journey allows us to see how he became a man filled with fury. A man who could have been a loving, kind husband and father, but succumbed to a life of hardship and regret.

Charley, a faithful woman who would be tested and pushed to the ultimate limits. Could she follow God's directives and put her own pride, safety and fears aside?

The questions brought up in the book are and were my questions. Questions that kept me separate from God for many years. Some have been answered, but others have not, not yet. The story contains miracles, some fictional but others are actual Heavenly encounters that I was cherished enough by God to experience.

I would love to hear about your reactions and thoughts.

karnpriester@gmail.com
www.facebook.com/karen.slimickarnpriester
twitter.com/KarenArnpriester
amazon.com/author/karenarnpriester
Blog: http://karenskoncepts.com/mythoughts

raidersvendetta.com

Long Ago

He tried many times to escape, but Itchy couldn't figure out how to undo the latch from the inside. *How long will she keep me in here this time?* he wondered.

It was a simple mistake; he hadn't meant to see Mrs. Anton naked. Itchy was just hanging out with his best friend, Marty Anton. When he threw open the unlocked bathroom door to relieve himself, he saw her standing in the tub. She hadn't removed the towel from the bar yet and Itchy saw all of her nakedness. Itchy quickly looked down and fell backwards as he scrambled to get away. The screams from Mrs. Anton blasted his ears as he peed his pants. The uncontrolled release was horrific for a fourteen-year-old boy.

Mrs. Anton was enraged. She threw on her robe and telephoned his Aunt Rose, screaming that Itchy was a pervert and Rose needed to keep him away from her son. She insisted that he would corrupt Marty and turn him into a "Peeping Tom." Itchy panicked and ran from the house as Marty's mom shrieked at him to never come back.

Itchy was afraid to go home. He knew that his Aunt Rose would use his latest misfortune to punish and shame him, but if he didn't go home right away, the punishment would be even harsher. She had a way of stacking sins on top of each other. He could already hear her screeches in his head. "It wasn't bad enough that you lusted after a grown woman, but then you refused to face your foul sin and suffer the consequences. God sees your filthy heart. You can't run away from Him!"

When Itchy slunk into the house through the back door, Aunt Rose was waiting for him. She looked at his soiled crotch and clucked with distain. Itchy didn't understand that his Aunt had mistakenly assumed the worst. The wooden paddle that she used for pulling bread from the oven was spinning in her hands. He knew what was coming next – he unzipped his pants and they, along with his boxers, fell around his ankles. She nodded toward the kitchen table and he placed both hands flat on the surface.

The beating was vicious this time. He tried not to cry, but the repeated swings of the paddle became unbearable. The tears rolled down his cheeks and puddles formed on the table.

While he endured her wrath, she quoted scripture to him. She always pulled scriptures out of context and Itchy was convinced that God expected him to suffer to be worthy of forgiveness and salvation. Aunt Rose would alternate scripture with demeaning statements, telling him that his pain was only a small measure of what he deserved. He was born a bastard to a mother who was cheap and easy with filthy men. Aunt Rose would do whatever it took to save him from himself.

After Aunt Rose felt the punishment had suited the crime, she stopped and opened the cabinet door to the vegetable bin, an outdated storage area for fresh produce. It was the cell Itchy must endure until he repented for his wrongdoings. Itchy carefully pulled up his pants. There was no longer enough room to sit, as there had been when he was smaller. He had to squat, bend over, and squeeze in to fit. The blisters on his backside were on fire and wet. Itchy was sure they were bleeding. This was typical when she suspected his punishable infraction was sexually motivated, which was more frequent as he became older.

The door closed and latched from the outside. There was no air circulation except for small holes drilled into the cabinet door. Originally, they had been drilled to keep the produce from rotting as quickly. Now, the holes were small windows into a kitchen filled with pain and horror.

Each time Aunt Rose walked past the bin, she would kick the door and scream at him to pray louder for forgiveness. This was the angriest she had ever been. It was quite evident to Itchy that she felt he had crossed over to a new level of depravity. When he was young, his prayers were heartfelt. He wanted to be clean, but after years of belittlement and reinforcement of his undeserving and vile nature, his prayers were hollow and solely to pacify this enraged woman. His knees and legs began to ache and his muscles throbbed.

Aunt Rose's rantings over the years filled in the holes of Itchy's history. His mother, June, had become pregnant at the age of sixteen. She was the youngest and the wild child in her family of staunch believers. She had run off to California with Itchy's daddy, Arthur, who was seventeen. They didn't have the decency to get married and lived in lustful sin. His father was blonde, handsome, and charming, like all demons were, and he'd tempted June beyond her strength to resist.

When Itchy was only six years old, his mother escaped and left Itchy to survive his father's brutality alone. No one heard from June again and Itchy didn't know if she was alive or dead. Most days, he hoped she was dead, a long, painful, lonely death.

Itchy had earned his name by contracting a severe case of head lice when he was young. His father's abuse included extreme neglect. When he did go to school, the kids were relentless with their taunting. Itchy hated the nickname, but hated his real name even more. His real name, Arthur, was his father's name.

Eventually, his father was arrested for manslaughter, a bar fight gone bad, and the police officers took Itchy to Langston Hall. Most kids would be scared in a children's home, but Itchy felt safe there. He had three meals a day, a clean bed, and clean clothes. He didn't make many friends but there was one girl who touched him deeply. Her name was Pagne. He didn't know her for long, but she would always be in his heart, one of the three females he would ever trust.

The county eventually located his widowed Aunt Rose and she begrudgingly agreed to take Itchy to live with her. "It is the Christian thing to do," she told the social worker. He was flown back to Boston to live with her and her son, Darrell. Itchy was excited to have a new home and an older brother. Darrell, however, was indifferent. He was too busy avoiding his mother's wrath and quickly learned that having Itchy around proved to be an advantage. If he lay low, Itchy caught most of the hell.

Before arriving, Itchy had no idea of the loathing his aunt harbored or the horror that awaited him.

Chapter 1

Friday

When Charley Abrams pulled into the bank's parking lot, Charley was relieved to find it empty. There was no one at the ATM. When she walked up to the machine, she saw an electronic message on the screen announcing that the ATM was offline for programming updates and would be offline for several hours. Charley was annoyed. She hated going into the bank for simple transactions. There was always a wait, but she needed to deposit a large check today. When she approached the reflective doors, Charley stared at her reflection. She had become her mother over the years. There were wrinkles, but they weren't deeply etched like a lot of women her age. Her body build was always meaty, gradually heavier as she got older. She liked to say that she wasn't overweight, just too short. When asked how tall she wasn't, Charley would smile and say, "four-twelve."

Charley kept her hair in a spiky short style and had recently allowed it to remain gray. This was a big adjustment in her appearance. Though she had watched the face of an old woman slowly appear as the years passed, she still admired her eyes. They were large and gray. They weren't as bright as they used to be, but still unique. Charley had never liked her mouth. She had thin lips and always envied women with pouty, full mouths. She had entertained the idea of Botox injections when younger, but it required needles and that was a definite deal breaker. When she pulled open the mirror of herself, she was glad to see that she was the only customer in the bank.

When her transaction was complete, Charley tucked her receipt into her pocket. As she turned toward the door to leave, she heard a loud commotion and looked up. Charley saw two men with ball caps pulled down low, bandanas over their mouths and noses, pushing a young woman through the doors. One of the men shoved the woman and she fell to the floor, landing on her hands and knees. Charley grimaced with sympathy pain. She had fallen recently and remembered how it had jarred her whole body. The second man, who was quite tall and had a large build, turned the dead bolt, pointed a gun at the group of tellers, and bellowed, "Everyone behind the counter, take three steps back with your hands over your head! Now!" The shorter man grabbed the fallen woman's arm and drug her further into the bank, then snarled at her to lay down flat on the floor.

"You," the larger man said, glaring at Charley, "get down on the floor." Charley slid down the front of the counter and sat down. "Down flat, face on the floor," the man screamed at her. Charley quickly lay down, staring at the floor

The shorter man, thin but muscular, moved behind the counter and raised his gun so everyone saw it. He also had a large, open black garbage bag. He swiftly moved from station to station, making each of the tellers step up and open their drawer. The money moved quickly from the drawers into the bag.

Once the drawers were emptied, the robber behind the counter herded all the tellers around to the front. Charley hoped that someone had triggered the silent alarm. She sensed the movement of bodies close to her as the tellers were told to lie flat on the floor. She was curious, but didn't look up. She wondered why the bank didn't have an armed security guard. Weren't all banks supposed to have a guard? If she survived this, she would find a new bank with big guards and big guns.

The shorter man made his way to the doors while pointing the gun at the group of people on the floor. "Let's get going!" he hollered at his companion.

No response.

"Man, we gotta go. Now!"

"We got time… wanna check the vault," the taller man threw back as he knelt by the teller closest to Charley.

"Who can open the vault?" he sputtered as he grabbed the young woman by her hair. His other hand held the gun next to her skull and tapped it hard. Charley heard her yelp in pain.

"The manager, Mr. Mitchell." Since there was only one man working in the bank, it was obvious who he was. Charley heard the masked man jump up and move to her right. She positioned her head slightly so she was able to see where the manager was lying. The robber grabbed him and pulled him up, holding the gun next to his chest. The tension was building as the shorter man continued to scream and curse at his partner who was dragging the manager back to the vault.

"Shut up! We're almost done here," the taller man yelled back.

Charley slowly shifted herself to get a better view of the room. The woman next to her looked like she was going to pass out. Charley smiled, hoping it would reassure her. Charley saw the man closest to the door. She had time to take in details now. Muscular, but not big, jeans, Nike tennis shoes, long sleeved blue shirt, red print bandana, and an Oakland Raiders cap. It was too hot to be wearing a long sleeved shirt. Charley assumed he had tattoos he was covering, but enough skin was showing to know that he was Caucasian. His hair was tucked under the hat, but a little blonde still showed. She decided to label that one Raider.

Once the vault was opened, the manager turned to face the bank robber. In that moment, the bandana slipped down off the robber's face. The two men locked eyes and the realization that the robber could now be identified registered with both men. The robber's eyes narrowed with an evil determination. Mr. Mitchell had only one option, to take the gun.

Charley jerked as she heard struggling and then the blast of the gun as it went off. She saw Raider move to the center of the bank and lift his gun. She squeezed her eyes shut, a natural reaction, as another shot rang through the bank. She heard the loud wail of a man and then the thud as he went down. "Darrell!" Raider bellowed. Charley heard another man cursing and moaning. "Damn it, Darrell, what did you do?"

Raider demanded that they all slide to the left wall and sit with their hands on their heads as he made his way to the counter. He kicked the young woman he'd pushed down earlier and screamed at her to move over with the others. She managed to make it to the wall without throwing up. Raider kept his gun pointed at the stricken group of women.

He looked over the counter and saw the manager in a crumpled heap and Darrell sitting on the floor. His hand clutched his chest as the blood oozed between his fingers.

"Holy crap, Darrell. How bad is it?"

"Bad enough to kill me I expect," Darrell managed to say with sarcasm. Darrell tried to stand but fell onto his back. "Get the hell outta here, I'm done."

"You ass, I should leave you," Raider snarled.

Raider moved around the end of the counter to get to Darrell, still trying to keep all the hostages in view. His partner lay on his back, unblinking eyes staring at the ceiling. He was obviously dead. Raider looked at the front doors, his expression frantic, like that of a trapped animal looking for a way to escape.

Charley, trying to make sense of what happened, assumed that Mr. Mitchell had grabbed the gun, killed the robber in the scuffle, and was shot by Raider before he got off another round. The coppery smell of blood filled the bank.

When Raider came around to the front of the counter, he saw several cars pulling in. They appeared to be customers. Charley could see that he had no idea what to do now. "In and out quick, you stupid idiot," he mumbled under his breath.

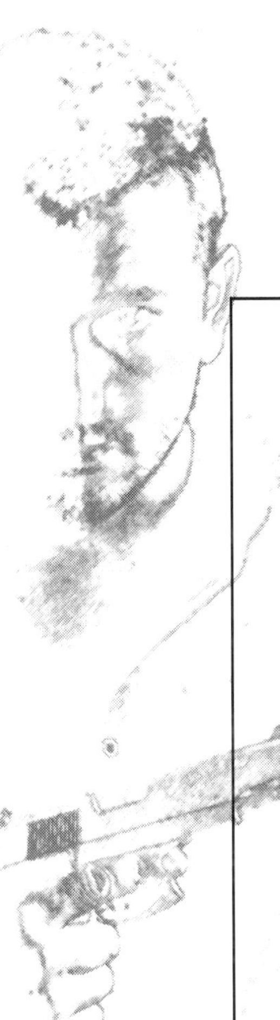

Chapter 2

As Charley scanned the room with her limited view, she saw an elderly man walk up to the bank entrance and try to open the door. The bank doors were tinted almost black, since they faced west, and she knew the man only saw his reflection in the doors, even though the people inside saw him. He looked confused, then looked at his watch and tried the door once more. He stood there, not knowing what to do next, baffled by the locked door.

It appeared to Charley, that Raider would rush the old man and get past him before he could react; might even shoot him. As Raider moved toward the doors, four construction workers moved in behind the old man. They tried the door, also looking confused. One of them knocked and waited. The conversation among the group was accented with shrugs and searching looks, seeking a sign or someone with an explanation. Several of the men pressed their faces against the glass, trying to see into the bank. They all stood there, waiting, discussing the situation. More people joined the group. A woman pulled out a cell phone and dialed. Charley heard the phone ringing from behind the counter. Each ring made the room vibrate as if a gong had been hit. Everyone held their breath. The woman hung up and tried again. The ringing continued. Raider appeared to be calm, but Charley was close enough to see his hand twitching as he held the gun. She feared the outcome for all of them. Charley silently began praying to God. The woman with the phone hung up again and dialed a short number. Charley assumed it was 911.

Charley heard Raider quietly repeating, "Leave." The

young woman on her cell phone became more animated, then suddenly became still, staring at the locked doors. She slowly began stepping back, instructing the others to do the same, keeping her eyes glued on the doors. Obviously, the police had warned them to move back for their safety. The construction workers hesitated but finally moved a short distance away. Charley identified the body language; the group of strong men were primed for a fight. They were ready to be heroes. She knew Raider would not be exiting through the front doors. The rest of the group moved to the far side of the parking lot and appeared to be waiting for the show to begin. Raider squatted on the floor, keeping the gun turned on the group, as he tried to use the bandana to wipe the sweat away from his eyes. This was difficult to do while keeping his face hidden. Charley thought how hot it must be in that disguise. By now, he would have been racing away in a fast car, air conditioner blasting, counting the money, if his partner had not gotten greedy.

They didn't have to wait long. A black and white cruiser pulled into the lot and several officers got out. They stayed on the far side of their cruiser. One officer took out a phone and dialed the bank's number.

The hostages were startled when they heard the phone begin to ring again. Raider jumped up and paced some more.

"Should we answer it?" one of the teller's asked. The bank robber seemed to be searching his brain for an idea.

"Yeah," he finally said. "Tell them the electricity is off and you had to close down for awhile." The teller, whose nametag said Anne, slowly got up and picked up the phone. Raider was pointing his gun at the young lady who had been pushed into the bank. He jerked the gun at her to remind Anne that he would shoot if she didn't do what he said.

"Hello, Ellisville Bank," she managed to say. Charley was impressed. She didn't know if she would be able to speak. "Everything is fine, Officer. Our power went out and it is procedure to lock the doors until everything is back up and running." Pause. "I assure you, we are all fine." Pause again. "I realize you have a job to do, but Mr. Mitchell is not here. Only he can authorize us to unlock the doors." Another pause. "I'm sorry, sir. Soon, sir," then she was quiet, listening to the other end of the line. From her facial expression, it was obvious to Charley that the officer was not buying her explanation.

Anne hesitated and looked at Raider. "They want to talk to you, sir. They know something is wrong." Raider began pacing and cursing again.

"Hang up you moron" he said through clenched teeth. Anne hung up the phone. She stood there, scared to move or speak. Raider walked over to her and smacked her across the face with the gun. She fell to the floor, whimpering. He pointed the gun at her and pulled back the hammer.

She managed to whisper between her sobs, "He knew. I didn't tell him, he already knew. You heard me. I tried to send them away." Charley felt her heart in her throat. She thought about trying to knock him off his feet with her legs, but he was too far away.

Dear God, please don't let him kill her! she screamed in her head. She heard the hammer slip back into position.

"All of you get behind the counter." They half crawled, half slid to the new location. Charley was able to get next to Anne and put her arm around her shoulder. She looked at the damage to her face and saw that, in spite of all the blood, the injuries were not serious. She would be bruised and swollen, but she would be okay. She felt Anne move in tighter next to her. Charley felt her whole body quivering.

They jumped when the phone began ringing again. No one moved to answer it. Raider squatted across from them, aiming the gun from one frantic face to another. The ringing kept going and going. It felt warmer inside the bank. Was it the closeness of the group, the sweat that comes with fear, or had they shut off the air conditioning? Charley had seen that happen in cop shows; make the criminals as uncomfortable as possible. She always felt bad for the hostages and now she would be the one sweating it out. The phone finally stopped ringing.

~

Now that they were behind the counter, they couldn't see anything outside, but Raider would stand periodically to check on things. More police cars had pulled in. Raider wasn't sure what to do now. He had to think quickly. They had always done hit and run robberies; gas stations, convenience stores, or drunks trying to find their cars. This was their first bank robbery and Darrell had said he had it all worked out. "Don't worry, it'll be a breeze. The drawers will have plenty. It's payday for most slobs and they load the drawers up just before lunch. We'll hit them hard and fast."

Darrell, you fool, you didn't say anything about the vault, he thought. Even Raider knew the vault required too much time, especially with just two guys.

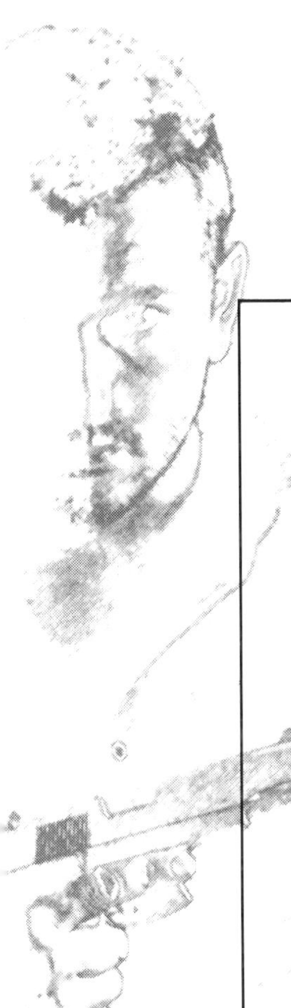

Chapter 3

A voice boomed through a bullhorn, "This is the police. We want to talk to whoever is in charge. We'll be calling you." After what felt like an eternity, the phone rang. Raider picked it up on the tenth ring. He held the phone to his ear, but didn't speak. Agent Morris was on the other end. "I'm Agent Megan Morris, with the FBI, and I want to help you help us resolve this situation. We don't want anyone hurt. What can we do for you?" After a few minutes of hesitation, he moved the receiver under the bandana.

"Look, I don't want anyone else killed. Just clear out and I'll leave."

"Anyone else? People have been killed? Wounded?"

"I'm not telling you anything. I just need you all to leave and no one will get hurt. If you don't, I will shoot someone."

"Can you tell me who is in there with you?" Raider slammed the phone down, hoping he burst the wanna-be cop's eardrum. Women with badges, just as bad as soldiers with boobs. Raider got up and looked around the bank. He needed to find a way to control the hostages while he searched the bank for a way out. He glanced over to the vault and saw that the metal bar door was standing open; the keys were still in the lock. "All of you, move into the vault, stay low."

They crawled past Mr. Mitchell's body and tried not to look into his shocked face, frozen in death. Then they crawled past the second body. It had been many years since this fifty-seven year old woman had been on her knees, let alone traveled on them. Blood had drained onto the floor from both bodies and their hands and knees were covered with the warm stickiness.

Charley made it into the vault first. The rest of the hostages followed her in and huddled in the far corner. Raider pulled the phone in the vault out of the wall and stepped out to shut the gate. Raider tested it with a hard tug. Once the hostages were locked in and no longer a threat, he knelt down and looked into Darrell's glazed over eyes. *What the hell did you get me into Darrell?* he thought. He saw the gun lying between his cousin's thighs. Raider picked it up and wiped the blood onto his jeans. He pocketed the keys, stuck the second gun in his waistband, and moved back into the bank to locate the cameras.

Raider entered each office and room looking for other employees or an exit. If a door was locked, he forced it open. He found the room with the recording boxes and surveillance equipment. He saw there were two screens. One was positioned to cover the front doors and the second would show the faces of people in line at the teller windows. He went back into the bank and smashed both cameras. He jumped when the phone rang. Raider decided to pick it up and see what they were offering.

"Thank you for picking up. I'd like to help," Agent Morris offered. Raider thought for a minute,

"Okay" he said with a smirk.

"How would you like for me to address you?" she asked.

"Sir will be just fine."

"I'm here to work with you. Tell me what you need."

"I want a helicopter and a pilot. If you provide that, I won't kill anyone. So you do what you gotta do to work that out." Raider slammed the phone down. He pulled the scarf off his face and the air, even though warm, felt good on his skin.

He continued to search for another way out. He knew he wasn't going out those front doors. He knew they would string him along, promise him anything, and wait for a sniper to get a clear shot. Raider figured he would find a way to slip out and be long gone before anyone knew he wasn't there. He checked the ducts, the windows, and the service doors. He saw that cruisers had surrounded the bank. He kicked himself for being disappointed. What did he think they would do? He checked for trap doors that would lead to the roof or under the building.

~

Charley knelt next to Anne to offer whatever comfort she could. She felt the bulk of her cell phone in her pocket. She looked out the vault gate bars, and didn't see or hear anything. She prayed that Raider wasn't on his way back. Charley looked at the huddled mass of women. "Is there anyone else in the bank, in any of the offices?"

"No," Geena answered. "We all come behind the counter for the lunch crowd."

Charley only had two bars on her phone and hoped it was enough to send a text. She texted her daughter, Mari, and told her where she was. When her daughter's return text flashed on the screen, Charley felt connected to the outside world again. She then entered the other hostages' names and phone numbers. There were a total of seven women: Charley; Angie, the lady they had pushed in the door; Anne, the teller hit with the gun; Lenore, the supervisor; Geena, the loan officer; Brittany, a teller; and Iris, another teller. Next, she texted that one of the robbers and the bank manager had been killed. She also told her to tell the police there was only one robber in the bank and all the hostages were locked in the vault. After assuring her daughter she was fine, she turned the volume off and hid the phone in the vault so she wouldn't be found with it. After getting the message from Mari, Angie's husband texted her to tell her that he loved her and he would be at the bank soon. Angie texted him back and told him they were all safe in the vault.

Charley saw the fear in the women's eyes. "I'd like to pray for our safety," Charley suggested.

Angie quickly straightened up and said, "Absolutely, we pray all the time; me, my husband and my three little ones.

The other women looked at Charley in disbelief. Lenore even snickered at the suggestion. "If God is so wonderful, why are we sitting in here? Why is Mr. Mitchell dead? He was a Christian. Just pray silently if you're going to pray. I don't want to hear it. The police will get us out of here."

Charley was surprised that the severity of their situation didn't lead them to want God's protection. Charley prayed silently while holding

Angie's hand. She felt Angie squeeze her hand several times. She felt blessed to know that they were united in their prayer. The Holy Spirit touched Charlie's soul with the understanding that she was needed in this crisis.

Chapter 4

Raider couldn't find a way out that wouldn't put him face to face with the police. He had been frantically searching for the last hour, no exit. He had found a pile of white tablecloths used for the bank's display tables and several boxes of promotional t-shirts. These could come in handy.

Raider pulled the bandana back up. He got to the vault door and then he heard the distinct vibration of a cell phone. No one is without a cell phone these days. He began cursing the women, unlocked the door, and pushed it open. "I want your phones, all of them." He pointed the gun at Lenore, "I'll blow her head off." Angie slid her phone over to his feet. The other ladies had been working, so no phones were on their person. He looked at Charley and she stared back. "I don't have a phone on me," she finally said. She wasn't lying; it certainly wasn't on her. He told her to stand up. He patted her down and when he was convinced she wasn't concealing a phone, he pushed her back to the floor.

It was a deranged sight, this man with a gun, looming over them, covered in blood. Charley knew this vision would terrorize any sane person. Raider picked up Angie's phone and checked her outgoing calls and then texts. Angie cringed with fear, realizing she should have deleted the message to her husband when she had the chance. He saw her last text sent and didn't bother to read any further. Raider glared at her through narrowed eyes. Without hesitation, he lifted the gun and shot her. He didn't shoot to kill, but hit her in the thigh. "You stupid, stupid woman," he muttered as she wailed in pain. Charley moved toward her and he lifted the gun to her face. Her nose was inches from the end of the barrel. She smelled the hot metal and the spent bullet. "Stay put or you're next," he growled. Charley wasn't a nurse, but she knew, if left unattended, Angie would bleed out.

"She's worth more to you alive," Charley stated calmly, even though she was terrified on the inside. "You may have hit a major artery. Just let me get a tourniquet on it so she doesn't die." Raider looked at the blood gushing from Angie's leg. He didn't respond but lowered the gun and stepped back. Charley pulled off Angie's t-shirt and wrapped it tightly around Angie's thigh above the bullet hole. She saw the mixture of terror, shock, and anguish in Angie's eyes. "God is with us," she mouthed to Angie. Angie seemed to relax a little.

The bank phone began to ring. Raider pointed the gun at Geena, "You answer it and tell them time is ticking. They now have a wounded hostage." Geena stood up slowly and Raider shoved her to the nearest phone, just outside the vault. She answered the phone and relayed his message word for word. They wanted to know details and Geena looked at Raider. "Hang up!" he screamed. He pushed Geena toward the storage closet and demanded, "Grab those T-shirts and take them into the vault." Geena obeyed. The women were instructed to rip the shirts into strips. Charley took one of them and helped Angie put it on. She knew Angie wouldn't want to be sitting there in just her bra. Raider started to stop her but found it curious that this old woman would worry about modesty. Charley also took several of the shirts and folded them into a compress for Angie's wound.

Raider then had all the women tie themselves together, just a few inches apart, with their arms extended. He looked at Angie and realized she wasn't mobile. To move her, they would have to drag her. She would have to be left in the vault. He had the remaining women at each end of the shredded T-shirt rope tie themselves together to make a circle. He looked at his shield and was pleased. Raider ducked under the rope and into the center of the circle. Now he would have their bodies as a shield. Any attempts to subdue him would jeopardize the women.

Raider kept his gun pointed in Geena's side. "Anyone try anything and I won't miss. At this range, the bullet will tear her in half." Charley was directly in front of Raider, face to face. She hadn't known what he was planning or she would have turned around before tying herself in. She walked backward as they moved into the bank. She could see the details of his eyes, deep green with gold veining. How did such beautiful eyes contain such hate? She found herself praying that she wouldn't trip. If she went down, the whole group would go down. The gun could easily go off and kill one of them.

Trying to walk past the bodies and maneuver across the blood-covered floor was difficult. The women could smell the mixture of their sweat as they shuffled together. It was soured and musty. Raider's was the strongest. His anxiety level combined with the heat in the bank made it ooze from his pores. The bank was warm and uncomfortable, but at least they were no longer sitting in the vault. It felt too much like a tomb. They were tied so close together, there was no airflow to help dissipate their body heat. Charley felt like she was suffocating.

The phone rang again. They shuffled their way to the desk and Raider picked up the receiver and waited.

"Sir," Agent Morris said. "We are working on getting your chopper. We can land it in the field just behind the bank, but we need to know that the ladies are safe and that you have not hurt them. We heard a shot."

"Well, one got shot for blabbing her mouth. She's alive but not for long."

"Sir, please allow her to leave the bank. You don't want a murder against you, especially of an innocent woman. Juries won't show mercy to a man who shoots an unarmed woman." Raider considered what she was saying.

"You're assuming that I will get caught and face a jury," Raider replied.

"It would show good faith with us if you let her go so she can get medical attention. We will see that you are a man of character."

Raider knew the routine. They were stalling, looking for an opportunity to take him out. He wasn't ready to make a move yet. He had worked out a plan now and needed to drag things out. "What about a trade?" he suggested. "The woman for some food and cold drinks."

"We can do that Sir. Give us twenty minutes. We will put the food at the front door. Just let her slip out and we can work out the rest of your demands once we have a show of good faith. How many people are there with you? We want to make sure we get enough food."

"You mean alive? Of course you do." Raider looked around him and there were six women in his circle of protection. "Seven including the wounded snitch," he supplied.

"Okay Sir, have the wounded lady come to the door. We will have the food shortly." Agent Morris quickly hung up and Raider suspected she had intentionally cut him off before he could protest. The group moved back to the vault and Raider unlocked the gate. Angie was unconscious and wouldn't wake up when Raider slapped her. He tried several times, using more force with each strike. In frustration, anger, and total disregard for her, he punched her hard in the face. She didn't stir. Charley saw how pale Angie was. The wound wasn't gushing, but the makeshift bandage was soaked through with her precious blood.

"Sir, we need to get her out now, she doesn't have long." Raider turned and Charley saw him searching their faces to see who had spoken. Charley took a deep breath, "Sir, please, let's get her to the door." Raider kept his gun in one hand and grabbed Angie's good leg with the other. He pulled until she slid down the wall and lay flat on her back. With the help of several of the women, they drug Angie into the main foyer of the bank, ten feet from the door. Raider knew that if they all struggled to get her out the door, the cops would pick him off even while surrounded by his shield. He instructed everyone to pull back into the center of the bank. He looked at Lenore who appeared to be the strongest of the women.

"Untie yourself. You will drag her through the door and bring in the food." He nodded toward Angie, still unconscious on the floor. "Remember, I have the gun shoved into your buddy's back," he had grabbed Iris. "You try to run and she's dead. Her blood is on your hands." Lenore looked into Iris's pleading eyes. Lenore nodded agreement and slowly untied herself from the shield of women. She moved over to Angie and saw the officers setting bags of food just outside the door. She slipped her arms under Angie's and backed over to the door, struggling to drag Angie by herself. She set Angie down and turned to unlock and open the door. Lenore pushed it open a few inches and blocked it from closing with her foot. She then reached down to pick up Angie. When her trembling hands were only an inch from Angie's dying body she lurched to her right and pushed through the doors, leaving Angie on the floor and Iris's fate up to Raider. By the time her escape registered with Raider, she was gone.

"Dammit!" he screamed. Iris body tightened. Suddenly, an officer dressed in full SWAT gear pulled open the door, grabbed Angie by the shoulders, and drug her out of the bank. Raider pulled the women tight around him, blocking any access.

~

The officer pulled Angie around the corner of the bank and to a waiting ambulance. She was rushed to the hospital with her husband sobbing at her side. Agent Morris asked what he could see.

"Well, there are five more women. Everyone is covered with blood, but they all look okay. Must have been a massacre in there. I only saw one suspect, but he had the women tied together as a human shield around him. Very clever," the officer observed.

"Yes, yes, it is. I think he's in over his head, but he's quick on his feet. That's not good." Agent Morris replied.

~

Raider picked up the ringing phone. "Sir," Agent Morris said, "Don't think things went the way you planned. Food is still out here and you're down two hostages." Raider was still reeling from Lenore's cowardly betrayal. He wasn't sure what to do about Iris. He should shoot her, but that hadn't worked out so well with the blonde in the vault. Did he want to kill her? No, he needed her; he needed all of the hostages.

"No, not at all how I planned. Didn't think she was a heartless bitch, but guess you all are down deep."

"Well, we're going to give you this one, tell the press you released two hostages. Looks good for you, Sir. Want to make sure those ladies get some food, been a rough day for them. I'll have the officer bring the food inside the door."

"No, *Megan*, no one is starving in here. Keep your food."

Raider slammed down the phone and moved his party back behind the counter. He had to regroup. The door was unlocked and he was a sitting duck. Raider found himself looking into the face of Charley. He thought he saw something in her eyes. Gratitude? "What's up with you?" he asked.

"Thank you for not shooting Iris," she said softly.

"If you care about these women, you'll go lock that door. If you take off, I will shoot her this time." He put the gun up to Iris's temple. There were several moments of intense eye contact between Raider and Charley. She untied her bindings and walked with determination to the door. She looked back at Iris and smiled a reassuring smile. Charley obviously decided to collect the food. She knelt down then opened the door a few inches. Raider saw an officer crouched on the far side of the food, reaching to grab Charley's arm to pull her out, but he pulled back. Charley pulled the food in, locked the door, moved back to the group, and retied her bindings. This woman intrigued Raider. *Why didn't she run? She could have escaped. Why didn't the officer try to grab her?*

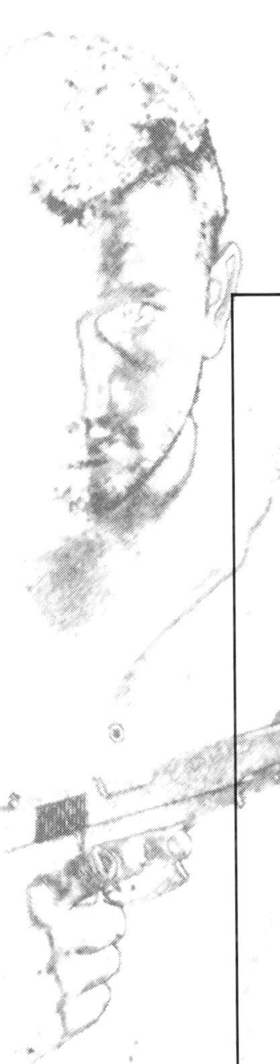

Chapter 5

Their appetites surprised the ladies. The events of the morning had drained them and their bodies begged for nourishment. Raider refrained from eating, even though the burritos smelled incredible. He didn't trust that they hadn't laced the food with something. He would wait to see if the ladies reacted and then eat later if they were okay. He took one of the sealed water bottles and searched for pinpricks before downing it. The cold water brought his body temperature down several degrees. The group sat on the floor, legs crossed, with Raider still in the center. He kept the bandana over his face, even with the sweltering heat.

Iris ate her burrito slowly, like a timid little bird picking at the edges. Raider watched her, wondering how someone so frail survived life. She caught his gaze and jerked when he said, "Boo." Her distress was obvious and she was ready to crumble.

Raider noticed that Charley didn't eat, and was suspicious and confused by Charley. He stared at her and when she looked up, they made eye contact. He nodded toward the burritos and she said, "No thanks, beans do not like me."

After everyone else had finished eating, they sat and waited. The phone rang. Geena was closest and answered when Raider nodded his head. She handed him the receiver. "Sir, Agent Morris here," Megan said.

"Yes, hello *Megan*," Raider responded with mock familiarity.

"Everyone get enough to eat?" she asked, feigning sincerity.

"Yes, yes we did," he said with sarcasm.

"Well, we are working on that chopper, and it should be here any time. Since this is wrapping up soon, think you can spare a hostage? Maybe someone older, someone with health issues?" Raider looked at the ladies. Charley was the only one he would consider as older. "Would go a long way with my bosses if I can show them you are willing to work with me."

"What do I get out of this? Why should I work with you? Going to get my chopper either way." Raider enjoyed toying with her, this woman with a badge – thinking she was more than any other tramp out there.

"What do you want, Sir?" She waited without breathing.

"You turn the air back on and I'll send someone out." It was dreadfully hot in the bank and Raider was having trouble thinking. He knew the cool air would revive him.

"We have to see a hostage released first; that's how it works."

"No, Megan, that's not how it works, air first. You can always shut it off if I don't deliver. I can't do a thing if you lie on your end. Oh, that's right, I can shoot someone. The advantage of having multiple hostages. Cushion."

Agent Morris hesitated and then responded, "Okay, Sir, we'll do it your way. Air, then you release a hostage."

"Great, I'll be waiting. Don't take too long though, you understand?"

"Yes, Sir, I do." Within ten minutes, they felt the cool air flowing into the bank. Everyone breathed a sigh of relief, but only for a moment. Raider wasn't ready to give up a hostage quite yet. He wanted the bank to cool down first, in case they shut off the air again once the hostage was released. He knew that this was a game of wits and deception. He couldn't count on anything they said. He had to rely on his military training and skills. He also knew he had to stall until sunset if his only option was going to work.

Iris spoke so quietly they almost didn't hear her. "How long will you keep us here?" she asked. Raider looked in the direction of the doors.

"I don't know," he lied.

Iris spoke again, an embarrassed tone in her voice. "I *really* need to use the restroom now." Raider had wondered when this would present itself. Raider wasn't surprised that Iris needed to relieve herself, but he had no idea how urgent the need was. They all stood and moved as a group to the restroom. During his earlier search of the bank, Raider had found a small bathroom that didn't have a window. They would not be able to escape. When they reached the bathroom, Iris untied herself and rushed in.

"If anyone else needs to go, do it now. I'm not going to be taking potty breaks all afternoon," snapped Raider. Panic began to creep up in Raider's mind. He realized that he also needed to use the restroom, and not just to pee. He tried to push down the urge, but this was not going to pass.

After the rest of the ladies had used the toilet, his own need had become urgent. He had not thought this part out. The ladies would be tied up tight, but he was concerned that the cops might have eyes inside the bank. A small wire with a camera could be pushed through small openings or vents. He could not be in the bathroom alone for any amount of time. The cops would rush in while he had his pants down. This presented an awkward situation, but he had no choice. He looked at the women and decided to have Charley and Iris tie up the other ladies. Charley was older and Iris was frail. He knew they weren't a threat if they decided to attack, he would easily kill them. He told them to tie the other hostages tight and threatened to kill them if anyone worked loose. Charley and Iris did their best not to hurt the ladies, but did not want to test him either. Once the ladies were tied up, he motioned for Charley and Iris to move into the bathroom with him. Iris's eyes showed panic. She was a young, attractive woman and Raider knew she thought he was going to violate them. Raider would have laughed if he had not felt such humiliation since his aunt was alive.

~

Once Raider positioned himself by the toilet and unzipped his pants, Charley knew that this was going to be awkward. The embarrassment was minimized when they were told to face the wall, shut their eyes, and not say a word. Charley considered making a run for it while he was indisposed, but she didn't know where the gun was pointed. It would be aimed at one of them and she knew she couldn't outrun a bullet. Once Raider was finished, they joined the others, and sat on the floor. No one had escaped.

Charley was distracted, staring at the clock, playing out all the ways this could end. She began praying silently and was surprised to get a word from the Holy Spirit. It was "Stay." No sooner than she heard this direction, Raider told her to untie herself from the other ladies.

"You'll be leaving us, Granny," Raider shared. Charley was relieved and quickly began to untie herself.

Again she heard the voice of the Holy Spirit say, "Stay." Charley sat back on her heels and tried to make sense of this direction. She wanted to argue, to plead for her release, but the Holy Spirit spoke again, firmly, and she knew the plan and purpose.

"Get moving you stupid woman, I'm telling you that you get to leave." Just as he finished speaking, Iris covered her mouth but could not stop the flow of vomit. "Are you kidding me?" Raider yelled as he moved back to avoid the gush of stinking bile mixed with burrito, releasing a flood of obscenities as he glared at her. Iris drew back as far as possible, terrified, waiting to see what he was going to do. Would he shoot her? Several ladies began to weep, which agitated him even more.

Charley had to do something before someone got shot, even if she brought his wrath on her. She lightly touched his shoulder and whispered, "Raider, please let Iris leave instead. Obviously, she is very ill." Charley suspected that Iris's frail demeanor was unable to withstand the terror of being held hostage.

"Why are you calling me Raider?"

"It's just a name. I don't know your real one." He looked confused. Charley pointed at his head, "Your hat, the Raiders?" Raider began laughing hysterically, not because of the name, but the insanity of his circumstance. "What's your name?"

Charley hesitated, she didn't want to stand out from the rest, but he was waïting. "Charley," she said quietly. He didn't react, she wasn't even sure he heard her. It didn't seem to matter any longer.

Raider stayed in the center of the women. When Iris wasn't in the bathroom, she was balled up on the floor, crying from the cramps that twisted her gut. "Please Raider, please let her go. She isn't getting any better," Charley pleaded. Raider looked at the quivering Iris and gagged at the smell of the vomit covering her clothes. Getting rid of that smell wasn't a terrible idea. "We don't want the air turned off, sir." Raider looked at Charley again, seeing the concern in her eyes.

"Can I get her to the door? She can't get there herself and I promise I won't run."

Raider knew she wouldn't. She could've escaped earlier and didn't. "Okay, but if you do run, I will shoot." He looked around at the remaining women, "What's your name?" Raider asked, looking at Geena.

"Geena," she said meekly.

"Okay Geena, you better hope Charley here is on the up and up." This threat was to scare the hostages, but he already knew Charley would be back. He was drained and losing his edge. He wanted them to know he was tough and mean, so he pulled the gun up to Geena's head and tapped several times. Not enough to hurt her but menacing none the less. Charley rolled her eyes and then caught herself. She didn't want to upset him. Raider caught her reaction but decided to pretend he hadn't. He was getting low on hostages and didn't want to shoot one unnecessarily. He had to stretch them out until the time was right.

~

Charley helped Iris to her feet and they slowly walked away from the others. When Charley got Iris to the doors, she set her down. "Now, when I open the doors, you crawl out. They will come grab you."

Iris looked up at Charley. "Why are you doing this? You could have left."

"You have a family at home?"

"Yes," said Iris.

"This is God's gift to them and you. He loves you Iris. Please take this opportunity to find Him."

Iris looked at her, confused, and then smiled. Charley saw several officers moving near the door. Once she opened the door and they saw two hostages, they would make a grab for both of them. She knew if she didn't step back, they would drag her out, too. She couldn't let that happen. "Okay Iris, after I unlock the door, you gotta push it open with your shoulder and just crawl." Iris positioned herself. Charley turned the lock and as she stepped back the two officers pulled open the doors, startling Charley. One officer grabbed Iris's arms and yanked her through the doors like a ragdoll. The second officer grabbed Charley's arm. She felt the tug and dropped to the floor. She heard Geena scream "No." Charley braced her feet on the doorjamb and prevented herself from being pulled out the door. The officer had to let go and pull back quickly, before Raider had time to react and shoot. As soon as the officer let go, Charley rolled back into the bank.

Charley lay there, breathing deep panting breaths. She knew they wouldn't expect her back at the door. She jumped up, ran over, and locked it, then ran back to the others. Raider looked at her in total disbelief. She winked at Geena and began tying herself back into the circle.

~

Raider hated women. They lied, connived, cheated, humiliated, and sucked the life out of men. Charley didn't make sense in his world.

The phone rang. Raider looked forward to this call. They moved as a group to the closest phone and Raider picked it up. "Yes, Megan?"

"Thanks for sending out Iris. You got your mom in there with you?" Agent Morris asked. Raider grinned at Charley. "Nope, just a loyal hostage. Guess she didn't want Geena's brains splattered on the walls."

"Do the ladies need anything?"

"They'll be just fine when I'm on that chopper and they can go home to their families. When is that gonna be *Megan*? Do I need to shoot another one to show you I'm getting irritated? I won't kill her, just a good wound, and one that bleeds fast. Do you work well under pressure, Megan? Would that help move things along? I got plenty of bullets left, got my partner's gun. I can spare another one if it will help motivate you."

"I'm on it Sir. You should hear it coming in soon." Raider heard Agent Morris slam her fist as she hung up. This triggered a satisfying grin.

~

Charley felt real hatred for this man. He was cruel and would do everything he threatened. She tried to give everyone the benefit of the doubt, but this is one time that she needed to remember that a snake is a snake and it doesn't think twice about biting.

Chapter 6

They could hear the constant hum of the air conditioner and Charley was thankful that they hadn't turned if off again. Brittany and Geena drifted in and out of a light doze. She looked over at Raider, who stared at the glass doors. Who was he and why was he so indifferent to life? He showed no remorse for killing the manager and he'd shot Angie without hesitation or emotion. How does a baby grow into such a monster?

Raider instructed them to return to the vault, bringing the tablecloths with them, and he moved out of the center. He took one of the t-shirts and tore eyeholes, then tied off the top of the shirt and, with his back turned, took off his bandana and hat. Next, he pulled the shirt over his head, pushing the sleeves into the shirt. He looked like a scarecrow when he turned around. He began to work on the tablecloths using a stapler.

It seemed like hours before the phone rang again and when Charley checked the clock, it had been. Why was Raider being so patient? She would have expected him to push for a quick escape. He seemed eerily calm, like a man with a plan.

Before entering the vault again, they had drug a phone close to the door. Raider picked up the phone and opened with, "I don't hear any blades whirling. Where is my chopper?"

"I'm sorry, Sir, my boss is stalling on me. He just doesn't think that you will keep your end of the bargain and let all of the hostages go. He wants to see another one come through those doors before he'll release the chopper."

"Well, Megan, I never said I'd let all the hostages go.

Now that would be foolish of me, wouldn't it? But, I'll tell you what. If your boss wants to see my intentions, have him listen to this." Raider set the receiver down and ignored Agent Morris's pleas and lies. Raider looked at Geena and spoke without any emotion in his voice, calm, like a stranger on the street giving you directions. "I'm going to have to shoot you. I'll be careful and aim for your thigh. I hope I don't hit an artery. Don't think they can move fast enough to save you if that happens." Geena jerked out of her exhausted stupor and began screaming. Raider had the look of someone determined and detached. Charley knew he would do this.

"Wait," yelled Charley. "Shoot me." Raider turned his head toward her.

"You're crazy! Are you out of the loony bin on a two-day pass?"

"No, just listen to me, please. I'm old, kids are grown, husband is dead. I've only got an old cat at home." Charley looked at Geena. "Geena, you got kids?"

"Yes, two little girls," she managed to whisper.

"How old are you, hon?" Charley kept switching her eyes from Geena to Raider, watching his finger on the trigger.

"I'm twenty-seven."

"Raider, she could be crippled for life or dead. I've lived a good, long life. Shoot me."

"You're screwing with me. Don't think I won't do it."

"I know you will. I know you have to. This is survival for you. I get that. But, does it matter who? Can just as easily be me, right? Let me do this for Geena and her kids." Raider's confusion was obvious, and then Charley heard the gun go off as she felt a fist punch her in the face. She screamed from the pain in her jaw and nose. Raider hung up the phone.

Charley saw stars. Her head had snapped back with the punch. Blood gushed from her nose. With tears rolling down her cheeks, she tenderly examined her jaw and nose with her fingers. Her nose felt like it was broken.

Once she could think clearly, she looked at Geena, relieved that she was not shot. Charley then looked at Raider. She saw a flicker of regret in his eyes when he saw the blood pouring from her nose, but it dissolved as soon as their eyes met. He glared at her and his words were an ominous whisper. "Next time, I will shoot you. Maybe I should anyway, put you out of your stinkin' misery. You are freakin' crazy." Geena was a mass of jelly, crying and shaking. Raider couldn't take it. "Shut up!" he screamed. Geena brought her hand to her mouth to smother her cries. The remaining ladies all sat there in silence, not wanting to draw Raider's attention.

~

It wasn't long before they heard the distinctive wop of a helicopter. Sunset was quickly approaching. The phone rang and it was Agent Morris. "Well, Sir, you hear that?"

"Yep, music to my ears."

"How's Charley. It was Charley you shot?"

"I don't know their names, not like we're ever going to hang out again."

"Well, is she okay?"

"Bleeding bad. Think she'll be okay if you guys follow directions."

"Let her come out, Sir. We need to get her to the hospital, right now."

"We put a tourniquet on her leg. I'll leave her in here. When we leave, you can come in and get her. Gotta apply pressure, Megan, you appear to work best under pressure."

"Okay, Sir. We'll do it your way. You need to come through the front and around to the right of the building." Raider hung up.

In a low whisper, "Geena, take these," Raider threw her several of the t-shirts, "soak them with blood from the bodies. If the blood on the floor has dried, you'll have to push on one of the bodies. It has to look like Charley is bleeding. Stay low, below the counter. I'm sure they have cameras hooked in and probably microphones." Geena obeyed. She had to push on the dead robber's body to force more blood onto the floor.

Raider looked at Charley. "If you tip off the cops when they come in, you'll get these women killed. You understand me?" he said just barely loud enough for Charley to hear. He then spoke in a much louder voice, hoping the police would hear, "The rest of you are coming with me. We'll move out to the chopper. I'm only taking one of you with me. The rest of you can run when I say. Got it?" They all nodded. Raider knew that dangling the carrot of freedom would buy compliance from the hostages and possibly the police if they were listening. They may refrain from any heroics if they thought most of the hostages would be released soon.

~

Charley felt a moment of relief that she would be rescued, but then the will of the Holy Spirit replayed in her head. She had to go to the helicopter. Charley wasn't clear what would come next, the Holy Spirit hadn't given her anymore, just that she was supposed to go to the helicopter with Raider. Charley looked into Geena's frantic face. She was clearly thinking *What if he takes me on the chopper?*

"Raider?" Charley said in a whisper.

"What now old lady?"

"Look, they won't know who's in here since you didn't give them a name. They'll just whisk whoever it is into the ambulance. Let Geena stay. Let her go home to her babies," she said quietly.

Raider looked at Charley in disbelief. "Who do you think you are? You runnin' some scam? You an old lady ninja who's going to take me down? You're up to something!" Raider whispered through clenched teeth.

Charley had to press, there wasn't much time. "Look Raider, you owe me one. I have done everything you said and I have done everything I promised. If you do this, I won't run. I will be the perfect hostage."

Raider looked in her eyes. She didn't blink or look away. He looked at Geena, and it was clear that she was barely functioning. "Okay, not because you asked, but because she is useless. Sit down." Raider instructed Geena. Charley wrapped Geena's leg in the bloody t-shirts and tied a strip around her thigh to look like a tourniquet.

"Not too tight is it?" she whispered to Geena.

"No, it's fine." Geena looked into Charley's determined face as she adjusted the deception to look real. "Just hold it and cry when they get to you. Don't talk to the police. You're in too much pain, okay? You can answer all their questions once we're off the ground. You don't want them to figure out you're not hurt before we get to the chopper. If they don't think he's a lunatic, they might kill us by trying to take him. Once Raider and I are up, the rest will be safe, too." Geena looked at Charley, bewildered.

"You and Raider?" she barely spoke.

"Yes, hon, me and Raider. I'm not letting him take one of these girls if I can stop it."

"But what about you? Don't you want this over? Why take my place?" Charley looked into her sweet face.

"This is a gift from God. Seek Him out once this is over. He wants to help you have an incredible life with your family. I'll be fine. He's looking out for me. Please tell Brittany and Anne that God loves them and He protected them today."

Geena was sitting in front of the spot where Charley had hidden her phone, so she quickly slipped it out of hiding and into her pocket. Luckily, she had turned it off before she hid it. Last thing Charley needed was to receive a call.

"Get over here," Raider barked. "We gotta go." Charley patted the top of Geena's head and joined the group. Charley tied herself into the shield circle and moved as Raider led. He tried dragging the garbage bag full of money from the registers, then stood for a moment, considering the logistics of holding two guns, maneuvering in a tight group, and bringing the money, before moving on again. On the way out of the vault, he grabbed the stapled tablecloths. Raider maneuvered them behind the counter, where he found a zippered cash bag, then had Anne fill the bag up with as much of the stolen money as she could hold before stuffing it into his shirt.

"I'm going to give you guys your directions. Don't screw with me and you'll be home tonight in your little beds. If you mess up, you'll be in the morgue. I will have a gun on two of you at all times," Raider threatened.

Agent Morris stood outside the bank, watching for any movement at the door. She had her best gunmen in position. They planned to shoot him in the head even though the hostages surrounded him. He would drop instantly. She would do everything possible to keep him from getting to the chopper.

The bank door slowly opened and, to Agent Morris's dismay, a huge white ghost slowly moved out. A large mass of white cloth covered the group. Using the stapler, Raider had converted the tablecloths into a large tent, cutting small slits in the sheet so they could see. The police couldn't even see their legs. Without a clear shot, the cops could not shoot.

Agent Morris considered rushing them, their visibility had to be horrible, but she wasn't dealing with a dummy. He had to have considered that possibility and his guns would be pointed at someone. Any attempt to take him down would result in the injury or death of one or more of the hostages. They could not be sure of getting to him before he pulled the trigger and, grouped so tightly together, he wouldn't miss his shot. Agent Morris signaled for everyone to back off and for the snipers to stand down.

"Anne, yell out and tell them to cut the engine," Raider instructed. Anne did as she was told.

Agent Morris bit her lip in frustration. She hadn't known he would come out covered, but had quickly realized the swirling air from the blades was to their advantage. They would get a break when the blades blew the sheet up, revealing the prize underneath. The white ghost stopped, waiting for her to comply. Agent Morris yelled, "Sir, you can't stand there all day. Give yourself up."

One of the ladies yelled out, "If you don't turn off that engine, he will shoot as many of us in the head as he can before you take him down. He is a dead man and he doesn't mind taking us with him. He has nothing to lose and he thinks you do."

There was no alternative; Agent Morris gave the signal to turn off the engine. The ghost continued its slow march to the field. It was the most bizarre picture – a circle of armed officers moving along with the huge white ghost, husbands and family members held back by more officers, and a lone helicopter sitting a short distance away.

When they got close to the helicopter, Charley slowly positioned herself to be the first one to reach their destination. When they made it to the open door of the cabin, she was where she needed to be. She knew that Raider had been watching her with a curious look on his face. She hoped that he wouldn't insist on one of the other women going.

"Charley, you're going with me," he said with authority. She heard the other hostages exhale with relief. It was then that Charley realized they had all been holding their breaths. "Drop down and crawl, then up into the chopper." Once Charley was in the helicopter, Raider slipped in next to her, still under the tent. The two remaining hostages were standing on the ground still under the drape and Raider had his gun pointed at Brittany. "Charley," he said in a low voice, "tell the pilot to get out of the cockpit."

"What?" Charley asked in disbelief.

"Tell him I have one gun on the hostages and one at the back of his seat." Charley repeated his instructions.

"I need to fly you out of here," the pilot argued, refusing to leave. Raider fired a shot through the back of the seat. The pilot was hit in his shoulder. Raider had missed the bulletproof vest and ripped a hole in the man's flesh. The SWAT pilot could not get a clear shot at Raider. He was losing blood quickly and was forced to abort the mission. He jumped from the cockpit. Charley's ears were still ringing from the gunshot.

"Charley, get up to the cockpit and shut the door." He then barked orders telling her how to start the engine. She could feel the vibration of the main rotor beginning to turn. Raider shoved the remaining hostages away from the copter, and slammed the door shut. He moved up to the cockpit and pushed Charley against the pilot's door. She shielded him from the officer's line of fire. He sat on the edge of her seat, and grabbed the controls. Charley could see the officers running toward the helicopter, shooting at the main rotor, and then felt the copter lifting off the ground. She assumed that the woman stomping the ground was Agent Morris.

"You've flown one of these before?" Charley asked with her heart in her throat.

"Yep, for Uncle Sam. I was in Iraq until my discharge." Once they were in the air and the field was behind them, Raider moved between the seats and ordered Charley to slide over to the other chair. The helicopter pitched as she struggled to obey.

"Dammit, be careful."

They sat quietly as they flew through the darkening sky. So many questions and fears raced through Charley's mind. Her journey to this seat, next to this criminal, felt surreal. Finally she dared to ask, "So, what are you going to do with me?"

"Do you really care?"

"Of course I care."

"You don't act like someone who cares. I can't figure out your game."

"I don't have a game," Charley responded.

"Everyone has a game," Raider said with conviction.

raidersvendetta.com

Reviews

A surprising twist for this new and rising author, Karen Arnpriester, Raider's Vendetta has all the action and edge-of-your-seat suspense required to captivate and hold its audience to its spectacular and unexpected ending. I loved, hated and will not soon forget the main character, Raider. Is there hope for Raider? Is anyone beyond God's reach? Will Charley survive? This book I could not put down until I had the answers I craved. I was hooked from the beginning and am hooked on this author! I'm already anticipating her next release that I hear is pending. Put me on the waiting list!!!
Pam Rich

A Christian drama with twists and turns, two people's journeys of self discovery and life lessons through a harrowing event. Rich characters, action, and deep Christian experiences.
J. Locke

After reading Karen Arnpriester's first book, and heard another was released, I had to give it a read since the first book, I could not put down. Now, with Raiders Revenge, it picks up more velocity with a fascinating character study that had me hooked. There were many twists and surprises and the writing style had me hooked again. I highly recommend this book to any reader who wants to be lost into the story, and delve deep into the mind of her characters. Bravo Karen.
Tom Allen

Made in the USA
Charleston, SC
09 September 2012